RECLAIM ME

THE NEW HAVEN SERIES
BOOK 4

J.L. SEEGARS

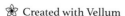 Created with Vellum

In Loving Memory of Mae Helen Seegars

"So do the shadows of our own desires stand between us and *our better angels*, and thus their brightness is eclipsed".

— CHARLES DICKENS

AUTHOR NOTE

Another day, another New Haven couple to break your heart and put it back together!

Many of you have wanted to know who Hunter and Rae are and how their story fits into the New Haven universe, so I'm really excited for you guys to get to meet them. A few things to know before you start:

- We first meet Hunter and Rae in Revive Me Pt. 1 when Mallory goes to a self-defense class that Chris picks her up from. While it's the briefest of encounters, we see a little glimpse of their connection, which is further explored here.
- The chapters labeled 'now' put us about two years removed from the end of Revive Me Pt. 3, so when the other couples pop up, which we know they will, we get to see them little more settled into their relationships.

Content and Trigger Warning:

Please be aware this story involves sensitive topics such as **drug addiction, overdose, terminal illness (cancer), parental and sibling** loss, suicidal ideation, mentions of stalking and intimate partner violence (not between the couple) as well as a graphic description of a fatal gunshot wound to the head in chapter five.

While I always endeavor to handle such topics with care, this story is in no, way, shape or form meant to be a guide to dealing with addiction, recovery or any of the other challenges we see Hunter and Rae face on the journey to reclaiming their love.

I strongly advise you to consider your own health and well-being before diving into this story.

THE PLAYLIST

01./ Renegade by Big Red Machine (ft. Taylor Swift)
02./ Anybody Else by JP Saxe
03./ Rescue by Lauren Daigle
04./ Godspeed by Frank Ocean
05./ Still in Love with You by Deeps
06./ Still Wonder by Alex Isley & Jack Dine (ft. Robert Glasper)
07./ What Keeps Me From It by JP Saxe
08./ How Does It Make You Feel by Victoria Monét
09./ Never Change by Adria Kain (ft. Leila Dey)
10./ JEANS by Jessie Reyes (ft. Miguel)
11./ At Least We Tried by GIVĒON
12./ Thinking 'bout Love by Wild Rivers
13./ oceans by Tori Kelley
14./ Orbit by Stefan Mahendra & Fika

1

RAE

The Proposal

There's bad decisions, and then there's *bad* decisions.

Ruinous, life-altering choices you know you'll regret when it's all said and done but somehow still manage to enjoy in the moment, and *God*, am I enjoying myself right now. My legs spread wide, the fabric of my birthday dress scrunched up around my waist, my panties pushed to the side because you don't get completely undressed when you're making a mistake, even when it's one as deliciously salacious as this.

The flat of his tongue rolls over my clit again, and my thighs twitch around his ears. I shouldn't be doing this. It shouldn't feel *so fucking good.*

But I am, and it does.

He grips my ass with rough fingertips, lifting my pussy up to his mouth like a bite of a forbidden meal, and I scream at the top of my lungs the way I never can at home with Aaron—not because his mother or my daughter might hear—but because in all the years we've been together he's never made me feel like this.

Wild. Reckless. Capable of ruining someone and desperate to be ruined in return.

No, that part of me can only be unlocked by the man between my legs. The man now holding my entire ass in the palm of one of his hands so he can use the fingers of the other to invade the walls of my dripping sex. My core contracts, and my eyes roll into the back of my head as pleasure pulses through me, incoherent words flow out of me as my body floats into a cloud of euphoria so thick it's able to keep me suspended for long moments, keeping me from the regret that's waiting for me on the ground.

I didn't come here for this.

That's the thought going through my mind as Hunter lowers me gently back down onto his desk. He doesn't even bother to fix my dress or my panties. Just leaves me wide open, my most intimate areas on display for him. I keep my eyes on the ceiling above me, focused on the heart in the middle of the ceiling tile directly above us that has our initials written in black paint.

"You should paint over that."

I don't know why I've chosen to start the conversation I came here to have this way. It's random and unnecessary, but it's the only way I know how to ease into telling him he has to let me go. I reach down and fix my clothes before sitting up and facing him. He's got his fingers clasped together, resting over the hard slabs of muscle that make up his stomach. For as long as I've known him, Hunter has never had a six-pack. He's just got one of those stomachs that's thick but solid and toned. I don't know what you call it, but it works for him.

He doesn't bother looking up because he knows exactly what I'm talking about. I hate that because I was hoping to buy myself a little bit of time without those eyes on my face.

"Why would I do that?"

"Because it's..." My throat is dry from all the moaning and screaming, so I swallow before continuing. "Because it's just a reminder of a failed past when you should be focused on the future."

One of his brows rises, a thick, dark line that makes my cheeks heat. "Is that what this was?" He asks, waving a large, tattooed hand between us. "You focusing on the future?"

"No." I slide off of his desk, skirting around his wide spread legs to put some space between us. "This was a momentary lapse in judgment. I didn't come here for this."

Hunter stands too, moving forward to delete every inch of space I've just given myself to breathe. Now, all the air I welcome into my lungs is infected with him, with his scent and arrogance, with his desire.

"Then what did you come here for, Rae?"

He brings his hand to my face, the same fingers that were just inside me tucking a strand of hair behind my ear. I suck in a ragged breath, and I should tell him to stop because now those fingers are moving down my neck, over my racing pulse to the pebbled nipples straining through the cotton of my sundress. Hunter cups my breast, and while I'm on the verge of coming apart in his hands, the muscles in his face don't move an inch.

It shouldn't matter that he appears to be so unaffected by me, but it does. It burns me up inside because I fall apart every time he touches me, every time he looks my way. I'm here with him when I should be with the man who helped me raise our daughter before Hunter ever knew she existed, but instead I'm here, courting ruin with a man who won't show me what I do to him.

Maybe it's madness or the pressing need for more of him, but I step closer when I should step back. I bring my hand to the nape of his neck and pull his lips down to mine when I should be coming to terms with the fact that they can't belong to me anymore. I slip my tongue into his mouth and wait for him to give me something in return.

He doesn't.

"Kiss me back, Hunter."

"Why?" He murmurs against my lips, his breathing annoyingly even. I step closer, committed to this act of desperation, and that's when I feel it. The thick, heated length of his erection nestled between us. With my free hand, I palm it, squeezing lightly just to prove to myself that it's real. Finally, his stoic facade breaks. It's a small fracture, a sharp intake of breath that he lets out in a low hiss that passes between his teeth, but it's enough.

"Because we both want the same thing."

The fire. The passion. The lost inhibitions we never miss when we're together.

Hunter makes me regret saying anything when he steps back and shakes his head. "No, Sunshine, we don't want the same thing." He swipes his thumb across his chin, an act of agitation I know too well, and stares at me with dark eyes that pierce my soul. "You came here to make a mistake, to make *me* a mistake, but I want to be more than that. I *deserve* to be more than that, but you won't let me."

"*I* won't let you?" Disbelief paints my tone in dark, broad strokes. It has no place here because we both know what he's saying is true.

"Yes, Rae, you. You're the only person who still looks at me and sees..." he trails off, but I don't need the words for my brain to conjure the image he's alluding to. An image of a broken man splayed on the ground with the tools of his destruction scattered around his prone form. He's not that person anymore. The time we've spent figuring out how our lives fit together for our daughter's sake has shown me as much, but I still see it in the back of my mind. Still hold it up as a reminder of how bad things can get. Still use it as a barrier between us in moments like this.

"I'm sorry. I wish I could see something else, anything else," I lie, exchanging his piercing gaze for the floorboards.

"No, you don't."

"Yes, I do, Hunter. Of course, I do." My voice trembles around the falsities. I've never had to double down on the lie before. Usually, he goes along with it, but I guess today he's tired of my little charade. Maybe he knows today is different. Maybe he feels the walls closing in, the clock running out.

"No, Rae, you don't. Because holding on to that version of me is the only thing keeping you from me and the only thing keeping you with *him*."

"That's not true," I shake my head for emphasis even though his words follow the same thread of logic as my thoughts. "Aaron and I are good together. You and I are a train wreck."

"Do you love him?" The question is wrapped around a broken growl that causes his top lip to curl. It's a sound that can only come from a wounded animal preparing to lash out in a final attempt to save their life.

I run a shaking hand over my messy hair as my stomach turns into knots. "Hunter."

"Say it, Rae, look me in the eyes and tell me that you love him, that you love him more than you've ever loved me."

He waits patiently for me to respond to his cruel request, and I hate him more with every silent second that passes. Why can't he just let this go? Why can't he just accept that the way I feel about Aaron doesn't matter because *we* don't work outside of the context of sated sighs and gut-wrenching moans. When a full minute goes by without me caving to his demand, he closes the space between us and cups my chin with gentle fingers. Slowly, he tips my head back, forcing me to meet his eye.

One dark slash of a brow raises. "Tell me you love him, Rae."

He's so close now, angling me to persuade me with proximity, and I don't back away. I stand firmly on the line between common sense and the bone-deep yearning for this man. For his hands on my hips and the warmth that spreads through my chest because of it. For his breath on my face as he lowers his forehead to mine and pulls in lungfuls of air just because it smells like me.

I close my eyes, staving off the unshed tears burning the backs of my eyes. "I need to tell you something," I whisper, scared to speak any louder because our connection is already tenuous and the words that are going to come out of my mouth next are going to destroy us both.

Hunter sighs, allowing me to shift gears. "I'm listening."

It's stupid, but I hold him tighter when I should be letting him go, when I know he'll probably let me go when he hears what I came here to say.

"Aaron asked me to marry him."

I open my eyes and find myself face to face with his devastation, and it destroys me. I feel like I should apologize, like I've broken some sacred vow, etched in stone and sealed with blood, that our souls have only just decided to acknowledge.

"Hunter, say something," I plead, wondering why I want his words when I already know they'll just make me feel worse. More guilty. More conflicted. More *wrong*.

His lips part, and my heart starts to pound, anticipating his wrath, his fire, his hurt, but he's remarkably calm as he takes my left hand in his right and runs his thumb across each of my ring-less digits.

"You didn't say yes."

I pull my hand back, tucking it behind my back. "I did. I took the ring off before I came in here because I didn't want you to see it."

Hunter studies me with dark eyes that see too much. "When did he ask you?"

"Tonight. At dinner."

He checks his watch, arching a brow when it reveals that it's not even ten yet. "You've been engaged for all of five minutes, and instead of spending the night celebrating with your fiance, you came here to me."

Something about his calm tone and even calmer demeanor makes me feel like I've been stripped down, lain bare, like the whole of every complication I've allowed to exist around the mess that is my life has suddenly been made simple.

"I—" My plan is to defend myself, to explain to him that I rushed over here because I wanted to be the person to tell him, that I didn't want Riley to call and let it slip, but once again, the big, elaborate speech deserts me, leaving me with a stupid response. "It doesn't mean anything."

But it does. Doesn't it? Just like my inability to say I love the man I've spent the last seven years of my life with means something. Just like the ease with which I say I love you to Hunter means something.

Hunter scoffs. "Of course, it means something, Sunshine. It means you said yes, but you didn't mean it. It means there's still time."

"Time for what?" I ask, thrown off kilter when he takes a sudden step back and turns back toward his desk. I watch him pull open the top drawer on the right-hand side and pluck something out. It's not until he's walking towards me again that I realize what it is.

A square, black box.

He doesn't open it until he's standing right in front of me, but I already know what's inside. Knowing doesn't stop me from being shocked when I see the gold band of a ring nestled inside the lines of the black silk. The small diamonds surrounding the larger center stone fan out into little triangles that look like a sunburst. I cover my mouth and shake my head in disbelief.

He can't be doing this.

There's no way he's actually doing this.

"Time," he says, finally answering the question I asked before I lost my ability to speak altogether, "for me to give you another option, a *better* option."

2

RAE

TWELVE WEEKS BEFORE THE PROPOSAL

Now

T he box in my hand is going to fall.

I see it happen in my mind's eye. The ancient glassware Aaron's mother, Marcy, has had since her wedding to his father forty years ago will go first, tumbling out of the poorly taped box and shattering all over the hand-scraped hardwoods under my bare feet. I'll have to feign regret as I sweep the shards of gold-rimmed glass up, frown, and sigh, and apologize every time it's mentioned, which, knowing Marcy, will be at least once a day for the rest of my life.

It still won't be enough to convince her I didn't do it on purpose, and that's fine because I won't be one hundred percent sure it wasn't.

"Whoa, babe, you're going to drop it." Aaron rushes toward me, swooping in just as the box slips free from my fingertips. He catches it midair and laughs at my clumsiness as he sets it on the counter in the middle of our brand-new kitchen. "Mom would have flipped if any of this stuff got broken. Her wedding china is in here."

I watch him start unpacking his mother's precious keepsakes and try not to roll my eyes. "Where's Marcy, anyway?"

Aaron glances over his shoulder toward the hallway that leads to the stairs then back at me with his brows pulled together in a tight line of disapproval. As far as looks go, this one is my least favorite of his. It's too close to the look he gives Riley when she eats her snacks on the couch.

"Rae, you know she doesn't like when you call her Marcy."

I move over to the fridge and pull out a bottle of water, cracking the top and taking a couple swigs before I respond to him. "Her name is Marcy, Aaron, what else am I supposed to call her?"

"I don't know, maybe Mom?"

The glare I turn on him makes him whither. "Why would I do that? She's not my mother."

Aaron knows this is a touchy subject for me, so I'm not sure why he's decided that today, of all days, is the best time to broach the topic again. After months of stressing about this move from Manhattan to New Haven and the addition of his mother to our household, I'm not in the mood to argue about something we've already discussed ad nauseam. Losing my mother when I was barely out of high school left a hole in my heart I have no intention of ever filling with Marcy Scott. Not because she's not a good mom, because she is—if helicopter moms are your thing—but because she's not *my* mom.

Her hugs bring me no comfort.

Her smiles offer me no reassurance, and all of her advice is biased towards her son.

"Sweetheart," Aaron coos, sidling over to me to wrap his arms around my waist and kiss my neck. "I know that, but one day, she will be your mother-in-law, and what are you going to call her then?"

"Marcy," I deadpan, ignoring the way my stomach knots at the mere allusion to marriage.

He stares at me, and despite being tired and sweaty and a bit annoyed, I can't help but appreciate how damn easy he is on the eyes. Between the honey-brown eyes, golden skin, and the jet black hair that he always keeps cropped close to his scalp, I'm usually prone to giving him whatever he wants, but I won't give him this.

Aaron must see the resolve in my eyes because he pushes out a breath of concession and leans in to kiss me on the lips. I reciprocate, allowing myself to relax into his arms, to let the anxiety of being back in New Haven and the stress of living with his mother fade into the background. I'm seconds away from slipping him some tongue when footfalls in the hallway announce that we're about to have company. We break apart at the same time, turning our attention to the doorway just in time to see my daughter, Riley, come barreling into the room with a phone in her hand.

"Auntie Dee is on the phone!"

Her voice bounces off of the bare quartz countertops and pings around the room, highlighting just how empty it is in here. Aaron plants a quick kiss on my cheek before he lets me go, knowing that a phone call from my best friend means unpacking the kitchen has just become his sole responsibility.

I pluck the phone from Riley's hands and run a hand over wild curls spilling out of the bun I wrangled them into this morning while an adoring smile pulls the corners of my mouth up. Chocolate brown eyes that are close to being squeezed shut by the chubby cheeks I hope she never grows out of reflect that same adoration back at me and my heart goes all warm.

"Thank you, Nugget. Did you finish unpacking all of your plushies before you decided to start playing games on my phone?" Silent shock is the only answer I get from my daughter. Luckily, it's the only one I need.

"Get back to work, missy," I demand, shooing her back in the direction she came from. She heads off without argument, or at least none that I can hear, and I put the phone to my ear. "Hey, Dee."

"You know she's talking shit about you as we speak, right?"

My best friend's unorthodox greeting makes me laugh. Deanna Tyson always makes me laugh. That's how we became friends in the first place. Her off-the-cuff, dry-as-a-bone sense of humor caught my attention on the third day of first grade. I was the only person in the class to laugh when she asked our teacher, Mrs. Mac, if her first name was Mary and followed it up with a question about why she wasn't wearing black. That shared giggle from across the classroom lost us both our recess that day and earned us both a friend for life.

"Yep, I'm probably being called everything but a child of God," I say, moving out of the kitchen and down the hall to the room Aaron will use as his home office. Right now, there's nothing in here besides his desk chair and stacks of boxes that contain his degrees from Stanford, as well as an array of accolades denoting the list of achievements leading to the promotion that brought us here to New Haven.

I plop down in the desk chair and turn my back to the closed door, gazing out into the massive, manicured backyard. When we viewed the house in early January, our realtor told us we would be stunned by how gorgeous the yard would be in Spring. It's the middle of March, so the season technically hasn't started yet, but Aaron and Marcy are already talking about all the elegant outdoor outings we can host for their family, friends and his co-workers. I advocated for a smaller place, something that wouldn't stretch us so thin financially, but in the end, the yard and all it's possibilities won out.

"Let's just hope she uses the curse words right this time. I can't have my niece going around calling people mother-shitters," Dee quips, reminding me of the first and last time I gave Riley permission to curse. We laughed for days at her odd combinations.

"As her mom, I think it's probably my job to hope she never gets them right."

"She's a smart kid, Rae. You know she's going to figure it out eventually. Those kids at her fancy little school will probably have her cursing like a pro by the end of her first day."

"Oh, God," I groan, knowing she's right because private school kids are the untamed monsters everyone wants us to believe public school kids are. "How long until she starts calling me 'mother' and rolling her eyes at everything I say?"

Dee snorts. "I'd say you probably have a good month or so left."

"Damn. I guess it was fun while it lasted."

"We had a good run," she agrees, a laugh slipping through the cracks of the severity she's forced into her tone. "How are you feeling about being back in New Haven?" she asks, switching gears now that we've gotten our signature banter out of the way.

Pulling my legs up into the chair to sit crisscross applesauce, I mentally prepare myself to answer such a loaded question. Over the last few weeks, I've had friends and even complete strangers ask me how I feel about moving back to my hometown. Each time, I've answered with the expected enthusiasm about sharing the place where I had all of my firsts with my daughter and putting down roots with Aaron. While none of those answers have been dishonest, Dee is the only person with whom I can be completely truthful because she knows everything.

The set of stairs I fell down and broke my arm.

The park bench where I had my first kiss.

The hospital room where I said goodbye to my mother.

The burial plot I picked for my brother.

The graves I've visited and the one I dug for a love I had to bury before it killed me.

"Rae?" Dee's voice is soft now, all traces of humor gone. "You okay?"

"It's weird," I answer, jumping straight in because there's no point in tiptoeing around it. "Everything is different but the same. It hasn't been home for a long time, but I don't feel like a stranger."

"You can leave New Haven, but New Haven will never leave you," she murmurs, repeating an old adage her mom, Emma, would recite whenever she'd hear us talking about how ready we were to put this small town behind us. She's been gone for two years now, but we still find ourselves quoting her at the most random times.

"The older you get, the more you sound like her," I muse, a soft smile playing on my lips even as my heart breaks for her again. Losing a mom is the kind of pain I wouldn't wish on anyone, especially my best friend and her little sister.

"Jayla says the same thing."

Even though I can't see it, I know she's rolling her eyes. Dee hates it when me and Jayla agree on anything. She swears we do it just to gang up on her, even if we express our similar thoughts at different times.

"Did she tell you we ran into each other at the mall yesterday?"

"Yeah, she said Riley and Sonia hit it off instantly."

"They did. Riley's already asking when we can have them over."

"Of course she is; that girl loves a gathering."

I laugh. "She really does. I don't know where she gets that from 'cause it's certainly not me."

"Well, there is a whole other set of DNA you have to account for," she reminds me, making my heart sink into my stomach.

Ever since Aaron drove us into New Haven city limits, I've been trying my hardest not to think about that other set of DNA, the man who contributed it, and what's going to happen when we run into each other here, in the very place I left him when his demons came to destroy us both.

3

RAE

I made a wrong turn.

Actually, I made several. A left when I should have gone right. Taking the fourth exit on the roundabout when it should have been the third.

"I fucking hate roundabouts," I sigh, making a U-turn in the middle of the street to get back to the counterproductive circle that should have just been a normal intersection.

"You're going to get yourself killed, Rae," Dee warns, her voice spilling through the speaker of my phone, which is nestled in between the two large Diet Cokes we slurped down on the last leg of our road trip. "You won't be much good to Will if you're laid up in the hospital beside him."

"I'm not going to be laid up beside him." The reassuring statement feels like a lie when it's punctuated by the blaring of a horn belonging to a pickup truck that looks more like a tank. The driver of said tank leans out of his window and flips me off, cursing me for ignoring the yield sign and pulling out in front of him. I don't make a habit of engaging with men in large trucks that are meant to compensate for their small dicks, so I peel off and pray that he doesn't follow me.

"What was that?"

"Nothing."

"Your driving is going to get you killed one day," she mutters, echoing a complaint I heard every other minute during our eleven-hour drive from Manhattan back to New Haven.

"My driving got us to New York and back, didn't it? What did you contribute exactly?"

"Fire playlists," she tosses back, not missing a beat. "And gas money."

"We both put in gas, girl."

And it took almost every dime the two of us had saved from years of babysitting and working odd jobs to cover the trip we'd been planning for half our lives. We'd done everything we said we were going to—walked the streets of Manhattan with slices of greasy pizza in hand, attended an open class at Steps on Broadway, took one of those cheesy tours where you sit on the top of a double-decker bus to see the sights while someone lays facts about the city over a hip-hop beat, and went to every show we could afford to see.

Broadway, off-Broadway, and off-off-Broadway too.

It was the best time. The kind of time I needed after spending eight months watching my mother die a slow, painful death, surrendering every ounce of her life to the hell that is breast cancer.

And now, with every mile I put between myself, Dee, and the goodness we found in the streets of New York, I can feel the happy fading. Shifting. My world turning slowly upside down with thoughts of hospital rooms and IV lines dripping saline into veins of a tired body curled under stark white sheets.

Once upon a time, that was Mommy, and now it might be Will. My brother. My best friend. The only family I have.

"What if he dies?"

"Stop being dramatic, Rae. Will is not gonna die!"

"But he's in the hospital."

"Yeah, and he called you himself and told you as much!"

Even through the anxiety and frustration burning a hole in my stomach, I can acknowledge the truth of that statement. Will did call me. He timed it just right, too. My phone started playing the ringtone I designated for him as soon as we pulled up at Dee's house. Since we'd been updating him on our location every hour on the hour, *per his request*, I figured he knew I'd made it to Dee's and just wanted to know how long I was going to stay over.

But what he'd actually called to say was that he wouldn't be home when I got there. Not understanding the gravity of the admission, I joked about him finally getting a life when I was out of town. He went quiet on me, the way he always does when he needs to say something but doesn't want me to worry. It took me longer than it should to get him to spit it out, and even then, it was in bits and pieces of reluctant information that I put all the way together when I heard a nurse come in and ask him if he was sure he didn't want something for the pain.

That's when my ears tuned in to the noise in the background. The opening and closing of doors. The faint chatter of voices over the intercom, paging doctors, calling codes. The melody of a hospital I've spent more time in than I care to admit.

"I'm still scared," I admit, pushing the words past the lump in my throat. Now that I'm turning into the hospital parking lot, it's fully formed. Large and imposing as it presses against my windpipe, strangling me with worse-case scenarios and flashes of every Grey's Anatomy episode I've ever seen.

"You can be scared, Rae, but don't let your feelings stop you from seeing the facts."

Her dulcet tone reminds me of her recently disclosed plan to pursue a career in psychology. We always planned to chase our dreams of principal roles in acclaimed ballet corps together, but apparently, Dee had a change of heart while she was away at school, completing her freshman year. She came clean on our last night in New York because she didn't want the trip to end without me knowing the truth. I tried not to be bitter about it—my best friend giving up on our lifelong dream, being left behind by yet another person in yet another facet of my life—but it was a hard pill to swallow. And now life is forcing me to swallow another one that's all chalk and dust with jagged edges that cut and scrape on their way down.

"Thank you for the advice, Dr. Dee."

"Dr. Dee," she muses. "I like the sound of that."

"I bet you do. It makes it sound like you're about to write a prescription for some dick."

"Rachel Renee Prince! Are you actually making dick jokes while your brother is on his deathbed?" She gasps, and I can practically see her hand on her chest in false indignation.

Cutting the ignition, I grab my purse, keys and the duffel bag full of clothes I didn't wear in New York and hop out the car.

"He's not on his deathbed," I remind her, double-clicking the lock button on my key.

"Exactly. That's exactly right. Now make sure you remember that when you see him."

I stop short just outside the entrance and push out a calming breath. "I'll try. Bye, Dee."

"Bye, babe. Text me if you need anything."

"Will do."

Ending the call, I rush inside the hospital, bypassing the information desk and heading straight to the elevator because I wouldn't let Will hang up with me until he gave me his room number. The seventh floor is pretty quiet, which I guess is technically a good sign as far as hospitals go, but it still gives me the creeps. Will's room is lively, though, buzzing with conversation and positive energy that flows between my brother's hospital bed and around the room, looping through the small spaces left between the bodies of the group of men and women standing shoulder to shoulder around his bed.

I pause just inside the threshold and place a hand on my hip. "Are you seriously running a meeting from your hospital bed?"

Everyone turns to look at me. None of the faces are familiar, but I suppose that's the point of Narcotics Anonymous—the anonymity.

"That you, Rae Rae?" Will asks, humor making his voice light.

The group of people surrounding his bed part like the Red Sea, creating an unobstructed path of sight that allows me to see the large smile stretched across his face. Annoyance rolls through me in a fierce wave. Seconds ago, I was worried about him dying, and now I'm contemplating killing him myself.

"How many times have I asked you not to call me that, Wilson?"

Wilson? Will is short for *Wilson*?" One of the men asks, hiding a smile behind his hand when Will glares at him. The glare shuts the man right up and puts an end to the meeting. One by one, the group of recovering addicts say their goodbyes and filter out of the room, leaving Will and me on our own.

We're used to it.

Since Mommy died, it's been that way. Me and Will watching TV on the couch, neither of us brave enough to sit in the recliner she loved so much. Will and me eating dinner at a table set for six. Two orphans holding each other close after having everything else ripped from their hands.

"Stop looking at me with those sad eyes, Rae. I'm not dying."

I drop my duffel on the floor beside the chair I'll be sleeping in tonight and climb onto the bed. There's not enough room for the both of us, but Will still moves over so I can curl into his side. His arm loops around my shoulder, and he holds me close, dropping a kiss on the top of my head.

"How was New York?"

I slap his leg, and he laughs, which makes me smile. "Tell me how you ended up in the hospital."

"My appendix burst. They had to remove it."

"When?"

"Friday night. I was running a meeting and nearly passed out from the pain."

"And no one thought to call me? *You* didn't think to call me?"

He squeezes me tight, pulling me in closer. "I didn't want you to cut your trip short."

There's no point in telling him I wouldn't have because we both know that would be a lie. If he had called me to say he was in the hospital, I would have dropped everything to get to him as soon as possible.

"When are you going to be discharged?"

"Tomorrow afternoon, as long as I get through the night without running a fever."

My hand immediately goes to his forehead, and he leans into my touch, indulging my need to verify his temperature. "You're not feverish now. Did you run one last night?"

"It was low grade and broke in the middle of the night. I'm fine," he assures me, moving my hand away.

"And they still let you have visitors? What if it's the start of an infection?"

"I wasn't going to miss a meeting. Addicts need consistency, Rae, you know that."

I do know. For the last five years, I've listened to him preach the gospel of routine and recovery to the people he sponsors while actively implementing it in his own life. He's more disciplined than some dancers I know, and that's saying a lot because there are a lot of ballerinas who can put Marines to shame.

"Someone else could have run the meeting."

My words come out muffled, rolled into the blurred edges of a yawn. Dee and I got on the road early, like while the moon was still in the sky early, and now that all the adrenaline and fear from worrying about Will has faded, I'm ready to crash.

"Tired?" he asks.

"A little."

"You should head home and get some sleep."

I sit up, pinning him with a hard stare. "We both know I'm not going home."

The look he gives me is just a reflection of mine, and in a mere second, we're locked in a staring contest reminiscent of the ones we used to engage in when I was younger. Will is ten years older than me, but he never made me feel like the annoying little sister, not even when I wanted to settle every argument and debate by seeing who could go the longest without blinking.

My eyes are burning from being open for far too long, but I refuse to lose. He's already spent two nights in this hospital by himself, and I'm not going to let it turn into three. Victory comes in the form of a twitch in Will's right eye that pulls his eyelids shut for a split second. We've been playing this game long enough for me to know that this counts as a blink, and I pump a celebratory fist in the air as I hop off the bed. Will rolls his eyes as I plop down in the recliner.

"Like I said, I'm not going home."

"Your back is going to hurt like hell after you spend a night in that chair."

"My back will be fine," I insist, letting the footrest out and crossing my arms over my chest.

"I'm glad you're back," he says, leaning back against the pillows as a familiar quiet settles between us. "I missed you."

"I missed you too, Will."

"Tell me about your trip. I want to know everything."

Despite the exhaustion settling deep in my bones, I give Will a detailed recount of the days Dee and I spent in New York. He listens intently, the way he always does when I talk, and asks questions that keep the one-sided conversation flowing until my heavy eyelids refuse to stay open any longer.

The room is dark when I come to, groggy and confused about where I am and what exactly has woken me up. At first, I think it's Will or a nurse coming in to check his vitals again, but he's asleep and we're alone. After a moment, I realize the sound that's woken me is Will's phone. It's on the counter next to the bag of clothes someone must have brought him from the house, vibrating loudly, threatening to wake every patient on the floor.

Will stirs, his face scrunched together in a pained expression that reminds me he hasn't taken anything except Tylenol since the surgery. I overheard the nurse say he's been restless all weekend, hardly sleeping. Now that he's resting, I don't want to let anything interrupt it, so I move fast, crossing the room and taking the phone into my hand to silence it. Once the ringer is off, I stare at the screen. It's a little after three in the morning, and the phone is *still* ringing, which means the person on the other end of the line is likely in the middle of a crisis.

And in Will's world, a crisis means relapse.

I cradle the phone in my hands, a nervous rush of energy sweeping down my spine as I envision one of my brother's sponsees in a dark room somewhere, a phone in one hand and the tools of their own destruction in the other. He always tells them that they can call him at any time. More than once, I've watched him leave the house in the middle of the night, his jaw clenched, shoulders set in determination, hands ready to pull someone from the depths of addiction. I glance at Will, knowing that if I wake him, he's likely to pull the IV out of his arm and leave this hospital with me and the entire nursing staff protesting.

The phone keeps ringing. Every vibration forcing my eyes to linger on the screen, to memorize the letters that make up the name of the person on the other end of the line.

Hunter Drake.

Someone's son. Someone's brother. Someone's friend. Someone who needs Will's help but will just get me instead.

Without thinking, I answer the phone, and my hands shake with the fear of inadequacy. I'm not equipped for this. I could make whatever this Hunter guy is going through worse. The thought echoes in my mind, amplified by the silence filling my ears.

"Will? You there?"

Hunter Drake is remarkably calm for a man in crisis. His voice is deep. A dark, riotous melody that wreaks havoc on my already pounding heart.

"Will's not—I mean, it's—" God, I can't get my words together. How is it that I'm supposed to be helping this man, and I can't even form a sentence? I clear my throat. "Sorry, Will isn't able to come to the phone right now."

"Is he alright?"

"Are *you*?" I blurt.

The line goes quiet again, and then Hunter laughs. It's not a joyful sound. The edges are sharp, the center bitter.

"What's your name?" he asks, and that's when I hear it, the forced intention pressing down on each word, how hard he's working to keep the lazy lilt of drug-induced euphoria from showing in his voice. I heard Will's voice sound like that once when I was ten, and he showed up to my birthday party high. Mommy forced him to leave, and then she went in her room and cried while Dee's mom, Emma, led everyone through the Happy Birthday song.

"Rae. I'm Will's sister."

"Didn't know Will had a sister." I don't know what to say to that, so I don't say anything at all, which is just as well since Hunter continues talking. "Can you give him a message for me?"

"Hold on a second. Let me get a pen."

"You won't need a pen. It's a short message."

There's a finality to the statement that has me glancing at Will, hoping he'll wake up and save me from this conversation and Hunter from whatever it is that's troubling him, but his eyes are still shut tight.

"Why don't you give him a call tomorrow?"

Hunter clicks his tongue. "Because I won't be here tomorrow, Rae."

My heart twists in on itself as the true meaning of his words settles inside my chest. A deep, harrowing sorrow pools in my stomach. The sensation of grieving someone I don't know before they've even gone. And Hunter is going. I hear the intent in his words, feel it in the silence on his end of the phone.

"Where are you going to be tomorrow, Hunter?"

He sighs, and it sounds like he's got the entire world pressing down on him, squeezing all the air out of his lungs. I imagine he must feel that way if he's thinking about ending his life.

"Not here. Can you just tell Will that I—" he pauses, and I imagine his lips pressed together into a hard, hesitant line. That hesitation gives me hope, makes me think that maybe he isn't as sure as I thought he was.

"Where are you?" The words spill past my lips in a rush. Hurried. Hopeful. "Maybe I can send someone to help you."

"There's no help for me, Rae."

"That's not true. You called Will because you thought he could help, right?"

"No, I called Will to say goodbye."

There goes my heart again, turning into knots of anguish for a perfect stranger. My mom always said I felt deeply for other people. That the world's problems weighed heavy on my heart. For as along as I can remember, she's referred to me as a gentle soul. Kind. Empathetic. Never a harsh word or a raised voice. Which is why nothing about my response to Hunter makes a bit of sense.

"Well, you'll have to wait to tell him yourself because I'm not going to pass along your message. After everything Will has done for you, I think he deserves more than a phone call, don't you agree?"

I don't have a clue in the world what Will has or hasn't done for Hunter, but I can imagine. My brother is the kind of person who gives everything he has to the people he cares about, and as one of his sponsees, Hunter fits the bill.

"You're probably right, but this is the best I can do, okay?"

Defeat casts a shadow over his words, bathing them in a darkness so thick and dense I feel it covering me as well. Any smart person would take a step back to avoid being engulfed by it, but I feel myself inching forward, reaching into it. Whether it's to save Hunter or lose myself, I'm not sure.

"I don't think that's true."

"I can assure you it is."

More silence. Another lung-emptying sigh filled with sadness that spells the end of this conversation and, if I let him go, the end of Hunter's life. I bite my lip, searching for something to say. My heart is telling me to keep him talking. My brain is screaming for me to wake Will. My mouth has a mind of its own.

"Have you eaten?"

"What?" he asks, an incredulous huff of amusement following the question.

"Have you eaten?" I repeat, like it makes total sense to ask someone in Hunter's state of mind about their eating habits.

"You think I want to die because I missed a meal?"

"No, but I do know you shouldn't make any big decisions on an empty stomach."

"So if I told you I had a five-course meal before I got high for the first time in two years and came up on this roof, you'd be okay with me stepping off of it?"

The image he paints makes my blood run cold. It's so vivid, so raw, so terrifyingly specific I'm stunned into a brief silence. Hunter chuckles, and it's a dark, condescending sound that tells me he thinks I know nothing about the kind of pain he's in. I resent that laugh and the assumption it represents. Pain is a familiar bedfellow of mine. The physical torture of dancing on open blisters and ingrown toenails. The emotional agony of holding my mom's hand while an oncologist explained that the chemo regimen she'd been following for months hadn't so much as slowed down the cancer.

It doesn't come from the same source, but pain is pain.

"Did you?" I ask, finally finding my voice.

"Did I what?"

"Have a five-course meal before you relapsed?"

"No, Rae, I didn't, and I don't think anyone would care if I left this world with an empty stomach."

"I would. I would care." My declaration gives him pause, and I use it to my advantage, choosing to fill the space with an offer I hope he won't refuse. "Which means you should let me buy you a meal."

4

HUNTER

"He bit my fucking nipple, Hunter!"

Mallory Kent's inappropriate declaration is punctuated by the sound of her taped and gloved fists colliding with the pads in my hand. She packs a hell of a punch, but there's not enough force behind it to make me move. When she realizes that, she spins and hits me with a roundhouse kick I'll happily take if it means that she's less likely to lose it on her son, Eric, who's apparently a little too enthusiastic about breastfeeding.

"Do three-month-olds even have teeth?" I ask, swinging the pads down so they absorb the brunt of the kick. There was a point in time when Mallory and I would train, and the only words I'd speak would be directives and critiques, but somehow—probably because of that one time years ago when I agreed to an impromptu session that ended up being more talking than fighting—this is our new norm.

Mallory talks.

I try to get her to shut up and fight.

She throws out a few combinations to show me she remembers

that I'm her trainer, not her therapist, and proceeds to treat me like one anyway.

Lather. Rinse. Repeat.

I'd be more upset about it if she wasn't such a good client, friend, and now business advisor. That last part of our relationship is still pretty new, something that happened when Mallory came to me with an investment proposal from the venture capitalist firm she works for and grand ideas about franchising. That was a little over a year ago, and now there are multiple Legacy Training Centers around the state, most of them in college towns, so we can serve young women in the same age range Mallory was in when she found me. All the new changes have been good for business, and even better for my pockets, but I won't lie and say that becoming the face of a brand that extends beyond New Haven hasn't been daunting.

I never wanted the gym to be more than what it was when I started it, when a dream that didn't spark in my heart became mine to make a reality, but here I am, doing branding shoots and filming self-defense videos for a YouTube channel that's seen by more people in a month than I'd ever want to know in a lifetime.

"That little jerk does," she says, huffing her way through a combination she used to execute with ease before her pregnancy with the twins. Now that she's fully recovered from her cesarean, she's determined to get back to where she was before becoming a mom.

"Widen your stance."

Her brows fold in on each other as she throws a jab that will cause her to stumble because her weight isn't evenly distributed. "My stance is fine," she grunts, following through with the move and proving me right. She stumbles forward, and I catch her, releasing her as soon as she's steady.

"Your center of gravity has changed, Mal, but you're still throwing moves like it hasn't. If you keep it up, you're going to hurt yourself or someone else."

Both of her shoulders drop, curved with defeat as she twists her lips to the side. I watch her process my words, the reluctance to accept the truth of the statement dancing in her brown eyes. Finally, she nods and begins to unwrap her hands.

"I guess we'll have to work on that later this week."

"You got it," I tap her on the shoulder with one of my padded hands and give her what I hope is an encouraging smile. "You still did good today. Not bad for a mom with a fucked up nipple."

This time, when she throws a jab—aimed directly at my stomach —her stance is perfect, and there's power behind the blow. It stings but not enough to steal my breath or anything, which makes her annoyed.

"My nipple isn't fucked up, asshole."

"That's how you made it sound. What am I supposed to think when you start talking about teeth and nipples?"

"I don't know. Not that."

We're both moving over to the bench where she dropped all of her shit when she stormed in here asking for a one-on-one session. I was on my way out the door when she showed up, and I paused my plans for the day to make time for her because she looked like she needed the physical outlet.

I toss my pads on the bench beside the bouquet of flowers I bought earlier, drawing Mallory's attention to them. Her brows lift and sparked interest makes her eyes light with a curiosity I don't want aimed in my direction.

"Who are the flowers for?"

"Nobody you know," I say, picking up the bouquet, my keys and phone. "You ready? I need to lock up."

She stands, grabbing her stuff too. "Really, Hunter?"

"Really, Mallory."

My answer is followed with a wave of my hand that indicates my impatience and, thankfully, gets her moving out the door. She's clearly annoyed but that doesn't stop her from waiting on me while I lock up.

"I'm not trying to be in your business," she says as we begin moving towards our cars. "But I do hope you're going to shower and change before you go on your date."

Even though she's got it all wrong, I still look down at what I'm wearing and ask, "What's wrong with what I have on?"

Mallory cocks a brow, sweeping her assessing gaze over the black shorts, shirt, and sneakers I'm wearing. "Are you serious? If a man showed up to a date wearing that, I'd walk right out."

"Good thing you're married, and you don't have to worry about things like that anymore."

Her jaw drops as she opens the driver's door. "Excuse you? Chris and I go on plenty of dates!"

Seeing her get so riled up is funny, especially when we both know that she's got an amazing husband and marriage. She and Chris went through some hard times over the years, but they're a great couple with one of the strongest bonds I've ever seen. Their little nipple-biting babies will grow up with two parents who are in love, which is nothing like the dysfunction of the family I grew up in thanks to my father, who left his first wife and son for my mother. A year after getting married, they had me, leaving me to grow up with a brother who despised me for having a full-time dad who constantly compared me to him.

"I know, I know, you and your husband are very in love."

"That's right, and you could be, too, if you put in a little effort before your date."

"Noted. See you on Thursday."

"Take a shower!" She calls out, and I wave her off, not bothering to respond as I make my way to my car.

THE DRIVE to the cemetery usually takes me twenty minutes, but today, I do it in fifteen. I sit in the car for a while, looking at a sky full of gray clouds and hoping the impending storm won't interfere with my plans to honor a life lost too soon. Eventually, I make the trek, walking a path I know by heart, remembering, as I always do, what it felt like to take these steps while sharing the burden of a casket with the members of a security team I left when the weight of my guilt got to be too much. When I reach her grave, I crouch down, brushing away dirt and random bits of debris until the letters of her name are clearly legible.

Legacy James.

A client turned friend whose death sent me flying off the edge of the wagon of sobriety. What felt like the end of the world at the moment actually resulted in the kind of goodness being brought into my life that didn't last long because I didn't know how to hold it, how to cherish it, how to feel like I deserved it.

"Happy Birthday, Legs. I can't believe you've been gone for so long."

The words are carried off by the wind, whipped around the headstones of lost loved ones. My parents are buried out here, and so are a few of my friends who failed to get a handle on the vices that brought us into each other's lives. Because of that, I spend a lot of time here, bringing flowers to graves that are my job to tend to, either because no one else can do it or because they just don't care enough to. I try to limit my visits to important dates—anniversaries of their deaths or their birthdays, or holidays like Mother's or Father's Day—so my whole life isn't marked by grief and loss, but even when I'm not here, I still feel it.

The emptiness.

The hollow.

The negative space in my heart, mind, and body that used to be taken up with good things and even better people. I miss one of them more than everyone else. Her absence isn't a result of a physical death but an emotional one. The loss of love that couldn't sustain the blows that refused to stop coming.

Visiting Legacy's grave makes me think of her more than usual, which is saying a lot because she's always a constant in my mind. The increase happens naturally, having something to do with the way Legacy's death overlaps with her arrival in my life. I used to be grateful for that overlap, convincing myself that good things could come out of even the worst situations, but now that I've lost them both, it just makes days like today hurt even more.

I've barely settled the flowers against the cold, granite slab when the first drop of rain breaks free from the gray clouds looming overhead and lands on my head in a fat, wet drop and rolls into my eye. Rising to my feet, I wipe the drop away, only for it to be replaced by several more in the span of a second. A clap of thunder sounds out, and the skies open up completely, prompting me to sprint up the path toward the parking lot. Ahead of me, there's a little girl holding the hand of a woman who is all but dragging her over the freshly formed puddles.

"Mommy, slow down. I want to splash," the girl pleads, her little legs working overtime to keep up with the long strides the woman is taking.

"Riley, no, you don't have on your rain boots," her mother replies, and I stop short, cocking my head to the side as the notes of her voice make their way to my ears, slipping in between heavy raindrops and claps of thunder with the sole intention of sending sparks of recognition down my spine.

The pause costs me precious time, allowing more rain to soak through my shirt and the duo in front of me to make it to their car, which is, by some twist of fate, right beside mine. The familiar stranger is now digging her keys out of her purse while the little girl —*Riley. Her daughter's name is Riley*—uses her mother's distraction to her advantage, driving her feet through the rainwater gathered on the ground around the car and giggling with delight.

"Riley, please, stop. You're going to be upset when you have to ride all the way home in wet socks."

"They're already wet, Mommy," Riley returns quickly. A little too quickly for a child her age, but I guess that's what happens when you have a mother like the one she does. You get to be all fire and sass, dancing in the rain without a care in the world.

Finally in possession of the keys, she unlocks the car and opens the rear passenger door, waving her hand to rush Riley into the dry confines of the vehicle. She goes without argument, happy to have gotten to splash in the puddles, even if it was for just a moment.

When she's settled in the seat, Riley's eyes collide with mine. She stares me down fiercely, unafraid even though I'm a stranger.

"Mommy, who's that man?" she asks, clicking her seat belt.

"What man, sweetie?"

Riley points at me, and I'm close now, closer than I should be to a stranger and her child. Closer than I should be to my lost love and the living, breathing representation of how far she's moved on from me. Closer than I should be but still too far away.

She turns away from Riley, closing the door to put a barrier between her child and the threat she's yet to identify. I stop near the trunk of my car and wait for her eyes to find my face. It takes too long because she starts at my feet, sizing me up the way I taught her to back when she spent all of her time inside the walls of the gym I named after the friend whose death brought her into my world.

In the time it takes her to meet my gaze, I've already marked every change she's made to her appearance since the last time I saw her a little over a decade ago. She's older, her brown eyes wiser, but she's still just as beautiful as she was the day she left me. Her hair is longer, hanging in thick layers of coiled, black curls that cling to her shoulders, a striking contrast against her caramel skin.

Her almond eyes are narrowed when they finally land on my face. When she realizes that it's me and not a complete stranger, they grow wide with recognition and surprise, but not fear.

"Hunter." Her lips curve around my name, but the sound of it is washed away as the rain picks up.

The torrent catches us both off guard, but it's still somehow the least surprising thing happening in this moment. We're more shocked by each other. By the reality of sharing air with someone you haven't seen or spoken to in years and, at least on my end, the pressing urge to know what it means for us both to be here—in New Haven, in this cemetery, in this moment—together after existing apart for so long.

"*Rae*."

5

HUNTER

Then

I don't know anything about Rae Prince.

I've never seen her in person. Before I called Will's phone, I didn't even know she existed. Still, the moment I walk into the Waffle House right off of the highway, I know exactly who she is. Maybe it's because she's the only person looking like she's about to meet up with a perfect stranger who, in their very first conversation, disclosed his intention to take his own life. It's the wrinkles between her brows that give her away. The lip pulled between her teeth. The fingers tapping on the linoleum table top. The general air of uncertainty and regret lingering around the booth near the back of the restaurant she chose to sit in. She's facing the door, watching the entrance, so she sees me at the same time I see her.

We both pause and share a look that's meant to confirm what we already know. That I'm me, and she's her. That we're two strangers meeting under the strangest of circumstances. She lifts her hand and waves, the beginnings of a smile playing on her lips before she strangles them into submission, forcing them to be something else, something more somber and fitting for the occasion.

My last supper.

How she convinced me to come here and share a meal with her, I'll never know. One moment I was on the roof of the building Legacy told me she intended to buy just a week ago, ready to put an end to it all, and the next I was agreeing to greasy hash browns and limp waffles all so Will's sister could feel good about letting me go off and die.

Because I still want to die...maybe.

Well, it's not so much of a want as it is a need. I *need* to go, to leave this world before I can hurt anyone else, before I can fail anyone else like I failed Legacy.

"You need a seat, sweetheart?" A waitress calls from behind the counter. She's got red, curly hair and frown lines in her ruddy skin as deep as the creases in her uniform.

"Nah." I tilt my chin in Rae's direction. "I'm meeting someone."

Speaking the words out loud is enough to get my feet moving, and in seconds, I'm casting a large shadow over Rae's table. She gazes up at me with almond-shaped eyes the color of roasted hazelnuts, and where I expect to find even a sliver of fear or intimidation because of my size and stature, I see nothing but interest and concern.

"Do you mind if I sit down?" I ask, giving her an out because God knows if I was in her situation, I'd want one.

"Unless you're going to eat standing up, I think you probably should take a seat, yeah."

The sass lacing her response surprises me so much it causes the muscles in my face to shift. It's not a smile. I haven't smiled since the day Legacy died. She's actually the last person I shared a smile with. We were laughing about some dumb joke Russ, the head of the detail, made, and that's when it happened. The ringing of a spent round, the melting smile that slipped off of her face as the life faded from her eyes. The wet squelching and hot splash of brain matter and shattered bone exploding onto me and the wall I was standing in front of.

When I decided to use tonight, that was the image in my mind.

Dissolved smiles and interrupted joy. I've seen death come for someone before. Soldiers in the unit I abandoned when I was dishonorably discharged from the military for not being a functioning addict like my commanding officer. My father, when he gripped his chest and collapsed, his eyes wide with anger and confusion at being betrayed by a heart his doctors had warned him for years would fail. My mother, whose body yielded to cancer so quickly, her life felt like sand slipping through my fingers. Like my parents, death had come quickly for Legacy, too, but the difference is she hadn't known to expect it.

Not right then, at least.

"Hunter?" Rae says my name like she's uncertain of whether she has the right to call me by it. Her brows fold in on themselves, thick, full, and perfectly shaped lines that ask me to sit because my continued standing is making her uncomfortable.

Finally, I drop down into the seat across from her, angling my legs to the side to ensure I don't accidentally bump her. The sigh she lets out is audible, and she keeps her eyes on me as I grab a menu and pretend to look over it.

"Are you actually looking at the menu or just avoiding making conversation with me?"

I cock a brow, lifting my gaze to meet hers. She's so confusing. One minute she's all steel and fire, and the next, she's soft and unsure, which makes her look as young as I think she is.

"You gonna judge all the choices I make today?"

"Only the bad ones."

"I guess it's a good thing I make a lot of those then."

"So how does this work?" she asks, reaching over to pluck the sticky menu from my hand. I watch her tuck it back into its designated spot between the ketchup, mustard, and hot sauce bottles. With nothing else to do with my hands, I clasp them together and try not to picture them covered in blood.

"How does what work?"

She gestures between the two of us with long, elegant fingers. "I don't know. This?"

"I don't know. I've never done this before."

I blink slowly, glancing around for our server because I need water. I'd forgotten how dry my mouth gets after using.

"Sure you have. If you're one of Will's sponsees, you go to meetings all the time."

"This isn't a meeting. You're not my sponsor."

Her jaw clenches, forming a surprisingly hard line for such a delicate curve, as she leans back against the booth and crosses her arms. "Your sponsor isn't available, so I'm all you've got. What would Will say to you right now?"

"He'd ask me what the fuck I'm doing here with his little sister." Self-consciousness ripples across her features, and she raises her chin, clearly annoyed with me for not taking her question seriously. I push out a long breath. "I don't know what he'd say to me right now, okay?"

"And you didn't want to find out. That's why you were planning to—"

Our server appearing out of thin air cuts her sentence short, and we pause our awkward conversation to order food I probably won't eat because the waves of nausea have started rolling, and they won't stop unless I use again. I'd planned to be gone before the effects of short-term withdrawal started, but now I'm here with Rae.

Alive and ashamed.

When the server leaves, Rae resumes tapping her fingers on the table, and I'm left with no choice but to put us both out of our misery.

"Will would remind me that recovery isn't linear," I offer. "And then he'd encourage me to talk about what led me to relapse because he knows there's always something that triggers the urge to use again after going through the hell of getting clean."

The way she smiles reveals everything I'd ever want to know about the way she feels about her big brother. Will is a hard ass who has never known a stranger in his life, but he's also an addict, which means Rae's love for him has probably been tried more than once. That she can project such positive feelings related to him even when he's not around says a lot about the work he must have done to repair what his addiction broke.

Like our own resident Houdini, the server comes back, setting plates and glasses down on the table before disappearing once more. I'm certain we won't see her again tonight. Picking up my glass, I take a slow sip of water, hoping it'll help with the dryness. It doesn't. Rae picks up her fork and starts to eat, taking an enthusiastic bite of her hash browns while maintaining eye contact with me.

"Would you tell him?"

My stomach twists. Will is the one person in the world I make a habit of being a hundred percent honest. He never required it of me, but it's just something I've given him because it's always what he gives everyone else. And there's something so wrong about lying to a guy who always tells the truth, no matter how ugly it is.

"Yeah, I would."

Rae plucks up two sugar packets from one of the canisters to her right and places them on the table next to the cup of coffee she ordered. I watch as she opens them one by one and dumps them into the stark, black liquid, wondering what she thinks about the likelihood of there being such a thing as an honest addict.

"Will you tell me?"

Despite the inflection at the end of the sentence and the quirked brow she pairs it with, it doesn't feel like a question. Her eyes make sure of it. They're hard and challenging, laughing at me for even considering denying her access to a story she's now a part of. The Hunter Drake saga. A tale of misfortune and woe that would already be over if it weren't for her.

"How old are you?"

She stirs the negligible amount of sugar into her coffee and then takes a long sip, closing her eyes to savor the flavor of burnt grounds that have probably been run through the machine more than once tonight. And it's that act that makes me realize why the question—which had been in my head since I first laid eyes on her—has finally made its way out of my mouth.

Rae is a conundrum.

Her face—all flawless, smooth brown skin with not a wrinkle or blemish in sight—expound her youth, but her mannerisms—the set of her shoulders, the steel of her gaze, the decision to drink hot, black coffee instead of those frilly iced drinks Legacy and all of her friends preferred—are that of someone much older than she must be.

"Nineteen." I choke on the water I've just welcomed into my mouth and it trickles back into the glass while Rae rolls her eyes. "Don't do that," she says. "If I'm old enough to watch my mom die, I'm old enough to hear about whatever made you use again."

"I watched my friend die."

The annoyance that had just made itself at home in her eyes fades away as her gaze softens with sympathy. "I'm sorry, Hunter."

Even though it is a big deal, I shrug like it's not. "I'm sorry about your mom."

Will had shared the news of her death in a meeting the day it happened. Confessing the burning desire to use again, to numb the pain of losing his mother before he got the chance to make up for all the fucked up shit he did before he was able to get clean. He never mentioned Rae directly, but he did allude to having other reasons to stay clean, other people depending on him to remain the version of himself they'd come to trust and rely on. Not knowing much about him besides his devotion to recovery, I'd thought he was talking about his sponsees, but now I know he was talking about Rae.

She takes another sip of coffee, this time to hide the quiver in her bottom lip inspired by my offered condolences. "Thanks."

We sit in a moment of silence before Rae speaks again.

"Breast cancer." I meet her eyes, imploring her to elaborate with a lift of my brows. "That's how my mom—*our* mom" —she corrects herself, leaving me to wonder how often she refers to their mother as just hers. There has to be at least a decade between her and Will, so it makes sense that she would think of their shared guardian that way. As someone belonging solely to her because she was raised alone for the most part—"she had breast cancer, and they caught it too late."

It's funny how unique, how utterly singular, an experience can feel until you come face to face with someone who has gone through the exact same thing. My mother's diagnosis came too late as well. Too late to save her. Too late to give me time to prepare to say good-bye. Too late to do anything but watch her die when all I wanted was her to live.

Using had made me numb for a moment, not long enough to make the years of sobriety I washed down the drain worth it, but for a while. That moment has passed now, though, the rush of euphoria is gone, and I'm open again. A sieve that won't stop catching pain even though all it can do is pass it on to something else and hope that it can hold it. Rae's pain passes through mine, collapsing into the endless gulf of heartache underneath me. There's barely enough room for it, but still, I take it because it's the least I can do.

"I'm sorry," I say again, more sincere this time. "My mom had breast cancer, too. By the time I convinced her to go to the doctor, it was already in her bones."

Rae's lips fold in on themselves, and her eyes turn glossy. Grief should be a private thing between strangers, but I can't bring myself to look away as a fresh wave of it washes over her. I want to witness it. To see something close to the pain I've known and carried for so long reflected back at me in something other than a mirror. It's a short-lived display, lasting only a few seconds before she reigns it back in and focuses on me more intently than before.

"You're not eating."

"I'm not hungry."

And I'm not. My stomach is all knots and nausea, and if I put anything other than water on it, I'm not going to make it through this makeshift meeting that's supposed to be saving my life.

"At least have some toast," Rae says. "It'll help with the nausea." She tucks a curly strand of hair behind her ear. "That's what my mom used to tell Will, anyway. I don't know how much good it actually does."

Not wanting to offend her or her mom, I pick up the slice of toasted white bread that came with my meal and take a bite, chewing slowly and praying it won't make a second appearance once I've choked it down. It doesn't make my stomach feel any better, but it does make Rae smile, so I guess it's a win.

"Did your mom help out a lot with Will's recovery?"

It feels like a violation of his privacy to ask this question, but I can't help myself. For some reason, I want to know, not about what getting cleaned looked like for Will, but what it looked and felt like for Rae. For someone who loves him. For someone who is just as invested in his sobriety as he is. I don't know what that's like. I started using after my mom died, and my dad was too busy berating me for finding yet another way to disgrace the Drake name to offer a kind or reassuring word. And then there's my older brother, Cal, who has hated me since birth because our dad left his mom for mine and would probably rejoice in the event of my death.

"Oh, no." Rae shakes her head. "She never let him come around me when he was using because she wanted to protect me, but I remember how he would call her crying, begging to come home, saying he was getting clean. She would always answer, always tell him she loved him, always tell him to eat and stay hydrated when he was going through withdrawal."

Not for the first time, I'm glad my mother wasn't alive to see me descend into addiction. It would have broken her heart.

"That must have been hard on your mom."

Rae nods. "She blamed herself for it even though he told her it wasn't her fault."

"Some people are just destined to carry the burden of responsibility, no matter how many times the people they love try to lift it."

"Do you feel responsible for your friend's death?"

I choke down another bite of toast before answering her. "Yes."

"Why? You didn't kill them."

"Her," I say, offering up the correct pronoun.

"Her," Rae repeats. "You didn't kill her."

"No, but I was supposed to keep her safe, and I failed." I shake my head, running a hand down my face, feeling the words, the anger, the shame all bubbling up in my throat. "And it would have been different if it was something unexpected or unpredictable like cancer or some shit, but it wasn't. It was her dumb ass ex-boyfriend who was the whole reason she hired a security team in the first place." Rae's eyes go wide, and I know I should stop talking, but I can't. "He said he was going to kill her. He promised. And Legacy, she did everything she was supposed to do. She filed the police reports. She got the restraining order. She moved and upped her security, and it still wasn't enough."

At the mention of Legacy's name, a flicker of recognition passes over Rae's face. I'm not surprised she knows who Legacy is. There isn't a single person in New Haven who hasn't heard her voice or seen her face on the six o'clock news. She is, or was, a local celebrity, loved by everyone except for the man who couldn't get over the fact that she decided to leave him after he started hitting her. Who made the last year of her short time on this Earth a living hell by harassing and stalking her until she had no choice but to hire the team that brought me into her life.

We became fast friends. I made her laugh, and she made me feel like I could be something other than a fuck up. I promised to teach her how to fight because she was obsessed with my MMA background, and she asked me to start a women's self-defense gym with her so we could teach women the things she didn't know about protecting herself when it mattered most. I wanted to say yes immediately but stopped myself because I was hesitant about leaving the stability of the firm for the uncertainty of entrepreneurship. Now, I can't help but wonder if things would have turned out differently if I'd said yes right then and there.

"But it was your best, right? You did everything you could for her?"

My eyes burn as tears gather in the corners. Ashamed, I turn to look out the window, watching the sky start to lighten. "I didn't save her."

"Maybe you were never meant to," Rae says softly. "Maybe you two were meant to know each other, to love each other for a short while, to learn whatever lessons you could only learn together, and then say goodbye. Is it tragic that she had to die in such a gruesome manner? Yes, absolutely. But is it your fault that an evil, violent man made good on a promise no one but God would be able to stop him from keeping? No."

Never in my life have I had someone attempt to absolve me of my guilt with such conviction. And maybe it shouldn't mean anything coming from Rae, but it does. My limbs are still heavy, and my heart is, too, but I feel something sliding underneath the edges of the weight on my chest, lifting it up and offering me just a second of relief.

A second where, for the first time since I literally washed Legacy's blood off of my hands, I can breathe.

6

RAE

"**M**ommy, you forgot to turn your windshield wipers on," Riley reminds me from the backseat, her voice calm even though I'm going sixty in a thirty-five to put some distance between us and the cemetery.

I push the lever down to activate the wipers and press the brake to force myself to slow down some because Hunter isn't after me. He didn't move an inch when I scurried around the car and into the driver's seat, nearly running him over as I pulled out of the parking spot. He just stood there, looking as stunned as I felt, as stunned as I still feel.

When I woke up this morning, I already knew it was going to be a hard day. We've been in New Haven for a week now, and it was on my heart to take Riley to the cemetery to meet her Nana and Uncle Will. Since she was a baby, I've shown her pictures and told her stories about them, letting her know how much they would have loved her. With Aaron starting his first day of work and Marcy distracting herself with cooking an extremely involved dinner to celebrate it, I thought today would be the perfect day to show Riley all of *my* New

Haven, which included the final resting place of my mother and brother.

Despite all the planning and thought put into the day, I wasn't expecting to run into the one person I've spent every day since my return to New Haven looking over my shoulder for. I thought I knew what the moment would look like, what it would feel like to have his eyes on me again, to breathe air infected with his scent and intensity for the first time in ten years, but God, it was nothing like I thought it would be. And to have Riley there to witness it? Well, that just made everything a million times worse.

She spotted him before I did, which has my mind all fucked up, making me think all kinds of crazy thoughts about biological bonds that are activated by proximity. I shake my head, trying to set the ridiculous thought free. That's not a thing. Men don't just look at a random child and know that they're theirs, even if that child is calling their ex-girlfriend Mommy and staring them down with eyes that are the same shade of brown as theirs.

Right?

God, I hope not.

"Who was that man?" Riley asks as I slow to a stop at a light around the corner from the house. She's been entranced by the rain for the duration of the ride, tracing the path of falling drops on the outside of the window with her finger. Normally, I'd warn her against leaving her little fingerprints on the inside of the window, but today I don't care.

I throw on my blinker and roll past the white line, looking both ways before turning right on red. The extra precaution is completely unnecessary because the intersection is empty, but it gives me more time to think, more time to come up with a lie I'll feel comfortable telling my daughter about the father she'll never know.

"What man, sweetie?"

The question pops out on its own, and I groan internally because Riley is a lot of things—smart, beautiful, headstrong, hard-headed as hell—but she's not stupid. She shoots me a quizzical look through the rearview mirror, and I hate that I can't unsee how much she looks like Hunter. The same eyes. The same thick, dark brows that dip inward when she's confused and go even lower when she's annoyed.

They're really low now.

"The man at the cemetery. Who was he?"

"Oh." I bite my lip as I pull into the driveway and put the car in park. "I'm not sure, sweetie."

I don't give her time to call me out on my lie, choosing instead to hop out of the car and rush to her side and open her door. She hops out, and I cringe when I hear the squish of her wet socks inside the sneakers I bought her for her first day at her new school. I'll have to wash and dry them tonight if they've got any chance of making it out the door tomorrow morning.

"Let's go, Nugget, we don't want to get rained on again."

Taking her hand, I rush us inside, and we make it in just as another shower begins. I busy myself with locking the door and shedding my wet jacket and shoes. Beside me, Riley is humming the theme song to Rugrats while she mirrors my movements. Recently, she's been into what she calls 'retro cartoons,' which is just her way of saying she's into the shows from when I was a kid and calling me old at the same time. Right now, she could call me an old hag, and I wouldn't care because I want her brilliant mind focused on something besides me dancing around her questions.

I glance at my watch and then at her, raising a conspiratorial brow. "If you hurry, you'll have time to watch an episode before dinner."

My offer has her moving twice as fast, and I laugh as she starts to race up the stairs, all thoughts of our previous conversation washed away by the promise of some screen time. Once she's gone, I make my way into the kitchen to find Marcy tending to multiple pots on the stove and Aaron sitting opposite her at the island with his laptop in front of him. He looks up as soon as I cross the threshold into the kitchen and treats me to a wide grin.

"Hey, babe. Did you get caught in the rain?"

"Yeah, it started to pour as we were leaving the cemetery, and of course, Riley wanted to splash in the puddles."

"Of course," he says, smiling indulgently as he opens his arms wide for me. I walk into his embrace, hoping the physical contact will help ground me. Aaron squeezes me tight and places a kiss on my cheek. It's soft and chaste. Decent. The kind of kiss that makes it impossible for me to forget that his mother is standing a few feet away, watching us.

"I hope you two didn't track in any mud because I spent the whole morning mopping the floors." Marcy's voice is soft with a perfect Southern lilt to it that makes it hard for you to suss out the bitchiness that's present in almost everything she says.

Pulling back from Aaron, I turn my attention to her, forcing a smile even though I want to tell her that I can cover the entire house in mud if I want because it's *my* damn house.

"Did you? I hope that wasn't too hard on your hip."

Marcy's eyes fly to mine, and I have to hold in the laugh her expression has building in my chest. She hates when I bring up her hip, but I'm going to continue to do so until Aaron realizes that her whole reason for having to move in with us was bullshit. A week after he got his promotion and told her we were moving to New Haven, she started complaining about hip pain and talking about how she might need to have a replacement soon because she could barely get up and down the stairs in her house some days. Aaron, being the loving and dedicated son that he is, immediately offered to help her find a place without stairs, but she made excuse after excuse about why that wouldn't work until, finally, he asked her to move in with us.

I could see the game she was running from a mile away, but I couldn't convince Aaron that he was being played by his own mom, so here we are, all living under one roof like she wanted. The only problem is I won't let her or Aaron forget why we're in this little arrangement from hell in the first place.

"No, my hip is just fine, Rae," she says, stirring a pot of greens while holding my gaze. "Thank you for asking."

"Of course, I'm glad to hear you're doing better. Maybe you won't need the hip replacement after all?" I cock my head to the side and lift a brow, which makes her serene expression falter. She doesn't like when I bring up the surgery I'm a hundred percent certain she was never told she needed.

Instead of answering, she places the top on the pot of greens and turns to the sink to wash her hands. "You should go freshen up, Rae, dinner will be ready soon."

As if anticipating me following his mother's order, Aaron releases his hold on my waist and turns back to his computer. I stand next to him, momentarily stunned by the dual dismissal, and then place my hand over his to still his fingers. He looks up at me with knit brows.

"You need to freshen up, too," I say, dropping my voice low as I bat my lashes at him.

Surprise etches itself into his features, and even though I can tell his interest has been piqued, he still chuckles and shakes his head. "It's not Wednesday, Rae."

The low reluctance in his voice as he reminds me of our agreed upon day for carnal indulgence makes my chest tight, but I push the frustration down, hiding it under a sultry smile that tells him I don't care that his mother isn't at bible study.

"I know what day it is, Aaron." Lifting my other hand, I rake my fingernails over the back of his neck. "And I want you, no, I *need* you today."

He licks his lips, glances at his mom, and then back at me. The short shift in his attention is almost enough to make me want to give up altogether, but then he closes his laptop and rises to his feet.

"We'll be back, Mom."

IT TAKES Aaron and I an hour to freshen up.

Forty-five minutes of that is me quietly begging him to go harder, deeper, and longer as if his dick could dislodge the memory of coming face-to-face with Hunter. As if a few orgasms could erase the mark he left on my soul. The other fifteen was spent showering and getting dressed for a dinner I didn't want but am currently forcing myself to eat.

"You should have gotten some of my noodles," Riley says to me from across the table where she's slurping down spaghetti noodles with nothing but grated Parmesan on them. She's been watching me push my food around my plate while Marcy fawns all over Aaron, who keeps giving her compliments on her dry-ass chicken. Now, they're both looking at me instead of each other.

"Something wrong with your food, dear?" Marcy asks.

I set my fork down on the side of the plate. "I guess I'm just not hungry. Riley and I had a late lunch." My fib would be more convincing if Riley wasn't currently scarfing down her food like she hasn't had a single meal today, but now that I've said it, I have no choice but to go with it. "We went to this cute cafe not far from your job, Aaron. It's called Twisted Sistas."

"It's my new favorite place," Riley adds.

"You have a new favorite place every other day, Ri," Aaron replies.

"So what?" She tosses back. "Favorites can change."

When I found out I was going to have a daughter, I decided that I wouldn't make her one of those little girls who don't know how to speak up for themselves. Riley is every bit of the girl I imagined she would be, sometimes a little too much so, and while I love that about her, other people don't always appreciate it. Marcy is one of those people. I watch her features crumple with disapproval and see her lips part to say something, probably to admonish Riley for being impolite, and feel a volatile reaction brewing inside of me. Thankfully, Aaron sees it too, and he jumps in, interrupting what would be his mom's reaction before it's a fully formed thought.

"You're right, Ri," he smiles wide, splitting the grin between the three of us, which seems to calm Marcy down a bit. "Tell us what other favorites you discovered today."

The request makes Riley's eyes light up, and she takes great pleasure in giving us a play by play of the entire day, undeterred by the fact that the moment she started talking Aaron pulled out his phone and started replying to emails.

I bump his leg with mine and whisper under my breath, "Seriously, Aaron?"

He doesn't even look at me. "What?"

"You asked her a question, the least you could do is pay attention while she answers it." His fingers fly over the keyboard at a rapid pace and tremors of annoyance rush down my spine with every letter he types.

"And then Mommy and me saw this man at the cemetery. She said she doesn't know who he is, but she said his name." Riley tilts her head to the side and looks at me; the spark in her eye indicates that she just remembered that fact. "How *did* you know his name was Hunter?"

"Hunter?" Aaron asks because, of course, he chooses now to tune back into the conversation. "Who's Hunter?"

"The man at the cemetery," my beautifully unaware daughter supplies, shoving the last of her noodles into her mouth. "Mommy knows him, but she said she doesn't."

Marcy arches a brow at me. "Oh, really?"

"Riley, don't talk with your mouth full."

After issuing the directive that also serves as a convenient deflection, I pick up my plate and leave the table. I can feel Marcy and Aaron's questioning gazes following me out of the room, but I don't stop until I'm in the kitchen, alone and able to breathe. I didn't realize Riley had heard me say Hunter's name. I don't know how she managed to with the door closed and the rain pouring and my heart beating so loudly every person in a ten-mile radius, both living and dead, must have been able to hear it skip a beat when I realized it was Hunter standing in front of me and not some dark figure who meant me harm.

For the first time since I saw him, I allow myself to acknowledge that he looked good. Not just handsome—because with the bald head, dark eyes, and mocha skin covered in tattoos he's always been handsome— but healthy. Like the man who was my best friend before he was ever my lover. Like the man I pictured a future with before I found out our present was all a lie.

I'm scraping my food into the trash can when Aaron comes in carrying Marcy and Riley's dishes in addition to his own. He comes up next to me, scraping what little is left on the plates and bowl into the bin on top of my uneaten meal.

"Mom took Riley upstairs to help her with her bedtime routine."

"She doesn't need to do that. Riley knows what she has to do."

"I asked her to."

"Why?"

"Because something is obviously wrong, and I wanted us to have a chance to talk in private."

My heart sinks into my stomach as I make my way over to the dishwasher on leaden feet. Aaron follows, watching me closely as I load plates, forks, bowls, and glasses into the machine at a snail's pace.

"Rae."

I sigh heavily and stand upright. "Nothing's wrong, Aaron."

He crosses his arms, studying my forced calm expression and calling it bullshit with an arched brow. "Who's Hunter, Rae?"

Swallowing is always impossible when my throat is as dry as it is, but I still try anyway because I need time to prepare myself to answer a question I never thought Aaron would ask. We've never talked about Hunter in any context. Our entire relationship is hinged on him loving the version of me that never knew or loved a man who chose his vices over her, and maintaining that illusion meant keeping a lot of things to myself, including Riley's paternity.

When we decided to move back to New Haven, I knew I was going to be giving up a lot of things. My dance career, the friends I'd made, the coffee shop I frequented too often, and the fifth-floor walk-up Riley and I had lived in since she was a baby, which I made Aaron move into because his place was too far from Riley's school. I knew this move would mean sacrifice, and I was willing to do it, happy to, even, as long as there were some things I got to keep for myself.

I want so desperately to keep this secret for myself, to guard my lies and carefully crafted illusions so that nothing else has to change, but when I look at Aaron, all I see is his determination to get the answer he feels he is owed. It's the same way he looked when I told him I wasn't leaving Manhattan to come back to New Haven. He pressed and pressed and pressed until I said yes, and now we're here, and everything is falling apart just like I knew it would.

"You can't ignore me forever, Rachel."

Bubbles of irritation flare in my chest. "Don't do that. Don't call me by my whole name like you're my dad or something."

"Then stop stalling and answer the question. Who's this Hunter guy, and why did you get all freaked out when Riley brought him up?"

"Because he's her father."

Aaron's eyes go wide with disbelief and then, after a few seconds of processing the fact that I've lied to him for years, narrow into slits. "I thought you didn't know who her father was!"

His elevated tone sends my eyes flying to the stairs to my left, searching for any sign of movement from Riley or Marcy because I don't need either one of them overhearing this conversation. When I'm satisfied that they're both oblivious to what's happening down here, I turn my focus back to Aaron. He's pacing the length of the floor in front of me with his wrists crossed over his head.

"Please keep your voice down, Aaron."

"Keep my—" he rounds on me, a dark laugh pouring out of him. "You've been lying to me for years, and you expect me to keep my voice down?"

"Yes, because Riley is upstairs, and I don't want her to hear you."

He shakes his head, but he does lower his voice, dropping it down to a dangerous, vicious pitch that's laced with disdain. "When you told me about Riley, I asked you. Do you remember? I asked you who her father was and if he was in her life; you looked me right in the eyes, Rae. You didn't even flinch. You looked me in the eyes, and you told me you didn't know who he was."

Somewhere in between Aaron's harsh tone and the anger dancing behind his eyes, my brain makes space for flashes of Hunter's face. For his concentrated stare and his calm but alert expression, for his even complexion and his thick, black beard that was neatly trimmed and perfectly tailored to the shape of his strong jaw.

Even when I thought he was clean back in the day, he never

looked as good as he did today, and I don't know what to do with that. I don't know what to do with him because I don't know this version of him. I didn't even know the version I thought I loved, which is why it was so easy to tell the lie Aaron now hates me for and why it's so easy to accept it now as a new, altered truth.

I don't know who Hunter Drake is, and for the sake of my daughter and the life I've built without him, it's best that I never find out.

7

HUNTER

The first thing I do after Rae speeds out of the parking lot of the cemetery is go to a meeting.

I was planning to go anyway since I'm the person who leads them, but after she walked away from me without saying anything other than my name, it felt like more of a necessity than a planned part of my monotonous life. Seeing her didn't make me want to use, but it did send emotions rushing through me in a wave strong enough to knock me off of my feet and flat on my ass.

"The only frame of reference I have for it is being slammed onto the mat." I laugh internally at my poor choice of a metaphor. No one else in my Tuesday meeting has fighting experience, so they don't really get it. Still, a few people nod, encouraging me to share the way I try to do for them when I'm on the other side of this dynamic.

"It's been over a decade since I've seen her, and now she has a kid..." I trail off, picturing the little girl whose face I only caught a glimpse of. She looks like Rae. I remember seeing pictures of her when she was a kid in the photo albums Will took great pride in showing me the first time they had me over for dinner after the relapse that brought her into my life.

"She's a mom." My voice shakes, and when I grip the edges of the podium, the wood creaks in protest. "I always thought I'd know her kid. I thought they'd be my kid, too. I didn't realize how tightly I'd held on to that idea until I was slapped in the face with the truth, which is that that won't ever happen. I won't know her or anything about the life she's built without me."

But it hasn't stopped me from picturing it. From building an image of the man who became everything we'd thought I'd be for her —guardian of her heart, keeper of her soul, father of her child. On the drive from the cemetery to the Baptist church where every NA meeting I've ever attended is held, I obsessed over it. What her life looks like. The peace she must have in her home now that she doesn't have to worry about hidden stashes and bathroom overdoses. I don't have to know the man she chose to know that's the case because I know Rae.

She wouldn't choose someone like me again. The lessons I taught her in disappointment have made sure of that. Which means the man she's with now, the father of her child, the partner who gives her peace and protection, is my opposite in every way.

Where I brought complications, he brings simplicity.

Where I brought chaos, he brings stability.

The only thing he doesn't have on me is love. No one in this world could ever love Rae more than I have, more than I still do. Of that much, I'm certain.

I blow out a harsh breath, knowing that my love for her is as irrelevant as my feelings about her being back here in New Haven. It's all my shit to deal with, to sort through, to process so it doesn't turn into an excuse for me to use.

"I guess we'll add it to the long list of things my addiction has cost me."

Out in the crowd, I see a few people nod their agreement. One of them is a kid in the last row chewing on his thumbnail. I've never seen him before, but that's not necessarily a red flag for me. Every day is someone's first day of sobriety, their first step toward a life without drugs, and when they make that decision, they usually end up in places like this, listening to people like me talk about the ups and downs on the road to sobriety. For that reason, I usually try to keep my shares on the lighter side. Not to sugarcoat things but to avoid being yet another person contributing to the shared weight we all carry when we leave this room.

That's what meetings with my sponsor, Nate, are for.

I lift a hand, rubbing at my forehead as the realization that I'm treating this meeting like my own personal therapy session settles on my shoulders. Shame eats away at my gut, and I rack my brain for a way to end this without it being weird.

Turns out, when you're in the middle of baring your soul to a room full of people, some of whom are the sponsees that depend on you to keep them grounded, there's no real way to do that.

"All of that to say, even when you're clean, there are still going to be moments like this. Moments when your past jumps out of the woodwork and reminds you of all the things your addiction has cost you, of all the ways you've been left behind. In those moments, you'll ask yourself what the point is. You'll think about giving up, but you can't because it might be too late to fix the past but you still have an entire future to show up for." Even though I'm not buying a single word that's just come out of my mouth, I steel my gaze and meet the eye of every person in the room, saving the new kid for last. "For some of us, that future starts today. Right here, in this room, with these people who are determined to help you show up as your best self, and I gotta tell you, my friend, you couldn't have picked a better place to be."

There's no applause when I leave the makeshift stage in the church basement, which is to be expected because this is a Narcotics Anonymous meeting, not an awards ceremony, but I'm still bothered by the silence. By the way, it settles around me when I take my seat at the back of the room, a collective but silent 'what the fuck?' from everyone in the room who won't say it out loud.

"Who else wants to share?" I ask, stretching my legs out in front of me and crossing my arms over my chest to appear relaxed when I feel anything but. Thankfully, a short, blonde woman from the middle row on the other side of the room stands and takes the stage. Her name is Jess, and she's been coming to these meetings since before I took them over. We've chatted a few times over the stale coffee in the back about how her addiction to opioids cost her custody of her children. Today, she shares about having an unsupervised visit with them for the first time in two years.

Once she's done sharing, the meeting moves along as normal. Nearly everyone shares except the kid in the back. He stays glued to his seat, chewing his nail and bouncing his leg, even after we wrap up. When I sit down beside him, his shame and anxiety is palpable. It scents the air around us, triggering the part of me that knows exactly how it feels to be where he is right now.

"I'm Hunter." I extend my hand to him, and he glances at it like I've just offered him a bomb, so I pull it back. "What's your name?"

He pulls his finger out of his mouth and wipes it on his pant leg. "Taurin."

"When's the last time you used, Taurin?"

Bloodshot brown eyes flick between my face and the front of the room, and at first, I think he's not going to answer me, but then he does. "Yesterday morning."

I let out a low whistle that's full of wonder. "First day is always the hardest."

"I know." Taurin curls in on himself, wrapping his long, thin arms around his stomach. He pins his chin to his chest and closes his eyes. "That's why I can never make it through day two."

"How many day ones have you had?"

"Five," he whispers, his voice a tremor or pain.

Five. Five attempts at getting clean at such a young age. He can't be any more than sixteen, and here he is, fighting demons I wasn't able to get a handle on until I was more than half his age.

I place my elbows on my knees and clasp my fingers together, studying his defeated posture. "You want it to stick this time?"

Taurin nods. "I *need* it to."

Something about the desperation in his tone resonates with the desperation inside of me. With that burning desire to be driven by something other than the need to have something you know will destroy you if you continue to hold on to it.

For Taurin, it's his drug of choice.

For me, it's Rae and all the things we lost when I stopped being able to hear my better angels because the voices of my demons got too loud.

I stand, and Taurin opens his eyes, watching to see if I'm going to stick around or abandon him like I'm sure so many people have before. I extend my hand again, and this time, he takes it, allowing me to help him out of his seat.

"Then we'll make sure it does."

8
RAE

After my post-dinner paternity confession, Aaron sleeps on the couch in his office. I spend the night curled up on my side of the bed, texting Dee about the fight and the run-in that inspired it. When she finished spamming my phone with voice notes that were nothing but her laughing manically at Riley being the one to put my business on front street, she pressed me for answers about Hunter, asking me questions that forced me to lay in the bed I share with Aaron and think about Hunter more than I have in years.

Okay, that's not true.

There hasn't been a single day since I left New Haven that I haven't thought about him. I mean, it's kind of impossible not to when I'm raising a little girl that's grumpy like he is in the morning and stubborn as a fucking mule, just like him. But outside of that, I've passed hours wondering how he is, if he's clean, if he's alone, if he's *alive*, torturing myself when I knew there was no safe way for me to find out the answer to any of those things. And now that I know, I wish I didn't because knowing has turned my life upside down.

I wake up the next morning on a mission to try and turn things right side up again. In my mind, that means putting on the sexiest, slinkiest nightie I own, tousling my curls into an intentionally effortless mess, and sneaking down the stairs to Aaron's office to make up with him so he doesn't go to work mad at me. To avoid going by Marcy's room and possibly waking her up, I take the back stairwell that leads to the kitchen, stopping short on the second to last step when the scent of coffee alerts me to the fact that someone is already up.

Aaron prefers espresso to a traditional brew, so the moment I hear the coffee maker going, I know it's Marcy waiting for me. Part of me wants to turn around and go back to my room, but I make myself move forward because I refuse to cower and hide in a house I help pay for. When I hit the last step, Marcy comes into view. She's standing at the island, fully dressed in a pair of khakis, a button-up with horizontal, pink lines running up and down the starched white fabric, and a white sweater tied around her neck. She looks like she's about to go play a round of golf at the country club, which is funny considering that it's six in the morning and the sun has barely risen. I would ask her what she's doing up so early, but I already know because everything, from the set of her shoulders to the half smirk she gives me before she takes a sip of her coffee, suggests that she's been lying in wait for me.

"Aaron has already left for work," she tells me, her voice laced with faux innocence while her eyes dance with spiteful glee. "He seemed upset. I think he slept in his office last night."

Although it's disappointing to hear that Aaron has left without saying goodbye to me or wishing Riley good luck on her first day at a new school, I don't let any of that show on my face. I can't give Marcy the satisfaction of having upset me the way she suspects I've upset her son.

"I think he had an early meeting," I offer, making my way over to the refrigerator to pull out the ingredients for the pancakes Riley requested I make for breakfast. If I time it right, they'll be done by the time she wakes up.

"A meeting?" She tilts her head to the side, studying my every move while also somehow managing to keep track of any changes to my expression. "Before six in the morning?"

I shrug. "I know it sounds ridiculous, but you'd be surprised by how many breakfast meetings I've watched Aaron spend the night prepping for before he was promoted to VP of Business Development."

Technically, it's not a lie. It's more of an exaggeration, meaning over the course of our entire relationship, I've only ever heard of Aaron having one breakfast meeting. And when that happened, he swore he'd never agree to have another one once he got promoted. Lucky for me, Marcy doesn't know any of that.

She rounds the island and takes a seat across from me with her coffee still in hand. I sigh internally, wishing she would go on with whatever plans she has for the day so I can have some time to figure out my next steps with Aaron. We never fight. Like ever. That's one of my favorite things about him, *about us*. We're steady. Everything about our life, from the restaurant we go to on date night to the day we have sex, is predictable. There are no surprises or variations, just smooth sailing on still waters.

No bumps.

No waves.

Just us.

I don't want that to change just because New Haven has thrown us curve balls in the form of my ex...and his mother.

"It's just that—" Marcy starts, pausing to take a sip of her coffee. "I could have sworn I heard you two arguing last night when I was upstairs with Riley."

"Nope," I say, slamming the buttermilk down a little harder than necessary. "Speaking of Riley, do you think you could go see if she's up?"

She glances up at the ceiling and then back at me. "I don't hear her, but I'm certain she'll get up when her alarm goes off."

Unable to think of a single response that doesn't involve me screaming, 'that's not what I asked you,' I focus all of my attention and frustration on assembling the batter while Marcy watches in silent judgment she doesn't voice until I'm moving the last pancake in the batch from the pan to Riley's plate.

"I never made Aaron pancakes for breakfast on a school day." She shakes her head to really emphasize her point. "All that sugar so early in the morning isn't good for kids."

Placing the plate in the microwave so the pancakes stay warm, I decide it's best to keep my response short. "Well, it's what she wanted for her first day breakfast."

"It's not good to give a child everything she wants, Rae. Pancakes for breakfast on a weekday. Special dinners when she doesn't like what's been prepared." Once again, her head goes from side to side, signaling her disapproval. "Keep it up, and you'll ruin her."

I wipe my hands on a dish towel and turn to face her, gifting her with my most insincere smile. "Well, I guess it's a good thing she's mine to ruin."

"That's a terrible way to look at things, dear. It takes a village to raise a child, and Aaron and I are your village. We have been since you and Riley came into our lives, which means Riley is just as much ours as she is yours."

My brows pull together, forming a line so tight it makes my head hurt. But the pain from the headache is nothing compared to the fire burning inside my chest, ignited by all of my maternal instincts coming online at the same time.

"Let's be clear about something, Marcy. I appreciate everything you and Aaron have done for Riley, but at the end of the day, she is my daughter. *Mine.* Which means I will always be in charge of making decisions for and about her. If I want to make her pancakes for breakfast, lunch, and dinner, I will do exactly that, and I won't so much as pause to ask what anyone else thinks about that choice."

"Pancakes for breakfast, lunch, *and* dinner?" Riley asks excitedly as she bounds into the kitchen with her school uniform already on. She looks at me with bugged-out eyes as she takes a sit next to Marcy. "For real, Mommy?"

Contrary to what Marcy might believe, I'm not actually fool enough to feed a nine-year-old pancakes three times a day, so I shake my head at Riley and force a laugh. "No, Nugget, I was just being hyperbolic."

"Hyperbolic," Riley repeats the word several times while I retrieve her plate from the microwave. By the time it's in front of her, along with a fork, knife, syrup, and a cup of milk, she's decided that she likes the way it feels on her tongue, and I hear her singing it to herself in between bites of her food.

"I'm going to get dressed," I say to no one in particular. "Riley, when you're done eating, put your dishes in the sink, and then come upstairs so we can wash your face and do your hair."

I don't bother waiting around for her response because I know she'll listen. Riley is a good kid, and I rarely have to repeat myself when I set clear expectations with her. For that reason, and so many more, I take offense to Marcy acting like taking my daughter's preferences into consideration is going to turn her into some entitled monster.

So many adults seem to forget that kids are people with their own thoughts and opinions and desires. As a parent, it's my job to give Riley space to express all of those things, and when her requests are reasonable, age-appropriate, and within the realm of possibility, I do my best to give her the things she asks for, so she knows that I care enough to go out of my way for her.

"Do you think the other kids in my class will know what hyperbolic means?" she asks as we pull up to Hartwick Academy, the best private school in New Haven. I glance at her through the rearview mirror and find that she's twiddling her thumbs.

"I'm not sure, Nugs. If they don't, I'm sure you'll do a great job of introducing them to it."

She nods, glancing out the window to take in the stately, white brick walls covered in vines of ivy. There are students pouring into the building from every direction in groups of varying sizes. My heart lurches as four girls around Riley's age pass by the car, talking and laughing with matching Coach satchels bouncing on their hips. They look like they've known each other forever, and their familiarity seems to drive home how new and unfamiliar everything will be for

Riley. The school. The teachers. The kids. The social scene. My baby won't know anything or anyone, and the thought makes me want to press the gas and take her far away from it all.

"Are you going to stop the car, Mommy?"

Her question draws my attention to the fact that I've been subconsciously accelerating instead of hitting the brake. The crossing guard gives me a strange look and holds up her stop sign, which only makes me more embarrassed. I lift my hand and mouth 'sorry' but she just shakes her head and turns the other way. After placing the car in park, I turn in my seat to check in with Riley before one of the teachers in charge of drop off opens the door and spirits her away.

"How you feeling, kid?"

"A little nervous," she confesses. "I don't know anybody."

"Yet. You don't know anybody yet, but by the end of the day, I'm sure you'll have at least one new friend."

Hope pulls her brows up into two high arches. "You think so?"

I nod, and even though I'm not certain, I say, "I know so."

To MY SURPRISE, and great relief, drop off goes well. Riley was retrieved from the car by Mrs. Marten, the school's headmistress, who we met when we first toured the school, and a little girl named Scarlett, who volunteered to be Riley's welcome buddy for the week. The moment she got out of the car, they started talking, bonding over their shared love of the rainbow stickers Riley had plastered all over the binder she was clutching in her arms.

Mrs. Marten and I watched the girls make a run for the entrance and shared a smile that made me feel comfortable leaving Riley to go and sort things out with Aaron.

His office is in the heart of the financial district, which is really just fancy terminology for a city block downtown that's heavily occupied by banks and venture capital firms that were drawn to New Haven because of its reasonable real estate prices and proximity to Atlanta. According to Aaron, it also doesn't hurt that it's the home of the Adlers—a family of Black billionaires that have a hand in everything from real estate to shipping. When I was a kid, I grew up hearing that name a lot, seeing it plastered on hospital wings and football stadiums for my high school. It never occurred to me that there were actual people behind the name, but Aaron's recent obsession with getting a meeting with the family's oldest son, Sebastian, has changed that.

That's probably why it doesn't surprise me to hear it gliding off of his tongue when his secretary, Eden, lets me into his office. She wasn't happy when I showed up out of the blue, insisting on seeing him, and she was even less enthused when I refused to accept her offers to have him call me when he had an opening in his schedule. All of that shows in her voice when she announces my arrival.

"Mr. Scott, your girlfriend is here to see you."

I brush past her, hating the way the cloying notes of her perfume get stuck in my throat, hating, even more, how she manages to make girlfriend sound like a slur. As if it's some kind of moral failure to not be someone's wife. I could have been Aaron's wife three times over by now if I wanted to, but I don't want to, not yet.

Maybe not ever, the voice in my head says, tacking the unwelcome addition onto the end of my thought. I don't know where it came from, and I don't have time to explore it because Aaron is sending daggers through me with his eyes.

I turn to Eden, needing to get her out of her before we start bickering in front of her. "Next time, refer to me by my name, or don't refer to me at all." With a flick of my wrist, I send the door flying toward the jamb and take sick satisfaction in being able to see the shocked expression that takes over her face before it closes.

When I turn to Aaron, annoyance is written all over his features, and he's no longer on the phone. He stands and strides over to me, robbing me of the chance to get comfortable in his space.

"What are you doing here, Rae?"

I slide my hands into my pockets, feeling self-conscious all of a sudden. "I came to see you. You left before we had a chance to talk, and you didn't even see Riley before her first day of school."

If I'm being honest, I think that bothers me more than anything. Aaron has been a part of Riley's life for as long as she can remember, and, father or not, he has a responsibility to support her through hard transitions like the one she's going through today. That shouldn't change just because he's mad at me.

"I'm sorry I missed it," he says, running a hand over his head. I search his face for any signs of remorse and come up empty. "I'll make it up to her."

"Don't worry about it."

Aaron sighs. "You can't just show up to my job like this, Rae."

"And you can't just leave the house without saying anything to me. I get that you're mad, okay? But you have to understand—"

"No," he says, cutting me off. "I don't have to understand anything. I've *been* understanding for seven years, and you've lied to my face every single day."

"I've already apologized for that, Aaron."

"And I'm just supposed to be over it? Would you have even told me if Riley hadn't brought up that you ran into him?"

"No." My instant answer sends his brows reaching for his hairline. "I had no intention of talking about Hunter with anyone, not even Riley, ever. He is my past; you are my future."

The declaration lacks conviction, and Aaron susses out the hollowness immediately. I guess it's easy to do when it's coming from a woman who's turned down your proposal three different times.

"I'm just having a really hard time believing that."

I close the space between us, relieved when he doesn't step back. "How can I fix it?"

"You already know the answer to that question."

Of course.

Of course, the one thing he needs is the one thing I'm not comfortable giving. I consider denying him once more. What Aaron is asking for is private. It's Hunter's and mine. It doesn't belong to him; it barely belongs to us, and it frustrates me that Aaron wants to own this part of me as well, that the things I've given up for him already aren't enough.

Pushing out a long, steadying breath, I prepare myself to give again because I know that if I don't, nothing will get better. And I need things to get better. I move over to the couch in the corner of Aaron's office and pat the cushion beside me, silently asking Aaron to come over. My stomach is in knots, but I breathe through the discomfort, telling myself I'll feel better once it's all out in the open, even though I know I won't.

"The night I met Hunter Drake, he was planning on killing himself..."

9

HUNTER

Now

There's a rhythm to the gym.

It's the crash and slap of padded gloves. Strained breathing and exerted grunts that are layered on top of the sound of bodies being slammed into mats. It's a melody I've grown accustomed to, one I depend on to keep me grounded when things outside of these doors are all flipped around.

I'm leaning on the metal railing that lines the lofted space I use to keep an eye on things when that rhythm changes. When the air turns thick and everything goes quiet because all of my senses have tuned into the woman striding into my gym like she owns the place.

Not the place, just me.

At first, I think my eyes are playing tricks on me, but then she looks up, using her hard-earned knowledge of my favorite hiding place in the gym to scope me out. When our eyes meet, she's not at all surprised to find that I'm looking at her, and I'm not shocked by the fact that being held in her gaze for more than a second takes my breath away.

We meet at the bottom of the stairs, and even though she sought me out, she seems thrown off by my proximity. Not uncomfortable, per se, but not fully settled in my space. It reminds me of the way strangers deal with me. The way all of their movements are slow and cautious, like their entire body is preparing for the moment when I decide to use my strength and size against them. Rae slides her hands into the back pockets of the jeans that are clinging to her long legs and toned thighs like a second skin. She's paired them with a buttery soft sweater and a pair of ballet flats. The corners of my mouth quirk, remembering a time when I would pester her about the irony of being a ballerina in ballet flats.

"Don't," she warns me, her eyes narrowed.

"I wasn't."

Silence settles between us, loud and uncomfortable. I don't know why she's here, and I don't know how to ask her, so I just wait for her to say something else. Instead of speaking, she looks around, marking the changes I've made over the years. I don't call them improvements. I never do because every updated mat or fresh coat of paint takes this place further away from what I built with her at my side.

"It looks really different in here," she says, finally, turning those eyes back on me. They're a luscious brown, deep and earthy like wild clay pulled from the bed of a winding river, and I've missed them so fucking much.

"Do you want a tour?"

Suddenly, all I want is to give her one. To walk her through the changes I've made to the gym in the hopes that it'll lead to a conversation about the changes I've made in me. I'd lead her through the five thousand square foot addition at the back of the warehouse and tell her we use the open space in the middle for everything from Zumba classes to goat yoga and that the rooms around the perimeter are rented out to content creators who specialize in fitness and want somewhere safe and comfortable to record their workouts.

I'd take her to my office and let her see that nothing much has changed in there because I won't let it. She'd see that my desk is still the same, a relic of our past, of a time when she'd perch on the edge and distract me from paperwork with nothing more than her smile. She'd see that the ceiling tile with the messy, lopsided, black heart with our initials in the center is still there, too.

She'd see everything, and maybe it'd mean nothing to her, but she'd still know there hasn't been a single day that's gone by where I haven't tried to find a way to hold on to her, to us, even though she let me go.

"No, that's okay." She tucks a curl behind her ear, and I remember what it was like to feel the delicate coils slip between my fingertips. "I wasn't planning on staying long."

"I'm surprised you came by in the first place."

"Why?"

"Because of the way you burned rubber to get away from me at the cemetery yesterday."

"Right." Her tongue darts out of her mouth, skating across her bottom lip before being replaced with the blunt edges of her teeth. "That's actually what I came to talk to you about."

I'm not quite sure where this conversation is going, so I forgo a verbal response, opting for a dip of my chin that tells her to continue. Rae gazes heavenward, taking time to gather her words, which is how I know I'm not going to be a fan of what she has to say.

"I need you to stay away from me," she blurts, catching me completely off guard. My head snaps back as if I've been struck, and a laugh spills past my lips.

She needs *me* to stay away from *her*?

Still laughing, I turn my head to the left and then the right, double-checking our surroundings before I respond. "You realize you're standing in my gym, right? That you came here and sought me out, not the other way around?"

I mean, obviously, I'd thought about seeking her out. Actually, after I wrapped things up with Taurin—leaving him at Waffle House despite my better judgment because he insisted his parents were on their way to pick him up—I drove around town aimlessly, hoping to run into her again, but she doesn't know that, which means this conversation is as random as it is uncalled for.

"Of course, I know that, Hunter." Rae rolls her eyes, and a shiver runs down my spine at the sound of my name on her lips. Maybe she's right to be warning me away. "I'm just trying to be preemptive, to rid you of any ideas about looking me up or showing up to my house or contacting my kid."

My brows fall together as a mixture of hurt and outrage filters through my body. "You think I'd do some shit like that? Just pop up on you or, worse, freak Riley the fuck out by showing up at her school and saying, 'hey, I used to be in love with your mommy?'"

When I say her daughter's name, all of her features go still. She takes a step back like the small space between our bodies poses a threat to Riley's safety, and it's so incredibly hurtful that I take a step back, too, reeling from the pain of watching the woman I once dreamed of building a family with physically recoil at the thought of me knowing anything about her kid.

I scrub a hand over my face and sigh. This is what addiction has earned me: distrust and skepticism. I've dealt with it before and talked my sponsees through their encounters with it as well, which means I know that being angry won't help. Using, but especially relapsing, breaks something fundamental in relationships, and as the addict, it's your job to try and repair it.

Most of the time, it's not a wound that's easily healed. It takes time and consistency, and with Rae, I have neither of those things. All I have is my word, and I already know it doesn't mean shit to her.

"I'm a lot of things, Rae, but I'm not, nor have I ever been, a stalker or a creep. I would never do anything to make you, your family, but most of all, your daughter, feel unsafe. You have my word that if I ever see you out in public, I will turn and go in the other direction before you even know I'm there."

Rae is stoic as she studies my features, almond-shaped eyes flitting from one part of my face to the other in search of sincerity. She must find what she's looking for because she swallows and nods.

"Thank you," she says before turning to leave just as quickly as she came.

"HEARD you kind of lost your shit in a meeting the other week. The fuck was that about?"

Nate poses the question seconds after taking a seat across from me with a cup of coffee in one hand and a chocolate croissant in the other. He's been out of town dealing with some family stuff, so this is the first face-to-face sit-down we've had in weeks. I'm not surprised that he's chosen to kick things off by calling me out about the way I acted when I ran into Rae on the first day of what I now affectionately refer to as 'Hell Week.'

"Who said that?"

He chomps down on his pastry, chewing thoughtfully before saying, "Everybody. The question is, why didn't you say anything to me about it?"

I shrug and take a sip of my water. "You were dealing with family shit, I didn't want to unload on you."

"So you chose to unload on a room full of your sponsees instead?"

"It wasn't supposed to happen like that."

"How was it supposed to happen then?"

"The way it always does."

"Meaning?" He lifts a brow, and the strands of silver that have just made it to the top of his face after months of staging a coup to take control of the hair hugging his chin dance under the fluorescent lights above us.

"Meaning, I was supposed to keep my shit tight, hold space for the meeting attendees and save all my trauma for you."

Nate dips his head in a faux bow. "I'm honored to be the keeper of your trauma."

"Of course you are," I toss back the last of my water and shake my head as memories from the meeting weeks ago assail me. "I fucked up, huh?"

"What makes you say that?"

"I mean, you just said that's what everyone else is saying, so…"

"That's not what I said." He takes another bite of his pastry and washes it down with coffee before continuing. "*I said everybody was talking about how you lost your shit.*"

"Right, which means that I fucked up."

"Hunter, since when does having a moment of vulnerability constitute a fuck up?"

That question gives me pause, which is exactly what Nate hoped it would do. His smug smile tells me as much.

"I guess never?"

Nate lets out a loud, boisterous laugh. "I mean, I'm sure there are some occasions when it does, but this definitely isn't one of them. A fuck up in our world is a relapse; anything else, including crying about your ex in front of your sponsees, is just a part of being human."

"I didn't cry."

"That's not what I heard." I flip him off, which does nothing except make him laugh. "Seriously though, Hunter, you've got to stop holding yourself to this impossible standard of perfection. You're an addict. The people you sponsor are addicts. That means they know, first and foremost, that you're not perfect. Hell, they probably prefer it."

Despite hating being called out in such plain terms, I find myself nodding and thinking of the conversation I had with Taurin after the meeting I'd written off as a failure. I took him to the same Waffle House I take all my sponsees to—the one where I met Rae on the night she saved my life—and we talked about how frustrated he'd been with all the examples of perfection during recovery that he'd been subjected to during his other attempts to get clean. He told me my impromptu share had made him stick around to hear more, and then he'd ask me to be his sponsor.

Watching him battle his way through turning days of sobriety into weeks is the one good thing that's come out of Rae's return to New Haven.

"Hey, kid, I've already told you one time that you can't do that in our bathrooms!" The loud and sudden outburst causes everyone in the cafe to turn towards the sound. Nate and I watch along with every other person in the building as the manager marches someone out of the back, where the bathrooms are, toward the front door. From where I'm sitting, I can see that the person is young, a teenager by the looks of it, but their face is obscured by the hood slung over their head. They say something to the manager, their voice too low for me to hear from this distance, and the guy shakes his head in disgust.

"I don't care. That's not an excuse for you to use our facilities like your own personal bath house."

"Hey."

I don't realize I'm standing until I look around and see that everyone I was just close to eye level with is now gazing up at me. The manager pauses as I cross the room, his features frozen in fear as I invade his space.

"H—how can I help you, sir?" he asks, tipping his head back to look up at me while the kid he's still holding in his clutches goes completely still.

"Well—" I pause, allowing my eyes time to rove over his scrawny chest and find the name attached to his employee badge. "*Tim*. You can start by letting the kid go."

"Oh, sir, you don't understand, this young man was—"

"Doesn't matter. Short of a few very specific things that would have necessitated a call to the police instead of a personal escort out of the building, there's nothing he could have done that would make this public spectacle necessary, so let him go before I'm forced to remove your fingers from him myself."

Most people take a threat of physical action from me very seriously. Tim is no exception. He peels the fingers of his right hand off of the kid's arm and drops the book bag he was carrying in his left on the floor, then he turns and scurries away.

"I'm sorry you had to experience that," I say, bending at the waist to pick up the book bag and pausing altogether when I realize that I recognize it and the pair of beat up Air Force One's it's sitting next to.

Snatching the bag up, I right myself immediately. "Taurin?"

He turns to me slowly, his eyes wide with fear and his shoulders slumped with shame. It's been a few days since I've seen him, and while he never looks particularly put together, I never assumed he was unhoused.

"We should go before they kick us out," Nate says, appearing on my left side while Taurin stands awkwardly to my right. It doesn't take but a second for Nate to realize that something is off. "Everything okay over here?"

"Yeah," Taurin says weakly, at the same time I say, "Hell, no."

Nate huffs out an uncertain laugh, glancing over his shoulder at the counter where Tim is glaring at the three of us. "I think it's safe to say that whatever is going on is going to have to get sorted out outside of here."

Without another word, Nate strides out of the cafe, and I fall into step behind him. Taurin sighs and comes along, too, but I think it's only because his book bag is still in my hands. We make it all the way to my car before Nate rounds on us with his brows lifted in a silent order for one of us to explain what's going on.

"Nate, this is Taurin, my newest sponsee. Taurin, this is Nate, my sponsor."

Nate extends his hand, leaving Taurin with no choice but to shake it. "Good to meet you."

"You say that to all the people you watch get dragged out of cafes?"

"Hey." I cut my eyes at Taurin. "Watch your tone, man."

"It's all good, Hunter," Nate says, easygoing as ever. "We're addicts, Taurin. I've met people under a lot worse circumstances and still said it was nice to meet them."

Taurin's eyes narrow into slits. "I'm not an addict. I've been clean for two weeks now."

"Son, I've been clean for twenty-five years, and I'm still an addict. It's just the truth of our condition. We'll always be addicts even when we don't remember what it feels like to be high."

"Kind of wish I was high right now," the kid mumbles under his breath.

"Don't say that," I growl. "Look, you're angry and embarrassed because of what happened back there, but that's not an excuse to be rude to someone who's just telling you the truth."

"Whatever." He pulls his hood down further until it's covering the sides of his face completely. "Can you just give me my bag so I can go?"

"Sure. I'd be happy to give you your bag just as soon as you tell me where exactly you're going to go."

Taurin shuffles his feet, kicking at the asphalt with the toe of one of his shoes. "Home."

Nate and I exchange a look. Neither of us believes Taurin's assertion, but as his sponsor, it's my job to call bullshit on it.

"You just got caught washing in a public restroom, kid. Let's try that again." Nothing but silence greets me, and while I can feel frustration digging its claws into my chest, I don't allow it to win. Instead, I square my shoulders and come back with a gentler approach that's still rooted in reality. "How long have you been living on the street, T?"

Tears pool in the corner of his eyes, but he's too stubborn to wipe them away. He's also too stubborn to meet my gaze, but he does answer me. Eventually.

"Since the day we met."

The moment the pain evident on his face causes his voice to fracture, my heart shatters along with it, and when he turns towards me, I open my arms on instinct, allowing him to find solace in the comfort of my embrace. It won't do a damn thing to heal the pain of being abandoned, of being pushed away and discarded by the people who are bound by blood to see you through your hardest moments, but it's better than nothing.

"My mom said I can't come back home," he whimpers. "The last time I used, I OD'd, and my little brother found me. I promised her I wouldn't do it anymore, but she doesn't believe me. She won't let me come home. I don't have anywhere to go."

The offer comes out quickly, as natural as taking my next breath, as familiar on my tongue as it was the last time I extended it to a friend in need.

"You're going to come home with me."

10

RAE

"So, you're *finally* going to tell him how you feel?" Dee asks, flinging herself onto the bed that's only recently become mine.

"Maybe."

I stand in front of the full length mirror and twist this way and that to determine whether I like the way the strapless romper fits. The shorts are *short,* the hem hitting the tops of my thigh and leaving everything else on display, while the tie-front and deep V of the neckline draw attention to the way the princess-seamed bodice turn my usually underwhelming cleavage into something to marvel at.

"Maybe? Rae, you've been crushing on Hunter for years. I think it's time to do something about it."

"But what if he doesn't feel the same way?"

Considering that Hunter has never so much as suggested that he thought of me as anything more than a friend, I think it's a fair question, but Dee's 'be fucking for real' expression tells me she disagrees. She hops off the bed, coming up behind me and placing her hands on my hips, forcing me to face myself head-on in the mirror.

"Look at you! He's going to be falling all over himself for a chance with you."

"You think so?" My voice is small, filled with the need for validation.

"I know so." To emphasize her point, she slaps my ass hard enough to make me yelp in pain and then darts out the door before I have the chance to react in any other way.

"I'm gonna get you back," I call out, letting the threat follow her out of the door because I have no interest in getting into a scuffle with her before the most important night of my life begins.

The sun is just starting to go down, so there are rays of golden light coming through the window of my bedroom, bathing the bed and boxes of clothes and other items Will brought with him to Hunter's when a mold in our walls made it necessary for him to leave our place two weeks ago. I was in the middle of finals when he called to tell me that things were going to look a little different when I came back from New York, where I've been doing a conservatory for the last semester, and while some people would be bummed about having to move in with their brother's sponsee turned friend for the summer, I was ecstatic because I love Hunter.

Not in *that* way.

Okay, maybe in that way, but also in the way that you love someone when they've become a constant in your life. When they've become someone you can call at any time, day or night, and they'll always pick up, always listen without judgment, and reassure you that everything is going to be alright. And after they've done all of that, they'll do everything in their power to *make* it alright. That's what Hunter is to me, what he's been since our worlds collided on the worst day of his life, and we realized everything got better when we had each other.

Initially, Will was pissed that I answered his phone that night and all around enraged to find out that I not only met up with someone in the middle of a relapse but also spent the night with them at a Waffle House, waiting for the sun to come up so I could take him to a meeting. Once he got past that, though, things got better. Hunter got clean again, and we built this bond that doesn't make sense to anyone but us. I encouraged him to start the gym to honor Legacy's memory, and he forced me to apply to New Haven University for their Bachelor in Fine Arts, and when I got in, he bought me waffles, and we toasted to our next chapters with cups of stale coffee.

That was four years ago, and I can't imagine my life without him in it. Being away for the last three months and not getting to see or talk to him everyday has made me realize that my need to have him around isn't just because I love him, it's because I'm *in* love with him.

And I'm determined to find out if he's in love with me, too.

A knock on my door pulls me out of my head and into the present. I turn and find Will standing just inside the threshold with a sour expression on his face.

"Is that what you're wearing?"

I glance down at myself and laugh. "The outfit is on my body, so yeah, this is what I'm wearing."

Will rubs at his forehead, his nose wrinkled with agitation. "Rae, you—please change. Our guests are going to be here any minute."

"*My* guests," I say, placing an emphasis on 'my' to remind him that everyone who's coming to the house tonight is coming to celebrate me. They're my friends and some of our extended family, and most importantly, they're all aware that I'm a grown woman who has breasts and thighs. "It's my party, Will. I can wear what I want."

He steps back as I move through the doorway and out into the hall. "Why does everything you wear these days have to be so....provocative?"

As I head down the stairs, I fight to hide my smirk. The realization that I'm in love with Hunter prompted a change in my wardrobe that Will hasn't really been a fan of. I would care more about his stances on my fashion choices if it wasn't having the intended effect on Hunter. In the week that I've been home, I've caught him eyeing me more than once. Last night, when I came downstairs for dinner in an old pair of cheer shorts and a cropped tank with no bra on, it took him a full minute to pick his jaw up off the floor. Will was out with some friends from work, so he wasn't there to see it, which was just as well because the last thing I wanted was for my big brother to see me sporting under boob at the dinner table.

Tonight, though, I don't have the option of sparing him from the art of my subtle seduction, so I hope he has the good sense to look away.

"It's a romper, not a lingerie set, Will. Please relax."

Even though he's behind me, tracing my steps as we move down the wooden stairs of the old house that's been in Hunter's family for generations, I know that he's rolling his eyes at me. He hates when I remind him that I'm not a little girl anymore.

"I'm relaxed," he insists, still on my heels when I enter the kitchen where Dee is standing at the island stealing a cup of the punch I made before I went upstairs to get dressed. "Don't I look relaxed, Dee?"

She lifts her ill-gotten gains to her lip and snorts into the cup. "You look like you're about to have a stroke."

"Who's stroking out?" Hunter asks. His voice a loud boom that fills the kitchen and settles low in the pit of my stomach as he comes in through the backdoor. He rarely wears an expression that isn't laced with stoicism, but today, he's all smiles. Both corners of his mouth pulling his full lips up into a curve that, to me, spells sin. I dreamed about that smile last night, about watching it disappear between my thighs as he kissed me in places I haven't let any other man explore at length.

"Is it you?" He turns a questioning, yet concerned gaze on me, crossing the room and taking my face into his hands. My breath leaves my body in a low wheeze that makes my knees weak and adds to Hunter's misplaced concern. "You okay? It's not too hot in your room, is it? I picked up a fan on my way back, and I'm going to set it up after I get the food on the grill."

This man.

How the hell can I not love him when he treats my every need, spoken and unspoken, like his own personal initiative?

"She's fine," Will says, tearing the moment apart with a dismissive wave of his hand on his way to the island to take Dee's cup of punch.

"I'm the one struggling to come to terms with my baby sister's new wardrobe."

He takes a long swig of the fruity concoction and closes his eyes like he wishes there was just a *little* bit of alcohol in there to ease his troubled mind.

"Oh." Hunter steps back and runs dark eyes over my body. There's not much to the outfit, but he takes his time looking me over. Goose-bumps pebble on my skin in every place his eyes touch, and I wonder if now is the moment to tell him that I never want him to look away from me. Finally, his gaze finds its way back to mine, and he smiles. "I think she looks nice."

I'd look even nicer in your bed.

The words are on the tip of my tongue, and I don't allow myself a second to think before my lips part to set them free. Caution be damned. I love this man. I want this man. And I don't care who knows.

"Nice? She looks sexy as hell, like she's trying to celebrate getting a degree and catch her a man at the same time."

I don't recognize the voice coming from behind Hunter, and he's so damn big I can't see them. No, not them, her. I can't see her, so I look to Dee and Will, but mostly Dee, for confirmation that they heard the phantom voice, too. Will is still lost in his head, probably tuning out all talking points that put me and the word 'sexy' in the same sentence, but Dee is completely in touch with what's happening right now. She's staring at the person behind Hunter, who I still can't see, and the expression on her face speaks straight to the alarm bells sounding off in my mind.

Something isn't right.

Hunter turns away from me, lifting one of his long, ridiculously muscular arms up and allowing it to come to rest on the shoulder of the woman whose disembodied voice I just heard. She's pretty. Even as I grow to hate her, to resent how comfortable she looks pressed against Hunter's body, I still can't bring myself to lie about that fact. Her face is round and full, her eyes twin pools of brown the color of hot cocoa, her nose a perfect, button shape that makes her seem adorable and delicate next to Hunter's rugged imperfections.

"I'm Indigo," she gushes, leaving the safety of Hunter's orbit to step into mine. At first, I think she's going to do the thing you're supposed to do when you meet a perfect stranger and try to shake my hand, but then she opens her arms wide and says, "I'm a hugger!"

And then we're hugging.

I stand with my arms pinned to my side for a long second while she squeezes me like we're the best of friends. Will stretches his eyes wide, silently imploring me to remember that our mother did raise me with manners, and I finally give in, wrapping my arms around her and holding on for just a second because I can't stand to go any longer.

Finally, the hug ends, but Indigo remains in my space. "Hunter has told me so much about you, Rae!"

"That's interesting because we haven't heard a thing about you."

For just a second, I think the words—which were swirling around in my head—have found their way out of my mouth on their own, but then Indigo's head full of honey blonde curls spins in Dee's direction, and her smile falters a bit.

My best friend, the angelic demon that she is, rounds the island with a fake smile plastered on her face. "I'm Deanna, Rae's best friend, and a frequent flier here at the Drake residence, which is why it's strange that I've never heard of you."

"At least act like you know how to be polite, Dee," Will warns in a tone far too authoritative for a man who was just crying into a cup of punch. He comes around the island, too, joining our little band of misfits and pulling Indigo into a hug that spells familiarity. "Nice to see you again, Indigo. Please forgive my little sister's feral best friend."

With at least one warm welcome under her belt, the interloper seems to relax. "Good to see you too, Will."

"How do you guys know each other?" I ask, infusing my voice with calm even though my heart feels like it's being squeezed by a giant, relentless fist.

Hunter, Indigo, and Will all share a look that makes me feel like

I'm standing on the outside of a unit I thought I was a part of, the fondness of a shared memory I'm not in possession of alight in all of their eyes. Silently, they agree that Indigo should answer, and she slips back under Hunter's arm before she begins.

"Well, Hunter and I met at the gym about—" she looks at him, like the words she's searching for are written on his face, "Two months ago, right babe?"

Babe.

She calls him babe. My hand curls into a fist. The edges of my nails dig into my palm, and I try not to scream when Hunter grins down at her indulgently.

"Three," he says. "You had just left for New York, Rae."

"That's right." Indigo grins, biting her lip as she brings her attention back to me. "We just clicked, and we've talked every day since. I've been trying to take things slow, but there's something about this man—" she pauses, placing a hand on his chest and shaking her head, "—that just makes you want to say the hell with caution and see where the wind takes you."

Dee folds her arms over her chest, arching a brow at Will. "And where do you fit in all of this?"

"I don't fit anywhere, Deanna," Will replies. "I ran into them when they were out on a date a few weeks ago, and unlike you, I'm in possession of something called social skills, so she's glad to see me again."

"Rae, you good?" Hunter asks, causing everyone to turn their attention to me and my stunned expression.

"Yeah, I'm fine." The lie is already a hard sell, but it becomes even harder when Indigo starts tracing the intricate lines of the flowers and thorns tatted on the inside of Hunter's forearm with her fingertips. It's an absent gesture, devoid of purpose or intention but full of meaning. Of intimacy. I blink several times as the tears burning the backs of my eyeballs fight to come forward. "I think I have something in my eye, so I'm just gonna go see if I can get it out."

The measly excuse comes out as more of a mumble, but I don't care, and no one, least of all Hunter, seems to mind when I rush out of the room and back up the stairs.

HOURS LATER, the sun has set on my romantic aspirations, and the party, leaving me desolate and hopeless under the cloud of fairy lights Hunter spent all day yesterday stringing through the canopies of the trees in his backyard. Music plays softly, and non-alcoholic drinks flow freely while laughter and food make their rounds, touching the souls and stomachs of every person who's come to celebrate me.

Unfortunately, I'm no longer in the mood for celebration. Ever since Indigo arrived this afternoon, all I've wanted to do is sulk and hide and cry tears of embarrassment into my pillow. Dee wouldn't allow me to, though. She stood in the center of my room preaching about how worthless men are and chastising me for even thinking about letting Hunter and his girlfriend, who he never mentioned before today, ruin my night.

For her sake, and mine, I tried to push through, and for a while there, I did a good job. I laughed and talked and ate. I did the Electric Slide to every oldie that came over the speakers and sat next to my Uncle Jake while he told me repeatedly how proud my mom would be of me. I even fielded questions about what I planned to do next from my former dance instructor, Ms. Alice, without dissolving into a pile of uncertainty and nerves.

I did everything I was supposed to do, all while hiding my broken heart, and now, I just want to sit with my sorrows for a moment.

My favorite spot in Hunter's yard is the large oak tree that stands at the very edge of his property next to a lake he once told me his dad loved to fish in. Hunter doesn't fish here anymore, but he does spend a lot of time sitting on the branch closest to the ground, and he never seems to mind if I sit out here, too. Sometimes, we sit together and talk about how much we miss our parents and how we wish life was a little less cruel. Other times, like before Will and I moved in, and we'd just come over so Hunter didn't end up having dinner alone, I'd come out here by myself and listen to the cicadas sing.

Tonight, I'm alone, and Hunter is somewhere with Indigo, blissfully unaware that I'm gone, that I'm hurt, that I'm regretting going to New York because it cost me my chance with him.

That I'm doubting whether I ever had a chance in the first place.

The shuffle and crack of feet trampling over fallen branches and grass alert me to the impending arrival of a person I can't identify because there are no lights out here. I go still, hoping that if I can't see them, they won't be able to see me.

"I already told you not to come out here by yourself when it's dark," Hunter says, walking up to the branch and stopping just in front of me. I can barely see his face, but I don't need to in order to know that he's a mix of anger, worry, and confusion. "The grass is too high. You could have run across a snake."

"You could have too, but here you are, standing in front of me."

Two big hands land on the hard wood on either side of my thighs, and he makes himself comfortable in the space between my legs. "I came out here for you. You came out here to, well, I don't know what you came out here for."

To cry over you.

I fold my response between my lips and study his face. "You're mad at me."

He grimaces; for some reason, he can never admit when he's mad at me. "No, I just don't like the idea of you putting yourself in danger for no good reason."

"I had a good reason."

"Oh, yeah, what was it?"

Damn, I kick myself internally for backing myself into a corner. Now, I have to tell him something true because he won't buy a lie. He knows me too well and cares too much to.

"I just needed a moment to myself."

All of his features go soft, and he raises a hand, bringing warm fingers up to grip my chin. "What's going on in that head of yours, Sunshine?"

My heart swells to the point of pain when he pulls out the nick-name only he calls me. He started using it a few weeks after we met, not to describe my particularly sunny disposition, but to express what I am to him. A ray of sunshine, light in his darkest moment, hope in a hopeless time.

I thought that depth of emotion would be easy to translate into love, but apparently, I was wrong.

In response to his touch, my hands begin to operate of their own volition. The right one cupping his jaw while the left runs an adoring line over the smooth skin of his scalp.

"Nothing you want to hear about," I reply, sighing when he leans into my touch.

"You worried about what's next?"

"A little, but I know it'll all work out."

The dance industry is a fickle bastard that has very little love for girls with melanated skin. My decision to take the conservatory in New York was informed solely by my belief that it would help me land a principal role in a prominent ballet corps. So far, that belief has been proven wrong. I've been turned away by companies all up and down the East Coast, and my list of preferred locations is shrinking by the minute, but I refuse to lose hope. I'm talented and determined, and my mother always told me that counts for something.

Hunter twists his lips to the side, thinking hard about what's upsetting me, even though I know he'll never guess correctly. "Are you mad that I haven't gotten you a graduation gift yet?"

I shake my head. "No."

"Because," he continues, acting like he doesn't hear me, "I was going to get you something, I was going to get you several some-things, but you told me not to because you wanted something from me that I wouldn't be able to buy in a store."

"I remember."

"But you never told me what you wanted."

"I know." My response is wrapped in a stuttered breath that's barely audible but still manages to meet Hunter's ears.

"You know I'd give you anything, Sunshine."

The reminder paired with the nickname sends a jolt of pain through me. It slices through my heart and splits my chest wide open. And it takes everything in me not to scream my frustration into the inky, black darkness that surrounds us because the one thing I want is the one thing I can't ask him for now.

I'd told Hunter not to buy me a graduation present because the only gift I wanted today was him. I wanted his love, his adoration, his heart, and in exchange, I was going to give him the only thing I hadn't already entrusted him with: my virginity.

11

HUNTER

"I know what I want for my graduation gift."

I look up just in time to see mischief take over the lovely brown of Rae's eyes and know, beyond the shadow of a doubt, that I'm in trouble.

Last night, I told her that I'd give her anything, and I meant it, but I should have specified that all of her requests should be mischief free.

Because when Rae is feeling mischievous, I go on high alert, looking out for every possible pitfall along the path I'm only going down because of her. A few months back, that path had led us to a bar on the whitest side of town for her to compete in a bull riding contest just because Dee told her she didn't think she could last more than a second on the mechanical animal's back.

Will's approach to Rae's rare moments of debauchery always involves a stern denial that's supposed to put an end to the conversation, but I know her well enough to know that that only makes her want to do it more.

Which is why the moment she sits down across from me at the

kitchen table with bright eyes and shoulders set with determination, I know I'll have no choice but to give her whatever she wants.

Pushing my plate to the side, I sit back and cross my arms. "Let's hear it."

Rae leans back against her seat, too, mirroring my posture. My eyes are drawn to the skin of her stomach, which is bared by the scrap of fabric she calls a top.

When I told Will they could move in, I knew I'd be seeing the two of them in a different light, discovering things about each of them that I'd never know if we weren't living under the same roof, but nothing could have prepared me for the amount of Rae's skin I've seen over the past week. Every time I turn around, she's across from me or next to me in something short and tight or long and clingy. It's all crop tops and cutouts and thoughts I shouldn't be having about the woman I consider my best friend.

Today, those thoughts are focused solely on the delicate curves of flesh peeping at me from under the frayed edges of her shirt because it's not long enough to cover the entirety of her breasts. Heat washes over me in a shameful wave, and I avert my eyes, focusing on her face instead of her chest.

"I want a tattoo."

"You want a tattoo," I repeat, incredulity coating each word.

She nods. "Yep. I want a tattoo, and I want you to take me to get it."

Everything about her expression tells me she expects me to refuse, but as far as requests go, this one isn't that bad, so I acquiesce immediately.

"Fine, as long as you let me pay for it."

Surprise cuts a line across her features, lighting up her almond eyes and turning her smile wild and bright. "Really?"

"Really. What'd you expect me to say no or something?"

"I mean, I figured you understood that I wasn't asking for your permission, so I wasn't worried about being told no. I did think you'd ask a few questions before you caved, though."

"Oh, I have questions, but I didn't want you on the defensive when I asked them, so I gave you what you wanted first so you'd be more willing to give me what I want."

Her leg starts to bounce, and I can't tell if it's from nerves or agitation. It doesn't really matter since it won't stop me from getting as much information as I can from her about this abrupt decision.

"What do you want to know?"

"Well, for starters, why did you choose a tattoo as your graduation gift from me?"

She arches a brow, eyes roving over my heavily inked skin. "Because you have more tattoos than anyone I know, and I knew you wouldn't take me to some shady spot that'll give me a staph infection."

There's no point in arguing with sound logic, so I move on to my next question. "Do you know what you want to get, or are you going to just decide when you get there?"

Her nose scrunches up into an adorably disgusted wrinkle. "Now you know me better than that. Of course, I've already decided."

I shrug. "I mean, there's no shame in not knowing either. When I got these—" I hold up my left hand, showing her the skeletal outlines on my fingers "—I had no idea what I wanted. I just walked into the parlor and told CoCo to fill in the space."

"Right, well, I won't be doing that. I've been thinking about this for a while now, and I want sunbursts here—" She uses her left arm to lift her breasts up to make it easier for me to see the index finger of her right hand tracing the same curves I was just obsessing over, and I nearly swallow my own tongue "—and here. I think I want to get them upside down, so the rays from the sunbursts come down like this—" another demonstration with her finger, this time it traces invisible lines over her ribs "—does that make sense, Hunter?"

"Yeah, Sunshine," I choke out. "That makes perfect sense."

"Do you know someone who can do that for me today?" she asks, bringing her arm back down to the table and allowing her breasts to return to their normal position. I make myself look away when the act causes them to bounce a little underneath her shirt.

I push to my feet and grab my plate, heading to the sink to give myself time and space to get my better angels back online so they can remind me that this is Rae I'm thinking about here. My best friend, my headache, my salvation in human form. I shouldn't be thinking about her in that way, especially when I'm with Indigo.

Things have been going really well with her, plus she's an appropriate choice for me. She's not my best friend. She's not Will's little sister. She's not the best thing that's ever happened to me, and therefore, someone I can't afford to lose. Rae, on the other hand, is all of those things and more, which is why it makes no sense that I can't stop thinking about what life might look like if we were something different.

If I felt worthy of her, and she thought of me as more than a drug addict with a heart of gold that she only gets to see.

"Hunter?" Rae has followed me over to the sink. She's got her hip leaning against the edge of the counter and her eyes on my face. "Did you hear me?"

"Yeah, I heard you. Why don't you go upstairs and get dressed, and I'll give CoCo a call to let them know we're heading their way soon."

She squeals and claps her hands before wrapping her arms around me from behind. When she comes up on her tiptoes to kiss my cheek, I lean over to make it easier for her and close my eyes to savor the brief moment of contact.

"Thank you, Hunter!" she gushes before rushing out of the room and up the stairs.

"Anything for you, Sunshine."

I REGRET PLAYING a part in Rae getting her first tattoos from the moment we walked into the parlor, and every male on staff tripped over their own feet trying to talk her into their chair, to the minutes spent holding her hand while she lay on the table with her taut belly and two-thirds of the most perfect breasts I've ever had the pleasure of pretending not to see on full display, to the weeks filled with daily and wholly unnecessary, inspections of said tattoos because she was afraid they were going to get infected.

But nothing, and I mean nothing, compares to the regret I feel in this moment, when the fine lines of ink are winking at me from underneath the edges of a yellow bathing suit that makes Rae look like a literal ray of sunshine even on a starless, summer night.

To be clear, it's not the tattoos or the bathing suit that have me filled with regret. No, that particular honor is reserved for Cameron Perdue—a six-foot-something pretty boy Rae used to date in high school—who hasn't been able to keep his eyes off of Rae or the tattoos since he arrived at my house a little over an hour ago with Dee and a few of their other friends from high school in tow.

Normally, I wouldn't be anywhere near this poor excuse for a high school reunion, but when they arrived, I was in the middle of grilling some steaks for Indie and me, and I refused to be run out of my own backyard by people I didn't invite over in the first place.

"You sure you okay with this?" Indigo asks, cutting her eyes at the group currently lounging in the pool. Dee and three of their other friends are negotiating the terms of a Marco Polo game while Rae and Cameron are lounging on the steps of the shallow end, their bodies only partially submerged while they catch up. Rae giggles when Cameron reaches over, ghosting his fingertips over skin and ink.

"No." I roll my head from one side to the other, trying to dispel some tension. "No, I'm not okay with that at all."

"Why don't you ask them to leave?" Indigo offers, misunderstanding my response. "I mean, Rae has to understand that you don't feel comfortable having strangers in your home like this. And if she doesn't, then maybe she can go stay with her friend until their house is done."

My brows furrow together, and when I look at her, I don't try to hide that I'm confused by her suggestion. "What?"

"You're uncomfortable, Hunter, and you shouldn't have to feel that way in your own home." She stands, coming over to the grill and wrapping both arms around my waist. "I think it's amazing that you've allowed Will and Rae into your home for as long as you have, but it's been almost a month, and it's okay if you want your space back."

I shrug her off. "You don't know what you're talking about, Indie."

And she doesn't. Rae and Will are as ready to get back into their home as she is ready to see them go. Maybe even more so. The problem is that with every problem they solve, comes a new one in need of a solution. Will has already apologized profusely about being here longer than planned, and he's working himself to the bone, trying to pay for all of the repairs. When he's not working, he's sleeping, and when he's not sleeping, he's working. The last thing I want to do is add an additional stressor to his plate by putting an expiration date on his stay here.

"Boundaries," she says, running a hand through her curls. "I'm talking about boundaries, and it's clear to me that you need some with Will and Rae. Especially Rae. She has to know she can't just have guests over at any time of night or traipse around in next to nothing in front of you."

I pull the steaks off the grill with the tongs in my hand and plate them up, barely maintaining my composure. "This is her home, Indie; she can wear what she wants, when she wants."

She shakes her head. "I just don't think that's appropriate."

"Noted." Past done with this conversation, I sit down at the picnic table where we set up everything we'd need for our now awkward dinner and gesture for Indigo to sit down too. She folds her arms over her chest and stares at me, obviously wanting to continue our talk. I sigh. "Indigo, please just sit down. I'm hungry and tired, and I've been looking forward to sharing a meal with you."

She doesn't budge, so I extend my hand, letting it linger in the air until she takes it. When she does, I pull her to me and wrap my arm around her waist to lower her down on the bench beside me. The sigh of contentment she lets out once she's settled next to me does very little to dispel the agitation bubbling in my chest because of her previous remarks.

Perhaps that agitation is why I'm so attuned to what's happening in the pool between Rae and Cameron. Why I'm hyper-focused on the way his lips graze the shell of her ear when he leans in to say something to her that makes her look more uncomfortable than anything else. Why I'm up and out of my seat when his fingers go to her neck, fiddling with the strings holding her top together with every intention of undoing them.

I make sure he doesn't get the chance.

My fingers are around the back of his neck in an instant. My grip tight enough to lift his lithe frame out of the water and away from Rae before anyone has the chance to react.

"What the fuck?!" he shouts, dangling in the air and kicking his feet. His body jerking like a fish caught on a hook. Wild, fearful eyes find mine while clammy hands try to pry my fingers open.

"Hunter!" Rae is out of the pool now, too, her body glistening as moonlight refracts off the droplets of water that refuse to leave her skin. "Put him down!"

"With pleasure." I let him go and frown when the bastard is lucky enough to land on his feet. Everyone—Rae, Dee, their little guests, and especially Indigo—look at me like I've lost my shit, so I don't bother being nice or hospitable. I look at Cameron, who is rubbing at the spot where I was just holding him with a pained expression, and say, "Get the fuck off my property and take your friends with you."

It takes all of two minutes for everyone to disperse. After their friends leave, Dee and Rae go inside, shooting me death glares over their shoulders and leaving me alone with Indigo, who also looks like she wants me to drop dead.

"What the hell was that, Hunter?" she asks, her usually delightful features crumpled in a mask of confusion. "You just attacked that guy for no reason."

"It wasn't for no reason. He was trying to untie Rae's top in front of everyone. I didn't think; I just acted on instinct."

"And your first instinct was to physically remove him from her space? You didn't stop to think whether or not she wanted him to do that?"

"Don't be ridiculous. Rae's not like that. She doesn't do stuff like that."

"Rae is a grown woman, Hunter. I'm sure she's done that and so much more. The question is, why did it inspire such a visceral reaction for you? I mean, if I didn't know any better, I'd think you were jealous or something."

She pauses, letting the accusation linger in the air to see if there's any merit to it. Then she bursts out laughing, and I'm so relieved the conversation is over, I join in on the laughter too.

"Good thing you know better."

12

RAE

"I'd put barres along this wall and mirrors on the opposite side so the girls can see themselves and make the necessary adjustments to their form."

With a grand sweep of my arm, I gesture to the wall of exposed brick and large, arched windows, letting in generous beams of natural sunlight I already know will make this space that much more magical when it's filled with the soft swishes of ballet skirts and little faces pinched with determination as they try to master fifth position. Aaron looks at the wall, too, but it's clear from his flat expression that he doesn't see what I see. Still, I continue, hoping that my words will help him see my vision.

"Oh! I forgot to mention that along with the reception area up front, we'll also sell pointe shoes with prep guides for the parents so they know how to get the shoes ready for the kids to wear, leotards, skirts, and t-shirts, hats, and bags all with the school logo."

I'm talking a mile a minute, an almost child-like excitement building in my voice with every idea that pops into my mind and flows off my tongue. Still, Aaron's face remains flat. Finally, when I can't take anymore, I march across the room to him and pin him with a hard stare.

"What's wrong?"

I feel like I've asked him that question a million times in the weeks since I laid myself bare in his office and gave him every sordid detail of my past with Hunter. Every now and again, I'll catch him just staring at me with this look on his face I don't understand and refuse to examine too closely because I'm scared I might not like what I find. When I ask him about it, he always says he's fine, so I leave it alone, hoping that with enough time and space, he'll work it out and come back to me.

In the meantime, I've been focusing on making my way back to myself because somewhere between the move, running into Hunter, trying not to strangle Marcy, getting Riley settled into her new school, and things falling apart with Aaron, I lost myself. I didn't really realize it until I picked Riley up from school after a full day of trying to make up with Aaron and warning Hunter away, but listening to her talk about her new best friend, Scarlett, and the robotics club she wants to join, made it clear that everyone has found their path in New Haven except for me.

Hunter's gym is doing better than ever. A quick Google search told me that in addition to the expansion of his original space, he's also opened multiple locations across the state.

Aaron's got his VP title and the corner office he's always dreamed of.

Marcy is living the high life and annoying the ever-living fuck out of me.

Riley is thriving in an entirely new environment and making new friends every day.

And I'm just...here. Flitting around from one place to the next, solving problems, issuing warnings, soothing egos, and missing the one thing that makes me feel like myself: ballet.

The idea of the school came to me during a conversation with Dee's sister Jayla, who spent the entirety of Riley's play date with her daughter, Sonia, plying me with margaritas and town gossip while we

FaceTimed with Dee, who was also partaking in Margarita Monday. I was explaining to them how much I miss dance when Jayla told me that she and a few other moms at Sonia's current ballet school were fed up with the attitudes they were getting from the lead teacher, Lena. Somewhere between Jayla's frustration and my longing for purpose, the idea of opening my own school was born. When I awoke the next morning, I was hungover but determined to make it become a reality.

It took me forever to find the perfect spot, and now that I'm here, standing in the middle of my dream, I'm a little frustrated that I have to pause to pull Aaron out of his feelings.

"Have you thought about how much this is going to cost?" he asks finally, his hands shoved into the pockets of the designer suit with a price tag that's the equivalent of a month's rent for most people.

"I've run the numbers, and I have enough in my savings to cover start-up costs and the first six months of operating costs."

Just enough.

If I don't spend another dollar out of it.

Aaron raises a brow. "The savings you're currently paying your half of our monthly expenses out of?"

My jaw clenches as I try to reign in my temper. I hate when he asks me questions we both already know the answer to. "Yes, Aaron, that same savings."

He nods, but there's no acceptance or support in the action, only condescension that he aims right at me with his next question. "So which one of our bills are we going to forgo paying to cover this dream of yours, Rae? The mortgage? My car note? Riley's tuition?"

"Aaron, please, stop being so dramatic."

"I'm not being dramatic. I'm being realistic" He widens his stance and lifts his shoulders in an exasperated shrug. "Go ahead, pick one."

The gauntlet he's just thrown lands at my feet, and my better angels appeal to me to leave it there, to do what's necessary to restore the peace Aaron has taken so much pleasure in destroying. I want to listen to them, but I can't, probably because something about Riley's tuition—which Aaron promised would be taken care of even after my savings ran out—being on that list unhinges me.

I run my tongue across my teeth and huff out an outraged laugh.

"*If* I had to choose, I'd probably start with the whole slew of bills we're paying for your mother. Then, I'd eliminate the membership fees for the country club you only got to impress your co-workers and the gym you've never set foot in. And if we still needed to tighten our belts a little more, I'd sell our five-bedroom house and move our family of *three* into a house that doesn't have a four hundred dollar HOA fee attached to it."

Shock takes over his features before they morph into a disappointed glare. "We're not having this conversation again."

"Why not? If you can question my choices, I can question yours. Or does it not work both ways?" I cock my head to the side in a gesture that is all sass and outrage, and Aaron shakes his head, clearly disapproving of my indignation.

"I'm asking questions about a decision you've yet to make, and you're bringing up stuff that's been decided for a long time now. I'm paying my mom's bills because she is on a fixed income and deserves to be able to do what she wants with what little money she has. We bought a five-bedroom house because we decided that we were going to start a family here in New Haven."

Everything about his answer pisses me off, but I only have the mental capacity to address the last part.

"*Start* a family? We already have a family, Aaron. You, me, and Riley are a family."

I leave Marcy out of it because...fuck Marcy.

Aaron's brows dip together. "You know what I mean, Rae."

"No, I don't think I do. Please elaborate."

We both know that we're walking down a path that spells disaster for the rest of our night, but Aaron can't turn us around, and I don't want to.

He licks his lips, racking his brain for the best way to deliver the bullshit on his tongue. "I love Riley, you know that." I nod even though sometimes I question it. Even though their bond is nothing like I thought it would be after seven years of him being in her life. She doesn't even call him Dad even though he's the only father figure that's ever been in her life, and he doesn't seem bothered by it, which is weird considering his recent push to have me call Marcy Mom. "But," he continues, putting his hands on my hips and pulling me in close. "I want my own kid. Someone with my eyes and my last name, who looks like my mom or somehow laughs just like my dad even though they've never met him."

His tone grows softer with every declaration while something inside me fractures because his vision doesn't account for the fact that any child we made together would still have some of me and Riley in them.

They could come out with my mom's eyes, Will's hands, or Riley's dimpled smile.

They could be more us than Aaron or Marcy, and the fact that he hasn't even considered that bothers me.

"I'm not ready for another child, Aaron."

I leave out that I might not ever be ready for another one, that going through pregnancy alone, without my mom, Will, or even Hunter by my side, scarred me in ways that I still haven't recovered from. Dee would have been there if she could, but she was all the way in Michigan being a psychological rock star, and I never let on how sad and lonely I was because I didn't want her to drop everything to come to New York and try to fix it, especially since I knew there was no way for her to.

When Aaron lets me go, it's a clear rebuke. A silent censure he only lends his voice to once he's paced from one end of the room to the next twice.

"You can't keep doing this to me, Rae."

I'm genuinely confused. "What am I doing *to* you, Aaron?"

"Yanking the rug out from under me with no warning. First, it was the whole Hunter thing. And now you want to take a gamble on entrepreneurship and delay starting—" My eyes narrow, and he pauses, changing the phrasing of his final grievance with me, "—

having a baby. It's like none of the plans we made matter to you anymore."

"Of course, our plans matter to me, but I matter too. Don't I?"

My chin wobbles, and tears blur my vision, not because I'm sad but because I'm so angry I want to scream, but I can't give the realtor waiting outside the building for us cause for concern.

In all the years that we've been together, Aaron has never seen me mad to the point of tears, so he mistakes them as a sign of despair. He rushes over and takes me into his arms, and I go reluctantly, which makes a hold that's supposed to be comforting feel awkward and unnatural.

"Of course, you matter, babe," he murmurs into my forehead before leaning back and giving me a reassuring smile. "We'll figure it out, okay?"

Relief flows through my veins, allowing the red to fade from my vision so I can see the man in front of me more clearly. I gaze up at Aaron, reminding myself that one of the reasons I fell in love with him is because he's a problem solver. If he says we'll figure out how to balance my dreams and his desires, then I trust that we will.

"Okay."

With things somewhat settled between us, Aaron drops a kiss on my lips and glances at his watch. "We should get going."

Truthfully, I'm worn out and not at all in the mood for the level of socializing that will be required to get through the event Aaron is so eager to get to, but I can't back out because it will just result in another argument.

Aaron grabs my hand, and I let him lead me down the hall and out of the building. Soledad, the realtor kind enough to let us do the walk-through alone, even though she's not supposed to, is waiting for us on the sidewalk.

"So, did you love it?" Her question is directed at Aaron because I already gushed to her about how perfect the space was for me when we did a showing earlier this week.

"It's great," Aaron says as he hands her the keys. The light, positive tone of his voice makes my heart lift. Hope bubbles up in my chest when he shakes Soledad's hand and says, "We'll be in touch."

THE FIRST TIME Aaron told me we had to attend the annual business award dinner hosted by New Haven's Chamber of Commerce, I wasn't all that excited about going. I thought it was going to be boring and filled with a bunch of old snobs who looked nothing like me.

Of course, there are some people who fit that description, but I'm too happy with the way our conversation with Soledad ended to let it get me down. It also doesn't hurt that within five minutes of us being in the room, we have drinks in our hands and have found ourselves in the presence of one of my old sparring partners from Hunter's gym, Mallory Kent. As soon as we locked eyes, she waved me and Aaron over and introduced us to her husband, Chris, her sister-in-law, Sloane, and her brother, Dominic. Although Mallory and I never hung out outside the gym, and this is my first time meeting her husband and siblings, everyone is extremely welcoming and, once we realize we're all NHU alums, conversation flows easily between us. The only interruption is the ringing of Chris' phone.

We all watch him weave through the crowd, concentrating intently on whatever the person on the other end of the line is saying. Mallory's gaze lingers the longest, and when she looks back at me, there's pure adoration in her amber eyes.

"Chris is a doctor," she explains, taking a sip of her champagne. "He's on call tonight, which means he'll probably be leaving us at some point because babies don't care that it's date night when they're ready to be born."

"They don't care once they're born either," Sloane says, smiling ruefully.

Mallory nods her head in agreement. "True."

"How old are your little ones?" I ask, genuinely curious, even though Aaron is shuffling his feet like he's uncomfortable with the turn the conversation has taken. I glance at him, apologizing with my eyes because I didn't mean to make things awkward for him.

Dominic is a quiet giant, but the moment my question reaches his ears, he's got his phone out with a picture of a chubby little baby girl with his dark eyes and her mama's curls.

"This is Ariel. She just turned four months old, and these little hellions are Eric and Jasmine. They were born two weeks after our demon child." He swipes to the right, and the screen changes, displaying a photo of two equally chubby babies with Mallory's ebony skin and amber eyes. They're carbon copies of her, which makes me laugh. Dominic laughs, too, reading my thoughts clearly. "I know, right? It's like Chris wasn't even in the room when they were conceived."

"Damn, Nic, leave it to you to whip out pictures of my kids before I can."

He shrugs, unapologetic. "Don't be mad at me because you got slow reflexes."

Mallory gapes at him. "My reflexes aren't slow. I'm just sleep-deprived."

Dominic continues showing me photos, sharing stories about each one as he goes while Sloane and Mallory add details he's forgotten to include.

"Do you two have kids?" Mallory asks once the baby show and tell is done.

I hate the way I pause because I'm not sure how to answer. Before the conversation earlier, it would have been an easy yes, but now I find myself hesitating, hoping that Aaron will heal what his words broke by whipping out his phone and showing everyone pictures of Riley.

He doesn't.

Instead, he just sips his champagne and looks around the room, probably planning what group of unsuspecting business owners he's going to infiltrate next, leaving me to answer, to wonder whether he even has any pictures of Riley on his phone to share.

"I have a daughter. Her name's Riley," I say, digging my phone out of my clutch and showing them the photo of her on my lock screen. It's a picture of us taken on our last day in New York. I'm sitting on the sill of the window of her old bedroom, and she's in my lap, grinning up at the camera.

"She's beautiful!" Mallory says, and Sloane nods her agreement before saying, "She looks just like you."

"Thank you."

I tuck my phone back into my purse and try to hide how embarrassed I am by Aaron's silence. Just as I pull myself together, he goes and makes it worse by making his first real contribution to the conversation since telling everyone his name an overzealous exclamation about some guy that just walked into the room with an entire entourage behind him.

"I didn't know Sebastian Adler was going to be here!"

I groan inwardly. Here we go again with the Sebastian Adler talk. These days he gets more excited about a complete stranger than he does me. Granted, the stranger in question is a billionaire and handsome as all get out, but still.

"He's always at these things even though he always claims he won't be," Dominic says, speaking with the kind of authority you only use when you know someone personally. He confirms my suspicion with his next words. "Do you want an introduction?"

Aaron's eyes turn into saucers. "Seriously?"

Dominic shrugs like it's no big deal, and judging by Mallory and Sloane's calm reaction, I get the sense that it's not, then he lifts his hand and waves the elusive billionaire down. Within seconds, our group has expanded, going from five to nearly a dozen. Sebastian greets Dominic first, dapping him up before turning his attention to Sloane and then Mallory, both of whom he greets by name.

"Seb, this is Rachel Prince and her partner, Aaron Scott," Dominic says, which then puts me in the crosshairs of the intimidating but surprisingly friendly man. He extends his hand, and I take it, shocked at the warmth and size of it.

"Nice to meet you, Rachel."

"Rae," I blurt, nervous for some reason. "You can call me Rae."

"Rae," he repeats, smiling like he's used to people losing their shit in front of him.

Aaron's hand appears between us, and Sebastian's brows dip down into a deep frown that Aaron either doesn't see or has just chosen to ignore. "I'm Aaron Scott, VP of Business Development at Statler and Fawn."

Sebastian is clearly unimpressed, but he still shakes Aaron's hand. "Statler and Fawn," he says thoughtfully. "You've been trying to get some time on my calendar for a while now."

Aaron's head bobs up and down, his eyes alight with an eagerness befitting a child. "That's right. You're a hard man to get a hold of."

"Yeah, that's intentional." Sebastian runs an assessing gaze over Aaron's face and laughs in a way that says this conversation is over. Then he pulls his hand back and smiles. "Now, if you'll excuse me, I see my wife across the room, and she'll have my head if I keep her waiting any longer."

And just like that, he's gone, leaving the group of men he came in with to follow closely behind. I'm not sure who they are, but since Sebastian didn't feel the need to introduce them to us, I'm going to assume they're security or maybe low-level employees. Either way, they move quickly, all of their gazes focused on the crowd surrounding us. At the tail end of the group are two men who move at a slower pace, their strides casual as they talk among themselves. Since I'm the only person in our group still paying attention to the processional, I'm the only one who notices when one of those men pauses, even though his partner is still moving.

To his credit, once Hunter realizes I am, in fact, standing in front of him, he tries to honor his vow to keep moving. He pulls his dark gaze from my face, even though I can't manage to look away from him, and begins to angle his body in the other direction. Unfortunately for both of us, Mallory spots him before he gets the chance to move.

"Hunter Drake, I know you weren't just going to walk past me without speaking," she says, and everybody, including Aaron who only recognizes the name because I told him it, turns to look at him, which means they see me looking at him too. And I'm not just looking at him, I'm devouring him visually, taking in every line of his hulking frame and silently cursing myself for being impressed by the way the fabric of his suit clings to it like a lover.

I've only ever seen him in a suit twice before. Once at my college graduation, and, later that same year, at my brother's funeral. Both times, he wore the same one. That suit was nice, and it fit him well, but this one? This one isn't just nice, and it doesn't just fit well. It looks like it was made for him, like every stitch was made with the composition of his form in mind.

Although Mallory is the one who called him out, Hunter looks to me before he makes a move to acknowledge her. It takes me one stuttered heartbeat to realize that he's waiting for me to give him permission to break his promise, and God, my brain must be broken because I give it to him with nothing more than a slight incline of my head.

"Russ, I'll catch up with you later." He tosses the words over his shoulder as he moves forward and brings Mallory in for a hug. Then, just like Sebastian, he spreads greetings around the group, saving me and Aaron for last.

"Hey," he says, standing in front of me with dark eyes that run greedy laps over my features and steal my breath.

I swallow hard, unable to drop his gaze even though I know I should look away. "Hi."

Aaron clears his throat and reaches for me, wrapping an arm around my waist. "Hunter, I've heard *so* much about you."

Aaron's tone is so nasty that I'm left with no choice but to glare at him, silently warning him to pull back. The act robs me of the opportunity to see how Hunter reacts to the fact that I've been talking about him but affords me the chance to see Aaron's smug smile be eaten up by shock when Hunter says, "And you are?"

I'm not feeling particularly charitable towards Aaron, but I still save him the embarrassment of answering the question himself. "This is Aaron Scott, my partner."

"Partner," Hunter repeats slowly, the time he takes to do so making the years Aaron and I have been together sound like nothing. He nods and presses his lips into a tight line before stepping back from us.

An awkward bout of silence follows the exchange, but Sloane clears it up by pulling us into an anecdotal story about one of her client's bizarre design requests. The change of topic allows me to relax just a little, but I grow tense once more when Aaron leans in close and whispers in my ear.

"I'm going to see if I can get us moved to Sebastian's table," he says, pressing a kiss to my temple before striding away.

I don't know whether to be glad he's gone or angry that he's on a mission to embarrass himself once again, so I just stand there stunned until Hunter sidles up beside me, the heat of his body turning me to mush.

"Thought you were married," he whispers, his voice pitched low so only I can hear.

"I never said that."

"You let me think he's your family, and he's not."

Against my better judgment, I look up at him just to find that he's already looking at me. "You and I both know that family can look a lot of different ways. It's not always rings and vows or bloodlines."

A thousand memories pass between us in a heartbeat, and between our individual streams of consciousness that are playing the same images in a different order, we each find the truth of my words.

We were family once, and now we're just strangers with a shared history.

Hunter's breath fans across my lashes. "Rae."

I shake my head, too aware of the fact that we're not alone. "Don't."

When I turn my attention back to the group, I notice that everyone is trying not to notice us. They're all intentionally averting their gazes, looking for something or someone in the crowd to distract them from Hunter and me. Lucky for them, that distraction comes in the form of Chris' return to the group. He's no longer on the phone, but he is wearing a slightly haggard expression on his face.

"What's wrong, baby?" Mallory asks, reaching a hand out for him.

Chris steps back into the fold and acknowledges Hunter with a slight lift of his chin before answering his wife. "Nothing, just the babysitter calling with a million and one questions. You'd think it was her first night on the job."

Mallory laughs. "First of all, stop calling her the babysitter like she's not your sister. Second, cut her some slack because it's her first time keeping both twins at once. Of course, she has questions."

"The Elliots' daughter didn't have any questions," Chris grumbles into his glass.

"The Elliots' daughter is also fifteen years old. I don't care how many damn CPR certifications she has, she's not watching my kids alone."

Hunter lets out a low whistle. "Fifteen?"

Dominic nods. "Yep, I was shocked too, but apparently, that's the norm around here."

"I had my first babysitting job when I was twelve," I offer. "It's a great way to make money, especially on the weekends. My friend Deanna and I used to have a whole roster of families we worked for. We'd use the money to pay for our dance gear when our moms couldn't."

"Okay, Black babysitter club," Sloane says, which makes us all laugh.

"Riley loves those books," I tell them, smiling fondly at the memory of introducing them to her. "She swears when she's old enough, she's going to start her own babysitting club."

"How old is she anyway?" Mallory asks.

"She's nine. She'll be ten in August," I answer immediately, not realizing my mistake until I feel Hunter's body go stiff beside me. One glance in his direction shows his face scrunched in concentration as he plays my confession back in his head. I watch the wheels turn in his brain, see the mental math he's doing, and then, the exact moment when it all clicks.

His eyes lock onto mine, and I must be wearing confirmation on my face because he sees it.

The thing he missed in the cemetery that day.

The signs he was too far gone to notice all those years ago.

The truth I can't stand here and acknowledge.

"I need to find Aaron," I murmur, backing away from the group of confused faces and turning to leave without so much as a goodbye. I don't realize I've moved toward the exit until I'm out in the hallway alone, save for the sound of Hunter's approaching footsteps. He's moving fast, so fast I hardly have time to round the corner that leads to the bathroom before he catches up to me.

It's been years since he's touched me, so the moment he catches me by the wrist, my entire body rocks with tremors of shock. I snatch away, holding the affected limb with the fingers of my other hand, and stumble back.

"Don't touch me."

"Riley's going to be ten in August?" he asks, his voice a low, broken tremor.

"Hunter, I need you to walk away. I need you to leave me alone."

He shakes his head, denying my request without a moment of consideration. "Answer me, Rae. Tell me I heard you correctly when you said your daughter is about to be ten."

"Yes! Okay?! You heard me right. Are you happy now?"

A humorless laugh echoes off of the walls of the hallway. "If she's turning ten this year, that means you gave birth in 2014, which means you got pregnant in 2013, which means..."

He trails off, leaving the gap open for me to fill. I can't do it. I won't do it. I shake my head, silently communicating that to him. Hunter puts his hands on top of his head and stares at me, crucifying me with his eyes, with Riley's eyes.

"It means—" he swallows roughly before starting again. "It means you were pregnant when you left New Haven. It means you were pregnant when you left me."

I lie a lot.

It's a fact that I'm aware of, and not really something I'm trying to fix about myself because every lie I tell is a lie of necessity. I lied to Aaron about not knowing who Riley's father was because I needed to be able to build a life with him without Hunter casting a shadow over it. I lied to myself about being okay with moving back to New Haven because I wanted the life I had with Aaron and foolishly thought I'd keep it if we were here.

And when Hunter's features are flooded with a thousand emotions that pull the lines of his handsome face into tight lines fraught with hurt, anger, panic and pain, I lie to myself and say that I only see the panic. I tell myself that I'm staring confirmation of my choice in the face, that ten years after the fact, Hunter is showing me that I did the right thing because not only was he not ready for the responsibility of a child, he didn't want it.

He didn't want *her*.

I repeat the lie so many times, I almost accept it as truth, but then Hunter does that thing he always does. He surprises me. He scrubs a hand over his face, and I watch acceptance wash away every bad feeling and negative thought until the only thing left is hope and a depth of emotion for my daughter I've never seen in Aaron's eyes.

"When can I meet her?"

13

HUNTER

Now

Right now.
Tomorrow.
Later this week.

Any of those would have been an acceptable answer to the question I posed to Rae on the night a slip of her tongue led to me finding out that her daughter is mine.

Mine.

Riley is mine.

She's Rae's, and she's mine.

She's ours.

I'd let go of the idea of sharing anything with Rae a long time ago, but now I'm consumed by it and thoughts of the little girl whose mother is still withholding her from me. She could have given me any answer. She could have said anything because anything would've been better than the silence I've sat in for the past forty-eight hours.

Silence I can't touch or break because I don't have any way of contacting Rae, and even if I did, I wouldn't use it because I know this must be hard for her, too. For nearly a decade, she's kept this secret, and it can't be easy to come to terms with the fact that it's all out in the open. My knowing, but most importantly my desire to be involved, has changed everything for her, and it will do the same thing for Riley. I keep reminding myself of that, hoping it will help me to be patient while Rae makes her decision, but patience is a hard thing to exercise when I've already missed so much of my daughter's life.

"What happens if she doesn't come around?" Nate asks, sitting cross-legged on the couch across from my desk while I pace in front of it. "What if she decides your past makes you unfit to be a father and says you can never be a part of Riley's life?"

I shake my head, unable to even consider that outcome. "Rae wouldn't do that."

"Rae is a mother with a little girl she has to think about, that she has to protect. She'll do anything to eliminate a threat, and that could easily include doing what's necessary to keep you away from her kid."

"Our kid," I correct him, stripping the agitation from my tone because I know he's just trying to push me to consider all possibilities, especially the most likely one. "She's our kid, Nate. She's my kid, and I—" I rub at the back of my neck "—I can't miss anything else."

"I hear you, Hunter, and I hope you don't have to, but I want you to consider what might happen if things don't go as smoothly as you want them to."

Tired of pacing, I lean against my desk and blow out a breath. "I'm going to be honest, Nate, I can't picture any scenario that doesn't end with me being a part of my daughter's life. It has to work out. It *has* to."

Nate nods. "Then, for your sake, I hope it does."

"Thanks."

"Don't thank me. I haven't done anything but cave into your delusion, which isn't at all my job as your sponsor." He stands and stretches, wincing in pain. "You need a new couch, that shit is uncomfortable."

I can't help but laugh. "Taurin said the same thing."

At the mention of my new live-in sponsee, Nate smiles. "How's the kid doing anyway?"

"He's alright, besides the whole mad at the world thing."

Taurin's only been staying with me for a few days, but I've already attuned myself to his anger. After the initial shock of having a roof over his head wore off, it set in. When he's not in school, he's pouting around the house. I got so tired of looking at him mope around and listening to him talk about how fucked up it all was, I made him come to work with me today just so he could be productive and pouty.

So far, it's been working well. He's committed himself to wiping off mats and other equipment as well as making sure the water bottles and other sports drinks stay stocked in the fridge. I told him if he keeps this up, he'll have a permanent place at the gym. He smiled and said he actually wouldn't mind that. It was the first real smile I'd seen from him since we've known each other.

As if we've spoken him up, Taurin comes striding through the door with a bottle of cleaning solution and a towel in his hand. Although he's already crossed the threshold, he taps his knuckles on the door.

"What's up, T?"

"Someone's here to see you."

"Well, I guess that's my cue," Nate says, waving to me on his way out the door. "Keep me updated, Hunter. Later, kid."

"Will do."

Taurin waves Nate off and turns to me. "Want me to send this guy in?"

"Nah, I'll come down."

"Cool."

We leave the office together, and when we get to the first floor, Taurin chucks his chin in the direction of the man in a suit standing awkwardly by the front desk. I recognize him instantly as Rae's *partner*, Aaron. I don't know how he's here or why, but I can only assume it's to tell me to stay away from his family. I mean, that's what I would be doing if I were him, facing the problem head-on, setting boundaries and expectations with no remorse or concern for the other guy's feelings.

His posture is rigid when I approach him, and I intentionally keep myself loose so I don't appear to be on the defensive. The last thing I need is to end up beating this guy's ass and having that held against me, used as another reason to keep me away from my daughter.

"Aaron." I pause just a few feet away from him and tuck my hands into the pockets of my shorts. "Good to see you again."

"Is it?" He asks, placing his hands in his pockets, too. We're a wild juxtaposition. I look like I just stepped out of a ring; he looks like he spends his days behind a desk. I'm covered in tattoos, and, from what I can see, he has none. There's a calm, calculated air to him, reflected in his flat, frigid expression, while there's a wildness brewing in me that's just waiting to be invited out. It's not just in my eyes, either. It's in my veins, crackling like static on a TV with fucked up settings.

Aaron doesn't know me, so he doesn't know that the still, stoic expression on my face and the forced politeness in my voice is an act, one I might have to drop if he keeps talking to me like he's fucking crazy.

"Right now, it is, but I guess that could change depending on how you say what you came here to say."

He nods and begins to glance around the gym. "This is a nice little place you've got here."

"Thanks. Rae said the same thing when she stopped by a few weeks ago."

That's not exactly true, but I say it just to get a rise out of him. His eyes flash with an anger that tells me he didn't know about the visit Rae paid me, which suggests that despite the fact that he's trying to come here and act as her representative, she doesn't tell him everything.

I would feel smug about that, considering that I can remember a time when there was nothing in this world I didn't know about Rae, but in the wake of finding out about the biggest secret she's ever kept from me, I don't feel smug at all. I just feel lost.

Not as lost as Aaron is, though. He looks completely out of his depth in here. Not just because he's wearing a suit in the middle of a gym on a Sunday afternoon but because his eyes are shifty and his posture is lined with uncertainty. Because he's just now realizing that coming here to threaten me was a mistake.

"You need to stay away from her."

Right. This old song and dance again.

"Is that what Rae told you to tell me?"

"Stop saying her name." His jaw tenses, which is all the confirmation I need to know that Rae isn't aware that he's here. "You two had your time together, and it didn't work out because you weren't man enough to keep your nose clean."

Even though he doesn't come right out and say it, I hear the knowledge of my struggles with addiction wrapped up in between the lines of the insult, and it stings because the only way he could have that information is if Rae gave it to him. Funny that she felt so comfortable giving him my truths when she didn't deem him worthy of holding hers.

"She's moved on now," Aaron continues. "We're happy and building a life together, and one day soon, we're going to start a family. I'm sure the last thing you want is to be the pathetic, druggie ex who doesn't know when to let go."

I bristle internally when he says he and Rae are going to start a family. What kind of shit is that to say when you're with a woman who already has a kid? Does he not consider Riley his family? Does he not look at her as his child? What kind of fucking asshole is Rae dealing with?

"My only interest in Rae is the access she might allow me to my daughter," I respond, catching us both off guard. The statement doesn't feel completely true. I love Rae. I'll always love her, but Riley is my priority.

Knowing her.

Loving her.

Showing up for her in all the ways the jackass in front of me probably hasn't.

"Oh," Aaron says, all the wind he'd been using to puff out his chest slipping out of him alongside the word. "She told you about Riley."

Now, I'm really confused.

"You didn't know?"

It takes a second for Aaron to recover and process my question. When he does, he chooses to lie, badly. "Of course, I knew. Rae and I talk about everything."

The other night, for the briefest of moments, Rae and Aaron looked like the perfect couple. Maybe it was their proximity to Mallory and Chris or Dominic and Sloane—couples who are in possession of the communication skills Aaron is trying to attribute to him and Rae—that fooled me, or maybe I'd just given them too much credit, but now I see the reality of them, and I can't look away.

"So she knows you're here?"

"We discussed it, but I didn't tell her I'd decided to stop by today and tell you to stay away from her."

"And Riley," I add, because I really can't believe he doesn't know that she's the priority here. Rae is a grown woman, and she's more than capable of setting boundaries with me if she needs to. She knows I will respect them. Riley is the vulnerable party. She's the one who needs to be protected in all this.

"Right," he says, annoyance bulging his eyes for a moment before he squares his shoulders and commits to acting like he cares about my daughter. "You need to stay away from them both. They've been just fine without you all this time, and I'll make sure that never changes."

When Rae came here to tell me our lives had to stay separate, she spoke with conviction that came from a place of selfless concern for her kid and left me with no choice but to yield to her demands. Today, Aaron stands in front of me speaking with that same conviction, except his comes from a well of self-serving entitlement. He hasn't spent a single second talking this over with Rae or thinking about what this conversation might mean for her or Riley. All he's thinking about is himself and how to protect what he has with Rae.

And all that makes me want to do is tell him to fuck off.

For the first time since I stood in front of him, I move, taking three steps forward to close the space between us. I loom over him, large and imposing and proud to be a big, scary motherfucker who can hold his own in the ring and out of it when necessary. Aaron tries to meet my gaze without adjusting his stance at all, but he's too short to make it happen, and I take great satisfaction in watching him tip his head back to fully witness the murder in my eyes.

"I'm gonna say this once, and then I want you to feel free to get the fuck out of my gym." I peer down at him, laughing internally at the false bravado he's projecting. "Whatever Rae and I decide to do about our daughter will be our decision. Not yours. And if I have it my way, I will be a very active part of Riley's life, which means I'll be a part of Rae's life, too. You might feel like you've got a leg up on me because you've been around, and I haven't, or because you've never struggled with addiction, and I have, but I want you to remember something." I lean down, placing my mouth near his ear. "You can recover from drug addiction. They have a whole twelve-step program for it and everything. But last I checked, there's no cure for being an insecure little bitch."

With a single finger to his chest, I send him stumbling back toward the exit, and he glares at me as he leaves, but he doesn't say another word. I watch him go, wondering how the fuck Rae ended up with an asshole like that.

14

RAE

Now

W hen I was a kid, I used to hate getting my hair done.

It took too long, and it hurt too much. The kitchen counter was always too cold, and my mom always managed to get water in my ears or shampoo in my eyes—sometimes both—before it was all said and done. She'd also get mad at me when I cried as she brushed out my curls. I remember because that was really the only time she ever raised her voice.

If you'd just hold still, we could get done quicker, Rae, she'd say, impatient hands raking through tangled curls with a rat-tail comb and not a lick of product because she didn't know a damn thing about detangling sprays, wide tooth combs or patience.

By the time I had Riley, I'd decided that our wash days weren't going to be anything like that. Now, don't get me wrong, she still cries sometimes when my fingers get caught on a particularly dreadful knot during the finger detangling portion or when the water isn't as cold as she likes it, but for the most part, it's not a traumatic time for her. I play her music and make sure she has plenty of snacks, and after I wash her hair twice—once with a clarifying shampoo and again with a moisturizing one—I do a deep condition and sit her under the hooded dryer on low for thirty minutes.

Usually, I use that time to clean up the mess I've made of the kitchen and to prepare myself for the styling portion of the day. That's what I'm in the middle of doing when Aaron walks through the door in a God-awful mood. He makes a beeline for me, which is odd because he knows we're not currently on speaking terms. I haven't said a word to him or his hag of a mother after I found out she got him to agree to pay for a full kitchen renovation in the house she no longer lives in so she can finally put it on the market. The sixty-thousand dollar invoice that came in Saturday's mail had Aaron's name on it and was back-dated to the week we moved to New Haven, which means Aaron knew on Friday—when he was standing in the middle of the place I wanted to build my dream in—that he'd already promised the money he could have used to cover my portion of our expenses to Marcy. And now, if I want to keep Riley at her school and a roof over our heads, I'll have to press pause on everything I wanted to do for myself.

Hell, I might need to go get a job at the school I was planning on putting out of business.

"We need to talk," Aaron says, standing close to me even though it's completely unnecessary.

I shake my head and pull down a few sheets of paper towel, using them to soak up the little bit of water on the counter I missed the first time. "I don't have anything to say to you, Aaron."

"Listen, Rae." He places a hand over mine, forcing me to stop what I'm doing. "I know you're mad at me, and I'm sorry I didn't tell you about the renovation, but can we just set it aside for right now? I have something to tell you."

A heavy, impatient sigh passes through my lips as I turn to him. "What is it, Aaron?"

He glances over at the breakfast nook where I have Riley set up under the dryer.

"Can we speak in private?"

"She can't hear us."

"Rae, please."

I cross my arms, letting him know I'm not budging. Whatever he has to say to me can be said right here, right now.

"I went to see Hunter."

Okay, anything except for that.

Grabbing his hand, I drag him out of the kitchen and down the hallway until we're near the front door. "What do you mean you went to see Hunter? You were supposed to be at the office!"

My heart is in my throat and yet, it's still managing to beat a million times per minute. I didn't get the chance to tell Aaron about Hunter discovering he was Riley's dad because I was in shock the night it happened. Then, on Saturday morning, when I intended to bring it up, I found the invoice that led to me giving him the silent treatment while sitting on his desk.

He sets his briefcase on the entryway table and tosses his keys down beside it. "I mean, after I finished working, I went to go see your ex and tell him to stay away from you, and, while I was there, I learned that you told him about Riley being his daughter."

"I didn't tell him. He put it together when he heard me mention that Riley was about to turn ten in August."

Aaron shrugs, his eyes disinterested. "Doesn't matter because he knows now, doesn't he? Which is funny because I seem to remember us having a conversation where you told me that you had no plans of ever making him privy to that information." He taps his index finger on his chin. "I also seem to recall, during that same conversation, you saying you never wanted to see him again, but today, I found out that you went to his gym."

"To tell him to stay away from us." I hate how it feels like I'm the one in trouble when Aaron just went and did the same thing I did for different reasons. "Why did *you* go see him?"

"To protect my family."

I scoff. "We both know that's not true."

He starts to loosen his tie, still staring at me. "You're calling *me* a liar?"

"Yeah, Aaron, I'm calling you a liar because we both know you going to see Hunter wasn't about your family. It was about your ego."

"You can't be serious right now, Rae. The man is a fucking drug addict, and you think I went down there to his sketchy ass gym on some kind of ego trip?"

"What am I supposed to think, Aaron? It's not like you called and asked my opinion on anything. You don't know if I want Hunter to stay away or if I want to try to integrate him into Riley's life, and you didn't ask before you went and spoke on behalf of me and my child."

"Oh, here we go with that '*my child*' shit," he says nastily.

"She is my child, Aaron."

"I know that, Rae." He spits the words out, and they land in a wet heap of resentment at my feet. "You never let any of us forget that she's yours, which means you don't leave any space for anyone else to try to know and love her."

"That's not true."

Is it?

"Yes, it is. You build this wall around Riley and then get mad when she's in there all alone. No one can get through. No one can get close. Not even me, and I've been trying for seven fucking years. Do you know how exhausting that is?"

His words strike a chord deep inside my chest. I step back, tears crowding my eyes. "Well, I'm sorry that we're so exhausting. I'm sorry that my past, my choices, my mistakes, and my child are so hard for you to deal with."

When the first tear falls, Aaron's face softens. He's still mad, and we're still broken, but I step into his arms when he holds them open for me.

"That's not what I meant," he murmurs softly. "I'm just saying I want you to make room for me in the little castle you've built around you and Ri. You're the one with the key, so please undo the lock so we can defend it together."

Aaron grips my chin gently, tipping my head back so I can look him in the eyes. The sincerity there confuses me because it says he truly believes what he's saying, that he really feels like I've been forcing him into the margins of Riley's life. Thinking back on the conversation I had with Marcy on the first day of school, I wince, realizing maybe that might be true.

"I'm sorry," I whisper. "From here on out, I want us to be honest with each other, okay? No more making decisions and hiding them from the other. No more taking on things alone. We have a lot going on, and I think it would be a lot easier to get through if we did it together."

Bubbles of hope and relief fill my chest when Aaron nods.

"Okay," he says. "But I'm going to follow your lead on this Hunter thing. Whatever you decide, whenever you decide, I'm going to be right here."

I lay my head on his chest, drawing comfort from the steady thump of his heartbeat.

"Hunter isn't dangerous," I tell him. Even though I haven't known him in a long time, I know that much to be true. Hunter cares about me, and although they've only been face-to-face one time, he loves Riley. He'd do anything to keep her safe, including lay down his own life. That truth was present in his eyes when he asked to meet her. It's the thing that's haunted me for the last two days while I've tried to think of a response to a question I should have already answered.

"We don't know that, Rae, and we have to consider everything before we decide whether or not we're going to let him in Riley's life."

Every time he says we, my heart skips a beat. This is what I've been wanting, what I've been waiting for: the united front. Me and Aaron facing every problem together instead of tackling them from opposite sides. It feels good to have it in this moment. So good, I grab onto it with both hands and hold on tight, letting all my anger and other simmering concerns fall by the wayside.

"You just said you were going to follow my lead," I remind him with an indulgent smile pulling at my lips.

"You're right. You're right." He pushes out a settling breath. "Tell me where your head is at."

I picture Hunter. Not just as he was the other night, all decked out in a suit, rubbing elbows with New Haven's elite, but as he was in the gym when I went to see him and at the cemetery when we ran into each other out of the blue. Every time I've come across him, I've been able to see his commitment to his sobriety. Will always used to say that once a person chose to do the work, you could see the determination on their face.

Back then, when Hunter and I were deep in the madness of our love, that determination wasn't there. He wanted to be clean, sure, but I think he wanted it more for me than himself. He wanted to be the kind of man who deserved me, and in doing so, he became the only version of himself that could have lost me. I'm confident that isn't the case today. He didn't get clean for me, or even for Riley; he got clean for himself, and knowing that makes me feel safe giving him access to my—no, *our*—daughter.

"EVERY DAY SHOULD BE a mental health day, Mommy!" Riley shouts as she pumps her little legs as hard as she can to make the swing go higher. I offered to push her, but she said that Scarlett said big girls don't need help, so I hopped on my own swing and channeled my energy into catching some air with her while also silently running through the advice Dee gave me last night about having this conversation with Riley. It all basically came down to being honest and open and not getting defensive if she gets upset.

When we were on the phone rehearsing, the words poured off my tongue easily, but every time I've tried to speak them today, I've gotten choked up, scared of ruining Riley's good mood, terrified to make her hate me.

Aaron assured me that wouldn't be the case when I expressed my fears to him last night. He's been extremely supportive of my decision to tell Riley about her dad, and even though we've only been back on track for a few days, I think we've finally found our footing in New Haven.

Let's just hope we can keep it.

"Every day can't be a mental health day, Ri."

"Why not?"

"Because we don't need one every day."

"But I needed one today?" she asks, still swinging high even though I've started to slow down.

"Yeah, baby, we both did."

She looks over at me, concern pouring out of those big, brown eyes. "Why did you need one? Is there something wrong with your brain?"

Her question surprises a laugh out of me. "Something like that."

"Wanna talk about it? You always say that sharing your feelings with a grown-up you trust can help you feel better. I'm not a grown-up, but you can trust me."

Motherhood is mostly saying things you hope make sense and praying your kid is not just listening, but absorbing your words. Most days, I don't know if anything I say sticks with Riley, but then, in moments when I least expect, she hits me with a line like that and I rejoice in the fact that the seeds I've planted have taken root.

"Thanks, Nugget." I flash her a grateful smile, then reach over and wrap my fingers around the rusted chain keeping the swing attached to the frame. Riley stops kicking her legs, helping me curb her momentum until she's completely still. "There is something I'd like to talk to you about."

Her eyes light up, and there's surprise lingering in the corners because she didn't expect me to take her up on her offer. "Okay."

I take a deep breath and send up a silent prayer that I'm making the right decision. "Remember when we went to Nana and Uncle Will's grave, and we talked about how important it is to love people while we have them?"

Riley nods. "I wish I could have met Nana and Uncle Will."

It's not the first time she's expressed that sentiment, nor is it the first time my eyes have filled with tears born solely from the knowledge that the three most important people in my life will never know each other.

"I know, baby. I wish you could have too." Reaching over, I brush an errant curl away from her face. "And I don't want you missing out on any more people who love you."

"What do you mean?"

"Well, you know that Aaron isn't your real dad, right?"

"Yeah, that's why I call him Aaron." Her deadpan response pulls a snort out of me that has her looking at me like I'm crazy. "When I meet my real dad, I won't call him his name because that'd be weird. I'll call him Daddy just like I call you Mommy."

The certainty in her tone catches me just as off guard as the words she's saying, and I find myself angling my body towards her. "Ri, have you been thinking about your real dad a lot?"

She nods and brings her hands into her lap to start twiddling her thumbs. "Yes."

"But you never asked me about him. Why?"

"I didn't want to make you sad," she whispers with her chin tucked into her chest so the words are barely audible. "It makes you sad when you talk about Uncle Will and Nana. I thought maybe talking about him would make you sad because you miss him like you miss them."

My teeth plunge into my lower lip to stop it from trembling. I don't know what to say, so I just follow Dee's advice and choose honesty. "It does make me sad to talk about your dad, but for different reasons than it makes me sad to talk about Nana and Uncle Will."

"How is it different?"

"Well, for starters, your dad isn't in heaven."

"Where is he?"

Here it is. The hardest part of this conversation. I run a hand down my neck and over my racing pulse. "He's here, in New Haven."

Sparks of wonder and excitement turn Riley's eyes bright. "Really?"

"Yep." I cough, pushing the words out past the lump in my throat that's made purely of fear because Riley has the same look in her eyes that Hunter did when the truth came out. It's steely resolve that tells me this train is moving full speed ahead whether I want it to or not.

"Can I see him?"

"Of course, you can."

"Right now?" She jumps out of her swing, and in an instant, she's standing in front of me, bouncing on her toes with excitement. "Can we go see him now?"

I should have expected this. Patience has never been a strong suit for Riley. Yet another thing she gets from Hunter. I open my mouth to tell her that we've had enough excitement and revelations for one day, but then I remember that she's been waiting her whole life for this, and I don't have the heart to make her wait anymore.

"Sure, Nugget."

I push to my feet and grab her by the hand. We're almost to the car when her steps slow to a stop, and she tugs on my arm. When our eyes meet, there's doubt swimming in her irises. Lowering myself down to her level, I search her face for any clues as to what's changed in the last sixty seconds and come up empty.

"What is it, Ri?"

"Does he love me?"

The question hits me right in the center of my chest, setting free a wave of shame stronger than any I've ever felt before. The consequences of my actions, of Hunter's choices, of our mistakes, are staring me right in the face, reflected in my daughter's questioning gaze, and while I'm sad she even has to ask, I'm happy to know the answer.

"Oh, honey. When you meet him, you'll see that you've got your dad's eyes and his ridiculously thick eyebrows—" Riley giggles when I make my brows wiggle "—but most importantly, you'll see that you have his heart."

15

HUNTER

Now

"I have questions."

Rae's voice pulls my attention to the door of my office, where she's currently standing with her hands in the back pockets of her jeans. It's been nearly a week since I last saw her, but her random statement makes it seem like we're in the middle of a conversation instead of at the beginning of one.

Dropping the pen in my hand onto the stack of papers on my desk, I gesture for her to come in and take a seat. To my surprise, she doesn't argue, opting to perch on the edge of my uncomfortable couch instead of one of the armchairs I got the other day. Taurin said it would have made more sense for me to get the armchairs and toss the couch, but I couldn't bring myself to part with it.

I have a lot of good memories on that couch, and most of them involve the woman sitting on it now with her legs crossed and her spine straight. There's no tension in her posture, just the kind of rigid perfection ballerinas exhibit even when they're not on the stage. With Rae settled in her seat, I choose to follow her lead, diving right into the conversation with no formalities or pretenses.

"I've been clean for ten years, three months, and" —I glance at the calendar, wanting to be as accurate as possible— "thirteen days. I go to meetings once a week—more often now that you're back in town—and have regular check-ins with Nate. He said that he'd be more than happy to talk to you about my recovery, and I've also asked some of my sponsees if they'd be willing to speak to you too. They all agreed, but if you want to be sure you're getting an unbiased opinion, I could give you Mallory's number."

When I reach for my phone, Rae shakes her head. "You don't have to do that."

"Then what do I have to do, Rae?" Desperation coats each word. I've waited for this moment for so long, hoping, praying, wishing that it would come, and now that it might be here, I'm eager to give her whatever she needs to see this through. "Tell me what you need to see, what you want to know because I'll do anything if it gets me her."

Rae's eyes shine with emotion. "You really mean that, don't you?"

"I've never meant anything more."

She rests her elbow on her knee and plops her chin into her palm then shakes her head. "Damn, you two have made this entire thing surprisingly easy."

I assume she's talking about me and Riley because the alternative means having to think about her little boyfriend, Aaron, and that's the last thing I want to do today. I don't like the guy, and one day, when Rae and I are more settled into this co-parenting thing, I'm going to tell her that he doesn't deserve her or Riley.

"You told her?"

My heart slows to a stop and then starts again, kicking into over-drive when Rae nods. She knows. My daughter knows about me, and I know about her, and things I didn't even know were broken in this world, and in me, are being healed.

"She wants to meet you," Rae says, her features calm and restrained even though I know there must be a riot of emotion happening inside her.

"And I want to meet her. Just tell me when and where, and I'll be there."

"Right now. Your parking lot."

"What?" Rae stands, and I do, too, because I heard what she said, even if my question suggests otherwise. "You left her in the car by herself?" I ask, following her down the stairs and out of the gym.

"I was gone for five minutes. The air is on, and she has her phone so she can call if there's an emergency." We're outside now, and Rae is parked right by the front door, which makes me feel a little better.

A little.

"That's still not safe," I tell her, my steps faltering when Riley looks out the window and meets my eyes. "Someone could have—"

"Hunter," Rae snaps, cutting me off. "She's fine. Everything is fine. Now, do you want to lecture me on my parenting decisions or meet your daughter?"

Part of me wants to do both, but I know that's not an option.

"I want to meet my daughter."

My daughter. Damn, do those words feel like heaven on my tongue. There's bliss in every syllable, euphoria in their meaning, and my feet are moving again, this time on their own accord, prepared to take me to Riley so I can find out if shaking her little hand makes me feel the same way.

Rae stops me with two palms on my chest, and the physical contact is a shock for us both. Currents of energy, sharp and decisive, rebound through me, stilling me once again. Rae feels it too. She steps back, her face warped into a mask of unreadable emotion.

"Just wait right here," she says finally, holding her palms up still but not touching me. "Let me bring her to you, okay?"

"Okay."

I don't know why it matters whether I go to her or she comes to me, but I know Rae has thought this part of our interaction through, so I follow her lead. I'm going to have to do a lot of that now, yielding to her, learning from her, letting her take the lead so I can figure out how to be as good at this as she is. From just a few paces away, I watch her open the car door and crouch down to Riley's level. Riley keeps her eyes on her mom's face, listening as she explains something I'm too far away to hear. I can guess what she's saying, though. She's probably telling her not to be afraid of me. That I might look big and scary, but I'm actually a teddy bear at heart, and while that's not really true, I'll go along with it, making it true for Riley the same way I used to make it true for her mom.

When their conversation is done, Rae grabs Riley's hand and helps her out of the car. They walk towards me looking like a hopeful future and a lost past, and my heart aches because they are both so fucking beautiful.

"Hunter, this is Riley," Rae says, yanking me back into the moment. "Riley, this is your dad, Hunter."

Most of the kids I know are either troubled like Taurin or....well, actually, I don't know any other kids outside of Taurin, but I can still say with confidence that Riley is nothing like any other kid in this world. Where I expect fear or the kind of bashfulness that makes kids cling to their mom's legs when they meet new people, I find nothing but courage. She looks me dead in the eye, and then, to my surprise and pure delight, she extends her hand to me and says, "Hey, I know you."

I drop down to my haunches, keeping her hand in mine. "You do?"

"Yep, you're the man from the cemetery."

Rae and I both laugh at her candidness, but I'm the only one who responds. "That's right. I did see you at the cemetery once. What were you doing out there, robbing graves?"

She scrunches up her little button nose. "Eww, no. We were visiting my Nana and Uncle Will."

"Oh, okay, I guess that makes more sense."

I glance at Rae, and we engage in a silent conversation over Riley's head. One where I tell her I'm sorry she had to do that alone, and she says it's fine because she's used to doing things like that alone.

"Were *you* robbing graves?" Riley asks, pulling my focus back to her.

"Of course not! That's against the law. Do I look like the kind of person who'd break the law?"

My daughter gives me a once-over with eyes that are just like mine and purses her lips. "A little bit."

I slap my free hand over my heart and let my mouth fall open in faux shock. "What is it, the tattoos?"

The question makes her giggle, and when I pull my eyes away from her precious face, I find that Rae is laughing, too. Their audible joy makes the air around me warm, and I bathe in it, hoping I never have to know another day without it.

"You're funny," Riley says. "Do you like ice cream?"

"I love ice cream."

Now Rae is pursing her lips, her eyes calling me a liar. She knows me and dairy don't really get down like that, but what am I gonna do? Tell my kid I'm lactose intolerant and miss a chance to have an ice cream date with her? I think not.

"Mommy, can we take him to get ice cream, please?"

Cute, smart and well-mannered? Oh, I can already feel myself turning into putty, my now pliable form being wrapped around Riley's pinky finger. Apparently, Rae already lives there because even though she tries to look stern, I can hear the surrender in her tone when she says, "Did you even ask him if he wants to go get ice cream with us?"

"Of course, I want to go get ice cream with you," I answer before Riley even has the chance to repeat the question. "And I know the perfect spot." I stand and train my gaze on Rae, studying her face for any signs of protest. "But we can only go if it's okay with Mommy."

Rae's eyes glaze over, and for a second, I think I've fucked it all up, but then she blinks and everything is back to normal. She forces a bright smile onto her face and splits it between me and the kid.

"Ice cream sounds good to me."

～

"LICK IS the only ice cream place in town with decent non-dairy options," I explain to Rae as we walk down the quiet city block with our frozen treats in hand. Riley is a few steps ahead of us, the vanilla ice cream on the cone she begged for melting rapidly onto her hands.

"Finally gave up your battle with lactose, huh?"

"Had to. It's important to know when you've been bested."

She rolls her eyes at my casual use of the phrase I was known for using on opponents when I fought in unofficial MMA rings during my army days. That part of my life was over by the time I met Rae, but I still regaled her with the stories, telling her all about my alter ego—The Reaper—and his favorite catchphrase.

"Ugh. Please don't tell me you're using that in everyday conversation now."

I laugh and take a bite of my gelato. "Whenever I can, however I can."

"I bet the people in your classes just *love* that." Sarcasm drips from every word, but it makes me smile. "Mallory and I used to hate those little catchphrases so much." She pulls her mouth down into a frown and deepens her voice so she can do a poor impression of me. '*Next time, let your actions match your knowledge*'"

"I remember." I join her in her laughter, making mine loud and exaggerated so it's really noticeable when it stops. "I also remember you being *a lot* better at mocking me."

Rae rolls her eyes. "Boy, please, my impression was spot on."

"If by spot on, you mean not even close."

She bumps me with her shoulder, and I try my damnedest not to add layers of meaning onto the casual touch because Rae isn't. She's just existing, just letting me exist with her and Riley.

"You're too far away, Ri," I call out, my voice carrying down the sidewalk. Riley pauses and turns, waving like I didn't just admonish her for breaking our agreement to stay within arms reach.

"Stay put, Nug," Rae says, and we both pick up the pace until we're close enough to Riley to see the streaks of vanilla running down her forearms. Given that she's not a fan of stickiness, I expect Rae to whip out a hand wipe or some tissue to clean up the mess, but she doesn't. In fact, she's not even looking at Riley or me because she's too preoccupied with the 'for rent' sign posted in the window of the building we're in front of.

It's an older building with faded red bricks and arched windows that tell a story of past grandiosity just waiting to be reawakened by someone. Because of its proximity to downtown and all the shops that have opened up around here that contribute a ton of foot traffic it's the perfect spot for a business of some sort.

"I can't believe someone hasn't snatched it up yet," she mutters under her breath, a faraway look in her eye.

Riley tries to use her mother's distraction to her advantage, but I see the intention to run off on her face and grab her by the hand to hold her in place. She squeezes my fingers and giggles when I squeeze them back.

"You know this spot?" I ask Rae, splitting my gaze between the building and her face because there's wonder and hope there that I don't know if I'm supposed to be witnessing.

My question seems to snap her out of her trance. "Yeah, I, um—" She bites her lip like she's trying to stop herself from telling me what her connection to the building is. Then she shrugs like it doesn't matter if I know or not and tells me anyway. "I was going to start a ballet school."

"Was? Why was?"

Rae glances at Riley and then back at me, and I'm aware of the internal battle she's fighting. She's already let me in so much today, and giving me this, a glimpse into a part of her life that has nothing to do with our daughter, feels like too much.

"We should head back," she says, tipping her head in the direction that we just came from.

I don't argue.

On the way back to her car, I run through a list of possible reasons why Rae wouldn't be able to rent that building and make her dreams of opening a school a reality, and the only plausible explanation is money. Starting a business is nothing more than one financial stress after the other, which is usually what stops people from taking the leap into entrepreneurship. I won't pretend to know what Rae or

Aaron's bank accounts look like, but I assumed they were well off. I mean, if they're doing well enough for Aaron to drive the latest Audi and rock suits with four-figure price tags, then I think he should be able to figure out how to get a building for Rae in one of the more reasonably priced parts of town.

If it were me....

Well, it's not you.

The mental reminder is enough to keep my thoughts and questions to myself for the remainder of our short walk. When we're standing in front of Rae's car, I drop down to one knee in front of Riley while her mom stands back, giving us some privacy.

"Thanks for the ice cream, Ri."

She smiles, and there's still a bit of vanilla on the corner of her mouth. "You're welcome."

I open my arms, hoping she'll grant my final request of the night, but more than okay if she doesn't. "Can I have a hug?"

To my surprise, she comes running, crashing into my body with the kind of force I wouldn't usually attribute to someone her size. She wraps her arms around me, dirty fingers sticking to my shirt. I can't bring myself to care as I fold her into my embrace, making sure not to squeeze too tight even though I don't ever want to let her go. My eyes turn misty as I breathe in her scent for the first time, pressing my nose into the cloud of curls that smell like shea butter and cocoa and Riley. It's the most perfect scent. The most perfect hug. She's the most perfect girl, and my heart is full of love that builds and builds and builds until I have no choice but to let it go.

"I love you, Ri." I release her, swallowing hard to keep the tears at bay. "I hope you have the best day at school tomorrow."

"Can I call you and tell you about it?"

"I would love that."

"You'll have to give Mommy your number, and then she'll give it to me," she says. Her little voice is full of authority as she backs away, turning toward the car. "Goodnight, Daddy."

There's nothing forced or unnatural about that word on her lips, but I'm still stunned by the ease with which she uses it. "Goodnight, Daughter."

Again, she giggles, trapping the innocent sound of happiness in the car with her when she closes the door. I turn to Rae, my eyes stretched wide. "Did I hear that right?"

She moves closer to me, tainting the air around me with the scent of pears and vanilla. "Yep, no first names over here, just titles."

My excitement wanes just a little. "Oh, so she calls Aaron..."

"No." Rae shakes her head. "She's never called him anything but Aaron. Apparently, she's been waiting to meet you before pulling the D word out."

In the small, pettiest part of my brain, I take extreme satisfaction in knowing I'm the only person Riley has ever referred to that way, and I have to change the subject just to make sure it doesn't show on my face.

"I told her she could call me after school tomorrow and tell me about her day."

"I heard. Dee isn't going to like that. She's usually Riley's first call after school."

A fond smile pulls at the corner of my lips at the mention of Rae's lifelong best friend. "How is Dee anyway?"

"She's good, living in Michigan and getting paid to gossip with the clients she's supposed to be helping."

"So, still up to her same shenanigans."

"Yep," Rae says, pulling out her phone and extending it to me once she's got it on the 'add a new contact' screen. "Put your number in and I'll make sure she calls as soon as she gets in the car. Pick-up is at three, and we'll be calling about ten minutes after that, so please make sure you answer."

"I will," I promise, typing my number in and then handing the phone back to her. She looks down, preparing to go through the motions of saving it, when she notices something.

"You still have the same number?"

"Yeah."

"Why?" My brows pull together, forming a tight line that says I don't appreciate the judgment in her tone. She rolls her eyes but still course-corrects. "I mean, I just don't think I know anyone who's had the same number for over twenty years. Why have you kept it for so long?"

I could lie. I probably should lie, but I don't like the idea of ending the first day of our new beginning on a dishonest note.

"Remember that time your car broke down on the highway in the middle of the night?" She nods, and I continue relaying the details even though we both know the story. "Your phone was dead, and you flagged down this creepy ass van that, thankfully, turned out to be full of a women's church group. They let you use their phone to call for help, and the only number you knew by heart was...."

"Yours," Rae says, finishing my sentence, understanding dawning on her features.

"When you left, I knew that you were gone for good. I deserved that, but I couldn't stand the thought of you reaching out to me for some reason or another and there being a stranger on the other end of the line."

Several different emotions play across Rae's features, and she quiets them all one by one, spiriting them away from my prying eyes. After a few moments of silence, she claps her hands and says, "I should get going. Do you need me to give you a ride back to the gym?"

Her polite tone is almost enough to make me ignore the way her eyes stretch wide with the hope that she won't have to spend another minute with me today. Although it's inconvenient, and unnatural, I decide the best thing to do is let her go.

"No, I'll just get an Uber back."

"Great," she says, turning to walk away from me without so much as a goodnight.

The abrupt end to such a good day doesn't sit right with me, so I reach for her, catching her by the wrist like I did the night I found out about Riley. This time, she doesn't snatch away; she just turns slowly, looking between her wrist and my face with a frown.

"I'm sorry." I release her. "I just had to say one last thing before I let you go."

"What is it, Hunter?"

She's not looking at me. Her gaze focused on a point somewhere above my head. It doesn't matter. I don't need her eye contact to know that my words will resonate in her heart.

"Thank you for today, for this chance to know her and learn you again. I know I made a mess of us before, but we really made something beautiful together, didn't we?"

All of her features go soft, and she finally meets my eyes. "Yeah, we really did."

16

RAE

Then

One of the first things I noticed about my room at Hunter's place is how close it is to his bedroom. I loved that when the house was quiet and still I could strain my ears and hear him breathing or tossing and turning in his sheets. I loved that I could hear his five o'clock alarm and the creak of his floorboards that told me he was getting dressed for his morning run. I loved everything about it, but tonight, or more accurately, this morning, I despise our shared wall because it's giving me a backstage pass to Indigo's first night in his bed.

Usually, they sleep over at her place because, despite her initial friendliness, she doesn't seem to be a huge fan of Will and I staying at Hunter's place. Every week, she finds new ways to keep him away from the house, dragging him deeper and deeper into her world with little to no concern for reciprocation. I don't know how Hunter talked her into coming over tonight, but I wish he hadn't because then I wouldn't be listening to *this*.

Her giggles of delight.

His low, rumbling tone that's supposed to be for her but is

speaking directly to the green-eyed monster living in my chest. Every time I see them together, or hear Hunter on the phone with her, all I can think is 'that should be me.' When I concocted my plan for the summer, I had a very specific vision for what things between Hunter and I would look like at this point, and Indigo wasn't a part of any of it.

Nor was the belly-burning jealousy and irrational sadness I've been dealing with since the night of my graduation party. I thought I'd be able to soothe those emotional wounds by putting us in situations created specifically to spark Hunter's desire, like the underboob tattoo and the kickback tonight with Cameron's handsy ass, but so far, nothing's worked. Every display of Hunter's protective, possessive side is fleeting, so short-lived that I'm not entirely sure I'm not imagining them.

I turn over and sigh, sandwiching my head between a pillow in hopes of blocking them out. For one blissful moment, I think it's working, but then Indigo snorts loudly at something Hunter said, and I'm left with no choice but to admit defeat. Sitting up, I grab the pillow and toss it at the wall.

"He's not even that damn funny."

"Right?" Dee adds from the other side of the bed. "I've never even heard him crack a joke, so she's definitely putting on."

"He makes jokes."

"Girl!" She throws an arm over her eyes and lets out an exasperated sigh. "You have got to pick a struggle. Either you want me to agree that he has no sense of humor, or you want me to call him the next King of Comedy; there is no in-between."

"Why can't it be both?" I ask, snickering when her annoyance leads to her turning her back to me.

"Good night, Rachel."

I roll my eyes. She knows I hate it when she calls me by my full name. "Are you really going to sleep, or are you just ignoring me?"

Her response comes in the form of a light snore that makes my jaw drop in disbelief. "Who falls asleep *that* fast?" I mutter, swinging my legs over the edge of the bed and grabbing my phone on my way out the door. When I step into the hallway, everything is quiet. I guess at some point during Dee and I's short conversation Hunter and Giggles found something else to do besides work my last nerve. I check the time on my phone and see that it's almost two in the morning, which means Will's alarm will be going off soon.

He's been picking up extra shifts at the factory to cover the growing cost of solving our mold problem, which means we haven't been seeing a lot of each other. When I do see him, he looks tired. His features gaunt and his complexion flat. He's lost weight, which I can only assume comes from him forgetting to pack food for his shifts. I pressed him about it a few days ago, and his excuses ranged from it not being a priority because he's too tired to have an appetite to him just not having the time to do it.

Since he won't let me contribute the little money I have in my savings to help with the house expenses, I've taken it upon myself to make sure he's nourished while he works himself to the bone.

I move down the stairs quickly and quietly, hoping to be done with Will's lunch by the time he comes down. A few of the lights are still on, which doesn't surprise me because Hunter always does that on nights when Will has to work, but what does surprise me is the fact that I'm not on the first floor alone.

Hunter is posted up against the counter by the sink, drinking a glass of water like he does every night before he goes to bed. We stare at each other for a long moment, and even though he looks good as fuck in the black tank and short combination I've come to think of as his uniform, I'm not all that glad to see him.

"Hey," he says, all casual and unbothered like he hasn't played a role in turning this night into a total shit show. First, by manhandling one of my guests—poor Cameron probably needs a neck brace—and then by making me an unwilling listener to the soundtrack of his and Indigo's nighttime routine.

I don't respond. I just make my way over to the cabinet where Will keeps his lunchbox and attempt to pull it down. My fingertips graze the end of the handle, but I fail to free the container from its perch on the highest shelf. I curse under my breath, wondering who put it all the way up there in the first place.

"Here, let me." Hunter comes up behind me, his broad chest and toned stomach brushing against my back and ass as he reaches up and makes light work of retrieving the stupid thing. He sets it on the counter and moves away, gone as quickly as he came.

"I could have gotten it," I say, lying right through my teeth even though we both know the truth.

"Sure, you could have." He places his abandoned glass in the sink and gives me a look that ensures I know he's being sarcastic.

"What's with you today?! You just keep butting into situations that no one asked you to be a part of."

Hunter pulls a face. "You're not seriously mad at me for kicking your little friends out, are you?"

"No, Hunter, I just *loved* seeing you manhandle my company just to turn around and snuggle up with your little girlfriend for the rest of the night." I turn to the fridge, yanking it open and pulling out the leftover steak he grilled earlier, not caring if he was saving it for him or Giggles. "I absolutely *adore* double standards."

He scoffs. "The only standards you should be worried about are yours."

"Mine?" I arch a brow. "What's wrong with my standards?"

"They're too low."

Now, I'm the one scoffing, tossing random items into Will's lunchbox without looking to see what any of it is. "*My* standards are low? Have you looked at your girlfriend lately?"

I expect him to take me to task for the stray bullet I've just sent flying in Indigo's direction, but he doesn't. Instead, he moves right past it, aiming his own verbal bullets at Cameron.

"Your high school sweetheart tried to undress you in front of everyone, including me." Something dark and dangerous passes behind his eyes. "He clearly doesn't respect you."

"Maybe I don't want to be respected, Hunter. Did you ever think of that?" His lips part, but no words come out, and I let out a vicious laugh in the face of his dumb founded expression. "It actually hasn't, huh?" I cackle again, unable to contain myself because I've just stumbled on an answer to a question I've been asking myself for weeks now. "You know what your problem is, Hunter? You think I'm a kid that needs your protection and guidance. You think I'm some helpless little girl with no desires or needs, which is laughable considering I was nineteen when we met."

Nineteen and a virgin, but still.

I don't even realize I've crossed the room to put my annoyance right in his face until I feel his breath on my lips, until I can taste the mint from his toothpaste and smell the alcohol from his mouthwash.

He glares down at me with dark, exasperated eyes. "I don't see you as a little girl, Rae," he whispers on an exhale. "I'm fully aware of the fact that you're a grown woman who can make her own choices and her own mistakes."

"Then treat me like it."

The air between us is thick and filled with heat. I wonder if Hunter knows that I've just issued a challenge to him, that those five words are as close as I'll probably ever get to asking him for what I really want. His eyes drop to my lips, and I lick them, preparing for a moment that won't ever happen.

"Act like one," he returns, and maybe it's just my imagination, but I swear I hear Hunter's own answering challenge in his response. Just the thought has me inching closer until my breasts are pressed into the top of his stomach and I can see his pulse start to pound. Until my stomach is brushing against the bulge in his shorts and my sex is clenched with anticipation of desires that won't be fulfilled.

Hunter feels everything I feel, but he doesn't step back, and he doesn't tell me to stop. He just stands there, a large and imposing figure casting a shadow over my body and my doubts. I lift up on my tip toes and hold myself there for a long second, more than enough time for him to see the intention in my eyes and change his mind.

He blinks, eyes low and hooded, and I lunge forward, taking a chance. The second our lips collide, Hunter's hands are at my waist. He lifts me up, suspending my body in the air like I weigh nothing, and I try to wrap my legs around him, but he won't allow it. I can't bring myself to care, though, because I'm kissing him, and he's kissing me back with all the fervor and passion I knew he would give me.

Our tongues crash together, and I moan into him, putting my hands around his neck so I can pull him closer. He comes willingly, turning his head to the side to get a better angle. In my mind, past the layers of surprise and delight, I curse because he's so fucking good at this. I want to spend the rest of my life kissing him.

The tell-tale creak of Will's door opening echoes through the house, breaking the silence around us and forcing Hunter and I's mouths apart. We're both panting when we pull away, and I want to smile because it was everything I thought it would be, but he's frowning, so I hold my giddiness close like a secret.

Hunter lowers me to the floor slowly, and I'm just getting my bearings, settling myself on the other side of the kitchen, far away from Hunter, when Will appears, looking just as worn out as he did when he went to sleep.

He rubs at bleary eyes and looks between me and Hunter. "Um, good morning?"

"I packed your lunch!" I chirp, forcing a smile as I hold the lunchbox up as proof.

Will walks over and gives me a peck on the cheek. "I already told you you don't need to do that, Rae."

"I know, but I wanted to."

"I'm heading up to bed," Hunter grunts, leaving the room before Will or I have a chance to respond.

"What was that about?" Will asks, staring at the doorway Hunter just passed through.

I bite my lip, my mind on the kiss and how he wanted it just as badly as I did. "I have no idea."

17

RAE

For as long as I can remember, Riley has always, and I mean *always*, loved science. Even when she was a toddler, she'd have me doing all kinds of homemade experiments—taping water bottles together so she could have a handheld tornado, mixing together hydrogen peroxide, yeast, and dish detergent to make elephant toothpaste, and buying every slime kit known to man. The first time I asked her what she wanted to be when she grew up, her answer was a mad scientist, and even though she dropped the 'mad' part somewhere between ages six and seven, her answer has stayed the same over the years.

As a dancer and born creative, I haven't always understood her interest, but I've made a commitment to supporting it, to showing her that I don't care if she never wears a pair of pointe shoes—which she hasn't—as long as she's doing what makes her happy. Science makes her happy.

Or at least it did.

"Ri, what's going on?" Dee asks through the phone. "You've been looking forward to the science fair all month."

I glance at Riley through the mirror of my vanity. She's sprawled out on the foot of my bed with the phone in her hand and a full-blown pout on her face. It's been there all week, and I'm not sure where it came from or what to do to get rid of it. When I tried to get the answer out of her, she said she didn't want to talk about it with me, so I had her pick someone from her list of trusted adults—which is basically just me, Dee, and sometimes Jayla—to discuss her feelings with. Unsurprisingly, she chose Dee and agreed to let me stay in the room while they talked. I was hopeful my best friend would be able to help her get her feelings sorted before we had to leave the house, but they've been on the phone for thirty minutes, and Riley has given her nothing.

"Are you worried about speaking to the judges?" I ask, risking being kicked out of the room for butting into the conversation. "Because I think you're going to do great. You practiced several times, and you have your note cards if you forget what you're going to say."

Riley glances at me and shakes her head. I breathe a sigh of relief and turn around, more confident about contributing to the conversation now.

"Y'all do know this is a phone call, right?" Dee asks. "You actually have to use your voices if you want me to be able to respond."

I encourage Riley to vocalize her answer with a lift of my brows. She sits up and hops off the bed, walking across the room to take a seat in my lap. Even though she's getting too tall for it, I cradle her in my arms like a baby and kiss the top of her head.

"She said she's not worried about the talking part, Dee."

The silence on the other end of the line tells me my best friend is at just as much a loss as I am, which makes me feel a little less shitty about not knowing how to help.

"Well, that's good," Dee says eventually. "Because you're an excellent orator, aren't you, Ri?"

Riley nods, and I jostle her around, hoping to free a smile from her. "Then let's hear you say it, Nugget."

"I'm an excellent orator," she says, her tone still flat even though there's a ghost of a smile playing on her lips.

"And you're going to blow those judges away, aren't you?" Dee asks, going full-blown motivational speaker. Riley already knows the drill when her auntie gets like this, and she falls in line like a good soldier.

"I'm going to blow the judges away," she repeats, and I can practically hear the eye roll she wants to deploy alongside the words she clearly doesn't want to be saying right now.

The door of our bedroom opens, and Aaron appears. "It's six o'clock."

"Alright, Nugs, we have to go." I tap Riley's hip, and she slides off my lap. "Dee, I'll call you and let you know how it goes."

"Okay. Love you guys!"

"Love you too," Riley and I say together before I end the call.

Tucking my phone into my purse, I take Riley's hand and give her a reassuring squeeze. "I don't know what you're worried about, Nugget, and I respect your choice not to discuss it with me, but I just want to remind you that things only have as much power as you give them. You can decide, right here, right now, not to give any more of your energy to whatever it is that you're worried about."

She stares at me with walls up behind those brown eyes I have no idea how to penetrate. I'm acutely aware of Aaron's presence lingering in the doorway and find myself wondering if right now is one of those moments where I could create space for Aaron in my dynamic with Riley. Ever since he told me he's felt like I've kept him on the outside of things, I've been trying to find a moment to show him that I don't want it to be that way anymore, but he's been so busy at work, and I've been so caught up in navigating co-parenting with Hunter and figuring out my next steps in New Haven, that we haven't had many chances to turn the desires we voiced in our heart to heart into action.

Maybe now is my chance.

"Isn't that right, Aaron?" I ask with forced enthusiasm because the integration feels unnatural to me. When nothing but silence follows my question, I glance over my shoulder and find him on his phone. "Isn't that right, *Aaron*?"

He jolts, wild eyes flying to my face as he lowers his phone to his side. "Yeah, that's right, Ri."

Riley's brows dip low, expressing just how unimpressed she is with his response, and now that I've seen her and Hunter make that same face side by side, I can't see her do it without thinking about how very similar she is to her dad and how much she's loved having him around. She even invited him to the science fair, and he promised he'd be in attendance. He called me three different times this week to confirm the time and the address, so I know he's going to come through for her. Maybe he'll be able to put a smile on her face.

"Alright, let's go. We don't want to keep your dad waiting."

Just like the first time Hunter was mentioned in our home, Aaron looks confused. He steps back, allowing Riley and I space to pass through the door.

"Hunter's coming?" he asks as we walk down the steps toward the front door.

"Yes, I told you that."

A knot starts to form in the pit of my stomach in the time it takes him to respond. I don't want to argue with him tonight, but if his silence means anything other than he's so happy that Riley's dad is choosing to be an active part of her life that he's actually speechless, then I can pretty much guarantee that's what's going to happen.

He waits until Riley is in the car to respond, offering me the excuse over the roof of the car. "I guess I forgot."

"Or maybe you were too busy on your phone to retain the information."

"You know things are hectic at work, Rae."

"Yes, Aaron, I know, but I also know that we don't have a chance in hell of having the kind of partnership you said you wanted if you're tuning me out when I'm trying to talk to you about things that matter."

He scrubs a hand down his face and nods. "You're right. I'm sorry. I'll do better."

"Okay, and hey—" I call out just as he's about to open his door. "I know this whole thing with Hunter isn't easy for you, but the only way we'll figure out how to make it work is if we keep talking to and leaning on each other."

Once again, he nods, and because we don't have time to continue to flesh this out, I accept the small gesture and choose to move on. The ride to Riley's school is only about fifteen minutes long, but I was hoping that in that time, she'd find something to be excited about. Unfortunately, she gets out of the car and leads Aaron and me to the gym with the same forlorn look on her face. I'm at a complete loss, but I know there's nothing I can do but give her the space to work through her feelings, so I follow along quietly, keeping my eyes peeled for Hunter.

I spot him in the middle of the gym, his large framed squeezed in between the small tables where the kids have set up their exhibits. Riley and I came in earlier this afternoon and got her table ready, so we wouldn't have to lug everything in tonight, and Hunter looks to be admiring our handiwork.

"Daddy!" Riley shouts, the first real smile I've seen all day taking over her face as she dashes over to him with her arms wide open.

There are over a dozen fathers in the building tonight, but some-how, Hunter knows that he's the one being addressed. I marvel at that fact as he turns just in time to catch Riley up in his arms, wondering how he's grown so attuned to her voice so quickly. I guess it's a thing parents can just do because I have the skill, too. We can be in a store, separated by aisles, people, and shopping carts, and I'll still be able to distinguish Riley's voice from every other child's.

Certain that Riley is fine, I reach for Aaron's hand, intending to present a united front when we approach Hunter, but come up empty. I turn around and see him standing right outside the gym door with his phone to his ear. Irritation rushes through me, pulling my face into a scowl that I don't hide or minimize when I catch his eye. To his credit, he does look apologetic, mouthing 'I'm sorry' before stepping out of sight, but it doesn't stop me from feeling like everything I just said to him before we left the house doesn't matter.

Determined not to let the night be further impacted by Aaron's job, I make my way across the gym to Hunter and Riley, noting almost instantly how animated she is while she's talking to him. I should be used to it by now; in the weeks since they met, I've seen her like this with him every time they're together in person or on FaceTime after school. He brings out a side of her that people only get to see when she feels safe with them, which makes me think it's time to add another name to Riley's list of trusted adults.

My suspicion is quickly confirmed when I finally make it to them and see Riley pointing her finger in the direction of a little boy a few tables over who has a group of other kids around his display. All of them are looking at my kid with varying, but no less unfriendly, expressions on their faces.

"Ri, who's that kid?" I ask, placing a hand over hers to stop her from pointing.

Hunter, who was just crouched down to Riley's level, stands, his face a picture of grim determination as he says. "Her bully."

"Bully?" I balk, incredulity coursing through me as I look at Riley for confirmation. I'm equal parts angry and sad. Angry because I want to end the little fucker who has the nerve to be mean to my little girl, and sad because she chose to share that information with Hunter instead of me. I make a mental note to ask him how he got her to tell him. Then, I school my features into a mask of calm and bury my feelings so I can focus on hers. "You have a bully?"

"Yeah, his name is Pierre, and he said that I have a boy name."

"She told him it was unisex," Hunter adds. "But then he started picking on her for saying 'sex,' and now every time he and his friends see her, they call her Unisex Riley."

I pull a face. *Unisex Riley?* That's not even a good insult. These private school kids wouldn't make it a day in the public schools Dee and I grew up in. Hunter gives me a look that says he agrees with my internal thoughts, and I bite back a laugh because while we both know the taunt is trash, we're still pissed that the words have hurt our kid.

"They said I was going to do my science fair presentation on sex," Riley says, pouting. "I told them my project was a water filtration system, but they just ignored me."

Tears spring in her eyes and the last thread of Hunter's sanity snaps. I watch it happen in real-time, and my heart starts to pound at the same time something I shouldn't be feeling and won't name unfurls low in my stomach.

"Come on, Ri," Hunter says, grabbing her hand and pulling her along with him. While I wasn't invited on this little side quest, I still follow them, damn near hitting a sprint to try and keep up.

"Hunter, you can't threaten a bunch of kids in the middle of a science fair," I hiss, throwing fake smiles in the direction of every concerned parent and teacher that is watching our processional.

"Relax, Rae. I'm not going to threaten any kids."

I wish that made me feel better, but as we arrive at the table where Pierre and his minions are standing, my heart is in my throat, and I'm mentally running through other school options for Riley once Hunter gets us kicked out of here.

"Which one of you is Pierre," Hunter asks, his voice a refined growl.

Every boy at the table steps back, leaving only one kid face-to-face with Hunter. He's a tiny little thing, shorter than Riley by at least two inches and thin. His translucent skin tinges with red when Hunter hones in on him, and when Hunter drops down to his level, he steps back, bumping into his table and nearly knocking the foam pipe and duct tape marble roller coaster off.

Hunter tilts his head in Riley's direction, eyes still focused on Pierre. "You know her?"

Quick as a flash, Pierre glances at Riley and then back at Hunter. "Yes, sir."

"Ah, you have manners. That's good to know. I didn't think that was the case once my daughter told me you'd been making fun of her name."Hunter looks at Riley, who's standing there with a satisfied glint in her eyes as she watches her dad take up for her. "What is it he calls you, Ri?"

"Unisex Riley."

Hunter swings his head back around, lifting a brow. "Is that true,

Pierre?" The boy shakes his head, and Hunter laughs. "Oh, so now you're calling my kid a liar?"

"N—n—n—no, sir," Pierre stutters, and I almost feel bad for him. *Almost.*

With a wave of his hand, Hunter dismisses the question. "You know what? It doesn't even matter, Pierre. The only thing that matters is your answer to my next question, so tell me when you're ready to hear it."

Pierre looks to me for help, but I remain stone-faced, feeling very little sympathy for the little brat who stole my baby's joy for a week.

"I'm ready, sir."

"Does your dad know how to fight?"

It takes everything in me to keep my jaw hinged. What the hell kind of question is that to ask a kid?

Pierre swallows hard. "Umm, yes?"

"You don't sound certain, Pierre, and I want you to be certain. Does your dad know how to fight?"

"*Yes,*" Pierre repeats, this time with more confidence.

"Do you think he could beat me?"

Every ounce of confidence Pierre just found leaves his body in an instant as he sweeps wide eyes over Hunter.

"I don't know."

"Do you want to find out?" Pierre presses his lips together and shakes his head, unable to lend his voice to his response. Hunter nods like he anticipated that answer. "I didn't think so, but I can promise you, Pierre, that the next time my daughter comes to me and says you or any of your little friends are being mean to her, we're going to find out."

"You would beat my dad up?"

"Your dad. Your uncles. Your grandpas." Hunter ticks each person off on his fingers, intentionally using his left hand because the skeletal bones outlining each digit help drive home how deathly serious he is. "Any man who was supposed to teach you that there's more to being a good person than knowing how to say 'yes, sir' and 'no, sir' will have to see me, and then when you're old enough, you'll have to see me too."

The boy's eyes bulge out of his head, the rims turning red like he's trying to hold back tears. I step forward, placing a hand on Hunter's shoulder. He glances at me, and we both ignore the jolt of electricity moving between my palm and his body.

"I think he's got the point, Hunter." To confirm, we both look at Pierre, who is nodding and definitely fighting back tears. Satisfied, Hunter stands and looks at Riley, who is beaming at him.

"Got anything else to add, Nugget?"

She shakes her head. "Nope."

He holds out his fist and she bumps it with her own. "Alright then, let's go win a science fair."

18

HUNTER

Riley's first-place trophy sits in the center of the table, gleaming under the dim lights in the restaurant and upstaging the dry excuse for bread sticks Aaron ordered when we sat down.

He doesn't want me here.

That much is clear from the way he glares at me every time Rae and I share a laugh over my interaction with Pierre. We're laughing about it right now, and while I'm tuned into the way Rae's lips curve every time she smiles, I'm also painfully aware of the daggers he's sending me from across the table.

"I don't think there's anything funny about threatening someone else's child," he says, plucking a bread stick from the basket and breaking a piece off. "You know Riley could get kicked out of school for the stunt you pulled."

Rae's smile falters. I watch her hide the crack in her joy behind a sip of water and find myself wondering for the millionth time why she's with this guy. I don't think I've seen them share a genuine moment of affection since we sat down at the table, and everything about Rae's posture suggests that they're not quite as solid as Aaron's arm draped over the back of her chair makes them seem.

"Don't say that, Aaron," she says through clenched teeth with her eyes on Riley to see if she heard what was said. Luckily, she's too caught up in solving the word search on the back of her kid's menu to notice.

"It's true," Aaron insists, unaware or unconcerned with the growing tension in Rae's shoulders. "All that kid would have to do is tell his parents about Hunter's brutish behavior, and they'd go to the headmaster—"

"Mistress," I correct.

The veins in both of his temples bulge at the same time. "Either way, all the parents would have to do is file a complaint, and then that'd be the end of that. They don't give refunds on tuition either, so in addition to the embarrassment of being dismissed from the school, we'd be out tens of thousands of dollars."

"That won't happen, Aaron."

"And what are you going to do if it does, Hunter? March up to the school and threaten the headmistress until she agrees to let Riley stay?"

One day, very, very soon, I'm going to give in to my urge to punch this asshole in the face, but today I settle for the satisfaction of blowing his mind by showing him that I have more than strength and good looks on my side.

"No, I'd probably just call up my good friend, Sorel Hartwick, and explain the situation, making sure she's aware that I was acting from a place of pure concern for my daughter. Since her name is on the door, and she sits on the Board of Directors for the school, I'm sure she'd be able to smooth over any bumps in the road *my brutish* approach might have caused."

"You know a Hartwick?" Rae asks, impressed even though she doesn't want to be.

"Sorel was a friend of Legacy's," I say, toying with my napkin. "We've stayed in touch over the years. She comes to the gym sometimes for goat yoga."

At the mention of Legacy, Rae's features soften. She holds my gaze and that thing that happens every time we look at each other in the eye for too long starts to happen. Threads of fate unravel between us. One end of each string is attached to my heart while the other roots around, trying to find a home in hers. Seconds pass in the form of memories only we can see, moving so slowly they create a new path for time. One where only Rae and I exist.

"Goat yoga?!" Riley exclaims, pulling us out of our bubble. "Who would want to do yoga with goats?"

Riley is the only person I'd never resent for interrupting a moment with Rae, so I turn an indulgent smile on her. "A lot of people."

"You?" she asks, brows furrowed together.

"I tried it once," I admit, which makes Riley and her mom laugh. "I had to see what it was about."

Even though I've managed to lighten the mood, Aaron seems determined to make it turn dim again. He doesn't share in our laughter, which causes Rae to pull back, too. She tries to make her fading humor look natural, so Riley or I don't notice.

But I do notice, and it pisses me the fuck off.

"Maybe you could ask her to give us a friend's and family discount on the outrageous tuition the next time you two are doing downward facing dog with a goat on your back," Aaron says, infusing false levity into his voice to make it sound like a joke even though every adult at the table knows it's not.

"*Aaron.*"

Rae is at her wit's end, so her tone is lethal and unforgiving. While she processes her feelings, I take the opportunity to jump on a topic I've been meaning to broach for a while now.

"A discount won't be necessary because I'll be taking over Riley's tuition payments."

I'm not asking, mainly because it doesn't sit right with me to have another man paying for anything that has to do with my daughter when I'm more than capable of doing so myself, but Rae still shakes her head and says, "No, I can't let you do that," while Aaron sits there like a slack jawed fool.

"You're not letting me do anything, Rae. She's my daughter, and it's my job to provide for her." I look at Riley, relieved to see that she's once again tuned us out. "I've missed out on nearly ten years of birthdays, Christmases, sports, and special interests, so I've got a lot of making up to do. Let me start with this."

I don't mention that taking over tuition payments is also the first step in my plan to help make Rae's ballet school a reality because I don't want to mention it in front of Aaron, and I'm still waiting for the other, most important, part of all of this to come together.

"Hunter, I—"

"Just say yes, Rae."

I don't mean for it to come out as an order, but it does, and heat flashes in her eyes as the authoritative growl unearths memories of a time when she never hesitated to say yes to me because she trusted me to take care of her mentally, emotionally, and physically.

"We'll consider it," Aaron says, placing his hand over Rae's.

My first instinct is to tell him to fuck off because I wasn't talking to him, but I think I've threatened enough little boys for today, so I nod like I don't plan to push Rae for an answer the next time we're alone and focus my attention on the menu.

The rest of our dinner passes by in an uneventful blur that's only tolerable because I get to sit next to Riley for the entirety of it. I get to watch her devour an entire plate of plain spaghetti noodles with nothing but grated Parmesan on top and decline Rae's offer to try her carbonara dish several times. Then I get to see Rae pout about how unfair it is that she takes a bite of my lasagna as soon as I offer it. Aaron stays quiet during all of these exchanges, spending most of his time slugging down the bottle of red wine he ordered—which made it necessary for me to explain to my nine-year-old what it means to be sober—and typing on his phone under the table.

Rae does the best she can to ignore his petulant behavior, but by the time we're making our way to our separate vehicles, she looks ready to explode. I don't feel all that comfortable with leaving Riley to ride with them when I can tell by how hard Rae is grasping the keys that she's going to lay into Aaron on the way home, but the curse of being a former absentee father is that you don't get a lot of say in situations like this. You get to pick one battle per day, and today, I chose tuition, which means I can't voice my opinions on the car ride or offer any kind of solution.

"Daddy, can you take me home?" Riley asks as we walk hand in hand to Aaron's car.

"Oh. I don't know, Ri, you'd have to ask your mom."

"Mommy! Can Daddy take me home?"

Nothing but a weary sigh proceeds Rae's response. "If he doesn't mind, baby."

"I don't mind."

I'd actually prefer to put them both in my car and take them far away from the human embodiment of misery that is Aaron Scott, but I know that's not an option right now. Rae flashes me a tight smile, and my heart aches as the desire to fix everything that's wrong in her life comes rushing to the surface, refusing to be held at bay any longer.

"Thanks," she says, unlocking the car doors. "You can just follow me. It's like a five-minute drive."

"Sounds good." I scoop Ri up, placing her on my back while she clutches her trophy tight. "Let's go, Nugget."

By the time I get Riley settled in my backseat and pull out of my parking spot, Rae is already waiting for us at the exit with her right blinker flashing. I put my blinker on, too, then flash my lights at her to let her know I'm ready to go. She whips the car onto the road and accelerates. From the back seat, Riley says, "Mommy drives fast when she's mad."

I don't laugh even though I want to, even though I remember the one time I let Rae get behind the wheel of my car when she was mad at me, and she flew through a stop sign and got upset with me when the other vehicles in the intersection blew their horns at her.

"How do you feel about winning first place at the science fair?" I ask, changing the subject to a safer topic.

"Good! I feel even better that you stopped Pierre and his friends from being mean to me. I can't wait to tell Scarlett all about it." From the rearview, I can see her wide smile as she looks out the window.

"Where was Scarlett tonight anyway? I was looking forward to meeting your new best friend."

Most of our post-school calls are filled with the Adventures of Riley and Scarlett. I was looking forward to meeting the little spitfire who has quickly become the Deanna to Riley's Rae.

"She was sick," Riley says. "She threw up in class, and Ms. Ryder made her mom come and get her."

Rae switches lanes, and I follow her lead, watching as she gestures wildly with one hand through the back window of the car. The evidence of her outrage illuminated by my headlights. Aaron is slumped down in his seat, probably too far gone on wine to engage or defend himself.

"Oh, that's too bad. I'm sure she was sad to miss your big win."

"Mommy took pictures. She said she'll send them to Scarlett's mom so she doesn't feel like she missed anything."

"That's cool. You have a pretty awesome mom, don't you?"

Riley nods enthusiastically, which makes my chest go warm. Watching Rae be a mother is one of the many things I thought I'd lost forever to my battle with addiction, so every time I get to see her and Riley together or just talk about how amazing she is with our kid, I feel a surge of pride.

"You're pretty awesome too, Daddy," she tells me, shredding my heart with the well-placed compliment. Emotion clogs my throat, making it hard for me to respond, but somehow, I manage to push the words out.

"Thanks, Nugget. You're not too bad yourself."

"Do you have a daddy?"

I should have seen this coming. Riley is one of those kids who notices everything, even if she doesn't comment on it right away. I should have known that she'd eventually bring up why I'm the only new person in her life. Dads usually come with a whole host of people in tow, grandparents, uncles, aunts, maybe even cousins, but all Riley's gotten out of the deal is me and an uncle who lives eight hours away and isn't yet aware of her existence because even though our relationship has improved the longer I've been clean, we still don't talk much.

"Uh, I had a dad, yeah, but he and my mom died before I met your mommy."

"Oh. That sucks."

I huff out a short laugh. "Yeah, it does. They would have spoiled you rotten."

"Marcy says being spoiled isn't a good thing."

I frown. "Who's Marcy?"

"Aaron's mom. She lives with us at our house."

Suddenly, everything about Aaron's fucked up personality makes sense to me. Of course, he's a little bitch boy with a buzzkill for a mother. I bet together, the two of them suck all the joy out of that house.

"Oh, well, I don't know why Marcy would say that, but there's nothing wrong with being spoiled unless, of course, you're a piece of fruit."

I've been a dad for all of two seconds, and I'm already making dad jokes. I shake my head, hating myself just a little but not caring because the joke serves its purpose. Riley giggles and forgets all about the misery awaiting her at home, and I join in, too, cracking more jokes to make her laugh and distract myself from the fact that at the end of this car ride, I'll have to let her go.

By the time we arrive at Rae's house, my face hurts from smiling so much. Rae parks Aaron's luxury vehicle next to the car I see her in all the time, and I pull up behind her, noting that she hasn't cut the engine yet. I wait for a moment to see if they're going to get out, but Riley gets impatient, unhooking her seat belt and grabbing her trophy, which leaves me with no choice but to hop out of my truck and help her down. When I decided to take the truck instead of the car, I didn't think she'd be riding home with me. I had no reason to since I've never driven her anywhere before, but that still doesn't stop me from feeling like an idiot for not choosing the vehicle that would have been easier for her to maneuver in and out of. To make myself feel better, and to put one last smile on Riley's face for the night, I scoop her up off her seat and sling her around until she's on my back for the second time tonight.

Her giggles of delight fill my ear as I bounce her all the way to the front door, only sparing the car where Aaron and Rae still are a passing glance. When we get to the door, I crouch down to make it easier for Riley to slide off, and she plants a kiss on my forehead.

I look up at her, fighting back the very real urge to cry at how precious she is. "What was that for?"

She shrugs her little shoulders, squeezing the base of the trophy tight. "Just because."

"Can I have a just-because hug too?" I ask, opening my arms wide.

"Sure." She wraps her arms around my neck and squeezes, allowing me just a second to squeeze her back.

"I love you, Nugget," I remind her, the way I have every time we've said goodbye since we've known each other. She's never said it back, but that's okay. I don't want her to give her love freely, to dispense it just because we share DNA. I want her to be stingy with it, discerning about who she gives it to. That way, it'll be so much sweeter when she chooses to give it to me.

When I let her go, she's smiling again, basking in the glow of a bond we've only just established. I watch that smile fall when the front door opens, the light from the entryway cutting a harsh line across Riley's face as an older woman steps onto the porch with us.

"Riley! What are you doing out here?" The woman, who I can only assume is Marcy, asks, literally clutching her pearls as she watches me straighten to my full height. "And who are you?"

I extend my hand, offering her a courteous smile. "I'm Hunter Drake, ma'am, Riley's father."

"Oh, hello." She doesn't take my hand; she just puts the one not at her neck on Riley's shoulder and guides her inside. "Where are Aaron and Rae?"

"They're in the car," Riley says, inside the house now but still lingering on the threshold because we haven't said a proper goodbye yet.

Marcy peeks her head out the door like she's looking for proof that the statement is true. When she sees the running car in the driveway in front of my truck, she sighs in relief.

"Okay, well, let's get you inside, Riley." She glances at me, judgment and disdain all in her eyes. "Thanks for bringing her to the door."

"No problem."

"Goodnight, Daddy," Riley says in a sing-song voice that makes me smile.

"Goodnight, Daughter." Marcy gives us both an odd look, so I tack on. "Goodnight, Mrs. Scott," just because I know it'll freak her the fuck out to know that I know her last name. Years of being my size and looking the way that I do have taught me that some people will go out of their way to find a reason to be afraid of me.

Aaron has probably told her all about my history of addiction and all the tattoos. He's probably made me out to be some caveman who grunts and resorts to violence at every turn, doing everything he can to paint an image of me his mother will go out of her way to uphold in an effort to support her son. Tonight, me standing on her doorstep with knowledge of her last name is that proof and it doesn't matter that I got the information from Rae or that there was nothing sinister in my tone when I said it. She chooses to be afraid because any alternative would be a direct affront to the narrative she and her son have crafted.

As expected, her eyes go wide, and she steps back even though I haven't advanced on her at all. "Good night," she says, rushing to close the door. I hear the deadbolt engage and laugh to myself as I walk down the steps. Meeting Marcy explains so much about Aaron, but it does nothing to help me understand how Rae can stomach the two of them every day.

When I reach the end of the short walkway that leads from the driveway to the door, I pause, battling with myself about whether I should check in on Rae before I go or just leave well enough alone.

Leaving would be the proper thing to do, but I don't like Aaron when he's sober, and I don't trust him when he's drunk, so that option doesn't sit right with me. I walk up to the car and rap on his window, gesturing for him to roll it down when he scowls at me through the glass.

"What do you—"

I hold a hand up, cutting him off so I can address the only person in the car I give a fuck about. "You good, Rae?"

She's not good. I can tell by the way her eyes are shining with unshed tears. I know from first-hand experience that those are tears of fury, not sadness, which means Aaron is in danger of losing his head if he doesn't tread carefully.

"I'm fine, Hunter. Thanks for getting Ri in the house and for being here tonight. It meant a lot to her."

"Of course, anything for my girls."

Rae was intentional about not saying my presence meant a lot to her, too, so I'm just as intentional about reminding her that Riley might be my first priority, but she's my second. I know she catches my meaning when her eyes take on that dazed look. Aaron fumes between us, but he doesn't say anything, which is preferable but also surprising. I knew he was weak, but I didn't think he was *that* weak. I mean sitting there pouting while another man reminds the woman you both love that she's his has to be a new low, even for him.

Satisfied that Rae is fine, I tap the top of the car. "Goodnight, Sunshine."

COMING HOME to all the lights in the house on and the sound of the TV blasting is something I haven't experienced since I shared my home with Rae over ten years ago, so it's taken some getting used to. And by getting used to, I mean pretending not to be annoyed every time I come home to it because I don't want Taurin to feel like he has to walk on eggshells around me.

We've been living together for almost a month now, and he's

comfortable here. Given that his parents have turned down every request to meet—despite him having close two months of sobriety under his belt, getting back in school and doing well, and working at the gym for me—his comfort here is a good thing, a necessary thing, the only thing that will keep him off the streets and on a path to the life he would have had if a basketball injury hadn't led him to a pain pill prescription that jump-started his opioid addiction.

Our arrangement isn't traditional by any means, but it's been working for us, and I hope it stays that way, even if he is the messiest housemate I've ever had.

"T!" I yell out as I enter through the backdoor and get slapped in the face with a pile of dishes in the sink and an open box of cereal on the counter. He comes running from the living room with a bowl of cereal in hand, sloshing milk around.

"Yeah?" I wave a hand in the general direction of the mess and give him a 'what the fuck' look. He shoves a spoonful of cereal into his mouth and nods. "I got you, man. Let me finish this bowl, and then I'll take care of it."

I cross my arms and stare at him, and he starts to chew faster, washing down his last bite with noisy slurps of his milk before making his way over to the sink.

"Strict as hell around here," he mutters under his breath.

"Gotta be when I'm dealing with gremlins like you."

"Speaking of gremlins, how's your kid?"

Taurin and I have spent a lot of time outside of meetings expanding on the things we've shared inside them. I've learned about the friends he grew up playing ball with, the girlfriend who's a cheerleader and a year older than him, the subjects he struggles with in school, and the bond he has with his little brother, Terrance. In return, I've shared details of my burgeoning bond with Riley, expressing some doubts about being good enough for her but still trying my best while he assured me that was enough.

"She's great. She won first place in the science fair."

"Cool. What'd she do?"

"Water filtration system," I tell him, pulling out my phone and walking over to the sink to show him pictures of Riley and her whole setup.

"Damn. That's like seventh-grade-level stuff. Isn't she just in third grade?"

"Fourth."

"Same grade as my little brother," he says, turning back to the dishes to hide the fact that his happy, open expression has morphed into one of sadness.

"You miss him a lot, huh?"

Taurin nods, running a soapy dishcloth over a plate that he's already washed. "Yeah, but I messed up, so I don't deserve to see him again."

Something about the statement pulls on my heartstrings because I know it's hard for addicts to feel worthy of second chances. Hell, I'm still trying to feel worthy of the one I've been given, but I don't want Taurin to be like me—doing the work but still holding the past against himself.

"Taurin." I place a hand on his shoulder. "That's not true. Whether or not you get it, you do deserve a second chance. The work you're doing to improve yourself is proof that you deserve one, so just keep doing the work, okay?"

"Okay."

Even though I'm tired, I stash my phone in my pocket and help Taurin finish cleaning the kitchen. Between the two of us, we have the place spotless in record time. Once we're done, I head up to bed, making sure to tell him to turn in soon since it's a school night. After my shower, I collapse into bed with every intention of falling asleep but find myself looking through the pictures of Riley on my phone. Most of them feature Rae in some way. She's always around, holding Riley's hand and walking down the sidewalk or running her fingers over Riley's hair when a trip down the slide has caused her wild curls to break away from the puff she occasionally wears.

There is one photo that's just of Rae, though. I took it one day when we were at the park by the gym, not noticing that Riley was out of frame. Rae is wearing a soft pink t-shirt and some light-washed jeans, a pair of crisp white Converses on her feet, and her head is thrown back as she laughs at something Riley has just said. Sunlight filters through the ends of her hair, kissing the tip of every curl. She looks happy and carefree, nothing like the tense and exasperated person she is when Aaron is around.

I liked the picture so much I made it her contact photo, so I could see it every time she reaches out. It's on my screen right now, accompanied by the vibrations that announce an incoming call that I answer immediately.

"Rae, what's wrong? Are you okay? Is Riley okay?"

My feet are already on the ground. My body refusing to wait for her voice to start making my way to her, to them.

"I'm fine, Hunter. Everything is fine," she says softly.

"Why are you whispering?"

"Because everyone is asleep, and I—" she pauses, the shuffling on the other end of the line telling me she's walking somewhere. While I wait for her to continue, I analyze her breathing, listening for any signs of distress, deflating into a heap of relief when I hear none. "—I needed to talk to you," she says, finally finishing her thought.

I relax back into my mattress. "About what?"

Rae is quiet, and I hear a door open and close, then she's back, talking at a normal volume. "I wanted to say thank you."

"You already thanked me once, Rae. You don't need to do it again. You didn't need to do it the first time."

"I know, but I just—" The line goes quiet again, and I wait patiently for her to finish her thought. "You're really good at this, Hunter," she breathes. "And I shouldn't be surprised. I'm *not* surprised because at one point in my life, I pictured you as a father on the daily, but then—"

"But then I messed it all up," I finish for her. "And you walked away because you didn't trust that I could be good for Riley."

Or for you.

I think the words, but I don't say them because they don't need to be said.

"I was wrong."

Regret coats those three words in heavy layers that drip remorse, and even though it would be so easy to agree, so easy to let Rae think she made a mistake back then, I can't.

"No, you weren't, Sunshine. The man you left, the one you walked away from, he wasn't any good for you, and he was no good for our daughter. You knew that, and you made the only decision you could. You left, and it was the wake-up call I needed. You left, and I became the best version of myself, and now you're back, and I get to be that man every day for Riley."

For you.

Again, I don't speak the words, but I know she senses them in the silence of the omission. She takes a shaky, gasping breath, and I close my eyes, praying to God she's not crying. I hate when Rae cries; it makes me want to murder someone.

"She loves you, you know?"

I picture our daughter's face, recalling her scent and smile. "I know. I love her too, so much. You've done an amazing job raising her for the most part."

"*For the most part?*" I can hear sass all in her tone, and I smile, happy my playful jab is bringing her out of whatever mood she was in when she called. "The fuck is that supposed to mean?"

I turn over on my side, letting the phone rest on my face. "It means you did an amazing job keeping her safe, making her smart and well-mannered, but you dropped the ball when it comes to shit-talking. Our girl definitely shouldn't have been bested by a little asshole who couldn't come up with something better than 'Unisex Riley.'"

"Oh my, God." Rae snorts, and there's humor laced all the way through it, and I smile, proud to be responsible for such a beautiful sound. "Why was I thinking the same thing?"

19

RAE

<u>*Now*</u>

After Hunter admonishes me for not arming our nine-year-old with an arsenal full of yo mama jokes, we hang up the phone, and I sit in Aaron's home office staring at the wall, wondering how I'm supposed to go sleep beside the man I just had to chastise like a child on the drive home.

Never in my life have I seen Aaron be so selfish, petulant, and *cheap*. He ordered a two hundred dollar bottle of wine and guzzled it down all by himself, heedless of the fact that alcohol consumption can be a trigger for some recovering addicts, and then when the bill came, he disappeared from the table to take a phone call. Hunter swooped in, refusing to let me touch it.

When I promised to pay him back for Aaron and I's food, he dismissed it with a wave of his Black card. Seeing the ease with which he settled the bill sent a rush of pride through my veins because I remember being broke with him. I remember times when he had to decide between the mortgage on the gym or the lights in his house, when he had to work part-time at the factory with Will just to make ends meet.

Clearly, he doesn't have those problems anymore.

He doesn't have a lot of the problems he used to have anymore.

Which isn't to say that he's perfect, because he's human and, most importantly, a man, but he's something different than the man I knew before. And it's not because he's changed all that much—he's still grumpy and too serious about most things—but because he's not drowning under the weight of guilt, shame, and insecurity. He's settled, confident in who he is and what he can be to the people he cares about, and it's so fucking sexy I don't know what to do with myself.

I blow out a breath and pick up my phone, dialing the number of the only person who can talk some sense into me right now: Dee. She answers on the second ring, and it's not until I hear the grogginess in her voice that I remember that ten o'clock is well past her self-imposed bedtime.

"What do you want, Rachel?"

I grimace. "I need some advice, Deanna."

"Yes, you should call Soledad back and see if the building is still available. If Aaron can do what he wants with his money, you can do what you want with yours."

"Well, damn, how long have you had that bullet loaded in the clip?" I ask, laughing at her unprompted advice.

"A while," she says through a yawn. "Please tell me I've fulfilled my best friend duties so I can go back to sleep."

"Not quite. I wasn't calling about the ballet school." Which is just another thing on the long list of nonsense I've had to deal with lately. "I wanted to talk about the dinner I just had with Riley, Hunter, and Aaron."

The line goes quiet, and I know she's fully processed that sentence when she gasps and says, "I'm up."

I fill her in on everything from the science fair to the phone call I just ended with Hunter, and by the time I'm done, she's in her kitchen sipping on the glass of wine she fixed when I told her that I did not pull Hunter to the side and give him some pussy as a reward for being such a good daddy. Her words, not mine.

"Why is Aaron being such a little bitch? Was he always that way?"

My feet are perched on the end of Aaron's desk while I lean back in his chair with the phone cradled between my shoulder and ear, trying to recall an instance in our seven-year history where Aaron showed me that he had this level of petty spitefulness inside him. I can't recall one.

"I don't think so. I mean, if he was, I don't think we'd still be together." Dee hums her disagreement, and my brows pull together, forming a tight line of confusion. "You think we would?"

Dee sighs. "I mean, you're with him now, aren't you?"

"Well, yeah, but things are different now, we have—"

"You and Aaron don't have anything now that y'all didn't have before. You don't have a child, you're not married, and your name isn't even on the deed to the house, so the only thing holding y'all together is you. The question is, why?"

"Because I love him."

It's a weak defense. Next to the picture of the bleak reality my best friend has just painted with her words, it feels like nothing. Less than nothing.

"I know you love him, Rae, but do you feel loved by him? Supported by him? I mean, integrating your estranged ex into your kid's life is hard as hell, and what has Aaron been doing to make it easier on you? On Ri? Has he even checked in with her? Reassured her that he'll still be there to love and support her even though Hunter is in the picture now?"

I bite my lip to stay the tears burning at the back of my eyes. "I don't think so."

"He didn't," Dee says with conviction.

"How do you know?"

"Because I asked Riley what Aaron thought of her dad, and she said they haven't talked about him at all."

"Oh." My voice is small, tinged with shame. "I didn't know that."

"Well, you can't know everything, Rae; that's why you have me."

"I don't want you. You're too mean."

She laughs, and I do, too, happy to let the heaviness of our conversation subside for a moment. I sigh softly, "I just don't know what to do, Dee. I mean, I can't tell if all the hostility I have towards Aaron is because he actually deserves it or if it's just because I have these rose-colored glasses on when I look at Hunter that makes everyone else look like shit."

It's my biggest fear: being unnecessarily critical of Aaron just because the newness of my situation with Hunter is making me feel like he can do no wrong. And it doesn't help that he and Riley are so connected, while Aaron's bond with her has suffered horribly from all the changes in our lives.

I've been guilty of it before, letting the rose-colored glasses give me tunnel vision, but I can't afford to take that kind of risk when Riley's heart and her life are on the line. Before I make a drastic decision like leaving Aaron, I have to make sure I'm seeing him clearly, through a lens unobstructed by the view of Hunter 'Just Call Me Super Dad' Drake.

THAT NIGHT, I have a fitful sleep on the couch in the living room and wake up grumpy. My bad mood persists for the rest of the day, only fading when Hunter texts me while I'm in the pickup line to get Riley from school.

> Hunter: Afternoon, Sunshine. Are you and the nugget down for an afternoon ice cream date?

There's a smile on my face as I type out my response that I tell myself is only there because I know the prospect of seeing Hunter two days in a row will make Riley happy.

> Rae: Sounds good. We can be there in fifteen.

> Hunter: I'll have your orders ready.

As promised, Hunter has my scoop of Rocky Road and Riley's sugar cone with vanilla in hand when we arrive at Lick. He's standing outside, smiling like he's won the lottery, when we emerge from the car. Riley gets to him first, exchanging her cone for a kiss on his cheek before taking off down the sidewalk, leaving us no choice but to follow behind her.

Hunter hands me my cup, and we fall into step.

"Thanks. I can't give you a kiss on the cheek, but I do appreciate the ice cream. I needed a pick me up."

"Wanna talk about it?" He asks, taking a bite of what looks to be raspberry gelato.

"No."

I can't talk about Aaron with Hunter because he'd probably be even harsher with me than Dee was last night, and I just can't take that right now. I expect him to argue or push me to share, but he doesn't.

"Can we talk about tuition then?"

Knowing I'm not going to get through this trap of an outing without discussing something with him, I nod. "Sure, what about it?"

"I want to pay it."

"I know, you already told me that."

"Right, and I'm telling you again so you can give me an answer."

"Oh."

"The answer should be yes, Rae. I'm offering to take a significant load off of you financially, leaving you free to pursue your dreams of opening up a ballet school, which is needed, by the way. I have it on good authority that a lot of moms are fed up with Ms. Lena at The Ballet Academy. They're thinking of taking their kids all the way to a school in Fairview, but none of them want to make that drive."

I scrunch up my nose and take another bite of my ice cream, chewing thoughtfully before I say, "Since when do you have your finger on the pulse of the ballet situation in New Haven?"

"Since Indigo enrolled her daughter in classes."

I almost choke on a chocolate-covered almond. "Indigo? You're still in touch with Indigo?"

My stomach burns with old jealousy made new, reawakened, and inappropriate because Hunter is not committed to me in any way, shape, form, or fashion.

He shrugs. "We text from time to time."

"A curse of having the same number for decades."

"Or a blessing, depends on who you ask." With a hand on my arm he interrupts my stride, causing me to pause on the sidewalk just a few feet from the building I wanted. "Listen, even though you didn't say it, I know that financial concerns have to be the reason why you couldn't make things happen with your school. I'm in a position to help you with that and contribute to our daughter's life in a meaningful way, so please just set your pride aside and say yes."

Maybe it's the warmth of his palm wrapped around my forearm or the soft eagerness of his eyes, but at this moment, I can't find a single reason to say no to him.

"Yes."

Hunter beams at me, and I yelp loudly when he wraps his arms around my waist and picks me up off of the ground, spinning me around the sidewalk. It's the closest we've been in years, and the familiar scent of his skin—all spiced earth and warmth— transports me back to a time when the only place I wanted to be was wrapped in the strength of his embrace.

When he sets me back on the ground, Riley is next to us, bouncing on her tiptoes.

"Do me next, Daddy! Do me next!"

Hunter obliges her request without hesitation, scooping her up and spinning her around in circles so fast I almost get dizzy looking at them. While they're caught up in their silliness, I walk the short distance to the building I fell in love with all those weeks ago, something like the hopeful flaps of butterfly wings fluttering in my stomach.

I can do this.

I can do this.

I can—

The thought dies a quiet, painful death when I stop in front of the building and see that the for rent sign is gone. In the grand scheme of things, it's not a big deal. With Hunter covering Riley's tuition, I'm still free to use my savings to start my school and let Aaron worry about everything else. The building being unavailable doesn't change that. It doesn't change anything, not really, but as I stand here, looking at nothing but the outline of the sign that welcomed me and my dream to the building, it feels like everything has changed.

"The sign is gone," I say quietly, turning to Hunter, prepared to repeat myself but stopping short when I see the gleam of silver keys dangling from his hand.

"I know," he says, dark eyes glued to my face, greedy for every change in my expression as I digest each word. "I came over and took it down as soon as I signed the paperwork this morning."

"Paperwork?" I gasp, confused by his words and the way my heart starts to pound with genuine excitement every time he says more of them. "You signed a lease for me?"

Hunter's lips curl into a slow grin that sets fire to my veins and melts me from the inside out. He moves forward—one hand in Riley's, the other hand holding the keys out towards me—and lifts his brows, silently ordering me to take them.

"No, Sunshine, I bought the building for you."

20

HUNTER

The first time I made Rae smile was a month after we met.

We hadn't seen much of each other because I was busy suffering through the task of getting clean again, and I didn't want anyone but Will to see me like that. On the one-month anniversary of our meeting, I got my thirty-day chip, and I looked out in the crowd and saw her there, pride shining in her eyes as she looked at me like I was holding an Academy Award instead of a piece of plastic that, at the time, just felt like a reminder that I was starting all over.

Again.

Will, the annoying bastard that he was, had me address the crowd, urging me to expose my missteps, so I could find acceptance among people who knew what it was like to start over. What was supposed to be a recounting of my fall from grace and a recommitment to my recovery, turned into a long, drawn out thank you speech that was just for her, and in the end, I called her my sunshine.

I think about the smile she gave me after that all the time. Sometimes, when I go to sleep at night, it's the first thing I see when I close my eyes. I remember exactly how long it took to form and how long it stayed on her face, but most of all, I remember what it felt like to witness it and know that I was responsible for something so beautiful, so pure.

When we were together, I thought I'd never top that smile, that moment. And when she left, I knew I'd never get another chance to try. Now, I know that neither of those is true because every day for weeks, I've had the chance to best myself, and today, I've succeeded.

The smile happens slowly, fragments of reluctant joy causing her lips to twitch and pull until they're left with no choice but to curve up into a grin so wide Rae covers it with her hand.

"WHAT?!" She screams through the trembling fingers hiding that smile from me.

"I bought the building for you," I repeat, even though I know she heard me the first time. "It's yours. Well, technically, it's mine, but I'm happy to sign the deed over to you if that will make you feel more comfortable."

"Hunter." She's still covering her mouth, so my name comes out garbled, wrapped around vocal tremors that are filled with disbelief. "Why would you do this? How did you do this? *When* did you do this?"

I can't tell if these are rhetorical questions, so I just answer them truthfully.

"Because I want to see you make your dreams come true." My brows furrow as I answer the second question because surely she knows how purchases work. "I tracked down the realtor and asked if the owner was interested in selling. They weren't initially, but then I submitted a letter to them and made an all-cash offer, hoping for a quick close, and they accepted." Her eyes go wide, and I'm not sure whether the mention of the letter or the cash is the cause, so I just keep pushing. "Like I said before, we closed this morning, but I started the whole process the day you showed me the building."

"Can we go inside?" Riley asks, her eyes wide, just like her mom's.

I hold the keys out to Rae again, hoping she'll take them. "Yeah, Mommy, can we go inside?"

Her hand trembles as she takes the keys from my hand, and I let out a shaky exhale when her fingertips brush the inside of my palm. Touching her is like nothing I've ever felt before. Even when it's rare and fleeting, I take it as a gift, knowing that even ephemeral things deserve to be treated with reverence.

"I can't believe you," Rae is saying now, tossing her incredulity over her shoulder while she slides the keys into the lock on the front door. As soon as it's open, Riley drops my hand and pushes her way inside. "Hey, say excuse me, young lady!"

"Excuse me!" She shouts as she runs down the hallway toward the back. If I hadn't just done a walk-through of the space in anticipation of this very thing, I would stop her in her tracks, but since I know there's nothing in here she can hurt herself with, I'm happy to let her explore. Her footsteps pound down the hallway as she flits from one room to the next, shouting her excitement just so she can hear her voice echo off the walls.

"Hunter, this is too much," Rae says, pulling my attention back to her. She's standing in the middle of her front room, which I assume she'll use for reception, with a hand over her mouth and the keys to her dream dangling off one delicate finger. "I can't accept it."

"You can, and you will." I close the space between us, needing to be in her orbit. "I don't have any use for this building, so you're going to take it and dedicate every square foot to your dream."

"But what if—"

My hand comes up, fingers acting on their own accord as they grip her chin and force her to keep her eyes on me. Rae pushes out a quivering breath, as overwhelmed by the sudden physical contact as I am, but she doesn't pull away. I shake my head, not in the mood to hear Aaron's doubts in Rae's voice. "Don't do that. Don't think about everything that could go wrong before you've had a chance to acknowledge what is going right. You have the space of your dreams, so tell me what you're going to do with it."

She looks around the empty room, and I can see the wheels turning in her mind, ideas that I'll go out of my way to make a reality taking root. I'm dying for her to share them with me, to give me another part of her to hold on to, but I also recognize that I can't make her. We've come a long way from her running away from me, but there are still walls up between us. She keeps them there to protect herself, and I let them stand because I know if we're going to have something that lasts this time, I can't just force my way in. She has to invite me.

Rae presses her lips together, trying to hold back, but then she sighs and looks at me with excitement and hope in her eyes. She turns, walking over to the wall across from us that faces the door.

"The reception desk will go here..."

RAE, Riley, and I spend an hour in the building daydreaming about what it's going to become, what *we're* going to make it, even though, for some reason, Rae's got it in her head that she's going to be doing everything alone. Everything was 'I should' or 'I'll need,' which made me angry for two different reasons.

Because, one, it drove home the fact that Aaron, for all his Rae and I this and my family that nonsense, doesn't do a damn thing to support her.

And two, it doesn't account for the fact that I'm going to be there with her every step of the way.

After Rae explained her vision for the space, I made a call to Archway Construction—Mallory's brother, Dominic's company—to have a team come out and build the desk and custom shelving she'd need in the reception area as well as cover the red brick of the exterior in a white, limewash paint to give it a charming refresh. Just like when I handed her the keys to the building, Rae stood there with her mouth agape, wondering why I was going out of my way to do things for her. I'd given her some speech about watching her chase her dreams being good for Riley, which earned me a hug and a kiss on the cheek, but the truth was something much simpler.

Something I can't voice but will continue to act on because the alternative is to pretend like I'm not madly in love with her, and I'm just not willing to do that.

Because I *am* in love with her.

And I've been in love with her since the first day we met. Since she answered the phone and challenged me to live, since she kissed me in the middle of my kitchen and made me realize that, up until that point, I had no idea what it was like to hold the flavor of destruction and desire on my tongue. Since she introduced me to my daughter and made my induction into fatherhood easier than I deserved.

I don't think I remember a time when I didn't love her, when I didn't want her, when I didn't crave her heat and the sweetness of her scent that has always felt like home to me.

That scent clings to me now as I walk into the gym to pick Taurin up and take him home, competing with the smell of exertion and sweat, and I fight to hold on to it. To hold on to her because every day I say goodbye to her and Riley, setting them free to return to the cold confines of the home they share with Norman and Norma Bates, the harder it gets not to do something stupid like tell her I never want to let her or Riley go again.

Pushing all thoughts of things I can't change to the side, I scour the first floor for any sign of Taurin. When I come up empty, finding it odd because I remember him specifically saying that he would be cleaning the locker room downstairs, I take the steps up to the second floor two at a time. My heart is in my throat, pumping out all my fears and anxieties at double speed. What if he's using? What if he OD'd? What if—

I stop short, and my thoughts come grinding to a halt when I pause outside of my office door and find it partially open with the sound of a teenage girl's giggles filtering through the crack mixed with the exaggerated low rumble of T's voice. The little relief I feel at knowing he's not somewhere relapsing is quickly overtaken by suspicion and dread because I have no idea what he and this mystery girl are doing in my office.

Since I know waiting around to find out is only an act of delaying the inevitable, I burst through the door with a frown on my face that almost turns into a mocking smile that would most definitely feature a laugh when they both jolt with surprise and jump away from each other even though, from what I can tell, they're not doing anything wrong except for being in my space without my permission.

The girl, who's closest to the door and, therefore, my wrath, shrinks in her seat, her eyes wide as they take in the scowl on my face. Taurin puts his hand on her thigh and pats it reassuringly.

"Chill, babe, this is my—" He pauses, not knowing how to categorize our relationship. I don't know how to either. When I told Rae about Taurin, I struggled with it the same way he is now. I'm more than his sponsor, but I'm not his friend, and I don't think I do anything to qualify as a mentor. He's not legally in my care, so I'm not even his guardian. We're just us. "This is Hunter," Taurin says finally. "He owns the gym. Hunter, this is my girlfriend, Alyssa."

Alyssa stands, tossing her knotless braids over her shoulder and extending her hand to me. She's a pretty girl with a sweet seriousness about her that I think is probably good for Taurin. When she stands, he follows suit, looking like he wished he had thought to stand when he made the introductions.

"It's nice to meet you, Mr. Hunter. Taurin has told me so much about you."

I take her hand, admiring the firmness of her shake. "Just Hunter, and it's nice to meet you too, Alyssa, though I would have appreciated it happening somewhere other than in my office."

Since it's not really her fault, I send my disdain in Taurin's direction, and he looks appropriately apologetic as he watches me drop Alyssa's hand.

"Sorry. We just wanted some privacy," he says.

"There's no one downstairs. Who exactly were you seeking privacy from?"

"It's my fault," Alyssa interjects. "When Taurin told me he was working at your gym, I asked if I could come down for a tour. I pushed him to bring me up here, so please don't be mad at him."

"I'm not mad," I assure both of them, adjusting my features to reflect that fact and thanking God that spending so much time with Riley has made me more aware of how surly I can come off sometimes. Taurin's girlfriend is nice, and she seems good for him, so the last thing I want to do is ruin the mood by overreacting. When both sets of their shoulders sag with relief, I know that I've succeeded. "In the future, I'd appreciate it if you didn't bring people up to my office without my permission, T."

"Noted." He nods, and I know I won't have to tell him again because as long as I set firm boundaries with him, he'll respect them. "Well, I should walk Alyssa to her car," Taurin says, putting his hand on her back and moving them towards the door.

"Bye, Hunter," Alyssa calls out over her shoulder.

"Bye, Alyssa," I say, sending them off with a wave and a smile that does nothing to convey how confused I am about going from having no one in my life to three someones I'd lay down my life for in such a short period of time.

21

HUNTER

Then

"Four years is such a big deal!" Indigo squeals. "We should be doing more than just going out to dinner. We should go dancing or get—"

She stops, catching herself before she suggests that I celebrate four years of sobriety by taking a trip to a bar, club, speakeasy, or whatever the fuck kind of haven for vices she frequents with her friends. I'm not judging. I know everyone doesn't have the same issues with self-control as I do, but I am tired of having to remind Indigo of my limits. I'm even more tired of her looking disappointed every time she remembers them.

"Never mind," she says, reaching up to fix the collar of my shirt even though it's fine. Her posture reeks of self-consciousness with an undercurrent of annoyance, and I wish I felt compelled to comfort her, but I don't.

I don't feel anything when I look at her but confused about why I'm still doing this thing with her, especially after knowing what it's like to kiss Rae. To hold her body in my hands and hear the sounds of her pleasure, *her desire*, in my ears.

"You look handsome," Indigo tells me, her smile too wide as she runs a hand down my chest.

"Thanks. You—" She looks at me expectantly, waiting for me to finish my sentence, but the compliment I was about to pay her gets all tangled up in my throat as Rae walks into the kitchen. She's wearing a sky-blue baby doll dress that matches the stripes in my shirt, and her hair is down around her shoulders. Recently, sometime after the kiss that we still haven't spoken of, she had Dee give her face-framing bangs that make her almond eyes look wider and even more brown.

And now those eyes are on me and Indigo, taking in our closeness while the scent of her perfume—an expensive formula with notes of pear and vanilla that I got her for her twenty-third birthday just last week—floats into the room around us.

"Oh, Indigo, you're here."

The snark in her tone isn't evident to Indigo, but I hear it.

"Yeah, Hunter asked me to come to his ceremony, and I thought it was important for me to be here to support him."

I can't read Rae at all. Her expression is flat, her eyes emotionless. It's the way she looks when she's got a million different things going through her mind, but it's not safe to let them out. She told me once that she mastered the skill when she first started dance, and her teacher, Ms. Alice, told her she needed thicker skin if she was going to make it as a Black ballerina. I've never, not once in the four years of us knowing each other, seen her deploy the skill. That she's doing it now means I've fucked up tremendously, and I don't even have to dig deep to know how because the answer to that question is standing right beside me, her arms wrapped around my waist possessively.

"Well, isn't that nice," Rae says finally, moving further into the kitchen. She moves parallel to us with long, graceful strides that carry her over to the shelf at the back door, where she always leaves her shoes.

And even though I want her to, even though I plead with her silently using only my eyes, she doesn't look at me. She just picks up her shoes and turns her back to me, planting a palm on the wall to steady herself as she lifts one leg and then the other to put them on.

"Is Will ready?" I ask, desperate to draw her into conversation.

"Yep," Will says, appearing out of nowhere and stealing my chance to talk to his sister. "Let's go get you chipped."

The drive to the church where we have our meetings is filled with Indigo and Will's chatter and Rae's silence, which is louder than anything else. Every chance I get, I try to catch her eye in the rearview, but she intentionally keeps her gaze on her phone. As I navigate the streets, I wonder if she's texting Dee, telling her all about my fuck up. I wonder if Dee knows about the kiss and if Rae has told her how hurt she is that I brought Indigo into a day she and I have celebrated together for years because it's not just the anniversary of my sobriety; it's a commemoration of us.

Truthfully, I didn't ask Indigo to be here. She invited herself when I told her I couldn't go to the movies with her tonight because I was getting my chip, and I was just too weak to tell her she couldn't come. I've been too weak for a lot of things lately.

To break up with Indigo.

To talk to Rae.

To stop thinking about that kiss.

It's still on my mind at the end of the meeting when Will calls me up to receive my chip, when Indigo slaps me on the ass and whoops loudly as I walk up to the podium, when I stand behind that podium, with the chip clutched in my fingers, and find her in the crowd. Indigo had insisted on sitting beside me, taking up a space in the rows reserved for addicts, while Rae stood towards the back of the room by the table with all the coffee and snacks.

Now that I'm up here, she doesn't seem to be able to look away from me, which is fine because I can't look away from her either.

"As many of you know, I hate public speaking," I say, smiling ruefully. "But I'm a fan of speaking up when there's something that needs to be said, and tonight, I need to say thank you to someone special." My gaze is still on Rae, but out of the corner of my eye, I can see Indigo shifting in her seat, the lines of her body fraught with anticipation. "Someone who has been by my side for the past four years, whose graceful steps and compassion have carved a path for me lined with love and acceptance, who's made it possible for me to be standing in front of you all today. Clean. Whole. Happy." Even from this distance, I can see the tears well up in Rae's eyes. They make her irises glossy, shimmering with emotion. "Rae—" There's a sharp intake of breath from the section where I left Indigo sitting, and I don't have to look to know it's from her. She must be pissed, but now that I've started, I have to finish. "Rae," I say again, swallowing past the lump of emotion in my throat. "I never had a best friend until you came along. I never knew what it meant to be witnessed in all my imperfections and faults and still be loved, so this" —I hold the chip up in the air, a silent toast to the person who means more to me than anything in this world—"this isn't just for me. It's for us, for everything we are and everything we'll become."

A single tear slips down Rae's cheek as I finish, and even though I want to go to her, to scoop her up in front of everyone and kiss her like she belongs to me, I don't. I return to my seat to the sound of scattered applause. As soon as I'm seated, Indigo clutches my hand and plants a smacking kiss on my cheek.

"You did so good, baby," she says loudly, as if she's trying to remind everyone, including me, that I'm here with her. Not wanting to embarrass her by pulling away, I give her a tight smile and turn my attention to Will, who's now cracking some joke about me delivering a whole monologue despite my aversion to being the center of attention. Everyone laughs, and we wrap the meeting on a good note a few minutes later.

When it's done, everyone comes up to me and congratulates me on making four years, and while I'm grateful for the well wishes, I'm eager to make my way out of the basement and find Rae. Indigo clings to me as we climb the steps that lead to the parking lot, her hand in mine, a weight I can't bear to carry anymore. When we get to my truck, Rae is there with Will and his sponsor, Nate—an older Black man with a kind smile and hard eyes.

"Everything okay?" I ask, noting the concerned look on Nate and Rae's faces.

"I think I tweaked my back at work," Will says, wincing in pain.

"You should go to the ER," Rae replies, rolling her eyes when he waves her off.

"Nah, I'm good. I just need to go home and ice it."

"You sure, Will?" Nate asks.

"I can take you to the ER," I offer, already digging out my keys.

"No. No." Will shakes his head. "You've got reservations at Hill House, and I'm not going to let you miss them."

"Hill House?" This, from Indigo, who can't read a room to save her fucking life. "I love Hill House."

"Then you and Hunter should go," Rae says, barely containing the urge to roll her eyes. "I'll ride with Nate, and we'll take Will to the ER."

"I'm not going to the ER!" Will insists, a little more forcefully than necessary. Everyone's brows rise in surprise, but Rae is the one who gives him the 'who the fuck are you talking to' look that makes him take a deep breath before trying again. "I'm sorry for yelling, but I don't have any interest in going to the hospital and racking up five thousand dollars in medical bills just for them to tell me what I already know and write a prescription I won't use. I pulled a muscle at work, and I'll be fine after I spend the night cuddled up with my heating pad." He straightens as best as he can and places a hand on Nate's shoulder. "Now, I'm going to get Nate here to take me home. You three,"—he waves a hand to indicate Rae, Indigo, and me— "go ahead and head out because your reservation is at eight."

"Oh, no, I'm not—" Rae starts, but Will holds up a hand to silence her.

"Rachel Renee Prince, you've been looking forward to the crème brûlée at Hill House all week, and we're not going to let a little back pain stop you from getting it, so get in the car, have a nice night, and bring me some home."

There's an authoritative boom to his voice that leaves no space for argument, so we don't argue. Rae and I watch Will hobble off with Nate at his side while Indigo claps her hands.

"I really do love Hill House!"

Awkward.

That's the only word for the dinner Will ordered us to have at Hill House. He couldn't have known it was going to be like this, or maybe he did know, and he faked back pain to get out of it. Maybe I should have faked back pain, too, or pulled out the oldest trick in the book and said my stomach was hurting.

Anything not to be sitting at this table in between Indigo, who can't stop talking, and Rae, who hasn't said a word to anyone but the waitress.

"Baby, you have to try this salmon," Indigo gushes. "The cream sauce is to die for."

"He's lactose intolerant," Rae blurts, surprising herself and Indigo. She's been so quiet, I think the girl actually forgot she was here.

"It's not an intolerance," I reply, and while I maintain that it's true, I don't take a bite of Indigo's salmon.

"Oh." Indigo shrugs, taking the bite for herself. She chews thoroughly and swallows before turning her attention from me to Rae. "So, I didn't realize Rae was short for Rachel."

"Yep," Rae says, pulling in a breath that screams impatience. She hates it when people use her full name.

"That's cool. Are you excited about returning to New York?"

Rae looks at me. Her brows arched in a way that asks me to get Indigo off her case, but I shrug like I'm helpless because I want to know the answer to that question too. The call to come back for another round of auditions with the American Ballet Theatre came in the day after the kiss, and Rae was so excited she screamed loud enough for everyone in the house, which unfortunately included Indigo, to hear. Despite her initial outward display of excitement, we haven't talked about it much since then. We haven't talked about much of anything since then, and I welcome the chance to hear the joy in her voice, even if Indigo is the reason why.

Setting her fork down, Rae nods. "I mean, I'm just going back for auditions. I'm not sure it'll turn into anything more."

"It will!" Indigo assures Rae, coming off a little too overzealous even to me. "And then you'll be out there on your own, living your dreams and figuring out how to be independent."

"I mean, the pay isn't that great," Rae says, her brows furrowed. "If I do get the job, I'll still probably have to have four roommates to afford to live there."

Indigo's eyes take on a dreamy look. "That's part of the charm, though, isn't it?"

"I guess." Rae shrugs, picking up her glass of water and taking a sip before muttering, "If you find poverty charming."

"No, not at all!" Indigo places a reassuring hand on Rae's arm. "I just meant that the whole roommate thing is part of the New Yorker aesthetic. You know, the struggling artist with the fifth-floor walk-up, working their ass off by day, sleeping around at night. I mean, you must be chomping at the bit to get back out there on your own, so you don't have to worry about this guy choking all your dates out, am I right?"

I'm not sure which part of that little diatribe is the final straw for Rae, but as soon as Indigo finishes talking, she stands, tossing her napkin onto her plate. "I'm going to go call Will and see if he's okay," she says, lying through her perfect teeth.

We watch her walk away, and Indigo turns to me with furrowed brows. "Why doesn't she like me?"

"She likes you just fine, Indie."

She scoffs. "Don't lie to me, Hunter. I see the way she looks at me even though I go out of my way to be friendly. I mean, you *see* that I'm trying to be friendly, right?"

"Maybe you shouldn't try so hard."

The sound of Indigo's fork crashing onto the ceramic plate in front of her draws the attention of nearly everyone in the dining room. Concerned eyes linger on us for a moment before everyone goes back to what they were doing.

"I try hard because I care about you, and you clearly care about her. Do you think I want to be friends with some twenty-something who thinks she knows everything about life already, Hunter? Hmm?

Well, I don't. I just want you, but apparently, I can't have you without her, so I'm trying, and it'd be nice if you encouraged the little brat to try, too."

"Don't call her a brat."

She looks at me like I've spontaneously sprouted a second head. "Are you serious right now? I say all of that to you, and all you care about is me calling her a brat?"

Her voice is growing louder by the second, and tension lines my shoulders as I think of all the ways this situation could go wrong. I'm a big, Black man with a history of drug addiction in the middle of a fancy, mostly white restaurant with a woman screaming at me, so there are a lot of them.

"Lower your voice, Indigo."

"Do you love her, Hunter?" She asks, her tone only marginally softer.

I know the answer to that question like I know the way back to my house. It comes to me easily, as natural as drawing my next breath, but I don't dare speak it out loud. I won't let the first time I acknowledge how I feel about Rae be wasted on a woman I shouldn't have gotten involved with in the first place.

"She's my best friend, Indigo."

"That's not what I asked, Hunter."

"But it's the only answer I'm willing to give." I reach across the table and grab her hand, but she snatches away. "Listen, Indie, this isn't working out."

Her open palm collides with the side of my face, and my head turns from its force. The lady at the table across from us gasps in shock, and I swallow the urge to laugh.

"Fuck you, Hunter!" Indigo shouts before storming out.

After she's gone, our waitress appears, her cheeks red with second-hand embarrassment. "Will you be needing any boxes, sir?"

I glance at Rae's uneaten plate. "Just one and two orders of your crème brûlée to go, please."

Once I've settled the bill and secured the leftovers and dessert, I set out to locate Rae for the second time tonight. When I find her, she's sitting on the bench outside of the entrance with her legs crossed and an odd expression on her face.

"I saw Indigo leave," she says, taking my hand when I extend it to her and allowing me to pull her up off the bench. "She seemed pretty upset."

"I told her it wasn't working out."

"Oh, I'm sorry."

She's not sorry. It's clear by the way the corners of her mouth twitch, but I let her believe the lie because correcting it will just lead us to a door neither one of us can walk through right now.

"Me too," I say, dropping her hand and giving her the bag of food. "Food and desserts are in there. Let's go home."

The ride back to the house is quiet. Mainly because I don't feel like talking, and I don't think Rae knows what to say. When we arrive, I put the car in park and sigh. Rae, who has already unhooked her seat belt and opened the door, pauses, turning to look at me.

"You wanna talk about it?"

I shake my head. "Nah, I think I'm just gonna ride around for a bit to clear my head."

She closes her door. "I'll go with you."

"You've already endured enough of my bullshit for the day. I'm sorry, by the way. I shouldn't have let Indigo come. I shouldn't have put you in the middle of my shit."

Rae shrugs. "You don't need to apologize. That's what happens when you love people. You have to deal with their triumphs and their mistakes."

I glance at her, keeping my eyes trained on her face even though they want to know everything there is to know about the expanse of her skin being exposed by the dress riding up her thigh.

"You think Indigo was a mistake?"

"I think she wanted you to be someone else when the people who know you love you for exactly who you are."

I consider her words for a moment before nodding. "Yeah, I think you're right."

"Of course I am."

Silence descends on us. Thick and suffocating because it's weighed down with all the things we won't say. "Are we ever going to talk about the kiss?"

My pulse quickens at the idea of letting everything I've felt and thought since the first time my lips met hers out into the open. It sounds like heaven. It sounds like hell. It sounds like a risk I can't take tonight.

"I don't think there's anything to say."

Rae shifts her body around, folding one leg up in the seat so she can face me head-on. "Are you serious?"

"Look, Rae—"

"Because I have plenty to say about it," she says, her voice taking on a low, sultry tone that only exists to unravel me. "Let's start with the fact that ever since we kissed, all I've wanted is to do it again."

"Rae, please," I beg, needing her to stop talking because, on a night that's all about acknowledging self-control, I'm surprised to find that I have very little.

"I think about kissing you all the time now, Hunter," she whispers, a confession meant for my ears and my ears alone. "When I fall asleep at night, I dream about you coming into my room and kissing me again, not just on my lips but—" She pauses, reaching over to grab my hand, and I'm weak, I'm so fucking weak because I let her take it. I let her place it on the inside of her thigh and guide it up, up, up, until the tips of my fingers graze the warmest, softest part of her. Rae pants, and my dick twitches. "Here," she says finally, rolling her hips into my hand.

"*Sunshine.*" I'm pleading with her, advocating for my sanity and the last shred of my restraint. "We can't."

"Yes, we can," she assures me, pushing up onto her knees and climbing across the center console into my lap. Her hands go to my shoulders, and her pussy is perfectly aligned with the growing bulge in my pants, and her titties, those perfect fucking titties, are right in my face.

"Jesus," I groan, my hands finding their way to her ass. My fingers are rough as they clutch two handfuls of her flesh, and I curse because nothing has ever felt as good in my hands as she does.

Holding Rae is like holding a firecracker, a burst of sunlight. She's strong; I know that because I've seen her strength, but she's also precious. I have to remind myself of that fact because I know the things my hands can do. These hands have been bloodied and broken, beaten a man within an inch of his life, demonstrated life-saving maneuvers to the women in my gym, held destruction in the form of powder, pills, and needles, and welcomed them like old friends, but they've never held perfection.

They've never held anything like Rae and what she's giving me at this moment, and I don't know if I can be gentle. I don't know if I can be patient and loving. I don't know if I can be the man she looks at me and sees.

She comes down, ghosting her lips over mine as she grinds into my lap. "I want you, Hunter. I want this. I want you to be my first."

Fucking hell.

I close my eyes, pushing out breaths that are meant to restore some of my calm. They don't.

"You haven't—" I swallow even though my throat has gone dry. "You've never?"

I stumble over the words like a teenage boy instead of a twenty-eight-year-old man, but Rae understands what I'm trying to ask. She shakes her head, gentle, uncertain fingers running tiny circuits across my scalp. "No, I was waiting for you."

My eyes fall shut again, and I shake my head. "Oh, Sunshine, you deserve so much better than me."

Rae leans back, and for a second, I think that's it, that she's finally come to her senses, but when her weight never moves off of my lap, I open my eyes once more to find myself face-to-face with berry brown nipples. I snake my hands around her waist, dragging them up her ribs and over those fucking tattoos before cupping her breasts. She gasps, licking her lips.

"Maybe I deserve more than you, Hunter, but you're all that I want."

22

RAE

Then

There's a moment, after I come as close to telling Hunter that I'm in love with him as I'll allow myself to get tonight, when he looks at me like he can't believe I'm real. It's dark in the truck, but I can see his eyes, and the wonder in them as he toys with my nipples makes my core melt.

He wants this.

He wants me.

And I've never been happier than I am right now.

I suck in a shaky breath as he lowers his mouth to one breast while continuing to pinch and pull at the nipple of the other. My head goes back, and I moan loudly when his warm, wet lips press into my skin, planting soft kisses along my flesh before he opens wide and sucks me into his mouth.

My hand is at the back of his head, nails digging into his scalp as I writhe in his lap. "*Hunter.*"

"Hmm?" He hums, swirling his tongue around my nipple before biting down on it gently.

"Let the seat back."

His left hand leaves me, abandoning my body for just a second, long enough to pull the lever that lets back his seat. Now that he's lying flat, gazing up at me with eyes that are greedy for every inch of skin I put on display when I shed my dress, I feel shy all of a sudden, which is stupid because I've been naked in front of other people before. I've even been naked in front of guys. Well, *a* guy. Cameron. We dated from ninth to twelfth grade and fooled around a lot in those few years, never going all the way because I wouldn't let it.

Something just didn't feel right, and I didn't know how to explain it to him because I wasn't like the other girls who were waiting for marriage or prom or the perfect night in the back of some guy's truck. I was just waiting for *it*. The right moment with the right person, and that moment is now. That person is Hunter.

Leaning over him, I take his mouth in an all-consuming kiss, aware of the way his hands are exploring every line and curve of my body. His tongue slips between my lips as his fingertips ghost down my spine, caressing every notch and disc on the way to my ass where he grabs two rough handfuls of flesh and squeezes, urging me forward. I pull back, looking into wild eyes that demand things his mouth has yet to say.

"Get up here," he orders me, the words rough and commanding. I don't move. I can't move. I'm too shocked because I've never seen him like this. Even the first night that we met, when he was just a few hours removed from using and still feeling the effects of the drugs, he didn't look as dazed as he does now. His eyes are so low, they're almost closed, and when he speaks again, giving me more explicit instructions because he's clearly taken my awe-induced paralysis for confusion, his voice is nothing more than a dark, dirty whisper. "Bring that pretty little pussy up here and sit it on my face, Sunshine. I want to taste you."

I clamber up his body, graceless and uncaring about looking sexy because I *feel* sexy. Under Hunter's watchful gaze, I feel beautiful. Hovering above his handsome face, I feel powerful and desired and perfect. And it doesn't matter that the cab of the truck is so low I have to curve my spine and rest my hands on the seats in the back row because Hunter's head is between my thighs and the wet heat of his mouth is centimeters away from my pussy and his fingers are moving my underwear to the side so he can nuzzle my clit with his nose before lapping at it with short, teasing licks of his tongue meant to drive me crazy.

My nails dig into the leather seats underneath my hands, and my thighs quiver around his ears, but Hunter takes his time. He savors me. He teases me. He drives me to the point of madness and brings me back, just to start the process all over, and when I'm close to sobbing and the insides of my thighs are raw from the constant rub of his beard, and the evidence of my need has made the bottom half of his face slick, he loosens his hold on my hip and brings his hand down, slipping two large fingers into me for the sole purpose of driving me insane.

"HUNTER!" I scream his name, and I feel the knowing smile forming on his lips nestled against the inside of my thigh.

"Don't worry, Sunshine. I'm going to let you come...eventually."

"Please," I sob, tears of disbelief mixed with pleasure squeezing out of the corners of my eyes as I move up and down on his fingers.

"That's it," he praises. "Fuck my fingers just like that. Show me how you're going to ride my dick when I give it to you."

My core contracts, rippling with the anticipation of what's to come, quivering because of what's already being given. His fingers move deeper, drawn in with every pulse of my walls, and it's not long before he's found that spot deep inside me that sends sparks of pleasure down my spine. I arch my back, working my hips in small, helpless circles as I chase that feeling. Hunter growls his approval, and because he's still eating my pussy like it's his job, I feel the vibrations of the sound right in my clit.

Everything grows slicker, hotter, wetter. Sweat is dripping down my back and lining the edges of my hairline. The windows have fogged up, turning the truck into our own personal bubble of sin, and it's everything.

Everything I wanted. Everything I needed. Everything I knew we'd be.

"You're ready now," Hunter tells me, coming up for a second of air before returning to his ministrations with renewed intensity. I want to laugh because I was ready ten minutes ago. Hell, I was ready the moment he used his tongue to part my lips, but I don't laugh. I don't breathe. I don't do anything except fall apart for him, baring down hard because my body demands it, and letting out helpless cry after helpless cry while I quite literally drown Hunter in my pleasure.

He drinks every bit of my release, not letting a single drop escape his attention while he reaches down and undoes his pants. I'm bone-less and exhausted, still recovering from the best orgasm of my life, but the clang of his belt and the quiet glide of his zipper energize me. And this time I don't want for his instructions because I know exactly where I need to be.I shimmy down his body, laughing when he nips at my breasts when they pass over his mouth.

When our mouths are aligned, I pause just to taste myself on his lips. His face is wet, every strand of his beard coated in my essence, and I laugh when, quick as a flash, he brings his hands up and grips either side of my face, holding me still so he can rub it all over me.

"You're a menace," I gasp, trying to wriggle out of his hold. It's a half-hearted attempt because I actually don't want to be anywhere but right here, in this moment with him. His eyes on my face, his hard body between my thighs. His dick, thick and erect and already trying to nudge its way inside me.

The moment turns serious all of a sudden as Hunter's thumb brushes over my lips, parting them slightly on its way down my chin to my neck. Long fingers span the width of my throat, fingertips dance over my pulse, a silent question I can only answer by covering his left hand with one of my own and using my fingers to apply the pressure he's afraid to. Heat flashes in his eyes, and I rock back onto his dick, needing to feel him inside me. He shakes his head, "Condom."

"It's fine—"

"No, it's not." His tone leaves no space for argument, and for some stupid reason, it makes me want to cry. I know it's not rational. I know this is our first time, and I don't even know if things between us will go any further than this moment, than this night, but I want that closeness with him. I want everything with him, and his insistence on a condom makes me feel like he doesn't want those things with me. "Hey," he says softly, sitting up so we're face to face. He drops a soft kiss on my lips. "I want everything you want, okay? But you've got a future to think about. You've got dreams to chase. I'm not going to be responsible for clipping your wings before you've even gotten a chance to fly."

"You don't know what I want," I say, tears clogging my throat because, of course, he knows what I want. He's my best friend. He's my first love. He's my Hunter.

"You want love, Sunshine. You want a house full of laughter. You want to fill up my house with babies that will run us ragged every day for the rest of our lives. You want a tree house in our tree and birthday parties out in the yard."

The image he paints of my desires is intoxicating. Every word is a memory of a moment, of a life, we've yet to live together, and I can't find a single, good reason why we can't start living it right now.

Hunter kisses me again, a slow, burning kiss. "But you also want to dance. You want the stage and the lights and the applause. You want little girls who look like you to see you and know they can be living, breathing art, too."

"Why can't I have both?" I punctuate my question with a roll of my hips that has him hissing out a curse through his teeth.

"One day you will, Sunshine, but that only happens if we make smart decisions today."

"Ughhh," I groan, throwing my head back in exasperation. "Why do you have to make sense at a time like this?"

"One of us has to," he says, grinning as he uses his free hand to lift the center console and fish out his wallet. I watch him remove the gold-foiled condom from the folded leather, entranced as he tears it open with his teeth and sheaths himself with just one hand. Once he's satisfied that the condom is secure, he lays back and stares at me, shaking his head. "You've never been more beautiful."

God, I love this man.

Reaching behind me, I grip his length and squeeze gently, just enough to make his pupils dilate and pull another gruff curse free from his throat. Then I lift up and guide him to my entrance, sucking in a breath when I feel the first thick inch of him breaching my walls.

Hunter's fingers flex around my throat, applying pressure to the sides, but just enough to bring my attention to his face. "Go slow, okay? We're not in a rush."

I nod and swallow when his right hand goes to my hip, easing me down as his hips lift to meet me. "Okay."

Hunter is a big man, so I wasn't expecting his dick to be small. I mean, everything about the way he carries himself suggests that he's got a fucking third leg, but knowing that hasn't prepared me for his girth or length. We work slowly, so fucking slowly that I'm panting by the time we've made any real progress, but I still feel like I'm being split open in the best possible way. I glance down at us, and seeing the lips of my sex hugging his shaft makes my eyes roll into the back of my head.

"Oh my God," I moan, lifting up slightly and coming back down to help him slide in further.

Hunter stills, his eyes trained on my face. "You okay?"

I nod, my vision blurry from tears and sweat and the delirium of passion. "I'm fine. I'm perfect."

"Ready for more?"

"Yes," I gasp, because more is all I've ever wanted from him.

When he strokes up into me the first time, breaking through that final bit of my body's resistance, I scream. Not because it hurts but because it's the most glorious moment of connection. A joining of bodies. A melding of our souls. Hunter feels it too; I can tell by the way his brows furrow, by the way, he bites his lip and looks at me like I'm some sort of goddess or witch.

I want to tell him that goddesses don't get ensnared by their own magic and witches can't be affected by their own spells, but I don't. I just channel all my energy into meeting him thrust for thrust, smiling wickedly when his eyes go wide with surprise when I tell him to go harder, to be rougher, to give me more than he's ever given anyone.

He submits to my requests, fulfilling my every need even as he runs his own pleasure down, and when I come again, with my nails digging into the flesh of the hand still wrapped around my throat, he falls over the edge with me.

Panting, I collapse on his chest. My eyes fall shut as Hunter drops kisses on the top of my head, and I struggle to keep those three little words, alive and impatient on my tongue, at bay. I've already given so much of myself, already pressed to get us here, I don't want to be the person to force us to the next step before we're ready. But I feel it. I've felt it for so long, it feels blasphemous to hold them from him, especially after what we've just shared.

"Sunshine?" he says, running his fingers down my side.

"Yeah?"

"You know I love you, right? I wouldn't have—we never would have done this if I didn't love you. If I didn't feel the same way about you that you feel about me."

Tears spring to my eyes, slipping out from underneath my closed lids. I bite my lip, reminding myself that I promised I wouldn't be the one to say it first, but I didn't say anything about saying it *back*.

"I love you too."

23

RAE

Now

I wake with a start, slick between the legs, with a moan parting my lips and Aaron's confused eyes on me. He's hovering over me, both brows knitted in confusion as I leave the warmth and safety of my dream—that involved a naked Hunter, a slew of mirrors and the main room of the empty building he purchased for me— for the stark reality of our bedroom. It's early, right around the time I should be getting up to prepare Riley for her school day, and Aaron is already dressed for work. The tie I got him for his birthday dangles in front of my face, and I'm distantly aware of the weight of his hand on my shoulder. The placement and grip he has on me suggests he was in the process of waking me up.

"You were moaning in your sleep," he says, removing his hand and stepping back to give me some space. There's tension in the lines of his forehead as he examines me with a sweeping gaze I can't read. "Are you okay?"

Another image from my dream washes over me when I sit up, and my hand goes to my throat, a pale imitation of Hunter's wide, heavy palm and thick fingers. "I'm fine."

"You sure?"

"Yes, Aaron," I snap, swinging my legs over the side of the bed and grabbing the glass of water I keep on my nightstand. He watches me drink it, waiting for me to finish before he continues with his unnecessary inquisition.

"You didn't sound okay. Were you having a nightmare?"

I push to my feet, brushing past him on my way to the bathroom. There's a cruel, shameful laugh building in my throat. "No, it wasn't a nightmare," I say, closing the door before he can follow me inside. "Far from it."

"What was that?" Aaron asks through the door.

"Nothing!" I shout. "Would you mind waking Riley up for me?"

Normally, I wouldn't ask him, especially since he's on his way out the door, but I just need a moment to breathe, a moment to process that dream without him hovering. Things have been weird with us since the science fair, not bad—since Aaron agreed that he deserved the reaming out I gave him after dinner—but not as good as they could be, and me having sex dreams about Hunter is only bound to make it worse.

"She's already up," he says. "Mom is downstairs with her, making breakfast. She said she's going to take her to school today."

I should feel relieved to hear that Marcy is helping with Riley, but I'm not because I know she only does that when Aaron asks her to, and Aaron only does that when he wants to talk to me about something that will likely lead to us arguing.

"Oh, that's nice of her." I try, and fail, to keep the suspicion out of my voice. "Could you thank her for me on your way out the door?"

"Actually, I'm going in late. I wanted to have a chance to talk to you."

My heart sinks. I don't know what he wants to discuss, but I do know that his opening the door for honest communication means I have to walk through it, and that means telling him about the building Hunter bought for me even though I still haven't wrapped my head around it yet. Since I'm in no rush to come clean, I take my time going through my morning routine, hoping that if I drag my feet enough, Aaron will run out of time or patience and leave for work.

No such luck.

When I emerge from the bathroom, wrapped in a towel with freshly washed hair and shaved legs, Aaron is sitting on the bench at the foot of our bed with his phone in his hand. He sets it down the moment I enter the room, a conscious display of his endeavor to be more present, and smiles. The sun is completely out now, and the clock on his nightstand says that it's a quarter till eight, which means Riley and Marcy have already left, and there will be no interruptions or distractions from this conversation.

Aaron watches as I cross the room to my side of the bed, where I keep all of my moisturizing products, remaining quiet until I take a seat.

"I found you a job."

I pause, my hand suspended in mid-air with a palm full of my favorite body oil dripping onto my thigh. "You did what?"

"I found you a job," he repeats, grinning like he's done some amazing thing, completely unconcerned with the frown on my face. "The Ballet Academy is hiring. They only need a receptionist right now, but it's an established school that's growing everyday, and I'm sure they'll have to take another teacher on eventually."

"Eventually?" Needing something to do with my hands so I don't launch myself across the bed and strangle this man, I begin rubbing the oil into my skin, hoping the scent of coconut and honey will calm my nerves.

"Yeah." Aaron stands, coming around the bed to sit close to me. "I'm sure once they need someone, they'll be looking to hire internally, and you'll be right there!"

"Mhmm." I hum, nodding like I understand his foolish logic.

"Exciting, right?" His eyes are so bright, filled with hope and selfish intentions. "I even asked the lead instructor, Lena, nice lady, by the way, if you could use the space to dance sometimes, you know, just to make sure you stay sharp, and she said that's something you two could discuss when you call her today."

"I'm not calling her, Aaron."

He rears back, responding to the sharpness of my tone the same way he would a smack to the face. "What? Why? It's a great opportunity for you."

"But it's not the opportunity that I want."

"Rachel," he says, pinching the bridge of his nose and gazing heavenward like he's praying for patience. "I thought we were past this whole school thing."

"No, we tabled the discussion after you made it financially impossible for us to take on the lease, but we never got past it. *I* never got past it."

"Well, maybe you should," he snaps, and now I'm the one rearing back like I've been hit. Except the difference between me and Aaron is that when I get hit, literally or figuratively, I don't just sit there and take it, I hit back.

"Hunter bought the building," I say slowly, clearly, so there's no mistaking the words that have just come out of my mouth. A shock of satisfaction rolls through me when Aaron's mouth drops, and I continue. "He gave me keys to it yesterday so I could start my school, and there was a part of me that didn't want to accept such a huge gift from him. There was a part of me that thought it wasn't right, that was worried about how upsetting it might be for you, but now that I know you're such a huge fan of resolving things with little to no discussion, I realize I shouldn't have been so worried. I mean you've only known about it for—" I glance at my wrist, checking an imaginary watch "—about a half a minute, and I bet you're already past it."

Using Aaron's shock to my advantage, I push to my feet and move over to my closet to pull down the beat-up black duffel I haven't opened since we left New York. It hits the ground with a loud thump, and then I step over it, reaching for the shelf that holds all the leotards, tights, and dance skirts I've accumulated over the years and slipping on the first ones I put my hands on.

Aaron appears in the doorway just as I'm securing the skirt around my waist, finally in possession of his voice but not his common sense. "You can't keep the building."

"I don't recall asking you for your permission, Aaron."

"You can't keep it," he says again and, judging by the petulance in his tone, barely containing the urge to stomp his foot.

I bend down and grab my bag, tossing it over my shoulder and using it to body-check him on my way out of the closet. "Watch me."

"THOSE SHOES ARE DEAD," Dee tells me, eyeing the box of the pointe shoes I'm holding in my hand through the camera.

She's probably right, but I still put them on just to be certain. Sure enough, the moment I go en pointe I feel the lack of resistance that can only mean one thing: a soft box. Sighing, I drop back down, lowering myself to the floor and unraveling the ribbon connecting the useless shoes to my ankles. Once I have them off, I toss them across the room.

"Someone's in a pissy mood today," Dee observes.

Reaching into my bag, I pull out a pair of brand-new shoes, along with the tools I need to break them in. "I just didn't have the best start to my day."

Dee watches as I take out my frustrations on the pointe shoes, rolling back the satin of the heel to expose the shank first then using the scissors I keep in my bag to cut down the hardened material that runs from one end of the shoe to the other.

"I know that, Rae," she says patiently, reminding me that I filled her in on my entire conversation with Aaron on the drive over. "I'm just wondering if you plan on letting Aaron ruin your first full day in your space."

"No, I just—" I blow out a breath, shifting to my knees and putting the shoe on the ground so I can use my weight to soften the box a bit. "I don't need his permission, you know? I can keep the building; I can use the money from my savings to pay for everything I need to get things off the ground. I don't need his permission," I repeat, sinking back to the floor.

"But you want his support," Dee says, nodding. I remember a time when I was upset with her for abandoning our shared dream of being professional dancers to pursue psychology, but now I'm more grateful than ever that she did. Her degrees have saved me thousands in therapy bills.

"Yes! I just don't understand why it's so hard for him to give it to me."

"Have you asked him?"

"No, because I'm tired of talking to him. I'm tired of fighting about every little thing."

"Every little thing or just one big thing?" she asks, lips pursed because she already knows the answer. I let the question live in the air while I repeat the breaking process on my other shoe. Dee is fine with the silence, opting to fill the time typing away on her computer while I avoid giving her an answer.

"You got a busy day today?" I ask.

"A few appointments, but nothing too crazy." She sighs and leans back in her seat. "I think I'm getting tired of Michigan," she confesses. "It's lonely out here."

"Where are you planning on going now?" I ask, a smile curving my lips. Dee is the most adventurous person I know. She doesn't mind packing up all of her shit and leaving where ever she is to start anew. It's the thing I love most about her.

"I haven't decided yet. What would you think about me coming back to New Haven?"

My heart squeezes with excitement at the thought of having my friend back within arms reach. "I think that would be amazing if it's something you want to do. Riley and I would love to have you here, and I know Jayla and Sonia would, too."

The mention of her goddaughter and niece makes her smile and then frown. "I just feel like I'm missing out on so much being out here when y'all are all over there. It was different when you were in New York because we were all spread out, but seeing you and Jayla together when we're on FaceTime has me feeling like I'm always missing out."

"Aww, babe, well, it sounds like you already have your answer."

"Maybe."

"Ain't no, maybe, Deanna; you just said you're sad and lonely. That means it's time to come on home."

"I didn't say I was sad, bitch."

I snort out a laugh. "Damn, why I gotta be all of that?"

"Because you're getting on my nerves. Now, pick up the phone and show me around this building your baby daddy bought you before Aaron burns it to the ground."

"He wouldn't do that," I tell her, wishing I had as much confidence in my relationship with Aaron as I do in his aversion to arson. Dee twists her lips to the side, letting me know she's not as certain as I am, but she doesn't say anything else on the topic, which allows me the chance to give her a full tour of the building before she has to hang up to tend to the clients that actually pay her.

Once our call ends, I pull up my favorite playlist and turn the volume up as high as it will go before putting on my freshly broken-in shoes and letting the music take me where it wants to go. Ballet is one of the most structured forms of dance, so there's not usually room for free-styling, but that's all I'm doing at this moment. There's no rhyme or reason or finesse to my movements, and because I'm out of practice, there are several moments when my shoulders and hips are not on the same line, but still, it feels good to move. To dance. To get back in touch with the part of me that loves the burn in my muscles when I stretch them to their limits and, as crazy as it sounds, the slight ache in my toes from the pressure of balancing the weight of my entire body on them when I'm en pointe.

There's madness to this art form, yes, but there's beauty too, and that's what I want to teach the kids that pass through the doors of my school. I want them to learn to appreciate the fundamentals like first position and then push themselves to perfect the harder skills like going en pointe, and I want them to leave here knowing that even if this world doesn't want them, they can still want it. They can still *have* it.

By the time I'm done, my ankles hurt, and my lungs are burning, but I'm happy, happier than I've been in a long time, about something that doesn't have to do with Riley. I collapse on the floor, wishing for a water bottle and maybe a snack, when my playlist stops, and my phone starts to ring, playing the ringtone I designated for Hunter. I lay there, staring up at the ceiling and contemplating letting him go to voicemail, but then I reconsider because he hasn't done anything to deserve that from me.

I pull myself up off the floor, hurrying over to the window sill where I sat the phone and scooping it up.

"Hello?" I'm breathless, a byproduct of pushing myself to physical exhaustion after months of doing nothing, and Hunter notices.

"Did I catch you at a bad time?" he asks, and I can practically see his eyebrows reaching for his non-existent hairline as he jumps to an inappropriate conclusion.

"No, this is a perfect time." I rub a hand down my face and over my neck, clutching at my dry throat. "I'm just down at the building... cleaning up." I close my eyes and groan silently at the poorly executed lie. I could have just told him I was dancing.

"Oh. Okay." There's a smile in his voice that teases me, calling me a liar.

"Did you need something?"

He never calls me. The one time we've talked on the phone since exchanging numbers, I initiated the phone call, and he's never returned the favor, until now.

"I wanted to know if Riley has a savings account."

God, why is that such an attractive combination of words?

I bite my lip, wondering if I'll dream about him again tonight, only this time, he won't be eating my pussy in the middle of a room full of mirrors; he'll be seducing me with finance terms like APY and compounding interest.

"Yeah, I, uh, I started her one when she was a baby with the money I got from Will's life insurance."

"Oh." His end of the line goes quiet, and I realize that it's the first time one of us has mentioned Will since we've been back in each other's lives. "That was smart."

"Thank you?"

"What's with the tone?"

"I don't know. I'm trying to figure out *your* tone."

"I don't have a tone," he insists, and I purse my lips even though he can't see me because we both know he's lying. "Okay, maybe there was a bit of a tone," he admits, which makes me smile.

"Do you want to tell me why there was a tone?"

Hunter blows out a breath. "You're just so good at this whole parenting thing."

"And that's a bad thing?"

His answer comes immediately. "No. I couldn't be prouder or more impressed with the mother that you are. I just—" he pauses, and I try to picture him now in this rare moment of self-doubt "—I'm just trying to catch up, to make up for fucking up so thoroughly that I ended up missing everything. I don't want to miss any more, Rae."

"You won't," I assure him because I can't picture going back to a reality where he's not a part of Riley's life, where he's not a part of mine. "I won't let you."

"Can you do something for me?" His voice is low and throaty, full of vulnerabilities he's not used to exposing, so I'm inclined to listen even though I know there's a high likelihood he might be preparing to ask me for something I'm not ready to give him just yet.

"What is it?"

"Can you consider letting me be around more consistently? Giving me a day to pick her up from school, help her with her homework, cook her dinner..."

"You know how to cook now?" I ask, trying to imagine him in somebody's kitchen.

"You've had my food before, Sunshine; you know I can cook."

There he goes with that damn nickname again, making me melt.

"Grilling is not the same as cooking, Hunter. You know your daughter barely eats meat, right?"

"I'm aware. Just like I'm aware that you're intentionally steering this conversation in another direction to avoid answering my question."

I kick at the window sill with the toe of my shoe. "Well, I don't know that I know exactly what you're asking."

"I'm asking to see her in person more than once a week for thirty minutes at a time. I know you wanted to take things slow, to try to ease all of us into this, but I think Riley is ready for more time with me, and I am more than ready for more time with her."

24

HUNTER

<u>Now</u>

Family dinner.

That's Rae's answer to my request. Weekly dinners at her place with her, Riley, Aaron and his mom. When she first offered it up as a way for me to have more time with my daughter, I almost laughed in her face, but then I saw she was serious and that Riley was excited about the prospect of showing me her room, and I was left with no choice but to agree.

If anyone ever needed proof that there's not a thing in this world I wouldn't do for the two of them, they'd just have to peek through the blinds in Rae's dining room every Thursday night at seven p.m. sharp to find it. This is my second week inside the shrine to perfection Rae calls a home, and I have to say, I don't understand her decision to be in this place, with these people, anymore now than I did when I was standing on the outside looking in.

The house, while beautiful and in the perfect, trendy neighborhood, is nothing like the home Rae once told me she wanted. There's no knick knacks on the shelves tinged with nostalgia and precious memories. No family pictures on the wall. No messes to stumble over or warmth to expel the chill in every room that emanates from the white furniture and metal surfaces.

"What happened to your hand, Daddy?" Riley's voice pulls me out of my head and back into this hellscape of a dinner. She keeps her touch light as she runs her fingertips around the perimeter of the scrape on my hand.

"Oh, that's nothing. I just hurt myself when Taurin and I were out in the yard the other day building—"

"Who's Taurin?" Aaron asks, cutting me off in the middle of my explanation. I turn my head slowly in his direction, working hard not to look as annoyed as I feel, and give him the attention he's so desperate to have from me.

He's sitting at the head of the table, his posture rigid and hostile, though not quite as unwelcoming as his mother's. She's all barely audible mumbles and disapproving eyes that will drill a hole into the side of my face until I leave.

"Taurin is one of my sponsees."

Aaron frowns. "Is doing yard work for you a part of his twelve-step program?"

Rae, who's sitting to Aaron's left, puts a hand on his forearm, a silent warning to pull back. She does that with him a lot. Warning him. Protecting him. Keeping him from tap dancing on my last nerve.

"No," I say, threading patience through my voice. "He's staying with me for a while, and when he saw me working on something, he offered to help."

Marcy's eyes go wide, and she chooses now to speak to me for the first time tonight. "Is that smart? Two addicts under one roof?"

I don't appreciate her tone or the way she makes my house sound like some kind of den of iniquity, and it's hard for me to keep my frustration and impatience off of my face. Rae must see me struggling because she jumps in, saving me from having to explain myself to a woman who just wants to see the worst in me anyway.

"Well, it's definitely not traditional, but I think it's better than the alternative, which was Hunter leaving him on the streets to fend for himself." Her voice is tight, packed with frustration, and, if I'm not mistaken, a bit of pride. "Getting clean is hard, but it's even harder to do when you don't have a safe, loving environment to do it in. Hunter is giving Taurin that, and I think that's amazing."

Yeah, that's definitely pride. It's in her voice and now in her eyes as she looks at me.

"I think Will would be proud of you," she says.

"Thank you, Sunshine."

I don't mean to use the nickname. It's a private thing. Something that belongs to Rae and me. Something I don't want tarnished by the other two adults at the table who kill everything with their judgment and negativity. I don't mean to use it, but it pops out anyway, the way it always does when I'm caught up in a moment where it feels like there's no one else in the world besides me and her. When I'm trapped in her gaze and have no intentions of looking for a way out. When my heart is brimming with unspent love that has no where to go.

Aaron clears his throat, snapping the moment in half, and Rae forces a smile, picking up her fork and spearing a green bean with it while I try not to watch the way her lips curve around the gleaming metal.

"What were you building?" Riley asks, bringing us back to the start of the conversation.

I focus my gaze back on her sweet face. "A treehouse."

Rae coughs, and everyone, including Riley, turns a concerned gaze in her direction. She waves her hand, assuring her silently that she's fine while Aaron claps her on the back.

"A treehouse?" She wheezes once she's finally recovered and taking slow sips of her water. "You're building a treehouse?"

The funny thing about history is that it will always find a way to make itself known, and when you have as much history with a person as I have with Rae, it happens more often than it doesn't. Every conversation we have, every look we share, is the equivalent to navigating a minefield. No matter how careful you are or how slow you move, every time you take a step, you run the risk of triggering a bomb.

No one else in this room knows that I did exactly that when I mentioned the tree house. They don't know that they're now standing at the site of an emotional explosion, covered in the shrapnel of a steamy night where four years of longing turned into lost inhibitions and confessions of love.

But Rae knows.

She remembers, and now she knows that I never let myself forget.

"A treehouse," she repeats, her eyes soft, her voice softer.

"A TREEHOUSE!" Riley shouts, bouncing in her seat. "That sounds so cool!"

"It is cool," I assure her when I manage to tear my eyes away from her mom again. "There's this big tree at the edge of my property that overlooks the lake my daddy and I used to fish in. That's where I'm building it."

Riley's eyes are as big as saucers. "Ohhh, can I see it?"

"Well, I don't have any pictures of it, but maybe one day, when you come to my house, I can take you out there so you can see it in person."

It takes me a second to realize my mistake, but when I do, I immediately wish I could take the words back. Rae and I haven't talked about Riley coming to my house. At all. Since becoming a part of Riley's life, I've been content to let Rae lead, only pushing for more when I felt it was likely I'd get the result I wanted. I'd love to bring Riley to the house, to bring her into my world just a little bit more, but I haven't asked Rae, and I don't want it to look like I'm trying to force her hand by mentioning it to Riley first.

The thing with kids, though, is that they always hold on tight to the things you want them to let go of. And judging by the curiosity dancing in Riley's eyes, she's not planning on letting go of this house thing any time soon.

"Can I come and see it today?" she asks.

"It's a school night, Ri," Rae responds, and I hope the reminder is enough to end this conversation, but it's Riley, so of course it's not.

"This weekend, then! I'll help you build the treehouse and make sure you don't hurt yourself again," she says, her eyes on me even though I don't have any power here. I hate that I don't have it, that I have to look to Rae for help while ignoring the smug smile on Aaron's face as he watches me flounder for a response.

Rae smiles gently at Riley, her tone soft. "I don't think that's a good idea, Nugget."

While I knew what her answer was going to be, I still feel unprepared for the pain that lances my heart when I hear it. I'm even less prepared for the way Riley's face crumples with disappointment.

"But why?" She whines, looking between Rae and me. "I want to help Daddy build the treehouse. I can be a good helper."

"You're a great helper, Ri," Rae assures her while I put a soothing hand on her back, rubbing small circles between her shoulder blades because it's all I can do. "But I'm not going to be here this weekend, so I can't take you over there."

"Aaron has planned a romantic weekend for him and Rae to reconnect," Marcy adds between bites of rice pilaf, chucking the information in my direction even though I don't want it.

"Two full days alone in Atlanta with no interruptions," Aaron says.

Rae's eyes flash with self-consciousness as she looks at me. "Riley's going to be staying with Jayla and her daughter, Sonia, for the weekend."

It hurts to know that I'm at the bottom of the list of childcare options for my daughter. Below Dee's little sister and Aaron's mom and a stranger on the fucking street, but I hold the pain in, swallowing it because nothing good will come from letting it out.

"You don't have to explain," I tell her, even though I do want an explanation. I want to know what I have to do to make my way to the top of the list of people she trusts to be alone with our daughter.

"I don't want to stay with Jayla and Sonia," Riley says, pounding a little fist on the table. "Their house is stupid. I want to stay with Daddy."

"Riley." Rae narrows her eyes, speaking her name like a warning. "We don't call people's houses stupid, and you can't stay with your dad because Taurin—"

"Taurin will be gone for the weekend," I interject, even though I'm not exactly sure how Rae was planning on using him to put Riley off. "His girlfriend, Alyssa, has asked him to go with her and her friends on a college tour."

For the first time since T brought up the trip, I'm grateful that I agreed to let him go. I'm still going to have to give him a long talk about setting boundaries and making good decisions when he's surrounded by temptation, but I'm willing to do that and a hell of a lot more if it means making Rae comfortable enough to let Riley stay with me this weekend.

Rae lets out a long, exasperated sigh that almost makes me feel bad for stripping her of another excuse. Almost. She picks up her glass of water and takes a sip before looking at Riley and me and saying, "I just don't think we're ready for an overnight visit yet."

Although I'm disappointed—with her answer and with myself for allowing even a modicum of hope to swell in my chest—I nod. "That's fair."

"No, it's not!" Riley wails, shooting to her feet. There are tears spilling down her cheeks and her bottom lip trembles with indignation. "That's not fair at all!"

"Nugg—" Rae starts, but before she can finish, Riley runs out of the dining room and up the stairs, sobbing all the way to the second floor. She ends her dramatic exit by slamming her room door.

Marcy tuts her disapproval, muttering something under her breath about the perils of never saying no to your child, and Rae silences her with a glare as she stands and tosses her napkin on her plate. "I'm going to go check on her."

Aaron places his hand on her arm. "Just let her work it out on her own, babe. You can't go running every time she throws a fit."

Now, I'm the one glaring. The one wishing my eyes were lasers so I could turn the fingers wrapped around Rae's arm, and the man they're attached to, to ash. Rae snatches away from him, rolling her eyes as she walks out, leaving me to sit in awkward silence with her little boyfriend and his helicopter mom until she returns.

Thankfully, it doesn't take long.

When Rae comes back into the room, she's alone but there are tear stains on her shoulder and chest, which I can only assume have come from Riley.

"Is she okay?" I ask, rising to my feet because the moment I know they're both good, I'm out of here.

"Yeah." She nods, running a hand over her dress. "She was pretty upset, but I managed to get her calm enough to talk to me, and we came to an understanding."

I don't know what it is exactly that tells me the tides have just turned in my favor. Maybe it's the way Rae keeps biting her lip and shifting her gaze between Aaron and me, or the gentle understanding in her eyes, or maybe it's just that I know her so well that I can get a line on her without her needing to say a thing. Whatever it is, I'm grateful for it because it means I get to sit in the glory of her decision before Aaron and his mom ruin it.

"I've decided to let Riley stay the weekend with Hunter," Rae says, her eyes trained on my face, cataloging exactly what her words have done to me. I make sure to show her the joy and the absolute appreciation, but I hide everything else—the love, the adoration, the desire to grab her by the shoulders and kiss her on the lips.

"Are you sure?" I ask, returning her intense stare with one of my own.

She nods. "Yeah, I'm sure. She wants to feel closer to you, to know more about you and your world, and she can't do that if I don't give her the chance to."

There's sincerity in her voice, but there's certainty, too, which tells me that she didn't change her mind because Riley shed a few tears or threw a temper tantrum. In fact, she didn't change her mind at all. Riley's raw reaction just acted as a catalyst, helping her to honor a choice she'd already made but was just too afraid to acknowledge.

"So you're just going to let your nine-year-old daughter spend the weekend alone with a virtual stranger?" Aaron asks, incredulity and an unmistakable hate glittering in his eyes as he looks between Rae and me.

"No," she says evenly, like she anticipated this question. "I'm going to stay too. If that's okay with you, Hunter."

"If that's what you need to feel comfortable, Sunshine," I say, my voice rough with emotion at the thought of having both of my girls under my roof for an entire weekend and my mind working overtime to try to figure out how to turn two measly days into a lifetime.

25

RAE

"**A**nd why does he keep calling you Sunshine?!" Aaron shouts. His voice a loud and annoying boom that I know is audible all the way upstairs. He's been on a full-blown rampage since Hunter left, following me around the kitchen as I clean up dinner and airing out his grievances with no care or concern about the child upstairs who can hear him.

"Keep. Your. Voice. Down." I say by way of response, bending over to put another plate in the dishwasher while he stands there doing nothing but puffing out his chest and complaining.

"Seriously?" he hisses. "You think my volume is the only thing we need to be concerned about right now?"

"No, Aaron, I don't. But if you actually want me to listen when you voice your other concerns, I'd suggest you bring it down a notch."

He scoffs in disdain, but the next time he speaks, his voice is at a more acceptable level. "You're unbelievable, you know that? I go out of my way to plan a romantic weekend for you, and you jump ship the first chance you get to go play house with your baby daddy."

The knife I'm holding slips out of my fingers and clatters to the ground, and I stand there for a second, stunned at the audacity of it and the man across from me. Shaking my head, I bend over and pick it up, shoving it into the utensil holder in the dishwasher.

"It's a work trip," I remind him, saying the thing I wanted to say when his mother brought it up at dinner in front of Hunter, and he chimed in, making it sound like some grand gesture instead of a thoughtless invitation he sprung on me at the last minute to try and smooth things over from the last fight we had. "You're going to Atlanta for work, which means I would have spent the entire weekend in a hotel without you."

"Don't make it sound like some hardship, Rachel. You'd be in a suite at the Waldorf Astoria."

I bristle, the way I always do, when he uses my full name to admonish me, to minimize my feelings and concerns while treating me like a child. "But I'd be alone, Aaron, and away from Riley for no good reason. You know how much I hate that. This way I get to be with her—"

"And Hunter," he says, cutting me off with a sneer. "You get to be with Riley and Hunter, which is exactly what she wanted, by the way. Do you feel good about that? Being played like a fucking fiddle by a nine-year-old."

"She didn't play me."

"Oh, yes she did." He laughs, and the sound is ripe with false humor. "She's always manipulating you."

"Feeling safe enough to express her emotions is not manipulation; it's a healthy way of communicating her needs."

"What about my needs, Rae?"

My head snaps up, and I stare at him in disbelief. "Did you seriously just ask me that?"

I used to think Aaron was a smart man. I mean, I don't think he's dumb now, but I do think he has to be missing that fundamental part of his brain that's dedicated to self-preservation because I know there's murder in my eyes right now, but instead of backing down, he keeps going, launching into a speech that's all about how fucking neglected he feels.

"Yes, Rae, I did because we haven't made love in weeks. All of your extra time and mental space is dedicated to your school, which I knew was going to happen, by the way, but I still agreed to let you keep it."

I grab the pan off the stove and shove it into the bottom rack. Marcy says it's supposed to be washed by hand, but I don't care. Tonight, everything in this damn kitchen is going in the dishwasher, so I don't end up chucking it at Aaron's head.

We both know he didn't have a choice in the matter when it came to me keeping the building.

"And when you're not at that building or talking to Dee about your school, you're focused on Riley and Hunter. I mean, it feels like the dude lives with us now. He's here every week."

"He's here once a week, Aaron, which you agreed to."

"Sometimes more than once," he insists, putting his hands on his hips. "Last week, he was here twice. I never agreed to that."

Wiping my hands on the dish towel on my shoulder, I gaze up at the sky, praying for patience and reminding myself that while I look good in a lot of colors, orange is not one of them.

"Hunter was here for all of five minutes on Wednesday because I had to ask him to pick Riley up from school when *your* mother forgot her."

Why he thinks it's wise to remind me of that little mishap right now, I'm not sure. All it does is make me more upset, more frustrated, and more confident that giving Hunter more time with Riley is the right choice because he came through when Aaron and Marcy let me down. And he didn't utter a single complaint when I called him, frantic and upset because Riley was waiting, and I couldn't get to her because I had to be at the building to sign for several deliveries. He dropped everything he was doing and picked her up, took her out for ice cream, and then brought her home and waited with her in the backyard until Marcy got home from the last-minute hair appointment she thought was more important than my kid.

Aaron, who hates when people point out his mother's flaws just as much, if not more than his own, grimaces. "You wouldn't have needed Mom to pick her up if you weren't opening that school."

My final thread of sanity snaps with a loud pop that turns everything in my vision red and blurry. Unfortunately for Aaron, his words hit me at the same time the rack I'm trying to push in to close up the dishwasher refuses to slide into place. I shove it hard several times, but each time it bounces back out because something is off. I bark out an enraged laugh and straighten to my full height, then snatch the dish towel on my shoulder off and throw it down. It lands in a defunct heap on top of the dirty dishes, and I don't care because I'm done.

I am *so* done.

"Well, I am!" I bellow, finally unleashing the madness Aaron has been trying to taunt out of me for the past hour. "I'm starting the fucking school, Aaron. It's happening, and I wish you would just get the fuck over it already." I blow out a breath, pushing the curls that have broken free from my bun out of my face. "We moved here for you, and you're living your dreams, aren't you? You've got the job you've always wanted, this big ass house we can barely afford, and your mom under our roof and all in our business; why should you be the only one who gets what they want, huh?"

A myriad of emotions plays across his features, chief among them anger, but I don't care. He wanted this fight, so I'm going to give it to him.

"Why can't I have my school?" I ask, my hand going to my chest before sweeping up to gesture at the ceiling. "Why can't Ri have her dad, hmm? Have you even taken a second to look at her lately? To notice how much happier she is now that Hunter is around?" Tears crowd my vision as the image of Riley's face the first time she met Hunter flashes in my mind. "It's like a piece of her was missing, and now she's whole. You say that you love her, so that should make you happy too, but all you've done since Hunter has been in the picture is sit around and bitch and moan about how it affects you."

Now that all the anger is out, I find myself deflating, my shoulders sagging with exhaustion. I shake my head at Aaron, hating that I can't see a hint of the man I fell in love with looking back at me. "I'm sorry this is hard for you, I truly am, but you've got to find a way to figure your shit out because Hunter isn't going anywhere. He's going to be a part of our lives for as long as Riley wants him to be."

"Riley or you?" Aaron asks, stone-faced.

"Both," I say, answering honestly because there's no reason to lie. I want Hunter around. I *like* having him around. He's a good man and an even better father, and when I'm not pushing him away, building up walls meant to protect Aaron's ego, he's a great friend.

With nothing more to say, I step around the open dishwasher and head for the stairs. Aaron doesn't make a move to stop me, and for that much, I'm grateful. I head straight to my room, lock the door, and get undressed on my way to the bathroom, knowing that a hot, steamy shower will help settle my nerves.

It does.

Once I'm clean and moisturized, I curl up on my side of the bed and grab my phone off the nightstand where I left it charging before dinner. I have a missed call from Dee and a few texts from Jayla, but the notifications that get my attention are from Hunter. There are several texts and a phone call that came in about thirty minutes ago. I open our text thread first and smile at the pictures he's sent along with message that says 'which one?'

My heart squeezes, compressed by emotions I don't fully under-stand. While I was downstairs arguing with Aaron, this man was at the store buying decorations for Riley's room. I let out a laugh that's part sob as I picture him, big and imposing in the aisles among all things pink, white, and frilly, excited about creating a space for our daughter in his home and needing a little bit of guidance from me. I feel bad about not being there for him, and as I dial his number, I lie and tell myself that I'm calling instead of texting, so I can give him a genuine apology for leaving him hanging, not because I'm hoping the gentle growl of his voice will soothe away the last of the tension in my body.

"Sunshine," he says, picking up on the first ring. "You good?"

I bite my lip, forcing back the sudden rush of tears clogging my throat. "Yeah, I'm fine." Hunter is quiet. His silence calls me a liar even though he won't. "I'm sorry I missed your call earlier. What'd you end up choosing?"

"It's okay. In the end, I didn't make any choices because your daughter made them all for me. She told me she wanted the unicorn comforter, matching PJs, and instructed me on which snacks to buy for her and you."

My brow furrows. "You talked to Ri?" She should have been asleep, not on the phone, helping Hunter prepare for our visit.

"Yeah, she called me." Even though it's a complete sentence, a fully formed thought, I get the sense that there's something more Hunter wants to add.

Flipping over onto my back, I stare up at the ceiling, wondering if I want to know what he's leaving out. "What aren't you saying?"

Hunter clears his throat, obviously uncomfortable. "She called me because she couldn't sleep. She said she could hear you and Aaron arguing, and she was worried that it was all her fault."

All at once, my heart breaks into a thousand little pieces, and the pain is enough to set the tears I've been holding back free. I've never wanted to be the kind of parent who subjected their child to loud, angry arguments. Before we moved back to New Haven, Aaron and I never had them. We never argued at all, but now that's all we ever seem to do. The thought that Riley feels responsible for it makes me feel sick to my stomach.

There's a desperate whimper pushing its way out of my mouth, proceeding my question. "What did you tell her?"

My face is hot, flushed with embarrassment, even though there's no judgment in Hunter's voice when he responds. "I told her grown-up problems belong to grown-ups, and they're never, ever the kid's fault."

When the dam inside me breaks, sending the tears I've been holding back out in hot, fat drops that roll down my cheeks and into my ears, I know it's time to hang up.

"Thank you for reassuring her," I shutter, hating how fucking broken I sound.

"Sunshine—" Hunter starts, his voice all gentle concern and comfort I can't let myself have right now.

"Goodnight, Hunter."

I end the call and toss the phone onto my nightstand before rolling out of bed and going to check on Riley. Her bedroom door is closed, so I push it open gently, hoping she's not still up worrying about me. When I see her curled into a tight little ball in the middle of the bed, I breathe a sigh of relief and pull the door closed, returning to my own room to play an unhelpful game of what if.

What if I didn't run?

What if Hunter hadn't relapsed?

What if, what if, what if.

26

HUNTER

Now

"You sure you got everything you need?" I ask Taurin, hovering outside his door as he packs his bag. "Toothbrush, toothpaste, deodorant? You're going to be doing a lot of walking; you don't want to smell."

"Hey, Hunter?" He zips up his bag, turning to face me with serious eyes.

I step forward, worried that he's about to get emotional or tell me that he doesn't want to go. While it'd throw a definite wrench in my plans for the weekend, I'm confident that I could come up with a solution that would keep Taurin safe and not make Rae rethink agreeing to this overnight.

"Yeah, T?"

"I've got this," he says, his voice confident and shoulders square. "Stop worrying about me and focus on you."

Crossing my arms, I lift a brow. "Me? What about me?"

"You're a nervous wreck, which is understandable since it's your first time having Rae and Riley over, but you can't keep projecting all of that energy onto me." He points at his chest with a hooked thumb to drive home his point. "I'm good."

I despise being called out so plainly, but I still find myself laughing. "You're right. I am nervous about Rae and Riley coming over, but that doesn't mean my concern for you isn't real."

"Of course it's real, but you gotta limit it a little bit." He holds his hand up, using his index finger and thumb to indicate the amount of worry I'm allowed to have for him. "I mean, you're giving me advice about packing hygiene products like I'm a little kid or something when what you're really worried about is me falling off the wagon as soon as I'm out of your sight."

He's right. Damn. I hate that I can't even hide the fact that he's spot-on with his assessment of my current state of mind. I hang my head in defeat. "I guess you're right."

Taurin moves over to the door and claps me on the shoulder. Brown eyes that used to be bloodshot and shifty are bright with humor and appreciation. "It's important to know when you've been bested," he tells me, smirking because he's finally gotten the opportunity to use my own catchphrase against me.

"Shut up." I laugh, shrugging him off. "Is Alyssa almost here?"

He pulls his phone out of his pocket. "She's been downstairs for like ten minutes. I told her to give us a minute so you could get all your big feelings out."

When I reach for him, intending to put his smart ass in a playful headlock, he dodges me with ease, ducking under my arm and dashing down the stairs leaving me no choice but to follow. We agreed that I'd get to meet Liz and Winston, Alyssa's best friend and her boyfriend, before they hit the road, but Taurin still groans in exasperation when I follow him out to the Jeep Wrangler, idling in the yard.

"Don't freak them out, okay?" He tosses the request over his shoulder before catching Alyssa in his arms.

"Hey, Hunter," she says, grinning at me. "Thanks for letting Taurin come with us."

In truth, I couldn't have stopped him from going even if I wanted to. Despite the respect he has for me and the responsibility I feel towards him, I don't have any actual authority over him.

"No problem, Alyssa," I grunt in surprise when she moves from Taurin's arms to mine, pulling me into an unexpected hug that's over just as quickly as it began.

"You packed so light, T," she says, teasing him as they walk around the back of the Jeep.

I noticed how little he'd put in his bag, too, but I didn't say anything. Didn't want to make him feel like I cared about him leaving his stuff behind because I don't. As far as I'm concerned, the room he's been sleeping in since his first night here is his, and it'll be his for as long as he wants it to.

"Yeah, well, it's just a weekend, and I knew you and Liz would have the trunk full," Taurin says, making the girl in the backseat with teal curls and a septum piercing giggle into her hand.

"We didn't pack that much, T," she says. Taurin shoots her a doubtful look as he opens the trunk, and they all share a laugh when several bags come tumbling out, falling at his feet.

I'm about to offer my help when the back doors fly open, and Liz and Winston, a lanky, dark-skinned kid with deep waves and a friendly smile, hop out and help set everything back to rights. Once they're done, and the trunk has been squeezed closed, Taurin sighs and looks at me. I've been quiet this whole time, just trying to get a feel for their group dynamic, so no introductions have been made yet. I figured I'd leave that to him.

"Uh, Liz, Win, this is Hunter. Hunter, this is Liz, Alyssa's best friend, and Winston, her boyfriend."

We exchange greetings, and I'm impressed when they both opt to shake my hand. Taurin's relief is palpable when I smile at them both, and I laugh because he clearly thinks I'm some sort of monster.

"Okay, well, I guess we should be heading out," he says, slipping his hand into Alyssa's.

"Not so fast. You still need to—" My sentence dies a quiet death on my lips as I watch another car pull up into the yard, officially marking the collision of my two worlds.

Rae said she was going to arrive around five o'clock, but it's not even four yet, which means she must have headed over right after picking Riley up from school. My heart starts to pound, and all the nerves and anxiety Taurin accused me of projecting onto him rush to the surface and distract me from finishing my thought.

"Still need to what?" Taurin asks, a teasing smile on his lips. He's never seen me and Rae together, but he's compared the way I look when I talk about her to the way he feels when he speaks about Alyssa. I respect what the two of them have, I really do, but I never miss an opportunity to tell him that what they have could never even come close to what I had with Rae or what I want to have with her again.

"Share your location with me," I tell him, my eyes still on Rae. She's parked her car next to my truck and is already out, holding Riley's hand as they make their way over to me.

"Daddy!" Riley shouts, dropping Rae's hand and running over to me. I crouch down just in time to scoop her up and into the air, spinning her around in a circle that makes her giggle and scream for me to stop. "You're making me dizzy," she says, still laughing as her eyes focus on Taurin, Alyssa, and the rest of their crew.

"Who are you?" she asks them as I set her back down on her feet.

"Riley." Rae's voice is all gentle admonishment as she walks up beside me, letting the warmth of her body and the scent of pears and vanilla mixed with a bit of coconut take over my nostrils. "Don't be rude."

Taurin steps forward first, splitting a smile between Riley and Rae. "It's okay," he tells Rae. "I have a little brother her age, so I'm used to the straightforwardness." Then he turns to Riley and offers her his hand. "I'm Taurin, and you must be Riley. Your dad has told me so much about you."

Riley glances at me for confirmation or permission to engage, and I nod, supplying both. She takes Taurin's hand, holding it with just the tips of her fingers, which makes Alyssa and Liz laugh.

"You let my daddy get hurt building the tree house." She delivers the accusation with narrowed eyes that make her seem so much older than her nine years.

"He didn't *let* me get hurt, Ri," I say, holding in a laugh.

"But he didn't stop it, so I feel like it's the same thing, right, Riley?" Alyssa asks, clearly trying to get on her good side.

Taurin's mouth drops, and his head swirls around as he glares at his girlfriend. "Who's side are you on, Alyssa?"

"Mine," Riley tells him, her voice filled with authority as she shares a conspiratorial grin with Alyssa. "Girl power, right?"

I look to Rae, whose brows are reaching for her hairline, as she watches our daughter turn all of Taurin's friends against him in a matter of seconds. Liz and Alyssa are fist-bumping her now, and Winston is trying to inch his way into her good graces by telling her about a time when Taurin let him run into a wall. She doesn't seem fully convinced by his story, but she allows it, letting him claim something called 'girl power by proxy' while Taurin watches on helplessly. He looks to me for help, and I shrug.

"It's important to know when you've been bested."

Not one to go down without a fight, Taurin works his way in between Riley and his friends and crouches down to her level, choosing to use his knowledge of the house to his advantage.

"Riley, did your dad tell you that he has a pool?"

"A POOL?!" She shouts, her eyes growing five times their normal size, which makes the older kids laugh. "You never said you had a pool, Daddy!"

"I can take you to see it," Taurin says, then pauses, looking up at me and Rae. "If that's okay?"

I look to Rae, who's looking at me, and it's such a small moment, such an inconsequential decision, but it feels good that we're making it together. "Yeah, T, just don't let her get in."

All of their eyes are lit up now, and I watch in awe as the entire group takes off behind Taurin with Riley in the center, allthoughts of the trip they were just so eager to leave for forgotten.

Rae sighs, and although I'm going to get to look at her all weekend, I find that my eyes are eager to consume every line of her face once they land on it. She's so damn beautiful, but she looks tired, like she hasn't been sleeping well. My heart twists in on itself, the need to hold her in my arms until she finds comfort and rest in my embrace, an urgent and demanding thump against my ribcage.

"You okay?"

She looks up at me and nods. "Sorry, we're so early. Riley was so excited, she made me promise we'd come over right after school."

"You don't have to apologize, Sunshine. You could have shown up at the crack of dawn, and I'd still be just as happy to see you."

We both know it's true, but I keep forgetting that our shared knowledge doesn't give me the right to speak those things out loud. To make Rae face my constant desire to share air with her and Riley.

Lifting my hand, I rub at the back of my neck, hoping to dispel some of the awkwardness I've infused into the air. "Do you need help getting your stuff out of the car?"

There's no mistaking the relief on her face at the change of subject. "Yeah, that'd be great."

I follow her over to her car and balk when she opens the trunk to reveal two duffel bags, one for her and the other for Riley, and several bags of groceries. Red tints her cheeks when I turn a questioning gaze on her.

"I didn't know what you'd have."

"Clearly, you didn't think I'd have anything," I say, laughing as I grab everything in one hand and close the trunk with the other. "If you would have called, I could have saved you the trip to the store."

We haven't spoken on the phone since the night of the dinner from hell. Just quick texts and greetings during my daily FaceTimes with Riley, so I'm not surprised that she didn't, I just hate that she preferred to spend a hundred dollars on unnecessary items rather than talk to me.

"It's fine," she says, following me up the steps of the back porch that will take us right to the kitchen. "I needed to get out of the house anyway."

"Are things that bad?"

The question slips out on its own accord, adding another pound of tension to the weight that began to settle between us the moment we entered the kitchen. I walk into this room every day, multiple times a day, and it still hits me like a brick every time I'm in here. Our history, but more specifically, the unexpected beginning of us that happened right where Rae is standing. I see it descend on her with a quickness, harsh and unrelenting, exacerbated by the presence of my knowing gaze on her face and the question she's yet to answer lingering in the air.

I set the bags on the counter and wait. For a reaction. For an answer. For something that's real, even though I know chances are, she won't give it to me. Sure enough, she reaches over the counter and pulls the grocery bags over to her side.

"Rae." I hadn't planned on starting our visit off by begging for details she doesn't want to share, but I'm concerned about her. She was sad and disoriented the other night, and even though she rushed me off the phone before they came, I know she shed tears over the fact that Riley overheard her argument with Aaron. "You can talk to me," I tell her, watching as she pulls out various snacks and sets them on the counter.

"No, I can't," she says, turning to put the jug of milk she bought in the fridge next to the one I replaced just this morning. "It wouldn't be fair to Aaron."

"What about what's fair to you?" I ask, pushing even though I know I should be pulling back. "You're not happy, Sunshine. Even a blind man can see that. I just don't understand why—"

"You don't have to understand, Hunter," she whispers, focusing her attention on the door because there are now footsteps and voices on the porch. "Look, I want this to be a good weekend for Ri, okay? Let's just concentrate on her."

My opportunity to respond is stolen by the sudden appearance of Riley, Taurin and the rest of the crew. I take one look at Riley's hand, which is clutched in Taurin's, and smile.

"Your plan worked, huh?"

He smirks. "Like a charm."

"I wish I would have packed my bathing suit," Riley says, pouting as she walks over to hug Rae around the waist. She's clearly laying it on thick, trying to get Rae to offer a solution to a problem she hasn't even fully voiced yet.

Rae runs a hand over her head, smiling down at her. "Your bathing suit is in your bag, Nugget."

"Really?!"

"Yes, it was the first thing I packed."

"Yes!" Riley shouts, pumping a fist in the air as she turns to Taurin and his friends. "Are you guys going to get in the pool too?"

They all look at each other, none of them wanting to break the bad news to Riley.

"They can't this time, Ri," I say, swooping in to save them. "They're about to leave for a trip."

"Sorry, Ri," they all say in unison, clearly regretful.

"Oh, man." The pout is back in full effect. "I don't want to get in the pool alone."

"You won't be alone, Nugg. I'll get in with you," I tell her.

"Me too," Rae adds, which immediately makes our daughter's face brighten while my mind struggles not to conjure images of Rae in a bathing suit.

"Alright, well, we're going to get going," Taurin says.

"Don't forget to share your location with me," I remind him, walking over to give him a hug. "And make good decisions," I say, keeping my voice low so only he can hear. I'm sure his friends know about his struggles, but I don't want to embarrass him. "Call me if you need me."

"I will," he promises, maintaining eye contact with me even as we let each other go. "Bye, Ri. Bye, Ms. Rae. I'm sorry we didn't get much time to talk."

Rae smiles brightly. "Just Rae, please, and that's okay. I'm used to coming in second to this little one. We can get to know each other better next time."

"I'd like that a lot."

"Me too, so have fun on your trip and get back safe, okay?"

Something in Taurin seems to come to life under the warmth of

Rae's kind words and the maternal lilt of her voice. It makes my heart hurt for him, knowing that his own mother won't even pick up the phone for him.

"Yes, ma'am," Taurin says finally, stepping back to allow room for everyone else to say their goodbyes to Riley, Rae, and me. When they're gone, I turn back to Rae and nearly melt under the heat of her gaze.

"What?" I ask, trying to decipher her mood.

"Nothing," she shakes her head. "Taurin seems like a good kid."

"He is. He's just had a rough go of it."

She's still looking at me. Her eyes warm and steady on my face, making it feel like I'm bathing in sunlight. "I'm glad he has you."

I don't know what to say to that. In fact, I can't find a single, proper response to her words, her eyes, or the way the combination of the two makes me feel that doesn't involve grabbing both sides of her face and kissing her, so I just nod and exchange her confusing expression for Riley's curious one.

She's still standing by her mom, looking around the house like she wants to explore but doesn't feel comfortable enough to just yet.

"Hey, Ri? You want a tour?"

Her eyes light up. "Yes!"

I drop down on a knee in front of her, offering my back. "Do you want to ride on the Daddy Express while you get one?"

She doesn't even answer; she just clambers up onto my back and giggles when I bounce her around and instruct her to put her seat belt on. With Riley secured on my back and Rae carrying the duffle bags behind me, we make our way through the house, going room by room until we make it upstairs, where all the bedrooms are. Rae has been quiet for most of the tour, letting me tell Riley stories about growing up here while she looks around and catalogs the few changes I've made since we lived here together.

There aren't many. Some of the furniture is new, some of the finishes have been upgraded out of necessity, but it's not the tribute to modernity that her house is. It's a home, not a shrine. It's old, but clean and comfortable. Well loved and lived in, which is what we always said we wanted the place we raised our children to be.

"And this—" I say, pausing just outside of the bedroom closest to mine "—is your room."

Still holding Ri with one hand, I push the door open with the other, smiling when she lets out a gasp of delight as everything comes into view.

"Let me down!" She orders, wiggling out of my hold until I do exactly as she says. When her feet hit the floor, she makes a mad dash for the bed in the center of the room. It's a twin-size bed with a white canopy around it and fairy lights woven around the posts. The comforter set is the one she picked out when we were on the phone the other night, and I got plushies to match it, which she's now clutching in her hands as she rolls around on the bed.

"Don't mess up the bed, Ri," Rae warns her in a voice that's pure indulgence and therefore carries no weight. "She's not even listening, is she?"

"Nope, not even a little bit."

"You did a good job with her room."

We're both in the doorway, but I'm taking up most of it. Rae is turned to the side, her breasts brushing my arm every time she pulls in a breath.

"Thanks," I grind out.

"Me and her are going to have a time in that twin-size bed, though," she says, shaking her head, completely unaware of what our close proximity is doing to me.

My brows pull together as I look down at her. "You're not sleeping in here."

Rae's eyes snap up to mine. "Oh, but I thought, well, with Taurin in the other room and you using the guest room downstairs as an office..."

"You're going to take my room, and I'm going to sleep on the couch."

"Hunter, I don't want to put you out of your bed."

"You're not putting me out of my bed. I'm putting you in it."

The innuendo hangs between us for several long moments, during which Rae waits for me to take it back, and I wait for her to accept that I'm not going to. In the end, neither of us gets what we want because we're forced to turn our attention to Riley as she sits up on the bed and says, "Can we get in the pool now?"

Rae answers first, probably because she's used to having to be the primary person to address Riley's wants and needs. "Yes, Nugget, just let me figure out what we're going to do for dinner first."

"Or," I cut in. "You two can go ahead and get in the pool while *I* take care of dinner."

Riley stands up on the bed and whoops with delight while Rae looks at me with surprise that breaks my heart etched into her features. I've always known that Aaron wasn't a great co-parent—his lack of a bond with Riley has shown me that—but seeing it written on Rae's face so plainly makes me want to break something.

Seven years.

He's had them for seven years, and he hasn't spent a single day cherishing them, supporting them, or loving them the way they deserve.

"Does that sound like a plan?" I ask, aiming the question in Rae's direction but unsurprised when Riley answers with a resounding yes.

"Alright, then!" I clap my hands and force myself to start moving because if I don't, I'm going to tell Rae she's never going back to that worthless asshole again, and I'm not sure that will go over well. "I'll see you two downstairs in your finest swimming gear."

When Riley and Rae emerge in their bathing suits, sunglasses, and matching hats, I'm standing next to the grill, tending to the burgers and hot dogs—the only meat Riley eats—while my brother, Cal, demonstrates his ability to make the same conversation we have every month feel even more awkward than it did four weeks ago.

"And, you're still," he hesitates, never knowing how to ask if I've relapsed even though he inquires about my sobriety every time we talk.

"Yeah, Cal," I snort, pulling a hot dog off of the grill before it burns. "I'm still clean, still working, still going to meetings and keeping my shit straight."

"Good. Good," he says, and even though it's been years since I've laid eyes on him in person, I can see the curt jerk of his chin as he nods his approval in my head. Usually, I'm annoyed by this point in our monthly call, when it's more of an inquisition than conversation, and everything, from the sharp, clipped tone he uses to the silences that follow, reminds me of our dad. Nicholas Drake.

Cal and I never talk about him, so he doesn't know how much I hate the way he reminds me of him, the way their similarities make me think of all the times growing up when he would demand that I be more like Cal. How those comparisons made me feel worse when I was already at my lowest, and made it easier for me to convince myself to use.

None of that is Cal's fault, though, so I try not to take it out on him. Besides, I'm sure he's got his own trauma surrounding our dad to deal with.

"How are you doing?" I ask him, feeling a little more patient with him than usual.

He clears his throat, surprised by the question. Usually, I don't ask because I don't expect him to share, but today, I've decided to take the chance, and he seems appreciative. "I'm good. Work has been hectic."

I don't bother asking for details because I know he won't give them; being a special agent in the Federal Bureau of Investigation for almost twenty years has made him incredibly secretive, and making the move to the Secret Service has only made it worse. The one and only time I got details about his work was some years ago when he and his partner, Lance Beckham, headed up a task force that took down some white supremacist group plotting to kill the President, and that was only because it was all over the news.

"How's Beck?"

"He's good."

Closing the grill, I turn my attention to the pool where Riley is trying to coax her mom up onto one of the huge floats Taurin, and I blew up earlier today. Rae doesn't look convinced that the oversized swan can hold her, but she tries anyway, giggling as she tries to climb aboard. If she wasn't laughing, and I mean hard down, cracking up, she'd probably be able to get a better grip, but since she can't seem to control herself, she ends up slipping off of the float and taking Riley down with her. They scream loudly and then come up for air, sputtering water and grinning.

"What was that?" Cal asks; those fucking Secret Service agent ears trained to hear everything. I didn't tell him I had company because I didn't want to tell him about Riley and run the risk of him tainting the situation with his doubts about my ability to be a father. "Hunter, you good?"

"Yeah, I'm good." I push the words out past the lump of fear in my throat, knowing that if I don't give him further details, he'll probably have a drone flying over the property in a matter of minutes. "That was just Rae and Riley you heard screaming. They're in the pool, and one of the floats flipped over."

"Rae? Your ex-girlfriend, Rae?"

The qualification burns, but I don't correct him because it's not like it's wrong. "Yeah, that Rae."

"And Riley is...?"

I bite my lip, pride swelling in my chest. "Our daughter."

"You have a daughter?" There's no mistaking the incredulity in my brother's voice, but I'm surprised that I don't hear disapproval. "Since when do you have a daughter?"

Blowing out a breath of relief, I launch into the full story, telling him everything about how I came to learn that the most perfect kid on Earth belongs to me.

"Wow, Hunter." Cal sighs. "That's a lot. How are you doing with all of that?"

"I'm good," I tell him. "I'm really good, happier than I've been in a long time."

As I look across the yard at the two lights of my life, paddling around on the float they just capsized mere moments ago, I realize that it's true.

27

RAE

I t's after eleven o'clock when we finally settle in for the night. Hunter cleaned up the kitchen and washed all of our swimming gear in preparation for another day in the pool, per Riley's request, while I got Riley in the bath and bed in record time. After getting her straight, I took my time getting myself together, opting to use the hallway bathroom instead of the one in Hunter's room because my heart started to race at the thought of going in there, and now I'm staring at myself in the mirror wondering what the protocol is from here.

Do I just go to bed without saying goodnight?

Do I go back downstairs and...hang out with Hunter?

Do I climb into bed with Riley and hope he has the good sense not to come looking for me?

I don't know.

The first and third options seem rude, especially after such a lovely evening, but the second option feels wrong. Like I'm inviting trouble inside after flirting with it on my doorstep all day. Sighing, I pick up my phone and shoot a quick message to the group chat I have with Jayla and Dee, hoping that one of them will respond. It's a long shot since they both go to bed before the sun sets, but I have to try. After five minutes of nothing but radio silence from them, I'm left with no choice but to make a decision on my own.

And by decision, I mean leave the bathroom and go wherever my feet take me, which is to the stairs that lead back to the first floor. The lights are still on down there, and I can hear the faint sound of the dryer turning, so I know Hunter is still up. I creep down the stairs, not wanting the creaking of the old wood to wake Riley, and breathe a sigh of relief when muscle memory from all the months of sneaking around to keep our relationship a secret from Will allows me to dodge the loudest one.

Once on the first floor, I let the bond I work so hard to ignore when I'm around Hunter lead me to him. It's a silent tugging of my heartstrings that moves my arms and legs, turning me into a lovesick marionette. When I find him outside on the patio with a glass of sweet tea in front of him and a glass of red wine waiting for me, I feel less ridiculous for giving in to that bond because he was clearly listening to it, too.

"Thank you," I whisper, feeling shy as I take the seat beside him. "I didn't know you kept wine in the house."

"I don't. I bought it for you," he says, stretching his long legs out in front of him. He showered at some point, probably when I was upstairs deciding whether or not I wanted to come down, and I'm delighted to find that he still wears a black tank and shorts to bed.

Picking the glass up, I note that the wine has been chilled, which means he planned this little rendezvous. "Does it bother you? Because I can have something else."

"No." He turns a dark gaze on me, catching me off guard. "You know alcohol has never been one of my vices."

The way he says it makes my throat dry, so I bring the glass to my lips and take a sip before turning my focus to the dark expanse of land in front of us. Hunter eventually moves his attention to it, too, and we fall into a comfortable silence that reminds me of how easily we used to exist together. We could sit in silence for hours, wrapped around each other, trading kisses and touches but not words. I miss the ease we used to have, especially because I've never found it with anyone else.

"Was Riley disappointed she didn't get to see the treehouse?" Hunter asks, breaking into my thoughts.

"A little bit, but I told her you said we could walk down tomorrow morning, and then she was fine."

"I love having her here," he says, his voice low and rough with emotion. "I love having you here."

"We love being here."

There's no point in lying about it. No point in trying to make him feel like he isn't single-handedly responsible for the best day we've had in New Haven since we moved here.

"You can be here whenever you want, for however long you want."

"Careful," I chide, infusing levity into my tone. "If you let Riley hear that, we'll be here all the time."

Hunter's eyes glitter with an intensity that melts the forced smile right off of my face. "I wouldn't mind that. In fact, I'd prefer it."

I don't know why I'm stunned. The man isn't exactly good at hiding his feelings. I see the way he looks at me, the way he looks at Riley. I hear the things he doesn't say lingering between the lines of the things he does. I know him, and I know that every day he's spent getting to know his daughter has also been spent falling back in love with me.

Maybe he never stopped.

Because I didn't, I never stopped loving him.

Maybe we're just destined to live forever like this, unable to love anyone else because our unresolved feelings for each other won't let us. I mean, that has to be what's happening with me and Aaron, right? We didn't start falling apart like this, all of our broken pieces and frayed edges exposed, until Hunter was back in the picture, dragging my love for him up to the surface, making everything complicated and messy. The way it always is with us.

I take another long pull of my wine. "Pretty sure Aaron wouldn't be happy about that, though. Not that he's happy with anything I do these days." When a full minute goes by without Hunter responding, I shoot him a look. "Are you really not going to say anything?"

"You said you didn't want to talk about Aaron with me, so I'm trying to respect your wishes."

I wave a dismissive hand in the air. "That was earlier. Now I'm on my way to being wine-drunk, and I've changed my mind."

He arches a thick brow at me. "You haven't even had a full glass yet."

"I'm a mom now, Hunter, which means I'm a lightweight."

We both know that even if I was a lightweight, I haven't had enough alcohol to impair my judgment or make me change my mind about something I was just dead set on a few hours ago. Even if I had, Hunter doesn't look like he's in the mood to take advantage of my preparedness to break my own boundaries.

"Sunshine, we can't talk about Aaron until you're ready to do something about Aaron. Until then, save all your complaints for Dee and Jayla."

Ouch.

Hunter must see the hurt on my face because his features soften just a bit. "Talk to me about something else, anything else. Just not him."

I press my lips together, fighting against the sudden urge to cry and racking my brain for something to say that has nothing to do with Aaron, or even Riley, something that just has to do with me, something that's all mine that I can give him.

"Oh!" I shift in my seat, pulling one leg up to face him. "I finally decided on a name for my school."

Hunter's entire face lights up, and my chest goes warm and fuzzy. This. This is the energy I want to be met with when good things are happening for me. Not the negative and, oftentimes, lackluster reactions I get from Aaron.

"Tell me."

"En Pointe," I emphasize the words with a dramatic flourish of my hand that makes Hunter smile. "It's perfect, right? Because it encapsulates the beauty and rigor of ballet all at once."

Pointe work has always been synonymous with ballet. It's not always the most challenging part of being a ballerina, but it is the most well-known. I want the dancers I produce to be that closely intertwined with their chosen craft, their names and faces as easily associated with ballet as the term that inspired the name of the studio they trained at.

He nods his agreement. "I love it. Now, you need a logo."

"Already done."

"Well, you'll also need some branded merchandise. I have a guy who does my stuff for the gym; I could see if he could get you some stuff before your opening. When is it again?"

I bite my lip, excited about being asked questions about the project I've been dedicating every waking hour to lately. "The opening is going to be at the end of this month."

His eyes go wide. "Rae, that's fast."

"I know, but I know I can pull it off. Jayla and the other moms from The Ballet Academy have already signed their girls up, and we've been working on a short, choreographed piece for the opening so we can do a little showcase."

Once again, I'm sharing something with him I've been keeping to myself. And once again, he doesn't disappoint. "That sounds adorable."

"It's so cute," I gush, pulling out my phone to show him the video I took yesterday evening when we were practicing. Hunter leans in close, watching with rapt attention.

"They look so serious," he says, shaking his head. "Little ballerina robots."

I laugh. "Don't call them robots."

He turns serious all of a sudden, pulling back to put some distance between us. "I'm proud of you," he murmurs, the words hitting me right in the chest. "You're really going for it, and you're not compromising your dreams for anyone, not even Aaron."

I pull back, too, putting both of my feet back on the ground in hopes that it will stop me from feeling like I'm floating on a cloud. "I thought you didn't want to talk about Aaron," I say, taking a sip of my wine.

"I don't," Hunter scoffs. "Fuck Aaron."

His candidness makes me choke, sending droplets of red wine flying out of my mouth and onto my thighs. Hunter pushes to his feet and rushes inside, grabbing a dish towel and returning in a second flat. He drops down to his haunches in front of me, using gentle strokes to dry the liquid up but still managing to graze my thighs with his fingertips.

"You really don't like him, huh?" I suck in a breath.

Hunter taps my right knee, ignoring my question. I allow him to nudge them open. His eyes stayed glued to my face as his fingers guide the towel up, stopping mere inches from my clenched sex. He knows what he's doing. The way he licks his lips tells me as much, and I still don't move a muscle to stop him. In fact, I do the exact opposite, parting my legs further in a silent challenge for him to continue, for him to act on the heat gathering in his eyes.

For one blissful second, it feels like he will. His fingers dance up the inside of my thighs, the towel long forgotten, and I slide down in my chair to grant him even more access. But just as he's about to reach the hem of my very short nightie, he stops and stands, backing away from me with regret etched into his features.

"Goodnight, Sunshine."

THE NEXT MORNING I wake up in sheets that smell like Hunter and just a tad bit hungover because after I thoroughly embarrassed myself and got left hanging high, dry, and horny, I stayed up and finished the bottle of wine Hunter opened for me.

The sun is already out, but that's not what woke me up. I lay in bed for a second, trying to figure out what exactly pulled me out of unconsciousness, and then I hear it again. The pitter-patter of little feet making their way toward the door I'm currently hiding behind. I know it can't be anyone but Riley, and so I sit up, bracing myself for her inevitable entry.

Seconds later, she comes bursting through the door, giggling like she's running from someone, and hops in the bed with me. Well, not with me, on top of me, which makes me grunt as the door swings back closed, shrouding us in silence once more.

"Good morning, Mommy," she says, knees in my stomach as she climbs over me and settles onto the pillows I just had my head on. "How did you sleep?"

"I slept just fine, Nugget. How about you?"

She gives me a thumbs up, indicating a great night's sleep and making me smile. I'm so glad she feels comfortable here. Hunter's house has always felt like a home to me, a place where you can be settled and safe, and it makes me happy that Riley feels that, too.

"How long have you been up?" I ask, turning onto my side and tossing an arm over her.

"A while. I woke up and went downstairs looking for you, but Daddy said you were still sleeping. We went on a walk to the tree house while it was still dark. We watched the sunrise."

My heart squeezes as a flurry of emotions runs through me inspired by the images rolling through my mind. Hunter took Riley to our tree. I rub at my chest, pushing back the tears brimming in my eyes, so I don't alarm Riley.

"That sounds like a beautiful morning."

"It was the best morning!" She smiles. "Now, Daddy's making pancakes, and I'm in charge of drinks."

"Oh, that's a big job for such a little girl. Are you sure you're ready for that kind of responsibility?"

Riley rolls her eyes. "It's just juice, Mommy. I can do that easy."

"Of course you can," I assure her, smiling because she hates when I forget that she's a big girl who can do hard things. "Can I ask you something?"

"Yep," she says, popping her lips on the 'p'

"If you're in charge of juice, what are you doing up here with me?"

"Well, I came to see if you wanted orange juice or apple. Daddy said he trusted me to make a good choice for you, but I didn't want to choose wrong."

"Rileyyyy!" Hunter's voice comes through the door, followed by the sound of his footsteps, and I look at Riley, stretching my eyes wide.

"Uh oh, sounds like the boss is looking for you."

She giggles as Hunter calls out for her again. "Where'd you go, Nugget?"

"I'm in here with Mommy!" she shouts, sitting up just as he pushes the door open slowly and peeks his head through.

I sit up, too, because it feels weird to be seen lounging around in his bed, but I immediately regret the decision when Hunter's eyes fall on me. My nightie, which is just a white version of the one I spilled wine all over last night, is sheer, leaving very little to the imagination. Hunter's mouth hangs open as he studies me, his eyes traveling from my face down my neck and then to my chest, where my nipples are standing at attention, straining towards him through the thin fabric.

"Can we have breakfast in bed?" Riley asks, slicing through the building tension the way only a child can.

Hunter swallows, and his lips part like he's preparing to answer her question, but no words come out. I jump in, intending to save him by supplying an answer but only managing to make everything worse when I say, "No, sweetie, we don't want to make a mess in Daddy's bed."

28

HUNTER

Now

Puddles.

The first time I took Rae in my bed, she left puddles in my sheets. Big, wet, mattress-ruining puddles that made it necessary for me to invest in a waterproof mattress topper. Those damn puddles are the only thing on my mind as I make breakfast, burning pancake after pancake as her words about making a mess in my bed play over and over again on a loop.

We don't want to make a mess in Daddy's bed.

Fucking hell.

I want her to make a mess in my bed. I was going to make a mess of her in my bed last night, but I just couldn't do it. I didn't want a conversation about her shitty-ass boyfriend to be the catalyst for our first moment together in years. When I take her—and I *am* going to take her because I don't give a fuck about the floundering commitment she's made to Aaron, it'll be about us and only us.

Not him.

"It's burning again, Daddy."

I curse under my breath, scooping another charred-to-a-crisp pancake out of the pan and onto the plate I've designated for myself while Riley looks on, swinging her legs from her perch on the countertop by the stove. She's as adorable as she can be in her unicorn PJs and matching bedroom slippers. When she came down the stairs early this morning, I'd just gotten back from my run, which I'd intentionally pushed up just so I could get back before she or Rae knew I was gone.

Turns out, I'd timed it perfectly because my sleepy girl came down rubbing her eyes and looking for her mom mere minutes after I walked through the door. Since it was our first time spending a morning together, I didn't know what to expect from her mood. Didn't know if she was a crier or a grump like me. Turns out, she's neither. Well, at least with me. I remember Rae mentioning something about Riley not being a morning person, but that wasn't my experience at all. I guess it's true what people say about some kids saving the drama for their mama because Riley and I had the chillest morning in history. She talked me into taking her to see the treehouse, and I caved, giving her a ride on the Daddy Express so the morning dew didn't make her slippers wet.

We chatted all the way down to the edge of my property, with Riley telling me all about her dreams and asking me about mine. I had to lie because none of the images my brain conjured during the few hours of sleep I got were appropriate to share with my kid. Riley is still talking, and my attention is split into thirds, trying to focus on Riley's voice as she talks about the birthday party she's now apparently having at my house, not burning the last of the pancake batter, and Rae moving around upstairs all at the same time.

She's on the phone. Her voice is a low and concentrated whisper that makes it impossible for me to make out anything she's saying or decipher who she's saying it to. I don't think it's Aaron. He's probably still mad about her being here with me this weekend, and while I know the decision has caused her some distress, I can't help but feel grateful that she made it. I would have been happy just having Riley here, but something about Rae being here too, invading my space with her scent and making herself at home between my sheets, just makes everything so much better.

"All the bubbles have popped. Mommy says that means it's time to flip it," Riley is telling me now, prompting me to flip the pancake before it's resigned to the same fate as the others.

"Thank you, Nugget." I smile at her, letting my appreciation show on my face. "I couldn't have done it without you."

"Who's going to eat those?" She asks, eyeing the burnt stack with a mildly horrified expression.

I can't help but laugh. "Those are for me. The pretty, golden ones are for you and Mommy."

"Oh, good," she says, relief rushing over her features. "I don't like burnt ones."

"What's burnt?"

The sound of Rae's voice makes me turn around just in time to see her striding into the kitchen on bare feet. She's got a lightweight sundress with flowers all over the skirt and bodice, which hugs her breasts and makes it clear that she's not wearing a bra.

"Daddy's pancakes."

"But not yours or hers," I assure Rae as I lift Riley off the counter and set her on her feet. She doesn't waste any time rushing over to the table, taking a seat next to Rae who's laughing at me with her eyes. "What?" I ask, smiling despite myself. She's so damn beautiful like this. Well-rested and relaxed, with the light from the window over the sink spilling onto her features.

"Nothing, just waiting for you to demonstrate those cooking skills you were bragging about the other day."

"You won't have to wait much longer."

To prove my point, I set about fixing our plates in record time, adding a serving of bacon and eggs to each of them before bringing them over to the table that Riley set after we came back downstairs to let Rae get dressed. Riley digs in first, dousing her stack of perfectly golden cakes in syrup before passing the bottle over to her mom.

"This looks good," Rae admits, adding butter and syrup to her stack.

"Told you I could cook."

"Don't get too cocky. I haven't even tasted them yet."

"I have," Riley chimes through a mouth full of food. "They're really good!"

I arch a brow at Rae, and she rolls her eyes before taking a dainty bite meant to convey her skepticism. I watch her chew, all of my attention on the way her lips move and then how her throat works as she swallows.

"Well?" I ask, my voice unnecessarily husky.

She picks up her glass of orange juice, taking a slow sip just to keep me on the edge of my seat. Then she smirks. "They're all right."

"All right?" I rear back, placing a hand on my chest to feign offense. "You hear that Riley? I think your mom just challenged me to a pancake war."

Riley's eyes get big, ignoring Rae as she shakes her head, trying to reel us back in. "Yes! I want to have a pancake war! Can I be on my own team?"

Clearly exasperated but also a little amused, Rae places a calming hand on our daughter's shoulder. "How about you be the judge?"

"Oh, yeah, I like that idea," Riley says, her face turning serious. "I'm a good judge."

I nod, already devising a plan to bribe her. "You're the best judge."

Rae sees right through me, and I catch her rolling her eyes. "But most of all, Ri, you have to be a fair judge, and that means not taking any bribes."

"I won't take bribes," Ri swears, placing her hand over her heart like she's taking an oath. It's the cutest thing I've ever seen. "I promise."

"So when are we doing this?" I ask, finally taking a bite of my pancakes and trying to hide the grimace on my face when the acrid flavor of burnt butter hits my taste buds. Rae snickers under her breath and stands, placing her hands on her hips.

"Now."

I look up at her, my gaze slow and studious as I drag it up her body. "Now?"

"Yep. Right now." She tosses the words over her shoulder, hips swaying as she moves over to the fridge. "Unless you're scared?"

I glance at Riley who is already looking at me with wide eyes that ask if I'm going to pick up the gauntlet her mom has just thrown down. They grow even wider when I set my palms on the table and push to my feet, and stay glued to me as I move over to the counter across from Rae and smile.

"Remember, Sunshine, you wanted this."

RAE BEATS my ass in the pancake war.

I maintain that I let her win while she and Riley insist that her victory means I have to call her Queen Pancake for the rest of the day.

I oblige because there's really not much I won't do for the two of them.

We spend the afternoon and early evening in the pool because that's what Riley wants to do, and she wears me out with round after round of Marco Polo while Rae alternates between playing with us and reading a book she said she's been trying to finish since the beginning of the year.

It's a good day. The best day, and I'm sad when the sun goes down and we have to come inside because I know that it puts me one step closer to saying goodbye to them. After showers and post-pool snacks, Riley and I stretch out on the couch in the living room, watching a movie while Rae cooks dinner and sings along to the music playing on her phone.

"Does she take the bus all the way back to Minnesota?" I ask Riley, needing to know how things turn out for the little girl with my daughter's name that's currently on my TV screen. When my inquiry is met with silence, I glance down at my real-life Riley and smile when I see that she's fallen asleep curled up in a ball next to me with her feet in my lap.

Pulling out my phone, I snap a picture of her, wanting to preserve the moment forever. Then I slip out from underneath her and head into the kitchen to show Rae. She's slicing up chicken for the burrito bowls she insisted on making for us, but she pauses when she hears me approaching.

"Let me guess, she's asleep?"

I nod. "Passed out. She didn't even make it through the movie."

"She's seen it a million times," Rae says, beginning to run the blade through the meat again. "It's one of her favorites."

"Figures. She knew every line." I inch closer to the counter where she's standing, every cell in my body begging to be closer to her. "It smells good in here, Queen Pancake."

Her lips curve into that smile she always gives me when she's not trying to pretend like I don't make her happy. I'm glad to see it. I want to see it every day, to make her give it to me so often it becomes instinct when I'm around.

"Thank you. I was going to make a cheese quesadilla for Ri, but I guess that's not necessary now."

"Will she sleep for the rest of the night?"

I don't mean for it to sound the way it does, like I'm angling for one-on-one time with her, but I can't take it back, so it just sits in between us. Rae glances at me, her eyes filled with the memories of last night when my fingers were inching up her thighs, and licks her lips.

"Probably."

The silence that follows is pregnant with all the things that could mean for us, with all the things we could do to each other, with all the things we could share. Rae's eyes don't stray from my face, but I can't seem to keep my eyes on hers. I'm too busy devouring her body language, reading every relaxed muscle and strained breath while the beginning notes of a love song I once said reminded me of her echo in the room around us. The sound suddenly loud and jarring. Rae lifts her hand, her intention to stop the music and interrupt this moment clear.

"Don't," I murmur, stepping forward and holding out my hand to her. "Dance with me."

Rae knows what this moment is. She knows exactly where it's

going to lead, and while I'm thinking about how fitting it is that we'll find our beginning in this same room for the second time, she's trying to talk herself out of wanting it. I watch her bite her lip, shuffling her weight between her feet while the wheels in her mind turn and turn and turn, trying to come up with a way to get out of this.

But there is no way out.

That's the beauty and the curse of us.

She sighs and sets the knife down, stepping out from around the counter and placing her hand in mine. Sparks that feel like finally fly out from the small point of connection, and I pull her into me, moving slowly, so she has time to retreat if she wants.

She doesn't. She wants *this*. She wants me. That much is clear by the contented sigh that passes through her lips when her body is pressed to mine, my hands on her hips, and my mouth at her ear, murmuring the lyrics of a song I haven't played since she left me.

Rae's hands are up around my back, her fingers clutching me like a lifeline as we sway back and forth. Desire is a slow, hot brew that burns our veins and soaks the room with the scent of possibility.

"We can't," she whispers, asking me to stop her as she lifts up on her tiptoes and lays her lips on my neck. "Hunter. We can't."

My hands slip down her body further, gripping her ass in my palms and lifting her up off of the ground because if she's going to kiss me, she doesn't need to struggle for it. Despite her verbal expression of wanting to stop, Rae keeps going, wrapping her legs around my waist and trailing kisses up my neck and over my jaw until her mouth is hovering over mine. She's got her eyes squeezed shut, blocking out everything that's not this, that's not me, but I've been dreaming of this moment for months now, and I want those eyes on me.

"Look at me." Rae's always been a good girl. She's always been responsive and eager to please me, so her eyes pop open when I order them to. "I love you," I tell her, unable to hold the words back any longer. Her eyes turn into puddles of heat and emotion.

"I love you too," she whispers the words back, resting her forehead against mine as her body sags with a mixture of defeat and relief that tells me she's been fighting those words back for as long as I have.

My grip on her tightens, and she gasps her delight as I pull the hem of her dress up to caress her skin. "You're still the best thing I've ever held in my hands, Sunshine. Tell me I can hold you tonight. Tell me I can *have* you tonight."

We both know I want more than tonight, but it's all I have the courage to ask for. Rae's answer comes in the form of a searing kiss that steals my breath and causes me to stumble forward so I can sit her on the counter. The moment she's on solid ground, my hands go to either side of her face, holding her mouth to mine so I can explore her thoroughly.

It's been years since I've tasted her, but she's still that perfect mixture of sweet and forbidden, of danger and destruction. When she moans into me, sweeping her tongue into my mouth to relearn the flavor of my desire, I can't help but moan back, giving her more and more until the kiss is as filthy as the images that crowded my mind last night.

I pull back, which makes Rae whimper, and then sigh when I kiss my way down her neck, over her chest, and then go further still until I'm kneeling on the floor before her, her legs over my shoulders and my lips on the inside of her thigh, making their way to the soft heat of her core.

Rae has the kind of pussy you dream about eating for days. Puffy brown lips with a perfect pink center that you could get lost in. And my favorite thing about her is that she knows how good it is, too; she's not shy or hesitant about offering it to you. As soon as I make my intentions known, she's shimming down on the counter to get closer, putting that shit right in my face, forcing me to acknowledge that she doesn't have any panties on.

"You've been waiting for this all day, haven't you?" I ask, my lips grazing hers as they move. She rolls her hips but remains quiet, so I nip at her clit and repeat myself. "Haven't you, Sunshine?"

"Yes," she hisses, using one of those long legs to force my face closer. "So give me what I want, Hunter."

Unwilling and unable to deny her, I dive in, using my tongue to part her folds and groaning when the sweetness of her essence explodes in my mouth. *"Fuck,* Rae, has this pussy gotten even sweeter?"

She doesn't answer, just moans and writhes under my touch and the relentless thrashing of my tongue until she comes apart around me so quickly and quietly that I almost don't realize that it's happened. I might have missed it if it wasn't for the quivering of her thighs and the fucking rainstorm of an orgasm that has her release dripping down my chin and onto my neck.

Puddles, I think, laughing to myself as I wonder how my girl can be sunshine and rain all at the same time.

Not one to waste a drop of the euphoria I worked so hard to wrench from her body, I lap at Rae until she's squirming and reaching down to push me away.

"Enough," she pants, chest heaving.

I shake her off, going in for more, desperate to make the moment last. "It's not enough, Sunshine. It'll never be enough."

She pushes up on her elbows, looking down the long line of her body at me. "I can't come again."

I frown, knowing for a fact that she's capable of more than one orgasm in a night. Once, on a really good day, I gave her five. I know because I made her count them.

"Yes, you can," I assure her, standing up so I can curve my body over hers. She shudders out a breath when I rub my erection against her, and I consume the sound in a quiet kiss.

Rae breaks it, shaking her head as she glances toward the living room where the ending credits of the movie are now playing. "Riley could wake up, we should—"

"Riley is sound asleep, Sunshine."

"But she could hear—"

I cut her sentence short by looping her legs around my waist and picking her up. Her eyes are wide as I carry her the short distance to the laundry room and kick the door closed. The dryer is going again, and the gentle hum creates a noise barrier that will make it impossible for any sound to escape. I pin Rae against the door and kiss her again.

"There. Now, you can be as loud as you want when you come again."

She lets her head rest against the door. "I already told you I can't."

"With him," I say, my voice a lethal whisper. "That might be true with him, but that's never been true with me, and you know it."

To demonstrate my intent to show her, I let my hands move from her hips to the band of my shorts and push them down just enough to free my dick. Rae gasps when she feels the tip brush her ass, and she moans when I drag it through her folds and up to her entrance.

Her hands go to my shoulders, nails digging into my skin. "Hunter."

"Do you want me to stop?"

She bites her lips, her body already betraying her act of hesitance as she rocks against me. "No," she says finally, the heat of her breath fanning over my lips. "I don't want you to stop."

I push forward, giving her just the tip first and loving the way her eyes flare with determination as she adjusts to the feel of me. Widening my stance, I stroke up, giving her a few inches more before pulling back and starting the maddening process all over again.

Rae's teeth dig into her bottom lip as one set of fingers leaves my shoulder to trail up my neck, gripping the back of my head to pull me down for a kiss. I love kissing Rae. I always have, but tonight, when I'm trying to be patient and careful, it's the kind of distraction I don't need. Still, I indulge her, worshiping her with reverent kisses while I feed my length into her inch by inch.

When I'm fully seated, she breaks the kiss with a hiss.

"You haven't gotten bigger, right?" She asks, panic in her eyes. "That's not a thing, is it?"

"No, Sunshine," I laugh. "That's not a thing." I pull back and stroke up into her again, watching her eyes roll back into her head. "You're just not used to taking a dick this big anymore."

"Oh my God," she cries, her face scrunching up in a mix of plea-surable pain as I start up a smooth rhythm that causes the flared head of my dick to hit that spot deep inside her I suspect hasn't been touched in years. She starts to move with me, meeting me thrust for thrust as we chase that feeling that's uniquely ours. That drugging brand of ecstasy that only exists when I'm inside of her, and she's wrapped around me, her walls rippling around me while my dick drives through her soaked channel until she succumbs to the inevitable.

Not just the pleasure of another orgasm, which I give her two more times before I let myself spill into her with long, hot spurts of cum that coat her walls, but the love that makes it possible. That makes it more powerful than anything we'll ever share with anyone else.

29

RAE

I'm not a person who gives in to their nerves easily. Being a ballerina doesn't allow for it. When I walk onto a stage, I have to be perfect, and there's no room for anxiety in perfection. There's only mastery. There's only certainty. There's only me and the trust that I have, not just in my training but in myself.

Most days, I'm living, breathing confidence on the outside, and deep, deep down, underneath all of the reminders to be two times better than my white counterparts to get half as much, is the anxiety, the fear, the doubt.

But that's most days.

Today, everything is upside down. The confidence of love is under layers of nerves and fear that have nothing to do with me leaving for New York tomorrow to start my career as a member of the American Ballet Theatre's corps de ballet, and everything to do with my big brother's narrowed eyes as they study my hand, which is clutched in Hunter's.

Hunter, who is always fearless and certain about everything, is stone-faced as he looks at Will, determined to be strong for me even though this must be hard for him, too. Will isn't just his sponsor—a source of support in his endeavor to stay clean—he's also his friend. Right now, the longevity of that bond rests on the words that are about to come out of my brother's mouth, and, judging by the frown marring his features, those words are not about to be good.

"Say something, Will," I plead, my eyes shifting around the restaurant. It was my idea to break the news to him in public, using my going away dinner as a cover. I thought it would help amend his reaction, keeping him from saying or doing something stupid, like trying to tell us that we can't do this because Hunter and I have already decided that we are.

It's been two months of us sneaking around the house when Will is home and fucking all over it when he's not, and while I thought it was time to come clean, I'm now thinking it would have been smarter to take this secret to the grave.

"Please," I add, reaching over with my free hand to take his.

For a moment, I think he's going to pull away, but he doesn't. I let out a sigh of relief and squeeze his fingers, urging him to look at me. When he does, his face, which is slightly thinner than it was at the beginning of the summer, is filled with tension.

"How long?"

"Since my four-year mark," Hunter says.

Will lifts a brow and lets out a low whistle. "Two months, which means I was only in the dark for one."

My jaw drops, which causes Will to crack. His shoulders start to shake first, and then his face breaks out into his signature smile. I let go of his hand and punch him in the shoulder.

"You're such an asshole!"

He clutches at his stomach, doubled over. "You two do know that I live in the same house as y'all, right? You know that I was at the meeting where Hunter held up a chip and said, 'This is for everything we are and everything we'll become'?"

Hunter grimaces at Will's poor imitation of him, but he's smiling. They're both smiling, which makes me smile even if I am still pissed at Will for sending my heart to live in my stomach.

"I'm honestly surprised it took y'all this long to work this out," Will is saying now, his face turning serious as he reaches for my hand again. "But I'm glad you did."

My chest is warm with relief. "So you're not mad?"

Will's brows furrow. "Rae, you're a grown woman. It's not my job to dictate who you can or can't be with, and as far as choices go, you could do a lot worse than this guy."

"Gee, thanks," Hunter says, his tone dripping with sarcasm.

Will grins at him, not at all bothered by his tone. "So what does this mean for New York?"

"Nothing has changed," Hunter tells him, not even giving me the chance to answer because he knows I've gone back and forth about my decision to leave. I want ballet, but I want him too. I want what we've been building for the past four years, what we've found in each other in the last two months. It feels wrong to just abandon it now, to just abandon him.

But he won't let me change my mind.

"I'm still leaving tomorrow," I confirm, my stomach filled with equal parts excitement and dread. "We're going to do long distance."

Hunter hears the pain in my voice, and he looks at me with eyes that are certain enough for the both of us. "I'm going to come visit once a month; we'll talk on the phone every day and do video calls once a week. We'll make it work."

Tears crowd my eyes, but I nod. "We'll make it work."

Will looks between us, and there's something odd in his expression as he picks up his glass of sparkling water and holds it in the air for a toast. Hunter and I join him, and I push my fears and doubts down, leaving only room for the happiness of this moment with the two most important men in my life.

"To your futures," Will says, clinking our glasses together. "May you always have love. May you always have each other."

30

HUNTER

Then

"I'm going to be Juliet!" Rae whisper-screams through the phone. It's the fifth time she's said it, and each time, there's a little less shock in her voice. "I can't believe it, Hunter. I don't think the company has ever had a Black Juliet before."

"Even if they have, she probably can't hold a candle to you." I push the words out past the lump in my throat that's all dashed hopes and disappointment I can't express.

Two months.

That's how long she's been gone. That's how long it's been since I've held her in my arms or woken up next to her. That's how long it's been since I've kissed her lips. We were supposed to do monthly visits; that's what we promised each other, but last month, when I scraped up enough to buy the flight, Rae had to call and cancel because a friend of a roommate's friend invited her to their Hamptons rental for the weekend.

Now we're going to miss out on each other again because one of the principal dancers hurt her ankle, which led to her roles being divided among a few of the girls in the corps de ballet. Rae, the little overachiever that she is, already knows all of the choreography, but now that she's officially going to be dancing the part, she wants to spend all of her time in the studio, which means she has none for me.

"Are you okay?" she asks, some of that excitement dying as she catches on to my mood. I try to shake it off, turning away from the packed duffel on my bed with the square, black box sitting on top of it.

"I'm good, Sunshine. I'm so proud of you. I know you're going to do an amazing job."

She sighs. "I'm really sorry I have to cancel again. I just—"

"You don't have to explain, and you don't have to apologize. This is what you're supposed to be doing, building your career, grabbing on to every opportunity."

Leaving me behind.

The words pop into my head on their own. An unwelcome addition to thoughts that were already hard for me to lend my voice to. Not because I don't mean them, because, of course, I do, but because it hurts to keep feeling like I'm getting lost in the shuffle.

"I miss you," she breathes, and my eyes fall shut at the severity in her tone when she delivers the words. "I miss you so much it hurts. This is so much harder than I thought it would be."

"I know, baby, but we can do hard things, can't we?"

Trying to encourage her when all I want to do is wallow in my own sorrow is a feat. A test of strength I find myself having to take more often than I'd like to these days. I knew this wasn't going to be easy, living over ten hours apart, never seeing each other, barely talking, and rarely being able to video chat, but I didn't think it would be this fucking hard.

"Yeah," she says, the small bit of confirmation drowned out by the abrupt melody of voices that signal the arrival of her roommates and their friends. They'll want to celebrate with her, take her out to dinner, snag cheap bottles of wine, and sneak them into the studio so they can make sure she knows every step and turn.

"You should go," I tell her, my heart aching as I prepare to say goodbye.

"What? No, this is the first time we've talked all day."

"I know. You can call me back when you get home from celebrating with your friends."

"Will you wait up for me?" she asks, her tone half regret, half excitement.

"Of course I will," I promise, even though I know that no matter how long I stay up, she won't remember to call. "I love you, Sunshine."

"I love you too, Hunter."

The line goes dead, and I turn back to my bed, pushing out sharp, even breaths to try and soothe the ache in my chest that's always with me in Rae's absence. I move over to the bed and begin to unpack, picking up the black box on top of my bag first. Despite knowing that looking at the piece of jewelry inside will only make the pain in my chest worse, I pop it open and brush a thumb over the gold band and sunbursts of diamonds I emptied out my savings for.

I planned to give it to Rae this weekend, to get down on one knee and ask her for forever, to tell her that I was willing to do whatever I needed to do to have that with her—sell the gym, the house, and my land, move to New York and get three different jobs just to afford the outlandish rent in whatever borough she felt most comfortable. But now, it's going into my sock drawer, set aside the same way I've been, hoping that one day soon, it'll get a chance to come back out.

Once I'm done unpacking, I grab my keys and hop in the car, deciding to hang with Will for the weekend. He was more than happy to entertain me last month when my trip got canceled, and I'm hoping he'll be even more understanding this time around when I tack myself onto all of his weekend plans because missing Rae is a little bit easier when I'm doing it with him. He feels her absence, but he's not destroyed by it. It's like he's perfected the art of loving her and letting her go. I don't know that I'll ever be able to do that.

As I turn on Will's street, taking note of the flashing lights of an ambulance in the near distance, it occurs to me that maybe I should figure it out. That maybe truly supporting her doesn't look like just encouraging her to fly but actually giving her space to spread her wings. Before I can determine whether I'm being wise or ridiculous, the whoop of the ambulance draws my attention again. And it's only as I'm approaching the house Rae and Will grew up in that I realize how close it is to where I'm going.

No, that's wrong.

It's not just close to my destination, it's *at* my destination. The large red and white vehicle with the siren still wailing is parked haphazardly in the driveway, right behind Will's car, and so I'm left with no choice but to park on the curb by the mailbox. To run across the grass to the open front door screaming Will's name while my brain tries to work out what the fuck I'm going to tell Rae.

Someone stops me with a hand on my chest right inside the door. "Sir, you can't be here."

I glance down at the woman, barely seeing her or the EMT uniform she's wearing because I'm too afraid, too angry at being stopped when I need to be moving, need to be helping, need to be figuring out what the fuck is going on.

"Wilson Prince," I tell her. "The guy who lives here. Where is he?"

"Are you family?" she asks, her voice stern, blue eyes serious.

I don't hesitate, don't think about the fact that there's not a drop of blood between us, that a random, injured ankle stole my one chance to make us family officially, I just answer. "Yes, I'm his brother."

31

RAE

"C ancer?!"

Bile rises in my throat, and I swallow it back down, determined not to get sick in the middle of the practice studio. It's already bad enough that the other dancers are staring, their eyes filled with concern and opportunity as they wonder if that one small word is going to take me out of the game the way Aaliyah's ankle took her out.

Not a chance in hell.

I think the words even as doubt swoops in, forcing me to face reality, to acknowledge the quiet tugging sensation in my gut as concern and fear draw me back to New Haven.

"Cancer?" I repeat, disbelief wrapped around the word.

"Yeah, Sunshine," Hunter breathes, his voice full of sorrow and apology. "The MRI revealed a mass on his prostate. The biopsy confirmed that it was cancerous."

I shudder, hating that I don't have any questions or confusion around the process. It's all so familiar to me, an echo of my experience with Mommy's diagnosis.

"Rachel, do you need a moment?" Marcelo asks from across the room. He's standing by the speaker, having stopped the music when I told him I needed to answer my phone. I've been waiting for this call from Hunter and Will all day, desperate to get some answers about the back pain that sent Will to the hospital a week ago. And now that I have it, I don't want it. I don't want the answer. I don't want a moment. I just want to dance, to lose myself in the predictability of the choreography, and leave the uncertainty of life to everyone else.

But I can't do that, so I look at Marcelo and hold up my hand, asking for five minutes. He nods and shoos me away, and I go, conscious of the fact that the remaining girls in the room huddle up as soon as I turn my back to them.

Fucking vultures.

When I step into the hallway, I lower myself to the floor and press my back against the wall, taking the time to rest because I've been at the studio all day, trying to perfect the timing of the pas de deux in the scene where Romeo and Juliet confess their love for each other.

"What stage?" I ask finally, closing my eyes as one lone tear escapes.

I know it's not going to be good when Hunter sighs heavily before he says, "Three."

"Fuck." I pull my legs up to my chest and hug my knees, images of the past few months rolling through my mind. All the signs were there. The weight loss. The lack of an appetite. The back pain. It was all right there in front of me, and I just ignored it. *"Fuck."*

"Don't cry, Rae Rae," Will says, his soft voice ensuring that I do exactly what he's just asked me not to. The tears come hot and fast, and I can't stop them. My brother is sick.

He's sick, and I'm not there.

He's sick, and I'm scared.

He's sick, and it's not fair.

"This is so unfair," I sob, my hand over my mouth as I try to quiet the pain. "Why does it have to be you?"

Why does it have to be me?

The unspoken question floats around in my head, bouncing off of the images of my mother's face, the memories of port placements, chemo infusions, and daily radiation appointments just for nothing to work. Just the thought of it all gives that tugging sensation strength, turning it into an incessant pull that I feel dragging me back to New Haven, demanding I surrender my life and my dreams to this beast of a disease that only exists to steal away everything I hold dear.

"It's not fair. It's not fair," I murmur over and over again, unable to stop.

"I know, Sunshine," Hunter says, and the gentle strength in his tone reminds me that he does know. "But we have to be strong for Will, okay?"

"And I'm going to be strong for y'all," Will chimes in. "Do you hear me, Rae? I'm going to fight, and I'm going to beat this thing, okay? I promise."

He can't promise.

He knows that.

Cancer patients aren't supposed to make promises to their family members. We're supposed to make promises to them. Vows of love and support and sacrifice. That's what I'm supposed to be giving Will right now, but my mouth won't open. The words won't come out, and I feel awful because I'm supposed to be able to give them to him. I'm supposed to be able to tell him that I'll come home and I'll take care of him. That while he's fighting, I'll be in his corner of the ring, but I can't do it. I can't bring myself to promise that I'll come home and watch him die.

"*We're* going to beat this thing," Hunter says to Will, but the words are a soothing, reassuring salve to my soul. "I don't want you to worry about anything, Sunshine. The doctors have already come up with a game plan, and we're going to follow their instructions to the letter. I'm going to take some time off from the gym so I can take him to all of his appointments. I've got him covered, okay?"

Relief mixed with the purest love courses through my veins. I nod, even though Hunter can't see me. "Okay."

32

HUNTER

Then

T he last person I watched suffer through the hell of cancer was my mother.

It took her quickly, so the battle didn't last long, but that doesn't mean that the days went quickly. Every second felt like an hour, every hour a decade, every breath a struggle. I've never seen time go by that slowly. If I hadn't lived it myself, hadn't sat by her bedside holding my breath and watching her chest, not breathing until she gasped and sputtered for air, I wouldn't have believed it could.

I used to look back at the short time between her diagnosis and her death and think God was cruel for not giving her time to truly fight, to show the disease what she was made of, but after the last few months of watching Will be decimated by the most aggressive forms of chemo and radiation, I've changed my mind.

This is cruelty.

The lingering and prolonged suffering. The volleying between hope and despair. The constant appointments, filled with poking and prodding and infusions that leave him weak and frail for days.

And the fatigue isn't even the worst side effect. No, that'd have to be the nausea that guarantees he'll vomit on the way home or the dryness that leaves sores in the roof of his mouth, or the darkened skin on his hands that make me feel like I'm watching him decay in real time.

But perhaps the cruelest thing of all is his smile because it hasn't changed even though he's dropped fourteen pounds in the last month. It's still as wide and awe-inspiring as it was the first day I met him. He likes to smile at me all the time, even when he's too weak to talk, and I take it as his way of letting me know he's alright, so I can pass the message along to everyone who calls to check on him because in-person visits stopped being a thing after a runny nose turned into pneumonia, which almost killed him.

"How is he?" Rae asks, her voice distant and far away, just like she's been for months. She came home to visit for a weekend right after Will got the diagnosis. That was back when things were more hopeful, when we could still go to meetings and our world hadn't shrunk down to include nothing but each other and the host of medical professionals trying to keep him alive.

"He's alright." I stretch out on the couch, my back aching from sleeping in the recliner in Will's room all night long. There are plenty of beds to choose from in this house, but I prefer to stay close, to make sure he doesn't need anything. "Sleeping right now."

"How many more treatments does he have left again?"

My jaw clenches. I don't know how to tell Rae that there is no number in mind now. That the doctors told me today that the infusions are the only thing staving off the cancer that's invaded everything, including his lungs.

"They've changed the protocol, so I'm not sure." I hate lying to her, but Will told me I had to. He made me promise to keep her in the dark about how bad things have gotten because, by some sick twist of fate, Rae's life is improving while his health is rapidly declining. Her successful debut as Juliet has led to her being promoted to a principal role, which has made her a shoo-in for the lead in other company productions. It won't be long before other, larger companies are looking to poach her, which means she'll have the world at her feet any day now.

Will told me he didn't want anything, not even him, to stop her from focusing on her dreams, and I'm not in any position to deny a dying man his last wishes.

"Oh, could you send me the new schedule?"

"Of course, Sunshine."

She goes quiet, and I listen to the hustle and bustle of the city through her end of the line, missing people more than I thought I ever would. It's hard being here alone with Will day in and day out, especially when he's sleeping most of the time and sick the rest of it. Before this little stint in quarantine, I thought I preferred to be alone, but now I'm desperate for human connection.

And I need a meeting, *badly*, because, as it turns out, watching someone you love die is triggering as hell.

"How are you doing?" Rae asks, pulling me out of my head. "I know spending all day, every day, catering to someone else's needs isn't easy."

There's a hint of guilt layered in between her words, and I hate it. I hate hearing it, hate the way it seems to be calling me a failure. When Will got the diagnosis, I swore to Rae that I would take care of him. I told her she didn't need to worry, but every time I hear that guilt, it feels like she is worrying, that she's concerned that I'm cracking under the pressure.

I am, but I won't tell her that.

"I'm fine, Rae. Finally got all my equipment delivered, so I can start working out again."

The equipment got here a week ago, and everything is still in boxes on the porch, but I don't mention that. I also don't mention that the urge to work out left me a long time ago, that ordering the equipment was a Hail Mary meant to jump-start the desire again, but now all the shit is on the porch, and the money is gone from my already dwindling bank account, and I can't bring myself to touch it, which just makes me feel worse.

"Good!" I can hear the smile in her voice, and it makes me smile.

It's the first time I've smiled since we last talked. She's the only bright spot in all of this, and our conversations are few and far between, which means I spend a lot of time in the bleak reality of her childhood home that feels like a hospice wing.

"Did you make it to the studio yet?"

"Just got here," she breathes, the smile in her voice fading right along with the one on my face. "I'll call you later, okay?"

"I'll wait by the phone."

Rae giggles, but I'm serious. My phone has become a lifeline, one that only operates correctly when she's the one on the other end.

"Bye, silly. I love you."

"Love you too, Sunshine."

After we hang up, I close my eyes, intending to rest for a second before going to check on Will, but ending up falling asleep. When I wake up, the house is eerily quiet, silent in a way that makes my blood run cold. My heart drops as I rise from my spot on the couch and creep down the hallway toward the bedroom to confirm what I already know to be true.

I know this silence.

I felt the weight of it sit like a brick on my chest when I came in from getting the mail and found my mom dead in the living room. Her eyes were still open, gazing out the window, wide and unseeing. I had to close them. God, I hope I don't have to close Will's too.

Tears have already gathered in my eyes, and my heart is pounding with fear and anticipated grief as I push the door open. Will is still. He's so fucking still, and his eyes are closed. If it wasn't for the absence of the rising and falling of his chest, he'd look like he was sleeping.

"Will?" I call his name even though I know he won't answer, and my voice breaks when I'm met with silence. My knees give out, and I hit the floor hard, which leaves me with no choice but to crawl over to him, sobbing as I put my fingers to his neck to confirm that there's no pulse.

He's still warm.

That's the thought that keeps playing in my mind over and over again as I dial 911 and explain to the operator that this isn't an emergency. It's what's on my mind as I open the door for the coroner and the police and go through the motions of gathering his medicine and doctor's information and everything else they need before they take him away. It's what's on my mind when everyone, including Will, is gone, and I'm left with nothing else to do but call Rae and let her know.

It's been hours since we spoke, which means she's probably at home now. Resting. Relaxing. Unaware that her world has changed forever.

"Hey, baby," she says, all cheer and ignorance. "What's up?"

"Rae..."

I can't say anything else. I don't need to. She hears it in my voice—the truth of her loss and my failure—and she doesn't respond. Not verbally, at least. She just wails. The sound is loud, long, and broken, and I slide down the wall across from the hospital bed that's all she has left of her brother and cry with her. We cry together until Rae drops the phone and someone else picks it up, until the chorus of voices I've come to associate with her roommates fills my ears, and one of them, a girl named Zoila, comes on the line.

"Hunter?"

We've never spoken, but I recognize her voice. She's the one always cooking for Rae. I wipe my eyes, trying to pull myself together. "Yeah?"

"When did it happen?"

"A few hours ago."

"Oh," she says, her voice soft as someone else shushes Rae and murmurs that it's going to be alright. It's a lie, but I should be the one telling her that. I should be the one comforting her right now.

"Can you put Rae back on the phone, please?"

"She's pretty upset," Zoila says. "Let me calm her down and have her give you a call back."

"No, I—" I start to protest, but the call has already ended. Bringing the phone down from my ear, I stare at it, letting all the rage of this loss and the abrupt dismissal build and build until I can't hold it anymore and send the phone flying across the room. It slams into the rail of the hospital bed and bounces off before clattering onto the floor and sliding underneath it.

For a moment, I consider leaving it there, thinking it might be for the best, but then it starts to ring. The light from the screen illuminates the underside of the bed, drawing me in like a moth to a flame. Realizing it might be Rae calling me back, I army crawl across the floor, lying on my stomach as I reach for the phone. I find it in seconds and coax it out with my fingertips, frowning when the move results in the sudden appearance of a bottle of pills.

It comes rolling out slowly, the round, white pills chiming lightly as they bounce off the plastic walls. The welcoming notes of destruction. I grab the bottle and sit up, bracing myself against the side of the bed while the phone lies forgotten next to me. I don't even know if it's still ringing. That's how focused I am on the bottle. How entranced I am by the white pills that were my introduction to addiction.

How fitting that they would appear now when I'm at my lowest.

Will refused to take any of the pain pills he was prescribed. He actually made me flush them every time his palliative care doctor would send us home with them, insisting that he'd need them, that his sobriety was the least of his concerns. I'm not sure how this bottle escaped our notice, but right now, when the pain is a blazing fire burning in my chest, and all I want is to be numb, I'm glad they did.

33

RAE

Then

There's this moment after someone you love dies when you realize that you'll have to spend every day of the rest of your life reminding yourself that they're gone. That you'll never hear their voice again, that no matter how many times you dial their number, they won't ever answer. For me, that moment comes when my plane lands and everyone pulls out their phones, turning off airplane mode and sending texts to let the people who are waiting for them know that they made it safely.

I pull my phone out too, send a text to Zoila, Dee, Hunter and then I type out a text to Will. My finger hovers over the send button, and I'm just about to press it when my brain catches up to reality. When I realize that I could hit send, and the text would go through, but Will won't receive it.

That reality destroys me.

It sets the tears I've been holding back for the week it's taken me to get the courage to return to New Haven free. It turns me into the weird lady who's crying on an airplane, in baggage claim, and in the passenger pick-up area that everyone sees but tries not to look at. It makes me a sad, sobbing mess that collapses into her boyfriend's arms the moment he loads her suitcases in the back of his truck and opens them for her.

"I'm right here, baby. I'm right here," Hunter murmurs into the rat's nest of curls I haven't washed in a week. He squeezes me tight, rocking me back and forth while the world moves on around us.

"Hey! You gotta keep moving," someone shouts at us, blowing a whistle that sets Hunter in motion. He lets me go, ushering me into the truck and slamming the door once I'm inside. Through the side mirror, I watch him turn toward the guy with the whistle, and even though I can't see his face, I can read his posture. I can see the tension lining his shoulders and the hostility in his body as he approaches the man. Despite being the authority in this space, the guy backs away, shaking his head as Hunter advances on him, heedless of the fact that he's got his hands up in a universal sign of surrender.

I roll my window down just in time to hear the man tell Hunter that he doesn't want a problem. Hunter puts one thick finger into the man's chest.

"Blow that fucking whistle at me again, and you'll have more than a problem," he growls. "You think I give a shit if people are upset about me spending five seconds comforting the love of my life when she's just flown in for *her brother's funeral*?"

"Sir, I understand, but this is a pickup zone. It's my job to keep things moving."

"Did you hear what I just said? I don't give a fuck about your job. I give a fuck about her." He hooks his thumb over his shoulder, pointing at me. "Your job description and your whistle don't mean shit to me." The pickup area is loud, filled with the sounds of idling engines, squealing brakes, and more, but Hunter is loud. Loud enough to draw the attention of several people standing around. One lady, a wiry, petite redhead in a yoga set, starts to look around, probably trying to find security, which is when I decide to hop out of the truck and intervene.

"Hunter, you've gotta stop," I tell him, placing a staying hand on his shoulder. When he turns around to look at me, his eyes are wide and wild, filled with anger that only dissipates a little when he realizes that it's me. "Please," I plead, tears born of fear and exhaustion brimming in my eyes, "I just want to go home." My hand slides down his arm until our fingers are linked together. "Can you please just take me home?"

For a moment, I think he's going to shrug me off, that's just how pissed he is, how far outside of himself he is, but then he calms. His eyes focus on my face, and he pushes out a steadying breath as he squeezes my fingers. Then he nods, and everyone around us, but especially the object of his aggression, breathes a sigh of relief.

"Yeah, Sunshine."

The drive from the airport is quiet and tense and sad, but Hunter holds my hand the whole way, which forces me to remember that I'm not alone. He's in this with me. He's sad like I'm sad, hurt like I'm hurt, but because he's here and we're together, I'm not alone in any of it.

When I realize that we're heading to my house and not Hunter's, I break the silence. "Why aren't we going to your place?"

Hunter glances at me. "You said you wanted to go home."

"I know, but not—" I swallow, pushing the words out past the lump of emotion in my throat that's inspired by the thought of going back to the house where my brother died. "I can't go there. I don't want to go there. I want to go to our home."

It's the last place I had good memories with Will. Where we celebrated my graduation from college and hugged each other goodbye when I left for New York, it's where I want to be because it's where Hunter is, where he's been since Will left, and I want to sit in our tree and cry.

"Okay," he says, changing lanes and heading in the direction of his house while I close my eyes, letting my brain wander from one heart breaking thought to the next until they're forced to pop open again.

"Why didn't you tell me it had gotten worse?" I whisper, voicing the question I've been asking myself since I got the call that changed my life. I've been meaning to ask Hunter, but between the crying and funeral arrangements—most of which he has handled—I could never find the time.

Hunter's knuckles bulge as he grips the steering wheel. "He didn't want you to know. When they told him it was in his lungs, I asked him to let me call you, to explain that his prognosis had changed, but he said if I did you'd drop everything and come home, and he didn't want you to do that."

More tears. This time, because Will's certainty in my dedication to him is a direct affront to the shaky commitment I've demonstrated over the past few months. I've called and texted and checked in after every appointment. I even came home right after the cancer was confirmed. But I wasn't committed to him. I wasn't here for him, not the way I was for Mommy. Not the way he would have been here if it was me.

I've spent a lot of time feeling guilty about that, but it was never enough to move me. To pull me out of the fear and pain-induced paralysis that's lived inside me since the care and well-being of my only parent fell on my shoulders. I didn't know that it was there until Will got sick. I didn't know that when faced with the choice to show up and fight or stay frozen in place, that I would freeze. That my muscles would seize up and my heart would go numb, and my mind would force out everything that was too serious and too painful, refusing to hold on to it for longer than a second.

My bottom lip trembles as the tears fall in hot streams that I can't bother to wipe. Hunter doesn't explain further. He just offers me his hand and lets me dig my nails into his skin because the pain is too much. And when we get home, he unloads my suitcase and takes it into the house while I leave a trail of tears on the way to our tree. I climb up on the lowest branch and sit out there for hours, shedding tears that are carried off by the chilly November air.

The sun has gone down by the time Hunter comes to get me, and I'm surprised that he's let me stay out here for so long. He's carrying a blanket that he slings around my shoulders before he wraps his arms around me and picks me up.

"You're going to catch a cold," he says, adjusting his grip to make sure he doesn't drop me. He's a little unsteady on his feet, and I don't know if it's because he's tired or because the ground is uneven, but he doesn't drop me, and I'm not worried for a single second that he will.

"I don't care if I get sick," I tell him, laying my head against his chest.

"I care."

And it's enough. His care. His concern. It's enough to stop me from arguing, enough for me to snuggle into his warmth and allow myself to be comforted by the beating of his heart.

When we're inside, Hunter sets me on the counter beside a bowl of soup. I'm not hungry, but I still open up when he stands between my legs with a spoon in his hand and orders me to.

"You cooked?" I ask, swallowing the warm broth, shredded chicken, and spiral noodles down without swallowing.

"Nate brought it by," he grimaces at the mention of Will's sponsor, and I wonder what the issue is with the two of them. "I just warmed it up."

"That was nice of him."

I make a mental note to call Nate and thank him. He's been trying to get in touch with me all week, probably just to check in, but I haven't answered. I haven't done a lot of things I'm supposed to do.

"His wife made it," Hunter says, feeding me another bite, this one full of perfectly tender carrots and onions. "All he did was drive it over so he could get in my ass about not returning his calls."

"You've been ignoring him too."

One corner of Hunter's mouth kicks up. It's not quite a smile, but he's no longer grimacing. He tries to put the spoon to my mouth again, but I push his hand away, guiding the spoon back to the bowl.

"Sunshine, you have to finish eating."

"I don't want to eat."

Hunter drops the spoon, and I shrug off the blanket before wrapping my arms around his neck and pulling him down for a kiss. He gives in easily; maybe he doesn't want to feel either. Maybe he needs the connection as much as I do. Whatever the reason, I'm grateful because it's exactly what I need. Everything else falls away as my hands start to explore his body and his do the same in return.

He cups my breasts, running his thumbs over my nipples before gripping the hem of my sweatshirt and pulling it up over my head. I shiver under the weight of his gaze and the heat of his lips when he lays kisses down my neck, across my chest, moving from one breast to the other while I cradle his head in my hands.

"I've missed you," he lays the confession over my heart, and tears blur my vision, so I close my eyes.

"I've missed you too. I'm sorry I didn't come back, Hunter. I'm sorry I—"

"Shhh. We don't have to talk about it."

His lips close over my nipple, and his tongue rolls around the hardened pebble until I cry out, desperate for more of the mind numbing pleasure he's just promised. It's been months since we've been together like this, but Hunter knows me, he knows my body, and he knows what I want. His fingers go to the elastic band of my leggings, pulling them down impatiently while I lift my hips to help him get them past my ass.

They hang around my ankles while Hunter spreads my thighs; his fingers are rough and perfect as they part my lips, two of them slipping inside of me with ease because I'm already wet. He brings his mouth back to mine, and I moan into him, rolling my hips because I want it harder, because I need him deeper.

"I love you," he says, biting my lip. "I love you so fucking much."

"I know," I whimper. "I love you too."

And I do love him. I love his head and his heart and the way he makes me feel. I love his fingers moving deep inside me, massaging that perfect spot that causes my walls to clench and my thighs to quake around his sides.

"That's right, Sunshine, give it to me," he says. "Give it all to me."

I don't have a choice. I couldn't hold back if I tried, if he asked me to, so it's a relief that he wants it all. That he wants my pleasure and the pain hiding behind it. I come with a shout that echoes through the kitchen, and Hunter doesn't stop fucking me with his fingers until everything I have to give has been wrenched from me, and the tears are flowing freely.

At the sight of them, the fire in Hunter's eyes tries to die, tries to transform into something softer, something more comforting. But I don't want comfort, at least not the kind that will come from words and not actions. I want this. I want his body and his hands. I want to forget.

"I'm fine," I assure him, reaching for the band of his sweatpants. He shakes his head, stopping me with gentle fingers wrapped around my wrists. His eyes rove over my face.

"You're not fine, Rae, and that's okay. We don't have to do this."

"But I want to." Desperation threads its way through my words. "I want to, Hunter. I *need* to. Please."

He sighs and lets go of my wrists, allowing me to continue undressing him. I wrap my fingers around his shaft, and his head falls back as he lets out a shuddered moan. The tortured sound is a call for connection that demands to be answered by my soul. I grip him tighter, running my hand up and down his length until his jaw turns rigid and there's precum leaking from his tip.

"*Rae.*"

"Come here," I tell him, and he steps forward, allowing me to circle his hips with my legs. I hold him close, the heels of my feet digging into his ass as his dick notches at my entrance. Hunter's eyes flare with the desire to continue, even as he shakes his head.

"Let me grab a condom."

"Don't stop," I whisper. "Stay right here with me, please."

I wrap him up tighter, pull him in closer, and he's strong enough to pull away, to stop this, but he doesn't. He stays with me like I've asked him to, and when I roll my hips in a silent invitation, he thrusts forward, giving me the first glorious inch of his dick and the feel of him unobstructed by anything else for the first time.

"More." I pull him down for another kiss, and he reciprocates, giving me exactly what I've asked for. It's like nothing I've ever felt. His bare skin, my slick channel. His lips on mine. The quiet, soft suction of my pussy as it clutches at his veined flesh every time he advances and retreats.

Hunter wraps his arms around me, lifting me up off of the counter so he's the only thing holding me up. And he does hold me; he holds me so tight I'll be surprised if I'm not bruised in the morning. His fingers dig into my hips as he lifts me up and then slams me back down, over and over again, until my pussy is spasming on his dick, and I'm filled with the heat of his cum.

And even once he's done, he doesn't put me down. He carries me up the stairs, into his bedroom, and then straight to the shower, where he cradles me in his arms and washes my hair and then my body, pretending not to notice when the tears return.

It rains on the day of Will's funeral.

Which makes the day feel that much more surreal. I cry when I put on my dress and again when Dee does my makeup. I cry when we walk into the church and when they lower his casket into the grave. I cry when it's all over, and the repast begins when everyone sheds their grief and brings out the smiles, trading memories over food brought by all the people Will helped keep alive.

I don't have an appetite, but I stay in the kitchen, fixing plates with Dee and her mom, Emma, by my side.

"Don't put that much," Emma says, eyeing the large scoop of macaroni and cheese I've just dug out of the pan in front of me. "We're going to run out."

Dee stretches her eyes to silently admonish her mother for fussing at me. "Things are winding down, Ma. Most everybody has already come and gone."

She's right. The only people still here are her, Emma, Jayla, and Nate, who is out in the yard with Hunter. I glance out the window to see if they're still in the backyard talking, and they are. Well, talking isn't exactly the right word because things look far too tense for them to just be having a normal conversation.

"But what if they get hungry later?" Emma asks. "You haven't eaten a bit of food today, Rae; you can't send it all out the door."

"I'm not hungry," I say, turning my attention from what's happening outside the window and back to the plate I'm fixing for Nate's wife.

Emma's disapproval is clear, but she doesn't say anything more. She just continues to cover the dish in her hand with aluminum foil and puts it in the fridge. When she's done, she comes over and wraps me up in a tight hug, kissing me on the cheek.

"I love you, baby girl."

"I love you too, Em."

"I'm going to go get Jayla," she says, releasing me. "Dee, meet me at the car in five."

"Yes, ma'am."

When we're alone, Dee gives me a sympathetic smile. "I can stay if you want me to."

"No, I think I'll be okay. I'm probably just going to spend the rest of the day in bed."

"Okay."

She gives easily, thinking I'm too fragile to be pushed. She's probably right. I feel too fragile for most things right now, too fragile to be awake, too fragile to be upright, too fragile to be wondering what's happening with Hunter and Nate in the backyard. All I want to do is sleep, and that's what I will do when the last of our visitors go.

Dee helps me finish making the plates for Nate's family and clean up the kitchen, and then she pulls me into a tight hug and presses a kiss to my forehead.

"Call me if you need me."

"I will," I promise her, waving goodbye as she walks out of the kitchen, leaving me to pack up the plates we fixed for Nate. I'm tying up the bag when he finally comes in to retrieve them.

"Heading out?"

"Yep," Nate says, taking the bag of plates from me. "I just wanted to say goodbye."

"Thank you for being here, Nate. I appreciate you."

"Of course." He scrubs a hand down his face, looking like he wants to say something but doesn't know if he should. "I'm always here for you; you know that, right?"

My brows pull together as I try to suss out what his tone is about. "Yeah, I know that."

"And I'm here for Hunter too," he says, glancing out the window where Hunter is still visible. I look, too, and for a moment, we're both quiet, watching Hunter pace.

I look away first, focusing on Nate because seeing the stress of the day settled on Hunter's shoulders is painful for me. "I know you are. He knows it too."

Nate raises his brows like he's not so sure. "He hasn't been to a meeting in months, Rae," he blurts. "I know you're both grieving, but he needs to get to one sooner rather than later, do you understand?"

There's a severity to his tone that I don't get. I mean, of course I know that going so long without the support found in meetings, and conversations with a sponsor, isn't a good thing. But Nate is making it sound like Hunter is falling apart, and he's not. He's not falling apart. He can't be because he's the only thing holding me together.

"I understand, Nate."

Something in his eyes tells me he doesn't think I do, but just like everyone else, he chooses not to push, and when he's gone, I breathe a sigh of relief, happy that silence has found me once again. I sit in that silence until Hunter comes in from the yard. He finds me in the living room, curled up on the couch in my funeral dress.

"You okay?" he asks, sitting down in the chair across from me.

"I'm fine. How are you?"

He slides down into his seat, resting his head on the cushion behind him and closing his eyes. "I'm tired."

He's tired a lot lately, which doesn't make a lot of sense for him. Hunter is the most active, energetic person I know, so the number of times I've seen him dozing off and sleeping in over the past few days has been out of character for him. I haven't minded it because I've enjoyed being still with him.

I sit up and go over to him, crawling into his lap. "Me too."

He runs a hand down my back. "Let's go to bed."

The offer is enticing, but I think we've spent enough time in bed. I think Nate is right, and maybe we should start trying to get back into a routine. "Or, maybe you should go to a meeting."

Hunter pops one eye open, his brow arched in offense. "What did you say?"

"I said you should probably go to a meeting. Nate said you haven't been to one in months—"

He sits up, and his rigid, defensive posture makes it impossible for me to stay comfortably on his lap, so I slide off, standing awkwardly in front of him while he glares at me.

"Why were you and Nate talking about me?"

"We weren't talking about you. I mean, it wasn't like that. He just brought it up, and I thought it could be good for you since it's been so long."

Hunter pushes to his feet and lets out a hollow laugh. "You're right. It has been a long time since I've gone to a meeting because it's hard to make meetings when you're running back and forth to doctor's appointments and pharmacies and making a thousand and one phone calls to insurance companies, trying to convince them to pay for medicine your friend needs to live. And you know what makes going to a meeting even harder, Rae?" It's a rhetorical question because he doesn't pause, doesn't give me a chance to answer. "Knowing that if you do attend one and bring back a single germ it can lead to an infection that will kill the person you are trying so desperately to keep alive."

My head rears back, and pain radiates through me, sharper and harsher with everything he lists off that he did for Will. That he did for me. The picture he paints is heartbreaking and familiar. Every sacrifice he made for Will and me is one that I made for my mother, but instead of the shared experience making us feel closer to one another, it feels like it's ripping us apart. Creating a gap in our bond that's filled with Hunter's unspoken resentment and my guilt.

"I appreciate everything you did, Hunter," I murmur, my voice dripping with shame.

God, why didn't I just come home? Why couldn't I just show up for Will, and for Hunter? Why couldn't I be brave and selfless instead of cowering in New York like a helpless little girl?

"I don't want your appreciation, Rae," he says, agitation laced in every word as he marches into the kitchen and grabs his keys off the counter. I follow him, confused—not by his anger because I'm angry with myself too—but by the determined set of his jaw as he prepares to walk out on me.

He's never walked out on me. He's always been the person standing by my side, holding my hand, offering love and support. I look for any traces of that man in the one standing in front of me and come up empty.

"Then what do you want?"

Hunter rounds on me, clutching the keys in his hands with wild eyes. "I want you and Nate and everybody else to get off my back! That's what I want. Is that too much to ask for?!"

He's yelling now, and I'm standing there in shock, unable to remember a single time when Hunter has ever raised his voice at me. This night is filled with ugly, painful firsts that I don't want with him.

"No." My chin wobbles as he stalks toward the door. "What are you doing?" I ask, even though it's clear. "Where are you going?" He remains silent as he places a hand on the doorknob, causing my heart to twist in on itself. Fresh tears have started to fall, but Hunter is unmoved. Maybe he doesn't see them. Maybe he can't see them through the haze of red he's viewing me through. "Please don't leave."

My voice breaks on the last word, but it's not enough to stop him. And the last thing I see before he walks out the door—leaving me alone with my grief, sadness and self-loathing—is his eyes that tell me he can't grant my request because I've already asked him for too much.

34

RAE

"Maybe you should go back home," Dee says, frowning at me through the phone. "You look miserable."

"Thanks, Dee." I manage to laugh even though the last thing I feel is amused.

"I mean, you're beautiful, of course," she says, strolling through the aisles of the grocery store. "But you don't smile anymore, Rae."

I lean my head back against the headrest of Hunter's truck and give her a sad smile. "Zoila said the same thing."

Everybody has been saying it to me lately, and I haven't been able to argue back or even take offense because it's true. I don't smile anymore. I don't laugh anymore. All I do is cry and try to figure out why Hunter and I can't seem to get along. All I do is sit around with my stomach in knots, grieving the loss of my brother and the apparent end of my relationship, wondering how everything fell apart so quickly.

"Well, when you've got two of your friends saying it, it's got to be true."

"I guess."

"Where have you been?" She asks, adding several pieces of fruit to the basket hanging from her arm. "Or, where are you going?"

"Same place you are now," I tell her. "I'm going to make dinner for Hunter."

Dee pulls a face but she doesn't say anything. She doesn't have to. I know that she's not a fan of Hunter right now. She's mad at him for spending all of his time at the gym when I've been home alone. I've defended his choice, reminding her that he took a lot of time off when he was taking care of Will, even though it hurts that I see him less now than I did when I was in New York.

"Toothpaste, air freshener, tampons," Dee mutters under her breath, repeating the list of random items over and over again until they're stuck in my head.

"Why don't you just make a list?"

"Because I have a system and it works for me."

"Sure, that's why you just walked past the aisle with the tampons on it without picking any up."

"Shit." She turns around, nearly running into someone as she does. "Damn, why are they always out of super plus?"

I open my mouth to make a joke about her heavy flow but stop short when the image of the box of tampons in Dee's hand makes me think about how I haven't bought any since I've been back in New Haven. Usually, Dee and I start our periods just a few days apart, with me starting first, and if she's buying tampons now then that means I'm late.

Shit.

My mind is suddenly flooded with images of Hunter and me on the night I came back to town. Him, insisting on a condom. Me, telling him not to stop. That was over two weeks ago, and now I'm late.

"Dee, I'm late."

"Late? You got a certain time you need to have dinner on the table?"

"No." I cut the engine and grab my purse, hopping out of the truck. "Late like, my period is late."

Dee's eyes bulge as she watches me rush inside the store, but I can tell she's trying to stay calm for me. "Don't panic, Rae. I mean, you've been under a lot of stress lately. Stress can throw your hormones all out of wack."

I want to be comforted by her words, but as I buy the test and take it in the grocery store bathroom, I can't shake the feeling that she's wrong. Confirmation of my gut instinct comes in the form of two pink lines that make Dee's mouth drop when I show them to her.

"Holy shit, Rae."

"I'm going to be sick."

Dee frowns. "Call me back after you're done vomiting."

Since she's known for compassionate vomiting, I don't take offense when she actually hangs up on me. I don't call her back when I'm done, though. Because as soon as I'm done purging what little food I had on my stomach, all I want to do is go home to Hunter.

As I make my way back to the house without a single grocery item, I convince myself that this could be a good thing. I tell myself that things have been hard lately, but they'll get better now that we have something good to focus on. A baby. A bright spot in the dark cloud that has been our lives lately. A gift from Will. Another reason for Hunter and I to hold on to each other.

"This will be good," I say to myself as I stand outside the door of Hunter's bathroom. When I got home, I heard the shower running upstairs, so I came up with the positive test in my hand and a smile on my face, ready to share the good news.

My heart is pounding, slapping against my ribcage as I place my hand on the doorknob and turn it. Steam greets me first, making it hard to see for a second.

"Hunter?" I look to my left towards the shower and come up empty. The water is still running, but the shower curtain is pushed back, so droplets are bouncing off of the bathtub and onto the floor, wetting Hunter's shirt.

I frown as I take in the scene in front of me. It's hard to make sense of it. Of the way Hunter's large form is slumped against the side of the bathtub. Of the way his head is lolling back and his eyes are closed. Of the way the needle I assume was in his hand is still sticking out of his arm even though he's no longer conscious enough to hold it.

The pregnancy test slips from my fingers, and it cracks under my feet as I run into the bathroom and fall to my knees beside him.

"HUNTER?!" I scream, slapping his face repeatedly with my right hand and pulling out my phone to call 911 with the left. "Come on, baby. Wake up. Please, wake up."

Tears stream down my face, familiar and foreign all at once. I'm no stranger to crying, not even to crying over Hunter, because I've been doing a lot of that lately, but I am a stranger to this pain, to this worry.

Despite my brother being an addict and me being in love with one for so long, I've never seen anyone high like this. I know that Will OD'd once, but Mommy went to great lengths to shield me from everything having to do with his drug use. She protected me as best she could. I wonder what she'd think if she could see me now, pregnant and afraid, trying to pull the father of my child out of a drug induced slumber.

"HUNTER!" I'm still screaming, and I strike him hard enough to make the palm of my hand burn with pain. His eyes flutter, but they don't focus. I don't think they can, but at least he's alive.

That's the first thing I tell the operator when I finally get someone on the line. And I repeat those words to myself in the minutes it takes for the paramedics to get there. They invade the bathroom, urging me out of the way as they administer Narcan and ask me questions like what he took and how long he's been using.

I don't know the answer to either of those questions, so I just stand there and cry, not speaking a word until they load him into the ambulance and ask if I want to ride with him to the hospital.

My eyes are wet.

My throat is dry.

And my heart hurts. It hurts so fucking bad I don't know how I'm ever going to recover from the pain. How *we* are ever going to recover from this.

We.

God, that word doesn't just include Hunter and me anymore. There's a whole other person in this equation now. Someone else I have to consider. Someone else I have to love more than I love Hunter, more than he loves the drugs that almost claimed his life.

"Ma'am?" The paramedic holds a hand out to me. "Are you riding to the hospital with him?"

I shake my head first because I know it'll hurt to say it, but then I find my voice, knowing I have to verbalize it to make it real for me. "No. I think he has to do this alone."

35

RAE

I spend a lot of time thinking about the last dinner Hunter and I had with Will. I think about the way he tricked me into believing he was upset about us, and how he laughed at my expense, but most of all I think about that last toast. How he seemed to cast a spell over Hunter and me, uttering words that made the lines of his fate and mine impossible to unlink. That made it necessary for us to keep finding each other, to keep loving each other, to keep ruining each other, over and over again.

That's what we do in his laundry room.

We ruin each other, and it is the most beautiful, perfect, stupid thing I've done in a long, long time. Which, of course, doesn't stop me from spending the night with him in his bed or letting him fuck me through his mattress for hours so that when I wake up the next morning, my stomach is knotted with anxiety and guilt, and the inside of my thighs are coated in his cum.

I groan and turn over on my stomach, surprised, and maybe a little disappointed, to find that I'm in bed alone. It's not like I wanted to wake up in Hunter's arms, but it might have been nice not to have to face the reality of what we've done all on my own. As I burrow into sheets that have gone from smelling like just him to now being soaked in the scent of us, I wonder where Hunter has gone. I don't hear him or Riley moving around downstairs, so I'm guessing she's still asleep, which means he's either out for a run or—

My thoughts are cut short by the sound of the shower in his bathroom turning on and the sensation of my blood running cold. I've never been triggered by the sound of a shower turning on before, so I'm unprepared for the way my body reacts, for the way my mind floods with images of the day that ended us, that made Will's toast nothing more than the wasted wishes of a dead man. I curl in on myself as they hit me, each one slamming into my chest and taking my breath away.

Hunter slumped on the floor, lingering on the edges of life with the evidence of his demon's victory plunged into his arm.

The broken pregnancy test forgotten on the threshold of the bathroom, the pieces of our future ground into the tile he's currently walking over.

My aching palms, red from slapping him multiple times to keep him conscious.

The droplets of water soaked into the fabric of his shirt, and the steam billowing around us, warming the room and making the effects of the drugs that much more potent.

For the length of Hunter's shower, I lay there, trapped in the memories and years old pain, berating myself for doing what we did last night, for letting him in so completely, for giving him my body and whispering truths that are only supposed to live in my heart. For forgetting that there are still so many things broken between us. And when the water stops, and he emerges from the bathroom moments later, his body wrapped in a towel and a wide smile on his face when he realizes I'm awake, I force myself out of it and out of his bed.

"Good morning," he says, striding over to greet me with a kiss as I push to my feet. I dodge it, stepping around him with an apologetic smile.

"I need to brush my teeth," I murmur, slipping out of the room and padding down the hallway to the only other bathroom on this floor. I take my time going through my morning routine and even consider showering just to help calm myself down, but then I remember that all of my clothes are in Hunter's room and decide it can wait until later.

When I walk back into his room, Hunter is sitting on the edge of the bed, still in that damn towel, taking his time rubbing lotion all over his body. I stand in the doorway, mesmerized at the sight of him and unable to hide it. I let my eyes run greedy circuits over his arms, legs, stomach, and chest, tracing over every line of ink.

There's a lot.

From his left shoulder to his wrist, there's a composite image that he said was a representation of shared struggle, proof that you can be going through your own storm and still pull someone else out of theirs. It starts at the top of his shoulder with a lightning-filled sky and turbulent clouds illuminated by a full moon. Where the clouds are the thickest, there's a hand, desperate and seeking, plunging out of it. The fingers of the hand stretch down, just barely gripping the fingers of the hand reaching up from a body of raging water.

I always found it funny that he chose to have such a meaningful image juxtaposed by the random presence of those damn skeletal tattoos on his fingers, but when he told me he just wanted something to fill the space, I accepted that everything doesn't have to have meaning. Some things just are.

They exist because they have to, because we need them to fill a void or scratch an itch. It occurs to me then, that maybe that's what last night was. A thing that had to happen. A lingering desire that had to be fulfilled.

"You know it's not polite to stare, right?" Hunter asks, snapping me out of my thoughts. I drag my eyes from the sun bursting with rays of light on his right elbow to his face, and he smiles indulgently. The way he used to smile at me when he'd tease me for always staring at him.

"Sorry." I edge around the bed, not wanting to risk getting caught up in his gravity and make my way to the closet where I stashed my stuff on Friday. I'm pulling out my clothes for the day, and trying not to vomit at the thought of having to return home and face Aaron after what I've done, when Hunter speaks again.

"Why is none of your stuff in my bathroom?"

I freeze, and my stomach clenches with anxiety as I assess his tone, trying to gauge whether he's asking because he's genuinely curious or because he somehow knows where my head is right now and wants to find a way to ease us into the conversation. I straighten and turn around to face him.

"I can't go in there," I admit. "Not after..."

His smile dies right in front of my eyes, and my heart breaks. There's something so devastating about the absence of joy on his face, about being the one that caused it to disappear.

He doesn't need me to finish my sentence. He doesn't need me to elaborate because he knows what I'm alluding to. Just like I know I've hurt him by bringing it up, by making us stand in the ugliness of his mistakes the morning after we made such a big one together.

Hunter rubs at his chin, and I watch him accept the painful truth, absorbing it into himself but not being ruined by it. I'm impressed by that. By the way he never shies away from being held accountable even when the transgression is old.

"I'm sorry," he breathes, his eyes all liquid regret and heated emotion. "I should have realized that would be difficult for you."

While I appreciate the apology, it feels so wrong to accept it, to be standing here making him feel bad about something as mundane as using his shower. Clearly, he's made peace with what happened in that bathroom, and I shouldn't be challenging that in any way.

"Don't apologize for using your bathroom, Hunter."

"I'm not apologizing for using my bathroom, Rae; I'm apologizing for not realizing how triggering it would be for you, for not thinking it through, for scaring you."

"You didn't scare me." I wave my hand, trying to dismiss my feelings even as tears spring in my eyes, conveying my fear. I bite my lip to try and hold them off. I don't want to cry. I don't want to make him feel bad. I don't want to relive this.

Hunter rises to his feet, coming over to wrap me up in the most comforting hug.

"Yes, I did," he murmurs. "And I'm sorry, okay? I'm good. I promise you, I'm good. And I'm going to keep being good for Riley and for you."

Maybe it's because I've already gone through the gauntlet of emotions this morning or because I didn't get much sleep last night, but something about Hunter including me in that promise sends panic bubbling up in my chest. The memories of the last time he attached his sobriety to me are so fresh in my mind, and I don't get how they're not fresh in Hunter's, how he can even say that when he has first hand knowledge of how terribly things went the last time he tried to be everything for me.

Once the panic begins, the reality of what I've done, what *we've* done, starts to sink in. When I left Hunter, I did it because I knew that I had to choose Riley, that I had to put her first in this life the way my mom put me first. And since he's come back in her life, I've put their bond ahead of everything else, knowing that Hunter would do the same, that if he focused on her, he wouldn't be in danger of breaking under the weight of our ill-fated love. But last night, for the first time since I became a mom, I put myself ahead of my daughter. I let freshly unearthed emotions and startling desire take over, fooling me into forgetting that this weekend was supposed to be about acclimating Riley into Hunter's world, not seeing if there is still a spot for me in it.

I step back, breaking Hunter's hold on me, and shake my head. "Just Riley."

"What?"

"You said you're going to be good for Riley and for me, but I'm not a part of that equation, Hunter. I can't be. The only considerations you have to make for me are from a co-parenting standpoint, nothing else."

His gaze wanders over to the bed, to the rumpled sheets that call me a liar, and then back to my face. Both of his brows are furrowed, and he's making that face that makes him look the most like Riley while his eyes pour out love and hope and desire for the stolen moments we shared in that bed to come out in the open, for the I love you's we exchanged to go from hidden secrets to kept promises lived out in the open.

"Rae, we just—"

"I know." I press my lips together, nodding. "I know what we did, and it was stupid. It was a mistake. And I mean, that's us isn't it? We get together, and we do stupid, reckless things. We put everything at risk, and we can't do that anymore, Hunter. We have a daughter to consider. You have your sobriety to protect and Taurin to take care of, and I have—"

Aaron's name gets trapped in my throat, and I feel myself crumbling as I attempt to resurrect the wall I've worked so hard to keep between us, using nothing but my bare, shaking hands and the fragments of the bricks we shattered with every kiss and touch we traded last night. Hunter watches me as I struggle, and there's pain in his eyes that radiates through me when he decides to help.

"Aaron," he says, clenching and unclenching his jaw as he uses the word to slide the final brick back into place. I can see his face through the gaping holes and jagged lines of the ruined wall, can smell his hurt lingering in the air, dancing along the edges of the scent of dust and construction debris. "You have Aaron."

"Yes. I have Aaron." My teeth plunge into my bottom lip, and Hunter just stares at me. His silence disconcerting, his pain unnerving. "I wish it could be different," I tell him. "I wish I could put it all behind me. Maybe then—"

I stop myself because I don't know where I was going with that thought. Because Hunter doesn't look like he wants to hear it. Because neither of us believe a single word I've said anyway.

RILEY and I get home around one in the afternoon, and Aaron meets us at the door. I'm surprised to see him because in our very brief conversation yesterday, he told me he wouldn't be home until the early evening. What's even more surprising than his presence, are the bouquets of flowers he has in his hand.

"My girls are finally home," he says, dropping to his knee to present a bunch of sunflowers to Riley with a dramatic flourish. "I missed you, Riley girl!"

Riley takes the flowers, her eyes wide with excitement. "These are pretty!"

"Say thank you, Ri," I remind her, correcting her lack of manners but saying nothing about her not returning Aaron's sentiment about missing her because she probably didn't miss him. She probably didn't think of him at all when she was with her dad, and that's okay.

I wasn't thinking of him either, but that's not okay.

"Thank you, Aaron."

"You're welcome. If you take them to the kitchen, I'm sure Ms. Marcy would be happy to help you put them in some water."

Riley looks at me for approval, and I nod. "Just set your bag on the bench and take off your shoes."

She's gone in a second, running through the house yelling for Marcy. I hear Aaron's mom respond, kicking off the conversation with a compliment on Riley's dress and saying nothing about the running and yelling, even though I know she hates when Riley does both. Then I look at Aaron and his big, grand smile and wonder if I've stepped into the Twilight Zone.

"These are for you," he says, handing me a large vase filled with red roses. It doesn't escape my notice that my flowers are already in water, and Riley's were not. It was a subtle way to distract her and carve out some alone time with me.

I take them, wincing slightly when our fingers touch in the exchange because after a night in Hunter's arms, anything else feels wrong. "Thank you."

"You're welcome." Aaron studies my face and frowns. "Are you okay? You look tired."

My cheeks heat. "I'm fine. It's just been a long weekend."

"Why don't you tell me about it while you take a bath," he says, taking my duffel bag and purse from my shoulder and slinging them over his own before linking our fingers together.

"Oh, um, a bath sounds nice, but I need to do laundry and get started on Riley's hair."

"We have plenty of time for that, babe, right now I just want a moment alone with you. Is that okay?"

After a weekend of excitement, I'm dying to get Riley back into the groove of our Sunday routine, but I don't feel like I can say no when Aaron is being so sweet and I feel this guilty.

"Yeah, that's okay."

I let him lead me up the stairs and into our bedroom. Aaron drops my things on the bed, and I'm careful not to look at it for fear that it might flood my mind with memories of Hunter's. I offered to strip the bed before I left, but he told me to leave it. That he'd take care of it. Him refusing to let me help him clean up the mess we made together made me feel even shittier than before.

And here I am, sinking even lower into the abyss of self-loathing because Aaron hasn't just drawn me a bath, he's covered the bathroom floor with rose petals and filled the tub with bubbles. He's sat a small table next to the tub and placed a bottle of wine and two wine glasses on top of it.

He's created a beautiful, thoughtful, special moment that I don't deserve.

"Aaron." I cover my mouth with my free hand, shaking my head as I look at him. He smiles again, his gaze filled with pride.

"Do you like it?"

"I—I don't deserve it."

He frowns and moves behind me, laying a kiss on my neck. "Don't be silly, babe. Of course, you do."

"Aaron, I—"

"Shhh." He stops me in the middle of my thought, bringing his hands to the straps of my dress and pushing them down until the fabric is lying at our feet. He repeats the process with my underwear, and then smacks my ass gently. "Get in the tub, baby. Let me take care of you."

I do what he asks because I don't know how not to, and when I sink down into the water, he pours a glass of wine and hands it to me.

"Thank you," I croak.

"You're welcome," he says, pouring himself a glass and taking a seat on the edge of the tub. "Tell me about your weekend."

I stutter and stumble my way through a summary of my time at Hunter's house, making sure to leave out the conversation on his patio the first night and everything that happened after we spent the whole day in the pool on Saturday. Aaron listens intently, which is unnerving because I'm worried about what he might see, but also because I'm just not used to having his undivided attention anymore.

"Sounds like you guys had a nice time."

I take a sip of my wine and nod before narrowing my eyes at him. "What's going on, Aaron?"

He sits his glass down on the table and chuckles, rubbing at the back of his neck. "Isn't it obvious?"

My poor heart, which at this point has spent more time racing than beating normally, starts to pound, and panic sends my eyes flying all around the bathroom looking for the ring box he's presented to me three times before. Each time, I've said no because saying yes didn't feel right, but today I'm afraid that I'll say yes just because I'm feeling guilty.

"I'm trying to apologize," Aaron says.

"Apologize?"

"Yes, baby. I've been a complete and total dick to you. When I was in Atlanta this weekend, all I could think about was how much I missed you, how much I've fucked up over the past few months." He reaches for my free hand, and I let him take hold of it, allowing him to bring it to his lips. "I know that I haven't been the man you fell in love with. I've been petty and selfish and jealous, and how could I not be? You have so much history with Hunter, and now you have this relationship you're building with him that's based around the most important person in your world, and I was scared there wasn't going to be room in any of that for me."

This is the most honest and vulnerable Aaron has been with me in a long time, and I hate that it's coming now, when I've already done something that could ruin us. Something that will hurt him when he finds out, and he's going to find out because I'm going to tell him. I hadn't decided before just now if I was going to come clean today, but I know now that I have to. There have been too many walls up between Aaron and me, too many things left unsaid, and if he can be honest and own his fuck ups, then I can too.

I reach over and place my glass of wine on the ledge of the tub on my other side. "Aaron, I need to tell you something."

"What is it?" he asks, his eyes filled with earnest while mine brim with tears that I swipe away because now isn't the time to shed them.

"I slept with Hunter."

Silence descends on us as my words register with Aaron. They settle on his head and trickle down into his ears, spilling onto his shoulders and rolling down the line of his arm to his fingers that are still cradling mine. The connection is short lived, severed with a decisive slice as Aaron releases me and pushes to his feet, starting to pace immediately.

Water sloshes around as I stand, reaching for the robe hanging on the hook next to the tub. It's brand new, another heartfelt gesture from the man I've just shattered with my words.

"Aaron, please say something," I plead, tying the robe tight around my waist.

He pauses, turning to me slowly with crossed arms and crazed eyes. "You *slept* with Hunter?"

"Yes, but it was—" Despite using the word with Hunter to describe what transpired between us last night, I can't bring myself to say it was a mistake to Aaron. I knew what I was doing. Hunter gave me ample opportunity to stop, but I kept going. I let him keep going. "I'm sorry. That's not what this weekend was supposed to be about, but it happened, and I don't want to lie to you about it."

"Well, thanks for your honesty," he scoffs. "How many times?"

I press my lips together, certain he can't really be asking for a number. He can't actually want to know how many times I told myself we'd stop only to find myself climbing on top of Hunter again or letting him hike my leg up as he slid into me from behind. There were too many times to count, so I didn't try.

"Before last night, we'd never..." My jaw clenches as shame digs its way through me. "When I left this morning, I told him it couldn't happen again." A wave of nausea lays claim to my stomach, and I don't know if it's because my body is physically rejecting the thought of never having Hunter again or just the stress of the situation. Whatever the reason, I find myself swallowing down bile as Aaron stares at me like he doesn't know who I am. "I'm so sorry. I know that I've hurt you, and I understand if you can't forgive me. I don't know if I'd be able to forgive me either."

With nothing more to say, I start to head toward the door, but as I move past Aaron he grabs my hand and stops me.

"Where are you going?"

"I don't know. I just thought maybe you wanted some space. Riley and I can go stay with Jayla and—"

"No." He shakes his head, still holding my hand. "I don't want you to leave, Rae."

"You don't?"

"No, but I do want you to promise me something."

Aaron and I both know that at this moment in time, there's nothing I wouldn't promise him. That's the funny thing about guilt, when it's strong enough, when it's potent enough, you'll do anything to get rid of it. You'll say anything. You'll do anything. You'll promise anything, even things you probably shouldn't.

There's an odd glint to Aaron's eyes as he considers me, as he waits for me to fold to his blank check of a demand. I swallow past the lump in my throat that's telling me not to make promises to a man I've just scorned and surrender to the part of me that feels like I owe him this because while he's been a lot of things over the past few months—petty, childish and insecure—he hasn't been unfaithful.

But I have.

"Anything."

He smiles—it's a small one, so faint it's just a ghost on his lips—and then brings his hand to my cheek, running a finger over my jawline and to my lips. "I can forgive you this one transgression." I push out a small, relieved breath, and the smile becomes real this time. "But," he continues, "this fuck up means things are about to change with you and Hunter's cozy little co-parenting situation. From here on out, I'm involved in every conversation and present for every visit."

"Aaron—" I start to protest, but he cuts me off with a finger on my lips.

"If you want to gain back my trust, you'll do this for me. And as long as things remain respectful, we won't have a problem. I won't speak to him. He won't speak to me or step foot in my house again. If Riley wants to spend time at his place, you're going to have to figure out a way for her to do that without you."

"That won't be a problem. Hunter and I already agreed that she could do visits with him every weekend."

"Good. We can do drop-offs together, and then we can spend our free time reconnecting, figuring out where things went wrong so we can fix them and get our relationship back on track." He runs his finger back and forth across my bottom lip. "I love you so much, Rachel. I know that we can get past this."

36

HUNTER

"Look who's awake," a voice from the far side of the room says, way too cheerful and loud for the throbbing happening at the back of my skull and the rolling wave of nausea in my stomach.

I'm barely awake.

And by barely, I mean I've just cracked a single eye open because when I slipped into consciousness, I couldn't figure out what the beeping sound that woke me was. Now, I know that beeping is coming from the monitor that keeps track of the amount of liquid in the IV bag that's dripping fluids meant to support hydration into my body.

I'm in the hospital.

The last thing I remember is being in the bathroom at the house, using the hour I knew it would take Rae at the store to get myself back right. I turned the shower on because I wanted to have an excuse to be in the bathroom if she came home early, but I didn't bother to get undressed, so I guess I wasn't too committed to the lie.

Not that it would have taken much to convince her. After I flipped out on her the night of Will's funeral, she stopped pushing. She stopped asking follow-up questions if things don't make sense, and a lot of things don't make sense anymore because I'm falling apart, and I'm tearing us up in the process.

Fuck. I try to sit up, my brain finally realizing that if I'm in the hospital, I must have done more than take the edge off, and there's only one person who could have found me, so now I need to explain. Now I need to fix it.

"Don't try to sit up, Mr. Drake," the nurse says, coming into view. She's a young, Black girl with a friendly face and more strength in her one hand than I apparently possess in my whole body. She forces me back down to the thin mattress without exerting much effort, and I go easily because my body is heavy and I'm so tired.

"Where's Rae?" I ask, glancing around the room for any signs of her and coming up empty. The scent of her perfume is absent from the air.

"Who?" The nurse—Carla, according to the badge clipped to her chest—asks. I frown up at her as she pulls the stethoscope from around her neck, preparing to listen to my broken heart.

"Rae," I repeat. "My girlfriend. Where is she?"

Carla doesn't answer, she just places the end of the stethoscope to different parts of my body and instructs me to breathe deeply at some points. When she's done, she loops the tool back around her neck and fixes me some water.

"She's not here, is she?" I ask, taking the cup from Carla's hand. She gives me a sad smile that answers my question.

"You came in alone."

Everything hurts.

My head, my stomach, my back, but the pain that lances my heart is the worst. I shouldn't be surprised that Rae left. I can only imagine what it must have been like for her to find me like that, knocking on death's door if the way my body feels now is any indication of how bad it was. But it still hurts to know that she did.

And I don't try to hide the tears. The shame. The anger, not at her, never at her, but at myself. I failed so fucking thoroughly. First with Will, and now with my recovery. But most importantly, I failed with Rae. I ruined us, and she left.

She fucking left.

Carla pats me on the shoulder, her face a mask of practiced, professional sympathy. "I'm sorry."

"Don't be. It's my own fault," I tell her, handing the cup of water back so she can set it on the table.

"You're right," she says, glancing at my chart, which tells her exactly how true my statement of ownership is. "But I'm still sorry."

"You can accept blame and compassion at the same time," someone says from behind Carla. She turns around and then steps to the side, revealing a face I'm not at all surprised to see.

"Nate."

He has his hands in his pockets as he walks into the room, and Carla slips out to give us some privacy. The last time I saw him, we argued for close to an hour because he could see right through the facade I was putting on down to my broken core. He knew I was using again, and he called me out on it. I hated him for it, and all of my responses were nasty and mean, but as he stands at the side of the hospital bed looking down at me, I don't see resentment or lingering anger. I just see concern and understanding.

I can't bear it, so I avert my gaze, looking at the white sheets.

"What are you doing here?" I ask.

"Rae called me." The mention of her name has hope bubbling in my chest, but when I look up at Nate, and he shakes his head, it dies. "She's gone. She went back to New York. She just wanted to make sure you had the support you needed to get through this."

To get through this.

I turn the words over in my mind, knowing that 'this' doesn't just refer to my relapse. It also refers to losing her because she hasn't just gone back to New York.

She hasn't just left New Haven.

She's left me.

The realization sets something free inside my chest, and I put my head in my hands, trying to muffle the sound of the broken sob that comes to destroy everything. To lay waste to my anger, heartache, and self-loathing, to leave behind nothing but acceptance.

37

HUNTER

Now

The first time Rae left me, I didn't fight.

I didn't catch a flight to New York and track her down even though it wouldn't have been hard to. I didn't call her every day and wear her down until she agreed to talk to me because I was afraid that I'd succeed in convincing her to come back to me. That I'd get her to come back just so I could ruin us some more.

When she walked out of my house almost two weeks ago after telling me we could never have what we'd found in each other again, I let her go because I was afraid there was nothing I could say that would make her choose me.

I've regretted that choice since the moment I made it, but I've only just gotten the courage to try to rectify my mistake. And I have Taurin to thank for that. Earlier this week, I saw him get the courage to reach out to his parents one more time because his little brother's birthday is coming up, and they not only responded positively but invited him to lunch at their house. I dropped him off, which gave me a chance to meet them and let them know how well he's been doing, and then I left and drove here.

Here, being En Pointe. Well, more specifically, the parking spot on the street outside of En Pointe, where I've been sitting for the better part of an hour trying to get the courage to go in. Rae is here; I know that because I parked right beside her car, so I know that's where I need to be, but I just can't bring myself to move, which isn't good for my objective or the bouquet of flowers wilting in my passenger seat.

"Are those for the school or for the owner?"

I nearly jump out of my skin when Dee's voice breaks into my thoughts. She's got her face damn near plastered to my passenger window, but she's still yelling to make sure that I heard her.

"Jesus!" I shout while she clutches her sides and laughs at my expense. I'm not someone who is usually caught off guard, so I'm sure she's getting a kick out of sneaking up on me. To further annoy me, she pulls at the door handle until I unlock it and allow her in.

"You've gotta pay attention to your surroundings," she chides, wagging a finger at me before turning her gaze to the flowers. I watch her eyes get round as she scoops them up out of the seat. "These are gorgeous, Hunter. Rae's going to love them."

Before I can say a word, she's got the flowers out of the car and is bumping the door closed with her hip. I roll my eyes and let out an exasperated sigh as I cut the engine and follow her inside the building. Dee has been back in New Haven for a week, and she's already managed to work every one of my last nerves.

Thanks to this new co-parenting arrangement where Rae uses everyone and everything to act as a buffer between us, I've seen more of Dee than I did when she used to practically live at my house. When I call Rae, she picks up the phone. When Rae brings Riley to the house to drop her off for the weekend, Dee is in the car. I love the girl, but I'm sick of looking at her.

"Who said they're for Rae?" I ask, hitting a jog to catch up with her. She tosses an incredulous look over her shoulder.

"Who else would they be for?"

"Oh, I don't know, maybe my daughter?"

Dee sets the vase, which is bigger than Riley, on the reception desk and plucks the card free. I wasn't going to get one, but I decided to just in case I changed my mind about coming in and opted to drop the flowers off in lieu of conversation.

"To everything you are and everything you'll become," Dee says loudly, reading the words off with an annoyingly dramatic flourish. "Congratulations, Sunshine." She taps the card on her chin. "Remind me, when did you start calling Riley 'Sunshine'?"

I grimace at her. "Don't you have anything better to do?"

"Nope. I've got all sorts of free time on my hands these days."

"Don't tell me they finally revoked your license because they realized you should be on the other side of the doctor/patient dynamic."

She flips me off. "There's nothing wrong with therapists being in therapy. In fact, that's the way it should be."

"True." I glance around, having lost all interest in the conversation, and my heart swells with pride as I take in the space. It's been completely transformed, and I'm dying to know if it's everything Rae wants it to be.

"She's in the back," Dee tells me, picking up the vase again and putting it in my hands. "Go and give her these. She'll love them."

Accepting that Dee is not going to let me out of here without seeing Rae, I take the flowers and head down the hall, going all the way to the end, where Rae's office is. Her door is open, but I still knock, not wanting to catch her off guard when she's clearly not all that comfortable being in a room alone with me.

"Come in," she calls without looking up from the papers on her desk. Once again, I feel that shock of pride roll through me.

"You're really doing it," I blurt, unable to keep the words in. Rae's head snaps up, and she shoots to her feet, the picture of elegance with her hair pulled back into a slick bun and a sage green pantsuit on. It's got three pieces: a form-fitting corset that hugs her breasts and allows her to flaunt her toned stomach, an oversized blazer that hangs open and stops at the top of her thigh, showing off the pleated waist.

All of her jewelry is gold, reminding me of the band of the engagement ring I bought for her all those years ago. I still have it. I hope one day soon I'll be able to give it to her. That reality only happens if I say what I've come here to say, though, so I can't lose my nerve. I can't let the wall I helped her rebuild between us continue to stand.

"Hunter." She smooths a hand down her legs even though she looks perfect. "Hey."

"Hey."

For a moment, we just stand there and look at each other. And it feels like it did when she first came back to New Haven. When we didn't know what to do with the charged air around us, so we just stood around, hoping the tension would dissipate.

It didn't then, and it doesn't now.

"These are for you," I tell her, advancing on her slowly to place the vase on the corner of her desk. Once it's settled, I step back, aware of the way Rae doesn't breathe until I'm out of her orbit.

"Thank you," she whispers.

"You're welcome."

Rae holds my face in her gaze. It feels like it's been years since she's looked at me when in reality, it's only been weeks. It doesn't matter because it's been too long.

"You've been avoiding me."

It's not a question or an accusation. Just an observation. Just a solid truth she can't deny even though she looks like she wants to.

"I have."

"Why?"

"Hunter, you know why."

"You're right." I'm taking slow steps towards her while her eyes beg me to stay away. My eyes tell her that she should ask me for anything else but that. I close the space between us in just a few seconds, and Rae stands her ground. Her chest heaves, and her eyes flare with restless indignation, but she stands her ground. "I do know why, so let's skip over that and get to the part where you tell me how to get you to stop."

Her eyes fall shut. "You can't."

I place one careful hand on her waist, and my thumb brushes

against the sliver of skin that's been neglected by her corset and pants. Rae sucks in a ragged breath.

"Rae."

"Don't do this, Hunter," she pleads, opening her eyes again.

"Don't do what? Don't make you remember what it was like when you weren't fighting me anymore? Don't remind you that every time I told you I loved you that night, you said it back? Don't tell you that I've missed you, that I regret letting you put that fucking wall back up between us when all I wanted to do is ask, no, *beg*, you to give us a real chance?"

It was my intention to come into this conversation with just a little bit of finesse, but it turns out that I'm incapable of doing that, so I just keep going.

"We deserve a real chance, Rae. You know it just as well as I do."

Something inside her awakens at my assertion, and she steps back, shaking her head as she puts space between us. "No, I don't know that, Hunter."

"Yes, you do. You're just too scared to admit it."

"I'm not scared," she lies, moving away further, this time rounding her desk to put a tangible barrier between us. "I'm just not willing to let one night of sex make me forget everything I know to be true."

I hate everything about her tone, about the way she's using it to keep me at arm's length.

"And what is it you know to be true, Rae?"

Her eyes are hard as they settle on me, and I see what she's trying to do. I see what the fear she swears she's not caving to is making her do, and it pisses me off.

"I know that you're not ready for this." She gestures between us. "You think you are, but you're not."

My jaw clenches with restrained rage, and I contain the urge to look around this building she's standing in and remind her of the million and one ways I've shown her that I am ready for this, for her, for Riley, for everything our life would entail.

"You don't get to tell me that I can't do this, Rae."

"If I can't, then who can?"

"I can!" I throw my hands up in exasperation. "I know myself. I know what I can handle and what I can't, and I can handle this. I can handle you and all the complications and stress that come along with building something real." I pause, and my throat aches around the broken words that come next. *"I'm strong enough this time."*

"I believed you when you said that before," Rae says, her voice deathly quiet. Her eyes razor sharp as they rove over my features with the kind of precision that tells me she's been thinking about this for a long time. "When everything happened with Will, I trusted you when you said you were good. I listened when you said you could handle the things you took off my plate, and you crumbled under the pressure. You fell apart, and you nearly died."

The pain on her face speaks a language that only the pain in my heart understands. They talk for a long time, their conversation filling the long, silent seconds when I can't even formulate a response to Rae because it hurts too much to address what she's said.

"Do you really have so little faith in me now?" I whisper. "After everything I've shown you? After all the ways I've shown up for Riley and for you?"

"I didn't ask you to show up for me," Rae says.

"But I did it anyway!" I roar, unable to keep my voice down, even though I know I shouldn't yell. It just hurts so fucking much to see her so steadfast in her resolve, so committed to thinking that I'm the same man I was when I failed her all those years ago. I push out a breath, forcing myself to lower my tone. "And I did it because I love you, Rae. I did it because I love Riley. Because I love our family, and I am at my best when I am with you."

Rae shakes her head. "I just don't think that's true."

"Am I interrupting something?"

Aaron's voice comes from behind me, and I don't move immediately. I stare at Rae, and she stares back at me with that same maddening resolute expression. I can't take it. I can't stomach it. I can't fucking believe it, so I stand there like a fool, waiting to be dismissed.

"No," Rae says, looking past me to Aaron. "Hunter was just leaving."

38

RAE

Now

"Those flowers Hunter brought you are gorgeous," Dee says, smiling at me over the rim of her champagne glass.

The opening for En Pointe is over, and despite the emotional storm cloud that's been hanging over my head since this afternoon, everything went incredibly well. It helps that Dee has been by my side for the entire week, helping me with whatever I needed to make things go smoothly and, now, reminding me to pause and celebrate an achievement that wouldn't have been possible without her or the man I've been trying not to think about that she just brought up.

My mind goes to the red orchids sitting on my desk. Their deep red hue a perfect match for the color I decided at the last minute to intersperse throughout my branding and space. I don't know how Hunter knew that my office was the only place in the building without a pop of red somewhere. And I don't know how to feel about the fact that he fixed it with such a simple, romantic gesture.

"Yeah, they're nice," I say, finally responding to Dee. She rolls her eyes at my nonchalance.

"Did you read the card?"

"Yes, Deanna, I read the card."

And when I was done crying over it, I put it in the back of a drawer in my desk so Aaron wouldn't see it. So he wouldn't tell me I should throw it away. So I wouldn't have to explain to him why I can't.

"It was sweet, right?"

I narrow my eyes at her and take a sip of my champagne. "What are you getting at?"

"I'm not getting at anything. I'm just trying to figure out why you're acting so weird when it comes to Hunter. You barely look at the man and don't think I haven't noticed that you've stopped talking about him altogether. Just a few weeks ago, everything was Hunter this and Hunter that."

"No, it wasn't."

Dee pins me with a hard stare. "Yes, it was. I felt like I'd been transported back to our college days where you spent all of your time talking about how in love you were with him." My lips part to deny her claim, but she silences me with one hand. "Don't you dare lie and say you didn't. I have the text messages and cryptic Facebook statuses to prove it."

That makes me crack up, and Dee joins in on the laughter, giving me a reprieve from her inquisition. It doesn't last long, though. Eventually, she turns serious again, eyeing me with concern and curiosity.

"Seriously, though, what changed between you guys? I thought y'all were doing good, and now you're being all cold with him, and he's looking all desperate and remorseful like he fucked up somehow." She pauses, her eyes going wide. "He didn't relapse again did he?"

"No!" I answer quickly, shaking my head for emphasis. "He didn't relapse. He's still clean."

"Okay, good." Dee places a relieved hand on her chest. "Then what's going on with y'all?"

I bite my lip. "I did something stupid."

We're sitting in the middle of the floor of the main classroom, surrounded by mirrors and barres that make it feel like no time has passed at all since our days as ballet students at Ms. Alice's. Except everything has changed. Instead of water bottles and granola bars, we're sipping on champagne and eating a charcuterie board in the middle of the floor, celebrating my transition from student to teacher. And instead of confessing to something stupid like forgetting my toe pads, I'm about to tell her that I slept with my ex.

"What'd you do?" She asks, plucking a grape off of the wooden board between us and dropping it into her mouth.

"I slept with Hunter," I whisper.

Dee is a notoriously loud eater, so I hear the moment she stops chewing. "You did what?!"

I bring my knees up to my chest and wrap my arms around them, resting my chin on top so I can see the disgust that must be gathering on her face. Except, there's not any disgust. There's just intrigue.

Dee reaches over and pokes me in the forehead. "You sneaky little bitch. When did this happen?"

The fact that she's not judging me in the slightest makes me feel better and worse at the same time. I deserve to be judged. I deserve to be admonished. I deserve to be anything other than celebrated.

"Remember when Ri and I stayed the weekend with him?"

"Rae! That was weeks ago!"

"I knowwww," I groan, closing my eyes. "I just couldn't bring myself to say anything because it was a stupid, one-time thing, and it won't happen again."

Outside of my dreams. It won't happen again outside of my dreams.

"Who are you trying to convince? Me or you?"

"Both," I say, releasing my hold on my legs and collapsing onto the hard floor beneath me. "It won't happen again. It *won't*," I recite the mantra I've had on repeat since I left Hunter's to the ceiling, hoping they'll find their way from my lips to God's ears.

Dee crawls over and lays on the floor beside me, and if I wasn't so distraught, I'd laugh at the fact that neither of us give a fuck about ruining our dress clothes. "You can say that as many times as you want, but until you figure out why it happened in the first place, you can't tell yourself it won't happen again."

My stomach clenches. I know she's right, but the last thing I want to do is dig any deeper into that night than I already have. Besides, I already know why it happened. It happened because I love Hunter, and he loves me. It happened because I'm weak, and we're cursed. It happened because I wanted it to.

But I can't say any of those things to Dee.

"I don't know why it happened."

"Bullshit. We both know you've already turned that moment over in your head a million and one times. You know exactly why it happened."

I glare at her. "Why are you so mean?"

"I'm not mean, I'm honest, and you need some honesty right now." She turns on her side, propping her head up on her hand. "Tell me what happened, and don't skimp out on any details."

Despite my better judgment, I give her a play by play of the entire weekend, starting with meeting Taurin and his friends on Friday and ending with me coming home and spilling my guts to Aaron.

"You told Aaron?!"

"Of course, I told him. What was I supposed to do?" She gives me a look that tells me I should have done anything but that, and I laugh. "You're a therapist. Isn't honesty and healthy communication supposed to be your thing?"

"I mean, yeah, and if I was your therapist, I would have absolutely encouraged you to be honest with your partner about what happened, but as your best friend? My advice is always to take that shit to your grave."

Most of the time, when I think about what Hunter and I did, I move between feeling sick with guilt and incredibly, shamefully, turned on, but I'm never amused. I've never laughed about it before tonight, so it feels good to let the laugh inspired by Dee's seriousness spill from my lips.

"You're awful, you know that?"

She nods. "I do, and that's why I've never been caught slipping. You can't let a man know you've fucked up, Rae, especially one as insecure as Aaron. They never actually want to work through it and figure out how you ended up there. And they never truly forgive you even though they say they have. They'll just keep finding new ways to make you pay for it, new ways to make you feel bad about it, new ways to use it to guilt you into putting up with their shitty behavior."

Everything about her response resonates deep in my chest, burrowing underneath the guilt to start working at the small part of me that thinks she might be right. Just as I start to consider it though, the emotional, guilt driven part of my brain kicks on, reminding me that I'm not the wronged party here.

And Aaron has been trying.

He's been more present with me, more patient and attentive with Riley. He's told Marcy that she'll need to move back into her house once the kitchen renovation is done at the beginning of June, which is just a few days away. We've figured out how to balance our relationship with co-parenting with Hunter and me running the school.

Over the last two weeks, we've been better than we've ever been before, and I know things will continue to improve as long as I stay the course. And I will stay the course because that's what's best for Riley and me. She needs stability on both sides, not the collision of chaos that would be me and Hunter.

"I don't think that's what Aaron is doing, Dee."

She doesn't look convinced. "I hope you're right."

"I am," I say, infusing my voice with conviction I don't completely feel.

We sit in the heavy aftermath of the conversation for a few short minutes before Dee cuts an eye at me. I already know what she's going to ask; I can tell by the sneaky little smirk curving her lips, but I still blush when she speaks the question out loud.

"Was the sex good?"

I roll over on my side, tucking my arm under my head so I can hide my smile in the crux of my elbow. "It was incredible."

39

HUNTER

Now

"You know you can come back to the house anytime." I toss the words out like they're meaningless, like it doesn't hurt for me to say them even though it does, and they land at Taurin's back as he leans over the bed, packing the last of his belongings into his book bag.

He's moving back in with his parents today, and while I'll miss him like mad, I'm happy for him. Happy that the lines of communication and understanding between him and his parents have opened back up. Happy that he's back to building a relationship with his little brother. Happy that I've played a part in making all of those things a reality, even if it was just a small one.

But I'm still sad for me. Devastated at the thought of letting go of yet another person I love. Torn up by the idea of coming home to silence every day except for on the weekends when Riley is here with me.

Taurin turns, his eyes glossy like mine. "I know."

"I still expect to see you at the gym in the afternoons and at meetings."

He nods. "You will. I promise."

"And I'm proud of you," I say finally, swallowing my tears just as his father, Jerome, comes up behind me. I move to the side, allowing him into the room. He walks over to Taurin and claps him on the shoulder as he places the car keys in his hand.

"I was thinking you could drive home today."

"For real?"

Jerome smiles down at his oldest son, who looks just like him. "Yeah, I mean, you have to practice if you're going to get your license any time soon."

When we met for lunch last week, we talked about how getting his license was a huge goal for Taurin since Alyssa is going to be leaving for college in a few months. Before Taurin met me, Jerome and his wife, Rose, had refused to let him behind the wheel because they were afraid he would end up killing someone if he did so while he was high. Clearly, their trust in their son, and my influence, has led them to this show of good faith.

Taurin holds the keys tightly, beaming up at his dad. "I guess you're right."

"Well, I guess I should walk you two out, then," I say, needing the moment to end so I can start the grueling work of feeling my feelings and not shoving them down into the finite box in the back of my mind that has, twice before, popped open and led to a relapse.

When we get outside, I pull Taurin into a tight hug before dapping up Jerome and sending them on their way. Once they're gone, I pull out my own keys and head to the gym to meet Nate for the workout I requested when I realized Taurin would be moving out today. He's already inside the gym when I arrive; his hands shoved in the pads I usually wear when other people are taking their frustration out on me.

I arch a brow at him as I start to tape my hands. "You sure you wanna do that?"

He shrugs, holding his hands up and bouncing around the mat on the tips of his toes to mimic the way boxers float around the ring.

He's surprisingly lithe for someone his age. "You said you wanted to work out, so let's work out."

"Fine." I lift my fists, beckoning him closer with one hand. "But remember, you asked for this."

Nate lasts ten minutes on the mat with me before he throws down his pads and puts his hands on his hips. "God damn, man. What are you trying to do, kill me?"

"No." I've barely even broken a sweat, but I let my hands fall to my sides and join him on the bench where he's sought sanctuary from my wrath. "I'm just working out some frustration."

"Yeah, well, you're going to have to use your words with me," he says, resting his back against the wall and closing his eyes while his chest heaves. I was a lot more mobile today than I would have been if I was the one holding the pads, which is why Nate is so worn out. I've been trying to get him in the gym with me for years now, but he's always maintained that he's in great shape. Maybe now that I've run him around a bit, he'll cut the shit and admit that he's not.

Once he's caught his breath, he sits up, resting his elbows on his knees as he studies me. "Today's a hard day," he says.

"Yeah," I admit. "Today's a hard day."

"Why?"

There is a whole list of reasons why, and even though I don't want to, I have to go through and name them all. "Taurin moved back in with his parents today. I'm going to miss him a lot."

"That's tough," Nate agrees. "But your objective was never to keep him with you forever. It was to give him a safe, loving place to heal while he worked his way back to his family."

I nod. "I know. I know."

"What else?"

"I don't have Riley this weekend."

That shit really pains me. It makes the cold void in my chest caused by Rae's silence and absence burn so much more, and when I couple it with the loss of Taurin, it makes it easy to feel like I've gone back to the time in my life when I had nothing and no one besides Nate and my recovery.

I know that's not true. I got a text from Riley this morning, and I FaceTimed her as Taurin packed so he could show her the new plushies he bought her for her growing collection. Before we hung up, she reminded me of our plans to have s'mores when she comes over next weekend.

So I have her.

I have my daughter, and that's the most important thing in the world to me, but it doesn't take away the sting of losing everything else.

"Why not?" Nate asks.

I grimace, recalling the phone call from Aaron, *of all fucking people*, who asked me to allow her to stay home this weekend so they could celebrate Rae's birthday as a family. He was cordial, friendly even, but there was smugness hiding underneath his tone, a gentle undercurrent that stomped all over my last nerve and made it necessary for me to voice my agreement through clenched teeth.

Of course, I was never planning to let Rae spend her birthday without Riley. That would have been cruel of me, and even though she broke my heart, I have no interest in doing anything to hurt her.

"It's Rae's birthday."

"Oh, they didn't want to include you in the festivities?"

"Nope." I grind my teeth, and the muscle in my jaw pulses. "Aaron wanted it to just be family, and apparently, I don't qualify."

"Sounds like you have feelings about being left out."

"I do." I push to my feet, moving over to the punching bag hanging up in the corner. Nate follows, positioning himself on the other side of the bag to hold it steady. When he's got a good grip on it, he nods. A silent green light for me to keep talking while I drive all of my anger and pain into the bag with my fists.

"He's not her family," I growl, throwing the first punch. It has so much force behind it that Nate has to let the bag go to keep it from colliding with his body. When it swings back to me, I spin into a kick that makes the chain securing the bag to the ceiling rattle. Nate steps out of the way, and I continue.

"He's not her family," I repeat, emphasizing each word with a blow to the bag. "Riley and me, we're her family. We'll always be bound together by blood and history, but she doesn't have any of that with Aaron." I'm panting now, wearing myself down with every punch and kick while Nate watches on. "They're not even married, Nate. All this fucking time, and he hasn't given her a ring. I mean, what the fuck is up with that?"

40

RAE

Now

Most people love their birthdays, but I've always kind of hated mine.

Not because I'm one of those women who's afraid of aging—I've always been a firm believer that I'm like a good bottle of wine, only getting better with time—but because it's hard to be excited about the day you were born when everyone who was there when you first entered the world is gone.

It's been over a decade since I've woken up to phone calls from anyone who can tell me what the weather was like on the day of my birth, how long Mommy was in labor, or what the nurse I was named after looked like. I mean, I know the stories because I haven't always been alone on this day, but I don't get to hear them anymore, and it sucks.

Since becoming a mom, most of my birthdays have been low-key, consisting of spending time with Riley or just lounging around with no bra on. That was my original plan for this year, too, but Aaron talked me into doing things differently. I still got to spend some time with Riley and relax at home, just not for long. We spent an hour this morning watching cartoons while munching on the breakfast Aaron and Marcy prepared for me, but after that, I had to get up and out the door to go to a spa day Aaron booked for me, Dee, and Jayla at the Cerros Hotel downtown.

We spent the entire afternoon being pampered and treated like queens, and now that we're dressed, relaxed, and all dolled up, we're on our way up to the rooftop restaurant for dinner.

"This has been such a great day," Jayla says, her ebony skin sparkling under the lights in the elevator. "I've always wanted to have dinner on the rooftop. People say it has the most amazing view of the city."

Dee smiles and wraps an arm around me. "Only the best for our girl."

"Not you acting like you planned the day," Jayla scoffs while I laugh at my best friend's silliness.

"You really think Aaron came up with all of this on his own? The whole spa day in the penthouse suite was my idea."

"Yeah, probably because you've been wanting to do it and didn't want to have to pay for it," I quip, not mad at all because I don't care how it's all happened; I'm just glad that it did. Today has been nice.

"Damn right," Dee returns, her eyes sparkling with mischief. "Cost him a pretty penny too."

She and Jayla high-five at that, and I just shake my head at the two of them. The elevator beeps, announcing our arrival at the rooftop, and the doors glide open, welcoming us to the outdoor dining experience.

"Hello, beautiful," Aaron says, extending a hand to me.

I take it with a smile on my face because I am actually glad to see him. "Hi, I didn't know you'd be here."

He pulls me into him, kissing me on the cheek. "Well, I have one more surprise for you."

Every time Aaron has proposed to me, he's gotten this look. It's a confusing mix of determination and fear that makes his eyes wild, but his features still in the most disconcerting way. He's got that look tonight, and as he leads me away from the elevator back toward the dining area, I glance back at Dee and Jayla to see if they know what we're about to walk into. They both shrug and shake their heads, and I don't know whether to feel relieved that Aaron hasn't mentioned proposing to them or freaked the fuck out that he's playing things close to the vest.

"SURPRISE!" The collective shout—which comes from a group of people that are mostly strangers to me—erupts as soon as we round the corner, and I jolt, placing my hand over my heart as I force myself not to scream.

"Oh!" I'm partly relieved to see so many people because Aaron has never proposed to me in public before, but I'm still on high alert because of that tell-tale expression. He's got it turned in my direction right now, only it's obscured by a smile as he gestures at the crowd of people gathered around one long, candle-lit table with a wide sweep of his arm.

"Do you like it?" He asks, searching my face. "It's a surprise party. Everyone came out to celebrate you."

"I love it," I whisper, willing the words to be true.

Aaron grins at me. "I knew you would! Come on, let me introduce you to everyone."

Using our linked hands, he drags me away from Dee and Jayla and into the sea of unfamiliar faces that are mostly his co-workers or old friends. Everyone, including his previously bitchy assistant, Eden, wishes me a happy birthday and tells me how beautiful I look tonight. The friendliness and generally positive vibes make me feel better about spending the last few hours of my birthday with these people. I tell Aaron as much after dinner when he's holding me close and spinning me around the small space in front of the table that's been designated as a dance floor.

"I wasn't sure if you were going to like it," he says. "I know you don't know them all that well, but I thought it was about time that both of my worlds collided, especially since I'm about to start working on a significant merger."

My brow furrows. "A merger? What kind of merger?"

Aaron pulls back, and my heart swan dives into my stomach as he sinks down to one knee. I cover my mouth with both my hands, aware that everyone in the crowd is now looking at us, and a few of them have their phones out.

"What are you doing?" I ask him, watching as he pulls a ring box out of his pocket. He doesn't answer my question, but I don't need him to because now he's opening the box, revealing a large diamond set in a platinum band.

I never wear silver.

That's the first thing I think when Aaron opens the box. The next thing I think is, 'Oh no,' because Aaron's lips are moving, but I'm not listening. I can't listen because my blood is roaring in my ears, and my heart is in my throat, and my knees feel weak.

This is good, right? This is how it's supposed to feel when someone is proposing to you, and you actually want to marry them. This is the feeling I was waiting for that I didn't have all those other times. Right? RIGHT?!

"....more than anything in this world," Aaron says. "We've had our share of ups and downs over the last three months, and we've both made mistakes." The emphasis he places on the word makes me sick to my stomach. "But I think the thing that's carried us through is the knowledge that at the end of the day, we were made for each other..."

Several of the women in the audience let out breathy sighs, but I can't draw in a single breath. My chest is tight, and there are black spots floating in my field of vision as Aaron looks up at me expectantly. And I don't realize that I've done or said anything, let alone yes, until the crowd erupts in applause, and Aaron is sliding the ring onto my finger.

He drops the box, and I watch it get kicked away by the toe of his shoe when he pushes to his feet and picks me up, spinning me around in circles while everyone cheers and whoops, shouting their congratulations. Aaron sets me back on my feet, and the crowd descends on us. I'm inundated with requests to see the ring, which I grant because I don't know what else to do. By the time I've finished playing the role of a hand model, Aaron has his phone out, grinning as he types out a message to someone.

I shake my head at him. "We've been engaged for five minutes, and you're already giving all of your attention to your phone."

The word 'engaged' feels all wrong in my mouth, but I tell myself that I'll get used to it, that I'll have to because I've said yes, and I only would have done that if I was ready to take the next step with Aaron.

"Relax, babe," he says, turning the phone to show me what he was doing. "I was just sending the video Eden took of the proposal to my mom. She's already shown it to Riley. She's so psyched about being a flower girl. You don't think Hunter will mind letting us have her the weekend of the wedding, do you?"

The moment Aaron speaks Hunter's name, my world stops, and a sharp and incessant pain cuts a jagged line through my chest. I place my hand over my heart, and my ribs buckle under the weight of Aaron's ring.

"Babe?" Aaron asks, confusion etching itself into his features as he watches me back away from him. "What's wrong?"

I don't answer him. I can't. I just turn and run to find Dee. She's in the corner with Jayla, and both of them look at me like I'm crazy when I stop short in front of them.

"I need your keys," I tell Dee.

"For what?"

"I don't have time to explain. Just give me your keys, Dee, please."

She looks like she wants to ask me all kinds of questions, but she doesn't. She just digs in her purse and puts the keys in my hand, letting me go without another word, even though I can feel her and Jayla's eyes on my back as I go. I manage to avoid Aaron on my way to the elevator, and by some strange twist of fate, it's empty and waiting when I press the call button. But I'm still impatient as I wait for it to take me down to the ground floor, as I search the parking garage for Dee's car, as I speed across town to Hunter's gym.

I spend the entire drive over alternating between a prayer that Riley hasn't already called her dad and broken the news to him and a speech meant to convey my intentions to follow through with an engagement I don't even remember agreeing to, but when I burst through the door of his office, finding him sitting at his desk doing paperwork that he immediately sets aside for me, I can't remember the lines of my speech or the reason for my prayer.

All I see is him.

All I feel is the magnetic pull between his heart and mine.

All I am is grateful that I had the foresight to take off Aaron's ring.

Hunter pushes back from his desk and tries to rise to his feet, but I shake my head.

"Don't." He cocks his head to the side, challenging my order. "Please," I swallow, crossing the room on unsteady legs. "Just stay right there."

When I'm right beside him, trying to angle my body between him and the desk, there's a moment where I think he won't move. Where I think he'll send me away because I deserve to be sent away. But he doesn't do that. He just glares at me silently and slides back, allowing me to sit on his desk.

"It's your birthday," he says finally, his voice a dark, gruff whisper. He's mad at me, but I can still see the love in his eyes, can still feel it pulling the love I'll always carry for him to the surface.

"I know." I place my feet on the armrests of his chair, hiking my dress up until my thighs are bared for him.

"I didn't get you a present." His eyes roam down my body, traveling from my face to my heaving chest and down further to my parted thighs.

"That's okay. I can only think of one thing I want right now anyway."

He wants it, too. Even though he's angry with me, he wants this, and it doesn't take him long to admit it, first to himself with a flare of his nostrils and a subtle shake of his head and then to me, with two hands under my knees that pull my ass down to the edge of his desk and leave me with no choice but to lay back and enjoy the only present I'll receive today that I actually wanted.

Hunter kisses the inside of my thigh, his lips rough and reverent. "Happy birthday, Sunshine."

41

RAE

Now

There's bad decisions, and then there's *bad* decisions.

Ruinous, life-altering choices you know you'll regret when it's all said and done but somehow still manage to enjoy in the moment, and *God*, am I enjoying myself right now. My legs spread wide, the fabric of my birthday dress scrunched up around my waist, my panties pushed to the side because you don't get completely undressed when you're making a mistake, even when it's one as deliciously salacious as this.

The flat of his tongue rolls over my clit again, and my thighs twitch around his ears. I shouldn't be doing this. It shouldn't feel *so fucking good.*

But I am, and it does.

He grips my ass with rough fingertips, lifting my pussy up to his mouth like a bite of a forbidden meal, and I scream at the top of my lungs the way I never can at home with Aaron—not because his mother or my daughter might hear—but because in all the years we've been together he's never made me feel like this.

Wild. Reckless. Capable of ruining someone and desperate to be ruined in return.

No, that part of me can only be unlocked by the man between my legs. The man now holding my entire ass in the palm of one of his hands so he can use the fingers of the other to invade the walls of my dripping sex. My core contracts, and my eyes roll into the back of my head as pleasure pulses through me, incoherent words flow out of me as my body floats into a cloud of euphoria so thick it's able to keep me suspended for long moments, keeping me from the regret that's waiting for me on the ground.

I didn't come here for this.

That's the thought going through my mind as Hunter lowers me gently back down onto his desk. He doesn't even bother to fix my dress or my panties. Just leaves me wide open, my most intimate areas on display for him. I keep my eyes on the ceiling above me, focused on the heart in the middle of the ceiling tile directly above us that has our initials written in black paint.

"You should paint over that."

I don't know why I've chosen to start the conversation I came here to have this way. It's random and unnecessary, but it's the only way I know how to ease into telling him he has to let me go. I reach down and fix my clothes before sitting up and facing him. He's got his fingers clasped together, resting over the hard slabs of muscle that make up his stomach. For as long as I've known him, Hunter has never had a six-pack. He's just got one of those stomachs that's thick but solid and toned. I don't know what you call it, but it works for him.

He doesn't bother looking up because he knows exactly what I'm talking about. I hate that because I was hoping to buy myself a little bit of time without those eyes on my face.

"Why would I do that?"

"Because it's..." My throat is dry from all the moaning and screaming, so I swallow before continuing. "Because it's just a reminder of a failed past when you should be focused on the future."

One of his brows rises, a thick, dark line that makes my cheeks heat. "Is that what this was?" He asks, waving a large, tattooed hand between us. "You focusing on the future?"

"No." I slide off of his desk, skirting around his wide spread legs to put some space between us. "This was a momentary lapse in judgment. I didn't come here for this."

Hunter stands too, moving forward to delete every inch of space I've just given myself to breathe. Now, all the air I welcome into my lungs is infected with him, with his scent and arrogance, with his desire.

"Then what did you come here for, Rae?"

He brings his hand to my face, the same fingers that were just inside me tucking a strand of hair behind my ear. I suck in a ragged breath, and I should tell him to stop because now those fingers are moving down my neck, over my racing pulse to the pebbled nipples straining through the cotton of my sundress. Hunter cups my breast, and while I'm on the verge of coming apart in his hands, the muscles in his face don't move an inch.

It shouldn't matter that he appears to be so unaffected by me, but it does. It burns me up inside because I fall apart every time he touches me, every time he looks my way. I'm here with him when I should be with the man who helped me raise our daughter before Hunter ever knew she existed, but instead I'm here, courting ruin with a man who won't show me what I do to him.

Maybe it's madness or the pressing need for more of him, but I step closer when I should step back. I bring my hand to the nape of his neck and pull his lips down to mine when I should be coming to terms with the fact that they can't belong to me anymore. I slip my tongue into his mouth and wait for him to give me something in return.

He doesn't.

"Kiss me back, Hunter."

"Why?" He murmurs against my lips, his breathing annoyingly even. I step closer, committed to this act of desperation, and that's when I feel it. The thick, heated length of his erection nestled between us. With my free hand, I palm it, squeezing lightly just to prove to myself that it's real. Finally, his stoic facade breaks. It's a small fracture, a sharp intake of breath that he lets out in a low hiss that passes between his teeth, but it's enough.

"Because we both want the same thing."

The fire. The passion. The lost inhibitions we never miss when we're together.

Hunter makes me regret saying anything when he steps back and shakes his head. "No, Sunshine, we don't want the same thing." He swipes his thumb across his chin, an act of agitation I know too well, and stares at me with dark eyes that pierce my soul. "You came here to make a mistake, to make *me* a mistake, but I want to be more than that. I *deserve* to be more than that, but you won't let me."

"*I* won't let you?" Disbelief paints my tone in dark, broad strokes. It has no place here because we both know what he's saying is true.

"Yes, Rae, you. You're the only person who still looks at me and sees..." he trails off, but I don't need the words for my brain to conjure the image he's alluding to. An image of a broken man splayed on the ground with the tools of his destruction scattered around his prone form. He's not that person anymore. The time we've spent figuring out how our lives fit together for our daughter's sake has shown me as much, but I still see it in the back of my mind. Still hold it up as a reminder of how bad things can get. Still use it as a barrier between us in moments like this.

"I'm sorry. I wish I could see something else, anything else," I lie, exchanging his piercing gaze for the floorboards.

"No, you don't."

"Yes, I do, Hunter. Of course, I do." My voice trembles around the falsities. I've never had to double down on the lie before. Usually, he goes along with it, but I guess today he's tired of my little charade. Maybe he knows today is different. Maybe he feels the walls closing in, the clock running out.

"No, Rae, you don't. Because holding on to that version of me is the only thing keeping you from me and the only thing keeping you with *him*."

"That's not true," I shake my head for emphasis even though his words follow the same thread of logic as my thoughts. "Aaron and I are good together. You and I are a train wreck."

"Do you love him?" The question is wrapped around a broken growl that causes his top lip to curl. It's a sound that can only come from a wounded animal preparing to lash out in a final attempt to save their life.

I run a shaking hand over my messy hair as my stomach turns into knots. "Hunter."

"Say it, Rae, look me in the eyes and tell me that you love him, that you love him more than you've ever loved me."

He waits patiently for me to respond to his cruel request, and I hate him more with every silent second that passes. Why can't he just let this go? Why can't he just accept that the way I feel about Aaron doesn't matter because *we* don't work outside of the context of sated sighs and gut-wrenching moans. When a full minute goes by without me caving to his demand, he closes the space between us and cups my chin with gentle fingers. Slowly, he tips my head back, forcing me to meet his eye.

One dark slash of a brow raises. "Tell me you love him, Rae."

He's so close now, angling me to persuade me with proximity, and I don't back away. I stand firmly on the line between common sense and the bone-deep yearning for this man. For his hands on my hips and the warmth that spreads through my chest because of it. For his breath on my face as he lowers his forehead to mine and pulls in lungfuls of air just because it smells like me.

I close my eyes, staving off the unshed tears burning the backs of my eyes. "I need to tell you something," I whisper, scared to speak any louder because our connection is already tenuous and the words that are going to come out of my mouth next are going to destroy us both.

Hunter sighs, allowing me to shift gears. "I'm listening."

It's stupid, but I hold him tighter when I should be letting him go, when I know he'll probably let me go when he hears what I came here to say.

"Aaron asked me to marry him."

I open my eyes and find myself face to face with his devastation, and it destroys me. I feel like I should apologize, like I've broken some sacred vow, etched in stone and sealed with blood, that our souls have only just decided to acknowledge.

"Hunter, say something," I plead, wondering why I want his words when I already know they'll just make me feel worse. More guilty. More conflicted. More *wrong*.

His lips part, and my heart starts to pound, anticipating his wrath, his fire, his hurt, but he's remarkably calm as he takes my left hand in his right and runs his thumb across each of my ring-less digits.

"You didn't say yes."

I pull my hand back, tucking it behind my back. "I did. I took the ring off before I came in here because I didn't want you to see it."

Hunter studies me with dark eyes that see too much. "When did he ask you?"

"Tonight. At dinner."

He checks his watch, arching a brow when it reveals that it's not even ten yet. "You've been engaged for all of five minutes, and instead of spending the night celebrating with your fiancé, you came here to me."

Something about his calm tone and even calmer demeanor makes me feel like I've been stripped down, lain bare, like the whole of every complication I've allowed to exist around the mess that is my life has suddenly been made simple.

"I—" My plan is to defend myself, to explain to him that I rushed over here because I wanted to be the person to tell him, that I didn't want Riley to call and let it slip, but once again, the big, elaborate speech deserts me, leaving me with a stupid response. "It doesn't mean anything."

But it does. Doesn't it? Just like my inability to say I love the man I've spent the last seven years of my life with means something. Just like the ease with which I say I love you to Hunter means something.

Hunter scoffs. "Of course, it means something, Sunshine. It means you said yes, but you didn't mean it. It means there's still time."

"Time for what?" I ask, thrown off kilter when he takes a sudden step back and turns back toward his desk. I watch him pull open the top drawer on the right-hand side and pluck something out. It's not until he's walking towards me again that I realize what it is.

A square, black box.

He doesn't open it until he's standing right in front of me, but I already know what's inside. Knowing doesn't stop me from being shocked when I see the gold band of a ring nestled inside the lines of the black silk. The small diamonds surrounding the larger center stone fan out into little triangles that look like a sunburst. I cover my mouth and shake my head in disbelief.

He can't be doing this.

There's no way he's actually doing this.

"Time," he says, finally answering the question I asked before I lost my ability to speak altogether, "for me to give you another option, a *better* option."

"Hunter."

"*I'm* the better option, Rae," he says, placing the box in my hand. It doesn't escape my notice that the fear and panic that swirled in my veins when Aaron was presenting me with a ring earlier tonight isn't there now. All I feel is the quiet hum of inevitability mixed with the very real dredging of doubt. Not about Hunter, per se, but about me, about us.

"You don't have to take the option right now," Hunter says. His eyes soft and sincere as they trace my features. "I've had that ring for over a decade, and it can wait a little longer. *I* can wait a little longer."

"How much longer?" I blurt, heat flooding my cheeks because I shouldn't be asking him that. I should be handing him back the ring and telling him I'm marrying Aaron. The only problem is, I can't.

Joy skates across Hunter's features, and it's so bright, so pure, anyone looking at him would think I'd just agreed to forever, not asked him how long he'd wait to have it with me.

"A year." He moves toward me again, bringing his hand up to cup my chin, urging me to look him in the eyes. "A year from now, when you trust me, when we're settled into raising our daughter and know all the ins and outs of co-parenting. If you still love me, *if you still want me*, then you'll meet me at the place where you saved my life, and we'll finally give ourselves the chance to live it together." He comes down, dropping a single, soft kiss on my lips before flicking his gaze up to mine. "Deal?"

For the second time tonight, I find myself making a commitment, but when I agree to Hunter's proposition, I don't feel a single ounce of regret. "Deal."

It's easy to feel like I've made the right decision when I'm standing in Hunter's orbit, surrounded by all the love we have for each other and the faith he has in us, but the moment I leave it, that certainty starts to wane.

Buckling under the weight of the realities I've yet to face. The first of which is Aaron, who is waiting outside of Dee and Jayla's house when I arrive because once I left my own birthday party, Dee smelled trouble and went to pick her up from Marcy. I don't think either of them would hurt Riley, but I'm grateful that she's with Dee all the same. Especially because it gives me a chance to have this conversation with Aaron without worrying about her over-hearing.

He's still in his car when I pull up in Dee's driveway, so I walk over and climb into the passenger seat with his ring in my hand instead of on it.

"You're not wearing your ring," he says, looking out the window and not at me.

I set the ring in question on the console between us. "I can't marry you, Aaron."

"You said yes." Anger and almost a decade's worth of resentment are packed into those three words. "You said yes in front of everyone I know, my co-workers, my boss, my clients, and now you're taking it back? What am I supposed to tell everybody?"

It should sting that he's more concerned about breaking the news to his friends than he is upset about losing me, but it doesn't, which is just more proof that we had no business holding on to each other for as long as we did.

"You should tell them the truth," I offer, which only makes him more incensed. He whips his head around, his lip curled in disgust as he looks at me.

"And what's that, Rachel?"

"That I hate being called Rachel, and you know that, but you still do it anyway. That your mom hates me, and I hate her right back. That you resent how much I love my daughter, and have never considered her yours. That we should have broken up after the first time you asked me to marry you, and I said no. That ever since that day, you've treated me as a challenge and not a partner, and I let you because I thought I'd never have what I truly wanted again, so I didn't care what I actually got."

Heat rushes to my cheeks at that admission. I don't know where it came from, but it rings true, so I don't take it back.

Aaron scoffs in disbelief, offended by my honesty. "And what you want, this prize you thought you never were going to have again, is your drug addict ex? You're choosing him over me?"

"No," I say, and it's not a lie because I'm not choosing Hunter.

Not yet.

Right now, I'm choosing me. I'm choosing to heal the broken pieces of my soul that kept rubbing up against the shattered pieces of Hunter's and left us both bleeding. I'm choosing to make peace with the fact that Hunter has done the work; he's sealed up his broken pieces with acceptance of his imperfections, grace for his mistakes, and the tools to try to make sure he doesn't make them again.

With the fact that he's wiped up all the blood and he's clean, but somehow, I'm still bleeding.

With the fact that I've been angry with him, and pushing him away because he's the only person who can see it. Who knows that underneath the band aid of faux perfection that's been my relationship with Aaron and the life I built without Hunter, there's a gaping wound that needs to be closed up.

I'm choosing to return to myself, to reclaim the version of me that faced down cancer by my mother's side and fought my way through the ranks of a cutthroat ballet corps, the warrior that swallowed heartbreak, grief, and depression to ensure the child she knew she would have to raise on her own came into this world safely, the bad ass who answered the phone for a stranger and saved his life.

Because she's the one I need.

She's the one who can do hard things, and I have a year to find her, to let her guide me down the path of healing, to forgiving myself and Hunter for all of our missteps, which is, perhaps, the hardest thing of all.

42

HUNTER

"Do you think Taurin and Alyssa will want to come to my birthday party?" Riley asks as I pull into the driveway of her mom's new place and cut the engine.

The rental is a one-story ranch-style house with three bedrooms and two bathrooms, which Rae says is more than enough space for her and Riley. They've only been in it for a few weeks, but they both seem to like it. I guess it helps that Dee, Jayla, and Sonia are just around the corner.

"I'm sure they'd love that, Ri."

"So, should I have Mommy send the invitation to Taurin's house, Alyssa's house, or both?"

"Uh—" I pause when I see Rae's front door open, and Aaron walks out. His car isn't in the driveway, so his appearance has caught me completely off guard. When he pauses on the bottom step of the front porch and glares at my car, I can tell that I've caught him off guard, too.

Riley, who has a concerning lack of spatial awareness, continues to chatter about the invitations as she clambers out of the truck and slams the door. The sound catapults me into action. I grab her weekend bag and yank my keys out of the ignition, catching up with Riley just as she's meeting Aaron on the short path to the front door.

"Hey, Aaron," she says, all casual cheer as she breezes by him and moves into the house. He doesn't speak to her, and he doesn't look at me. I don't really care about him paying me dust, but it burns me up inside to see him ignore Riley, which means I have to address it.

I step in front of him, blocking his path. He tilts his head back, glaring at me with unrestrained hate. This is the first time we've seen each other since I helped Rae move her shit out of his house. He looked at me then the same way that he's looking at me now: like he wishes he could beat my ass. I smirk, inviting him to try, so I can have a reason to lay him out.

"Get out of my way, Hunter."

"Believe me, the last thing I want to be doing right now is breathing the same air as you, so I'm going to say this and let you get on with your day. The next time my daughter speaks to you, make sure you open your mouth and speak back. I don't care how you feel about Rae or how you feel about me, but she—" I lift my hand, using one finger to point at the door Riley just passed through "—she doesn't have anything to do with our bullshit. You were a part of her life for seven years, which means you'll always mean something to her, so if she speaks, you speak back. If she calls because she wants to converse with you for some odd reason, you'll answer. You got me?"

If I had it my way, Riley would miraculously forget that the piece of shit in front of me exists, but I know that probably won't ever happen, so I'm left with no choice but to make sure he understands what's expected of him if he ever finds himself in her presence again.

"Yeah," he says through clenched teeth. "I got you."

I step to the side. "Then you can go."

With one last hateful look, he leaves, clearing the path to the front door, which I take with a smile on my face. When I step through the door, I'm deposited right into the living room and the chaos that is Rae trying to build furniture. She doesn't even look up, probably because she knows it's me.

"We've have to make sure Riley remembers to close the door behind her when she comes in the house."

"She said you were coming in behind her."

"I was; I had to pause to talk to Aaron for a second," I tell her, crouching down to grab the instructions she's squinting at.

Rae looks up, searching my face to see if I'm upset. I'm not, but I appreciate her concern. "He just came by to drop off some mail that came to his place by mistake."

I shrug. "I don't need an explanation, Sunshine."

And I really don't. Even though we're not together yet, I know Rae isn't going back to Aaron. She's too focused on moving forward.

"Okay," She says, reaching for the instructions in my hand. I hold them out of her reach, which makes her narrow her eyes at me. "I need those, Hunter."

"Why? We both know you're not going to follow them."

Rae is one of the smartest women I know, but she sucks at reading instructions and is even worse at building things. Something about the words, letters, and tools just don't click for her. I've built every piece of furniture in her place, so I'm not sure why she's chosen today to act like Mrs. Independent.

The corners of her lips quirk. "I can follow instructions."

A month.

It's been a month since I've kissed her, since I've tasted her, since we've done a single thing to act on the heat that is always coursing between us. I know she can follow instructions. Just like she knows I'm good at giving them to her. That shared knowledge passes between us in an invisible wave of passion we can't act on because we decided that taking sex out of the equation was the best way to ensure we kept our heads on straight during this year of waiting and working our way back to each other.

I end our staring contest first, dropping my gaze to the instructions for the TV stand and holding out my hand for the drill Rae has clutched in her fingers. "Give me that. I'll finish this up while you get started on Riley's hair."

"Aww, man," Riley whines from the kitchen, having heard me sick her mother on her. "I don't want my hair done."

Rae rolls her eyes at me, handing me the drill before she rises from her spot on the floor. She rubs her hands down her thighs, which are bared by the short-ass shorts she's wearing, and starts to make her way to the kitchen.

"Fine, Ri, let's just cut it all off," she jokes, which makes Riley giggle. They have this conversation every Sunday afternoon when I bring Riley home, but it never gets old for them, and it never gets old for me.

While Rae takes down Riley's previous style, I undo the little progress she made on the TV stand, because it's wrong, and then put it together the right way. It takes me fifteen minutes to complete the job, which I'm a little sad about because it means I don't have a reason to hang around the house any longer. After I put the finished piece on the wall Rae told me she wanted the TV on and set the seventy-inch behemoth on top, I put all the trash in the box and set it by the door so I can take it with me when I go.

"Alright," I say, walking into the kitchen to see Riley hopping up on the counter to get her hair washed. "I'm out of here."

Rae glances over her shoulder at me. "Did you finish with the TV stand?"

"Of course." I give her a look that asks her if she's forgotten who she's talking to, and she turns away from me to hide her smile. I still see it, though, because I'm walking up to her to give Riley a kiss on the cheek before her head goes under the running water. "Have a great week, Nugget."

She giggles and squirms as I tickle her armpits, splashing water everywhere. Rae swats me away. "Alright, alright, that's enough of that."

Not wanting to get myself or Riley in further trouble, I back away with my hands up and a smile on my face. "Goodbye, Ms. Prince."

"Goodbye, Mr. Drake," Rae says, her voice all sass and humor that makes my chest fill with warmth.

"Goodbye, Daughter. I love you."

Even though her mom is currently drenching her head, and a little bit of her face, in water, Riley waves. "Bye, Daddy. I love you too."

Her little voice, and those three words, stop me dead in my tracks. I look to Rae for confirmation that I heard right, and she's already looking at me, tears in her eyes as she nods.

We agreed that when Riley finally said I love you to me, we wouldn't make a big deal out of it, but now I want to make a big deal. Now, I want to scoop her up off the counter and spin her around in circles to make her squeal with joy while I beg her to say it again and again.

I don't do any of those things, though. I remain calm. I back out of the kitchen with tears in my eyes, a hand over my heart, and a look on my face that thanks Rae for the precious gift that is our daughter and the chance to have both of them in my life.

43

RAE

"Mommy. Daddy. Look at me!" Riley shouts before doing the most graceless cannonball ever into Hunter's pool. She lands with a huge splash that sends water spraying all over Taurin, Alyssa, and their friends Winston and Liz, who are all responsible for turning my daughter's 10th birthday party into a diving competition. They've been in the water with Riley, Scarlett, Sonia, and a few of the girls from En Pointe all day long, acting as the on-site babysitters while the adults remain dry and entertained on the patio, where Hunter is manning the grill.

"Encore! Encore!" Hunter shouts while I marvel at his enthusiasm. Even though I don't want to spend the rest of the day mustering up a new compliment for the same trick, I lend my voice to his chant, loving the way our chaotic harmony makes our daughter smile and giggle as she pulls herself up out of the pool and dives into it again.

"Y'all are crazy," Dee says, waltzing up to the grill with a half-eaten plate in hand with her eyes trained on the steak Hunter is about to pull off the fire.

"Please." I wave a hand at her, taking a sip of the watermelon lemonade Hunter's brother, Cal, made this morning. "We're adorable."

Hunter looks over his shoulder at me, one of those heart-melting smiles on his lips. He loves it when I refer to us as a unit, and I love the way that it feels right on my tongue and in my heart.

"Damn right, we are."

Dee rolls her eyes, exasperated with us the way she always is, even though she loves that we're slowly working our way back to each other. "Y'all are also sickening," she says, shoving her plate in Hunter's direction when the steak is finally done. "You can just drop that right here."

"Save some steak for somebody else, Dee," I tell her, laughing when she cuts an eye at me. "I don't think Cal or Beck have had any."

"We haven't," Cal chimes in, rising from his spot at the picnic table behind me. Beck isn't far behind, and Dee, who can't decide which one of them she wants to try to get into her bed, blushes and starts batting her eyes at them both.

"We could always share," she says, her voice dropping to a shamelessly low octave. Cal and Beck share a look that is part humor and part something else, and I look away because whatever the something else is, it's none of my business.

"I have some more steak marinating in the fridge," Hunter adds, harshing Dee's vibe with the addition of logic. "There's no need to share."

"I'll go grab it," Beck offers, already heading toward the back door.

Dee's eyes light up as she follows behind him. "I'll come with you!"

Cal watches them go with an odd look on his face, and I feel the need to fill the awkward silence with words.

"Dee's harmless," I assure him, causing him to bring his attention back to me. He's got kind eyes, and even though they're serious like his brother's, they don't really look alike. I know, from conversations Hunter and I had a lifetime ago, that they don't share a mother, which is probably why Cal's skin is a few shades darker than

Hunter's, and his features are composed differently but no less handsome.

The corners of his lips tip up into a smile as he sips his lemonade. "Even if she wasn't, I'm sure Beck can handle himself."

"You're right."

Beck, like Cal, is a former FBI agent who now works for the Secret Service, which means he's dealt with more pressing threats than Dee's horniness. Last night, when we all went out to dinner so that Riley's first time meeting her uncle wasn't on the day of her party, they told Hunter and me they were about to start a new assignment but couldn't disclose any more details. With the election coming up, I guessed they were about to be tasked with protecting one of the candidates, but they wouldn't confirm or deny anything when I started throwing out names.

Either way, it's cool as hell to know that my daughter has so many fiercely protective men in her life who could, and would, literally kill for her if necessary.

"Uncle Cal!" Riley shouts, bounding over to us with pool water dripping down her body that she gets on Cal when she hugs him around the waist. "Are you going to get in the pool with me now?"

Cal, who is just as weak for Riley as Hunter is, sets down his drink and any hopes of getting steak and allows Riley to pull him over to the pool, leaving me and Hunter alone. He's distracted with the grill, and I want to be close to him, so I allow myself the chance. I slip an arm around his waist and sigh contentedly when he stops what he's doing to turn into me.

"What's up, Sunshine?"

My eyes are on his lips, and I want to kiss him so badly my muscles ache with the restraint I'm using to hold myself back. I force my gaze up so I'm looking him in his eyes, but they're not any safer than his lips. There's just too much wanting there. Too much desire, too much knowing how it is when we're together, and too many days since we have been.

"Oh, nothing." I breathe, reaching for humor to stop me from jumping his bones and scarring everyone here for life. "Just wondering how you feel about Cal trying to edge you out of your position as Riley's favorite Drake man."

We both look over at the pool, watching Cal lift Riley onto his shoulders so she can have a leg up on the older kids as they play Marco Polo. Hunter considers my question for a second and then shrugs.

"He's a good uncle and all, but he can't hold a candle to me when it comes to my girl."

His certainty is so sexy it almost makes me forget that I'm trying not to want to kiss him on the lips.

"I think you're right about that."

He gives me a cocky grin. "I am."

"I have a question for you," I blurt the words out, and Hunter's brows rise.

"What's up?"

My heart starts to pound, and I swallow past the ball of nerves in my throat, telling myself it makes no sense to be nervous because what I'm about to say next could only ever make him happy.

"Would you want to look into adding your last name to Riley's so she can be Riley Prince-Drake or, if she wants, just Riley Drake?"

His eyes sparkle with liquid emotion as he searches my face to make sure I'm serious. "You want that?"

"Yeah, I want that. I think it makes sense."

Because one day, my last name is going to be Drake, too.

I don't say the words, but the way Hunter looks at me tells me he doesn't need to hear them because he knows.

44

HUNTER

Six Months to Decision Day.

"Thanks for coming."

Rae's appreciation is unnecessary, and I'm about to tell her that when I notice her teeth chattering. We're standing outside En Pointe, and it's a little after nine on a chilly December night a few days before Christmas, which means the sun has been down for hours. It also means that Rae should know better than to be standing on the sidewalk in nothing but a long-sleeved leotard, tights, and long socks that come up over her knee.

"Where's your coat?" I ask, pulling my hoodie over my head and handing it to her before she even has the chance to answer. I don't like the idea of her being cold, even if she is just walking the short distance from the building to the car.

She swats my hand away, but I glare at her, and she caves, taking the hoodie and slipping on even as she protests. "This is completely unnecessary, and, if you must know, I left my coat at home because I wasn't planning on being outside for long."

Her plan changed when she inserted her key into the lock, and it got stuck, making it impossible for her to get into the building. She called me, hoping I could help her free it, and I came running because I never miss an opportunity to be in her presence. Especially on a rare night, like tonight, when neither one of us has Riley in tow. She was supposed to be with me because it's the weekend, but she opted to take a trip with Dee, Jayla, and Sonia to Disney instead.

"Yeah." I rub at the back of my neck, catching the bit of shade she's cast in my direction. "I'm sorry I made the problem worse."

And by worse I mean snapping the key in half and making it necessary for us to call a locksmith who won't be able to come out until tomorrow morning.

Rae laughs. "It's fine."

We're moving slowly down the block, walking side by side because an influx of last-minute Christmas shoppers made it impossible for either of us to get a spot close to her building. Rae's car is all the way down by Lick, and my truck is a few spaces away in front of the little Italian place that just opened up.

"Have you eaten there?" I ask, tipping my chin in the direction of the restaurant. Rae's eyes follow my gaze and then come back to my face, intrigued.

"No," she says, fiddling with the hoodie sleeves hanging well past her hands. She looks adorable and happy, swimming in fabric drenched with my scent. "Do you wanna buy me dinner?"

"Always, Sunshine."

She reaches out, wrapping her fingers around mine and leading me down the sidewalk, only letting go when I move ahead to open the door before she can pass through it. There aren't many people inside, but it smells divine, so I'm not worried that the small number of patrons—which are primarily couples—is a sign of bad food. We're seated immediately, placed at the back of the restaurant where the lighting is low, and there's no one else around.

Rae's got the menu in her hand, perusing the offerings while I stare at her. "This is nice," she says, and I nod when she looks up at me, unable to put into words how nice it is to just sit across from her for no other reason than because we wanted to.

"Yeah, it is."

"I do appreciate you coming out in the cold to help me. I mean, I'm sure I could have called someone else, but—"

"No." I cut in, shaking my head. "You don't need to call anyone else. Ever. I'll always come when you call."

"I know that," she breathes, pressing her lips together. "I know you will."

Our waitress appears with complimentary bread sticks and water, telling us about the night's specials while filling our glasses. When she's done with her introductory spiel, Rae says she already knows what she wants to eat, which leaves me with mere seconds to choose which dish I want. Truthfully, I'm not all that hungry, but I still get the carbonara because it's Rae's favorite and for some odd reason, she chose chicken Marsala this time.

"Ohh," she moans regretfully when the waitress leaves to put in our food. "I love carbonara."

"I know."

She plucks a bread stick from the basket and breaks it in half, taking a bite. "Will you share with me?"

"Why didn't you order it if that's what you wanted?"

"Because my therapist suggested that I make one small, random choice every day as a way to prove to myself that things can turn out okay even if I don't try to control every aspect of them." She shrugs, taking another bite of her bread stick. "Apparently, I have control issues."

Picking up my glass, I take a sip of water to try and tamp down the vast amount of questions that have just popped in my mind. I want to know everything. Like when she started therapy and how long she's been going and if, by chance, she's talked to her therapist about the answer she's supposed to be giving me in six months. When I trust that none of those things will come out of my mouth, I respond.

"Really?" I ask, arching a brow. "I never would have thought."

Rae is a lot of things, but flexible isn't one of them. There's a reason why ballet—one of the most rigorous dance forms—is her chosen craft, a reason why she keeps Riley on a strict routine and takes the same way home every day when she picks our kid up from school. Growing up loving, and being in love with, an addict means a life of chaos, of ups and downs and highs and lows that you have no way to anticipate or control, so it makes sense to me that her reaction to the unpredictability of life with Will and with me, resulted in a fierce rigidity.

Her jaw drops in surprise and a tiny bit of offense, but she laughs. "Shut up. I'm working on it."

"Good." I smile, turning my glass of water around in small circles just to have something to do with my hands. "How's the support group Nate suggested?"

"It's nice. Did you know Taurin's mom is a part of it?"

"No, I didn't."

"She shared about him the other day, talking about how she's looking forward to them spending Christmas together," Rae says, then she slaps a hand over her mouth, her eyes wide. "Damn. I wasn't supposed to tell you that, was I? Aren't these things supposed to be anonymous?"

"I think it's fine, especially considering that she told me the same thing when I talked to her earlier this week when she came by the gym to try a yoga class."

Her nose scrunches up. "It wasn't goat yoga, was it?"

My laughter echoes between us, making our server smile as she appears with our plates. I wait until she leaves us alone again to ask, "What do you and your daughter have against goats?"

"Nothing." She picks up her fork and knife, cutting into the chicken and taking a bit, nodding her approval before continuing. "I just don't think they belong in yoga."

"Don't knock it until you try it, Sunshine."

We fall into a comfortable silence, both of us enjoying our meals, only really speaking when we feel it's necessary. For Rae, that necessity comes in the form of bullying me out of large bites of my carbonara, which is fine because I ordered it for her anyway. Towards the end of the meal, when we're pretty much the only people in the restaurant, and we're just sitting at the table because neither of us wants to leave the presence of the other, she turns serious almond eyes on me.

"I owe you an apology."

My brow furrows. "An apology? For what?"

"For the way I acted when I came back." She bites her lip. "For not seeing or appreciating the person you are now and using our past to push you away. That wasn't fair to you, and I'm sorry for that."

"Hey." I reach across the table, offering her comfort with an upturned palm, which she takes with a sigh. "You don't need to apologize. You were trying to protect yourself from being hurt again."

Since we've been back in each other's lives, we've had a lot of conversations. Most of them have been about Riley and what she needs, wants, and deserves from both of us. And while that's the way it should be, I can't help but feel like we should have made some time to have this conversation, too.

I rub my thumb over the inside of Rae's wrist. "I'm sorry too, Sunshine," I murmur, shaking my head as tears fill her eyes. "For fucking up so badly. For scaring you away. For leaving you alone when you needed me the most."

"I left you alone," Rae gasps, tears flowing freely now. "I should have come home when Will was sick. I should have been there to support him and you. I regret staying in New York so much, Hunter. More than you'll ever know."

"You think that's why I relapsed?" I ask, incredulity skating across my features as she nods.

"Of course, it is. I put too much pressure on you, and you broke. I broke you," she whimpers. "I broke us."

"Oh, baby. Come here." I tug on her hand, and she's up in a second, rounding the table on shaky legs that give out as soon as she's close enough for me to catch her. I pull her in, helping her get situated on my lap. "You didn't break me, Rae. I was already broken. Taking care of Will brought up so much shit I hadn't dealt with around losing my mom."

"But if I had been there, you wouldn't have—"

"Yes, I would have," I tell her, absolutely certain that's the truth.

"Because even if you were there every single day, I would have still been watching someone I love suffer. You wouldn't have been able to distract me from that. Watching you suffer through that loss might have made the situation that much more triggering. I was happy to be there for you, to protect you from that pain even if I couldn't do it forever." My hand moves up and down her back, trying to soothe her as she cries harder, silent sobs shaking both of us. "But the break was always coming, Sunshine. That's what happens when you try to walk around on a fracture and don't give it time to heal."

My mom was my fracture. Her death was the catalyst for my drug addiction, and losing Will opened up every wound I thought I had sealed up with the love I'd found in the family I'd created with him and Rae.

None of that was her fault, and I can't believe she's been walking around for so long thinking it was.

"You have saved me, Sunshine." I lay a kiss on her temple, allowing us both a bit more comfort from physical touch. "Your love has saved me more times than I can count. It could *never* break me."

45

RAE

Three Weeks to Decision Day

Hunter opens the door for me, looking remarkably calm for a man who called me fifteen minutes ago to let me know our daughter had locked herself in the bathroom and was asking for me. He wouldn't tell me what was wrong, just that I needed to come now, so I ran out of my house in a ratty old T-shirt and pair of basketball shorts I stole from him months ago when my washer went out, and doing laundry at his house resulted in them getting mixed in with my clothes.

"What's wrong?!" I yell, pushing past him to get into the house.

"Are those my shorts?" he asks, tilting his head to the side as he examines me.

"Not now, Hunter! What's wrong with my baby?"

"She started her period."

"What?!" I round on him. "You couldn't have told me that before I left the house without my purse and, therefore, zero reinforcements to deal with this situation."

"Rae." He walks over, places two big hands on my shoulders, and levels me with a stare. "Breathe."

I do as he says, pushing out one deep breath and then another until I no longer feel like I'm going to throw up. "She's only ten," I tell him, shaking my head as stupid tears gather in my eyes. "She's just a baby."

One of Hunter's hands slips around to grip my nape, pulling me into his chest. "I know. Apparently periods are starting earlier and earlier for this generation."

I wrinkle my nose, pulling back to look at him. "How do you know that?"

"Research."

"You've researched periods?"

"I have a preteen daughter, Rae; of course, I researched periods. I've also got a full stash of period products upstairs just in case this happened."

God, I love this man. Anybody else would be losing their shit right alongside me, but not Hunter. He's all calm, collected, fatherly grace while I'm a blubbering mess.

"Well," I sniffle, reluctantly leaving the warmth of his embrace. "If you've got everything covered, why did you call me?"

"Because she asked for you, and I knew you'd kill me if you didn't get to walk her through this. You've been there for all of her firsts, and I wasn't going to let you miss this one."

My heart is all mush and emotions I've been holding back for the better part of a year. We're just a few weeks out from what Dee and Jayla have jokingly been calling Decision Day, which also happens to be my birthday, and I'm tired of pretending I don't know what I want. I've told everyone except Hunter that because I know he's committed to waiting the whole year, but I grow a little more impatient every day I look at the ring box that lives on my dresser.

That impatience comes spilling out of me in the form of a quick, chaste kiss to Hunter's lips that makes his eyes glow with heat.

"I love you," I tell him, just because I can. "You're an amazing co-parent and an even better dad. Riley and I are so lucky to have you."

"I love you too, Sunshine."

With that out of the way, I back away from him and head towards the stairs, praying Riley is as together as her dad is.

She is not.

"I can't believe I have to go through this EVERY MONTH," she whines, her shrill voice bouncing around the small confines of the bathroom we're currently locked in because she refused to come out.

"I know, baby, but that's the curse of having a uterus."

"I don't want a uterus anymore."

I burst out laughing, which she doesn't appreciate. She glares at me from inside the bathtub where she apparently thought it was smart to set up camp for the night.

"You're going to be okay, Nugget," I tell her, running a hand over her curls. "It last for a few days, and I won't lie, some of those days are going to suck, but I'll teach you everything I know about getting through it alive."

"Why are you making it sound like I'm about to go to war?"

"Because you are," I laugh softly. "Periods can be really tough on your body, so it's important that you know how to take care of yourself. When to rest, what to eat, the medicine to take to manage the pain."

"So that's why my stomach hurts?"

"Yep." I nod, giving her a sympathetic smile. "I like to take a warm shower and then lay down with a heating pad on my stomach to help the cramps. You've seen me do that before, right?"

"Yeah. I don't think Daddy has a heating pad, though," she says, nodding toward the basket of period preparedness Hunter put together. She's right. There isn't a heating pad.

"Okay. I'll see if he has one, but first, let's get out of the bathtub and into bed, okay?"

Riley sighs, but when I stand up and extend my hand to her, she takes it and lets me lead her to her bedroom. Once I've gotten her settled, I head back downstairs to find Hunter. He's in the kitchen, twiddling his thumbs while he sits at the island, probably feeling as helpless as I do.

"I've got her in bed." He looks up at me and gives me a relieved smile.

"Good. I was afraid she was going to try to live in that bathtub."

"Me too."

"Was the basket helpful?"

"It was perfect; the only thing you were missing was a heating pad."

"I thought I had one in there." He twists his lips as he contemplates where it might have gone, and then realization smooths out the lines in his face. "It's in my bathroom," he says, already pushing to his feet to go and retrieve it.

"No." I lift a hand to stop him, which causes him to pause. "I can get it."

"Rae, you don't have to."

His features are tense, drawn tight with the awareness of my feelings around his bathroom. What he doesn't know is that I've been working through it in therapy, using EMDR to reprocess the trauma I associate with that room. I haven't had cause to test out how effective it's been until now, and I don't want to miss the chance. It's the last thing I want to check off of my list before I finally give Hunter his answer, and I've been determined to do it because before the break, this was the place I envisioned us raising a family, and I don't want to let go of it just because of one bad day in one room. Of course, I know that if I needed him to, Hunter would, but I don't want to need him to.

I want the treehouse in our tree.

I want a nursery in Will's old room.

I want him and this house.

I want our home.

"But I need to," I tell Hunter, turning before he can stop me and heading back up the steps. When I enter his room, it's quiet. His bed is neatly made, and everything smells like him. The bathroom door is partially open, and I take cautious steps towards it, making note of what I feel in my body as I approach.

Mostly, I feel calm, which is good, and when I push the door open, I feel silly because it's just a bathroom. It's different than it was when I lived here. The tub is gone, and now it's just a grand, walk-in shower with a waterfall shower head. The vanity has been updated, and there's different tile on the floor, but the configuration is the same.

It's still the same room, and there's no changing what happened here, but I'm different now, and so is Hunter, and that's why this time, this chance we've decided to take on each other, will be different too.

46

HUNTER

Decision Day.

I should have told her a time.

That's the first thing that crosses my mind when the numbers on my watch go from eleven fifty-nine to twelve o'clock. It's noon, and I've been waiting for Rae to show up for hours.

Around the third hour of sitting in the booth at the back of the restaurant where she waited for me all those years ago, it occurred to me that she might not come. That after everything, she might have decided we weren't worth it. That I wasn't worth it. But instead of panicking, I breathed. Instead of worrying, I talked to our waitress and told her that I was waiting for someone and tipped her handsomely to have our order out as soon as she got here.

But now, I'm all out of calm breaths and the waitress is looking at me like I've constructed some elaborate story just to spend the whole day sitting in her section. I pull out my phone, preparing to text Dee, and ask her if she knows if Rae is coming, but then I hear the bell above the door chime and feel the air in the entire building shift with the weight of her presence.

I've got my back to the door, mainly because I didn't want to sit there staring at it all day, but also because this is where I sat when we first met. The scent of pear and vanilla hits my nostrils as Rae runs her fingers across the top of my back on her way around the table. She drags her hand down my arm as she lowers herself into the booth, and I smile at the casual, familiar touch.

"Happy birthday, Sunshine."

"Thank you."

My eyes rush over her features, greedy to consume her. "You look beautiful today."

She grins. "I know."

I can't help but laugh at her cockiness, letting humor and relief that she's here thread their way through the sound that Rae soaks up happily until the waitress sits our plates down in front of us.

Her brows furrow as she looks down at the steaming, hot food. "You already ordered?"

"Yeah. I had to ensure you ate because someone once told me you can't make big decisions on an empty stomach."

"Well, I've already convened with my better angels and made a decision." She bites her lip, and my heart drops. "It was a tough choice, but I think I made the right one."

I force out a calming breath. "And what did you choose, Sunshine?"

It should be enough that she's here, that we've done the work to get to this moment, but I need her to say the words aloud. Her left hand comes up slowly, and she places it on the table, sliding it toward me. At first, I think she's just reaching for me, trying to hold my hand, but then I see it.

The gold band I've waited a lifetime to see wrapped around her delicate ring finger.

The diamonds fashioned in the shape of sunbursts glinting up at me.

The smile on her face that spells forever.

"You," she says simply. "I chose you."

The End

ABOUT THE AUTHOR

J.L. Seegars is a dedicated smut peddler and lifelong nerd who's always had a love of words, storytelling and drama. When she isn't writing messy and emotionally complex characters like the ones she grew up around, she's watching reality TV, supporting her fellow authors by devouring their work or spending time with her husband and son.

ALSO BY J.L. SEEGARS

Restore Me: The New Haven Series (Book #1)

Again: A Marriage Redemption Novella

Revive Me Part One: The New Haven Series (Book #2)

Revive Me Part Two: The New Haven Series (Book #2)

Revive Me Part Three: The New Haven Series (Book #2)

Release Me: The New Haven Series (Book #3)

Printed in Great Britain
by Amazon

4674397R00208